BREATHE

BREATHE

Inspired by a true story

Elena Kravchenko

Matador
9 Priory Business Park,
Wistow Road, Kibworth Beauchamp,
Leicestershire. LE8 0RX
Tel: 0116 279 2299
Email: books@troubador.co.uk
Web: www.troubador.co.uk/matador
Twitter: @matadorbooks

ISBN 978 1800463 066

British Library Cataloguing in Publication Data.
A catalogue record for this book is available from the British Library.

Printed and bound in the UK by TJ Books Ltd, Padstow, Cornwall
Typeset in 10.5pt Aldine by Troubador Publishing Ltd, Leicester, UK

Matador is an imprint of Troubador Publishing Ltd

In memory of Thomas and Thisbe Ander

Prologue

She had no breath left.

The torrent tossed her upside down, threw her in all directions, pulled her apart. Her lungs were bursting. Her face, her whole body, tightened and spasmed as cold fear flooded her mind. For a moment she stared at the planks floating near the surface, beams of light piercing the cracks between them.

She wrestled against the flow, and with all her strength pushed one more time for the surface.

Air.

A wave slapped her in the face, then gulped her down like a dry leaf.

She fought back and broke the surface again, choking and gasping, thrashing her arms in blind panic.

A man's head popped up among the waves, four metres away, five. She swam, grabbed his shoulder. He jerked back, his eyes dark with terror, his mouth wide open.

"Help me! Hel …"

He pushed her away.

She reached out and clenched his arm. He grabbed her wrist and pulled her hand away.

"No, no, plea—"

Something sharp and heavy pushed into her back, and she yelled in pain.

She sank.

She began coughing beneath the water. All sound was fading. She was feeling weightless. She didn't know where the surface was anymore. The current was sucking her deeper.

Kristoffer's face was there, indistinct, right in front of her.

She felt his hands on her shoulders, on her numb skin, warm and strong. She inhaled the inky water. Her heart froze. Her mind stood still.

Darkness.

She inhaled again.

One

When all his life was ahead of him, he imagined it to be perfect. Everybody does. And everybody fails. And some learn how to live the imperfect life happily – to see the beauty in every mundane day. Because frankly, most days of life are mundane.

His friend Kristoffer was one of those people. He was a happy man. He believed that a truly happy life was a chain of good mundane days, where you relish your day, sunshine or rain, and the smell of coffee in the morning. You go to work, spend time with people that make your heart warm, smile at strangers. Closing your eyes at night, you feel that it was a good day. And then your whole life is a network of good days and if you look at one you see all the others reflected in it.

Kristoffer accepted life the way it was. Unfair. But mostly a wonder.

Carl never felt that way. That morning he had woken up with a huge hangover. That was a state of affairs that he could almost call mundane, but never a wonder.

An earthquake of magnitude 8.9, the strongest in forty years, has occurred in the Indian Ocean off the western coast of Sumatra. A tsunami has struck a large section of coastline in South East Asia and four thousand people are thought to have perished.

Even from behind his bedroom door, Carl could hear every word. His dad must have switched the set on at full volume. Back in Sweden, he would listen to his transistor radio first thing in the morning. It had been that way since Carl was a child, and clearly, he was not about to abandon the habit, even on Boxing Day morning on a rare visit to London. An aroma of cinnamon, thick and warm, wafted under the door – the smell of his childhood. Carl threw the blanket off and sat on the edge of the bed, rubbing his temples. He popped two Nuromols and gulped down a whole bottle of water.

He shuffled from his room. The coffee pot was on the table and his cap next to it.

"Morning, Mum." He poured himself a coffee.

Columbia's FARC guerrillas last night kidnapped a group of between seven and ten holidaymakers from a spa resort near San Rafael …

Carl plonked onto the sofa next to his dad.

British charity organisation Save the Children has announced it will withdraw from Darfur, following the death of a number of aid workers at the hands of rebels …

Asteroid 2004 MN4 is estimated to have a roughly one-in-forty chance of colliding with Earth in 2029.

Carl stared at the screen, wondering if they ever broadcast good news any more. It seemed the world was only interested in war and death. And money. But it was Christmas and the financial markets were closed. Carl caught himself wishing for the first time that they'd talk about the Pope and his dull annual blessing to the faithful. He reached for the remote.

"There's got to be something better," he said, scrolling through the channels.

"It's Kalle Anka!" His dad grabbed his arm.

"Sort of. It's Donald Duck on a twenty-four-hour cartoon channel." But his dad wasn't listening. He sat leaning forward at the very edge of the sofa, his eyes glued to the screen. Donald Duck oddly translated into Swedish as 'Kalle Anka', and his dad didn't seem to know the difference between the Christmas show and the duck. As a kid, Carl used to wonder if they gave him the name 'Kalle' because of Disney's duck. But half of his friends had the same name so probably not. Anyway, that wasn't what kids bullied him for.

"Would have been the first year I missed it," his dad said without looking at him.

Carl covered his smile with his fist. "I'm glad we saved your Christmas."

"Mum, come to watch Kalle Anka!"

She was already behind him with a tray full of cinnamon buns just out of the oven. Carl stood up and gave her his seat.

All Carl wanted was to shave and take a shower but he felt he had to stay, at least for a few episodes. It was one of the most unfathomable Swedish traditions – to watch a set of old Disney cartoons every Christmas Eve at 3 p.m. Every year. The same set of cartoons. At the same time. The clips were dated, randomly dubbed and had hardly anything to do with Christmas. Carl had read that 1997 had been a record year, when nearly half of all Swedes watched the show. It was insane. In national terms, the most popular show in the world. That particular year he wasn't among the audience; he had left Sweden for good to live in London, and he and his new friends were climbing Kilimanjaro. But as a child, he would never have made that trade. Then, it was a long-awaited family affair and they all froze in front of the little black and white TV and nobody spoke unless to recite familiar lines with the characters. One year, the powers that be tried to refresh the cartoon assortment, and it ended in a countrywide burst of indignation. Carl could still remember how upset he was. It was his worst Christmas ever, his world was shaken, he cried into his pillow because he knew his life would never be the same again.

"I was thinking again about the summer house," Carl said during an ad break, when his dad had rushed to the bathroom. "You can't sell it."

"If Lars and Nils insist then we have to." His mum pursed her lips.

Carl knew that selling the house would break her heart. Grandad had been gone four years but she and her brothers still couldn't decide how to share the family house. It wasn't even a proper house – it was a cabin with bunk beds suitable only for the short Swedish summer, lost among lakes and forest at the edge of the Arctic Circle.

"Lars' wife has a summer house in the Archipelago. He doesn't need it. And Nils wants to buy something small on the west coast," his mum said.

"It's not as if you can buy anything if you sell it."

"I know but they don't want to travel that far any more. Even you stopped going."

Carl felt the reproach in her voice. He avoided the gaze of her grey eyes.

The night before their summer trips, his heart would race in his chest as he wrestled with his pillow, trying to sleep. Then in the morning they'd all squeeze into Dad's old Volvo with a pile of sandwiches and flasks, their suitcases in the boot and strapped to the roof, and drive more than fifteen hours and a thousand kilometres up north. Days were easy back then – raise a Swedish flag on a high flagpole first thing in the morning, climb a tall pine tree behind the house to check if there was a Soviet submarine intruding into their lake waters, carve a catapult and, if he was lucky, find a wild deer track with his grandad by the lake, where it had come to drink from the forest. He was never happier than there, running barefoot after his football on the sandy beach and splashing naked in the reassuringly cold water of the lake. There was no tomorrow and no yesterday, only a momentary but endless summer day.

These days Carl never dwelt on it. Why would he? He grew up, and childhood dreams were left behind with the skinny boy swinging his afternoons away in the hammock between two old birch trees.

"I'm busy here in London. You know that," Carl said. He thought a moment about those trees. They had been cut down years ago and fashioned into a fireplace.

He slowly chewed a piece of a cinnamon bun and poured the crumbs he had collected in his hand onto the plate. The truth was he hadn't gone there for the last three summers. Last year he had changed the Lulea trip to a later date because Ralf had invited him to sail the Mediterranean on his new thirty-five-metre yacht. Then Ralf's girlfriend brought her model girlfriends and he never managed to leave the boat in time for Sweden.

"What if I buy out my uncles?"

"It's so much money." His mum sighed.

"I have a good job. We can afford it." Carl expected a good bonus next year. Though if he did buy the summer house any mortgage on a flat in London would have to wait.

"Why would you do that?"

Carl thought for a moment. He watched his mother's hands as they wrapped around her coffee cup, the webs of wrinkles stretched tight. He was looking for the right words to describe something so familiar, yet he couldn't find them.

Like with so many things in life, he felt it but didn't know how to say it.

"It's our family legacy," he finally said quietly. "It's where I come from." He felt a slight shiver in his chest.

His mother's eyes blazed with tears but she remained composed.

"What about your sister?"

"What about her?"

"Will you share it with her when we die?"

"Oh, who thinks about death?"

"Carl, we're old. One day it will come."

"I'll share the house with her equally. Promise. And I'll find a time to come this summer. Maybe with Kristoffer."

"How is he?"

"He's good. Eva's pregnant. They're very happy."

The M4 from Heathrow was empty and in less than half an hour Carl was back in Chelsea. He turned off the engine and checked his phone. A couple of missed calls and a text from his mum that they had boarded their flight to Stockholm. A voicemail from Ralf, complaining about the snow and that it could interfere with the flight taking off in the morning. It occurred to Carl that he hadn't packed his luggage. He couldn't remember whether he had picked up his ski suit from the dry cleaner. He yawned and stretched and looked at his windows on the second floor. Lights from his Christmas tree blinked in the dark. It was his first tree since arriving in London ten years ago. He was glad his mother had insisted. It was their first Christmas with him in London and he had wanted them to have an amazing time.

When did they get so old that they thought about death?

Snow began swirling around the car, falling obliquely against a street light. The flakes were large and fluffy, as they often were in Sweden. He closed his eyes and saw an endless white landscape, the trees and roofs covered in soft snow-hats. He saw the Northern Lights.

A bang on the car window shook him out of his daydream. Carl slid the window down.

"Are you stalking your neighbours?" Luka thrust his head inside the car. His nose was red and running.

"Hi, Carl." A girl in a white hat with a fur pompom peeked out from behind Luka's shoulder. She looked familiar. Ciara? Lora? Whatever. Carl wondered how Luka remembered them all. More than once Luka had had casual sex with one girl, who turned out to know another girl with whom he had a fling, and a drama would ensue. Their anger, their fighting over him amused him but his best entertainment was from watching them try to hurt him by cooperating with each other. He didn't care about any of them after he'd slept with them, but somehow the girls came back for more. Carl's old-fashioned courting style, as Luka called it, was utterly unsuccessful compared to Luka's policy of open disregard.

"Hi, guys. What are you doing here?" Carl said.

"I called you twice. And left a voicemail."

"I didn't check my phone." He clasped his mobile in his pockct.

"Come with us to the Mandarin Oriental. A friend is joining us. She's a marvel." Luka blew half-melted snowflakes from the edges of his furry hood.

It was quite admirable that Luka always had a new girl to introduce him to. He tried hard to set Carl up, usually with someone beautiful, sometimes interesting. But they nearly always fell for Luka in the end.

"You still don't have a companion to go skiing tomorrow, do you?"

Carl shook his head. Did he need to bother asking?

"So …?" Luka said.

"I need to pack. And do some work."

Luka looked at him as if he was ill.

"You don't usually refuse a drink invitation."

"You know I have to prepare for the meeting the day after."

Luka pulled his chin into his neck and twisted his lips. "Sometimes I have a feeling you work enough for both of us."

Carl smiled. He often thought so too.

"I can drop you to the Mandarin," he said. Luka's girl was dressed in a short leather jacket and mini skirt and was dancing on her stilettos on the spot, trying to warm herself. "It doesn't look like there are many taxis tonight."

"Thanks, mate. Babe, jump in the back." Luka inclined the front seat to let her in.

"Can I smoke?" she said as soon as she sat down.

"Definitely not." Carl looked at her in the rear-view mirror. She was young, not much more than twenty, with a thick layer of make-up which made her look … tired. Did Luka call her 'babe' because he didn't remember her name?

"How is your brother? Why don't you call him to join you for a drink?" he said to Luka.

"Giovanni went to Phuket with his fiancée."

"Of course, he got engaged. So, you're without your partner in crime."

"I am indeed," Luka said in low voice. "You didn't hear what happened?"

"Go on."

"He was caught in the tsunami. He's in hospital."

"What?"

"Haven't you seen the news?"

"I saw the news, but I thought it was in Indonesia?"

"The earthquake was near Sumatra but the wave went all the way across the Indian Ocean. It hit Thailand too."

Thailand? Carl held his breath in for a few seconds. "Casualties?"

"Not much clear information but they say more than a hundred people killed in Phuket and even more injured, including tourists."

Carl gripped the wheel tightly. Kristoffer … Where was it he had gone? His mind was blank.

"What happened to your brother?"

"He called Dad this afternoon. Couldn't speak coherently. His doctor said his pelvis was fractured, minor injuries to his legs, a few scratches." Luka went silent, then stared at Carl. "What I can't work out is, if you see the wave approaching why don't you get away from the beach? I don't get it."

"Is his fiancée with him?"

"Can you imagine that? A tsunami in Thailand? On Boxing Day!"

"No," Carl said. "So, is his fiancée fine?"

"He doesn't know where she is. He lost her in the water."

"Are you going to Thailand?"

"No, no, it's too dangerous." Luka waved his hand in the air. "They're warning people not to travel to the affected area."

"Really?"

"Of course. Every earthquake has after-quakes and they're worried about a new one."

"But your brother …"

"Dad spoke to the Italian embassy in Thailand. They said once he's safe to travel they'll send him back on a medical plane."

"And his fiancée?"

"I'm sure she's fine. She probably can't find her way around. No mobile phone. Roads are destroyed. And how can she know that Giovanni is in a hospital? They say it's chaotic there. Power supplies interrupted, telephone lines jammed or down."

Carl listened without hearing. Luka was speaking fast, talking about a chance of something. His girlfriend shared her view and Luka rolled his eyes. Carl had exchanged texts with Kristoffer three days ago, or maybe four. They had landed in Bangkok, Kristoffer said. Where did they go from there? It was their honeymoon, for God's sake. How could anything happen to them?

"There's Liv. Stop. Stop here." Luka's girlfriend tapped on Carl's shoulder and pointed to a brunette in a full-length wool coat at the corner near a post box, standing in the pool of a street light. Her long dark hair fell over a shawl of indeterminate colour, a leather belt accentuated her thin waist. She was tall. Boots without heels and still probably as tall as him. One of the models Luka liked to hang out with, he concluded.

"She could be your Santa's present for being a good boy." Luka leaned across him and the window slid down.

Liv peered inside the car. Carl could make out the colour of the shawl now – a deep burgundy. Her lips were full and the same colour as the shawl.

"Hi, guys," she said in a quiet, cashmere-like voice and rested her blue eyes on Carl. Inside, he swooned.

"Hi, Liv," he said, trying to sound casual.

"Merry Christmas, *bellissima*," Luka said.

"*Grazie mille*. Merry Christmas to you all."

"Liv, come around. I'll get in the back next to *mia bell'angelo*." Luka winked at Carl.

She slid in and opened the top buttons of her coat. A gentle scent filled the car, the delicate aroma of jasmine.

"*Ar do Svensk?*" Carl said.

"I am." She smiled, revealing a perfect line of white teeth. "You too?"

"*Ja.*"

14

"I'd have never guessed it from your looks." She raised an eyebrow. "Italian, maybe."

"I wish I was," Carl said without looking at her. He had always wanted to be anything but Swedish.

"*Bella, c'è solo un Italiano. Ed sono io!*" Luka leaned forward between the seats. Liv laughed and ruffled his curls.

Luka said something else and Liv replied in fluent Italian and they both laughed. Amber was about to change to red. Carl knew there was no time to get through the lights but he pressed hard on the accelerator anyway and the car jerked forwards, sending everyone back into their seats.

"I don't wear a seat belt, dude," Luka growled.

"Sorry," Carl said, not feeling so.

"Where are you from in Sweden?" Liv said.

Her skin had a peach tan with a warm golden shade – the glow of the sun. She'd probably just returned from some tropical island. Or maybe she spent the autumn in Rome, improving her Italian, sitting under the warm sun in street cafés, sipping prosecco.

"A small town. You've probably never heard of it."

"Maybe I have."

"Finspång." He felt his cheeks reddening. He cleared his throat and added quickly, "It's near Norrkoping. My parents, as young teachers, were sent there after their study at Umea University. But never left."

"You're right, I've never heard of it. Is it nice?"

"No."

"That's not something people often say about their home town." She lifted an eyebrow and half-smiled.

"Just being honest," he said. "It's a boring industrial town. It often feels like a ghost town when I visit as there are so few people around." If there was anything that gave him ambition in life, it was a pulsing desire to leave the town and never go back, but he didn't say it aloud.

"I grew up in Stockholm."

"I could guess it."

"How?" When she tilted her head to the side, her earrings, thin golden leaves with crystals, sparkled in the street lights.

"Your accent," he said. It was a safe bet. He saw the same pattern in people from Stockholm or any other capital, and actually it wasn't really the accent. It was more the delivery – they didn't have to prove anything.

Carl parked in front of the Mandarin Oriental. The entrance was unabashed Christmas splendour, the towering columns opulently decorated with pine branches and candy canes and apples in sugar, silver and ruby ribbons, all studded with hundreds of blinking lights. A doorman in a scarlet tunic and top hat with golden ribbon stepped forward to open the car door.

"Mr Lundmark, a pleasure to see you again."

"Hi, George. Not tonight. I just drove my friends."

"Why not?" Liv said. There was a note of disappointment in her voice.

"I have to work."

"Oh. That answer –" she frowned, as if looking for the right word "–is devoid of life." She stood against the glittering lights of the Edwardian façade, large snowflakes landing on her silky hair. Carl felt a tightness in his chest and broke away from her gaze.

"Why? Because it's Christmas and everyone has to be merry?" He turned the ignition key. "I've important meetings coming up I need to prepare for. My job is my priority. I'm not alone in that." He wanted to say more but felt silly trying to explain himself to someone he had met five minutes ago. And yet something in what she had said left him unsettled, angry.

"Do you have a tendency to live in the future?" Liv said.

"Maybe. But I think most people live either in the future or the past, right?"

"And it doesn't bother you?"

"No, why would it?"

Liv half-shrugged.

"Life in London," he said, "is fast-paced. Everyone is on the run. I have things planned for a year ahead. And that includes travel, friends, family … Not just work."

"But isn't life always like that?"

"Meaning?" His foot was on the brake, ready to release it.

"You go running after something with high hopes, then once you get it you find it's never as good as running and hoping?"

Carl pushed the front door, a loud rasp announcing his arrival to an otherwise silent flat. A slight smell of cinnamon was still in the air and the flat was dark but for blueish squares on the carpet from the street light outside the window. Normally, before leaving his flat, he'd leave at least a table lamp on by the entrance. It gave him comfort when he returned, a little warmth, a deceiving feeling that the place wasn't empty.

Carl fumbled along the wall and turned on the lights. He took off his coat and shoes and went to his office. At his desk, he picked up a Morgan Stanley report from the top of the pile of documents and mindlessly flipped through its pages. The thought of working the whole night filled him with dread. He lifted his eyes from the report and gazed at a picture in a silver-plate frame with rusted corners on a bookshelf. He and Kristoffer at their graduation. What always struck him about that picture was how different they both looked. With their bronzed skin they stood out from a blond cluster of their friends, summer sun intensifying the contrast.

He remembered that mix of sadness and excitement. Anxiety, too, about the next step. "Do you know what my favourite stories are?" Kristoffer had said before the photographer asked them all to smile. "When you think it's the end of a story, unaware that it's only the beginning."

Carl walked to the world map on the wall. Where did he and Eva go in Thailand? It wasn't Phuket. Kristoffer had said they found a special place for their honeymoon, a pristine beach away from the crowd. There were so many places in Thailand they could choose from. He peered at the Gulf of Thailand, the eastern coast. Samui. Koh Tao. That sounded familiar. Was that where Kristoffer had said he wanted to go? He had become passionate about diving since they went together on a bucket-list trip to the Red Sea. And after manta rays in Hawaii, passion had turned into obsession and now he was chasing whale sharks. Carl pulled his phone from his jeans pocket and turned it in his hands. There must be a six- or seven-hour time difference with Thailand – they were surely asleep. And if something had happened Kristoffer would have called him. If he could. No, it wasn't Phuket. He shoved his phone into his pocket and returned to the desk.

The Torekov letter. Carl rushed out to the hall and pulled open the console drawer where he had stuffed a pile of correspondence from before Christmas. He flipped through the usual junk – advertisements, leaflets for home deliveries – and then he saw it. A thick envelope with jagged edges and Swedish stamps. Inside, a card with a picture from Kristoffer's wedding, elegantly handwritten by Eva. Warm Christmas wishes. Nothing about the honeymoon destination.

They must have gone to Koh Tao, Carl decided. He squatted near the Christmas tree, the pine aroma filling his nostrils, and put the card on a low side table along with other Christmas cards, arranging it so it was right in the middle.

He stared at the photo. It was taken after the church as they were walking a bright green carpet of grass with daisies to the shore. The wind blew Eva's hair and her golden curls rushed over Kristoffer's face. It was a small and intimate wedding, only a few close friends and family, on the southwest coast. There was nothing fancy about it, no pretentious ceremony or lavish reception, just a stainless steel champagne bucket and tall glasses with frozen berries balanced on the rocks, and waves crashing against a monolithic altar. Yet it was the most beautiful wedding Carl had ever been to. The dramatic, breathtaking Nordic landscape only emphasised the purity of the occasion and the fragility of their feelings as well as the resounding greatness of the promise they had made to each other.

He tipped the envelope and three photos slid out into his hand. On one, he was sitting between Eva's two sisters at the dinner the night before the wedding. He had been asking Eva to introduce him to her sisters since Kristoffer had started to date her but she always teased him that they were too good for him, that he had to man up. It was Kristoffer who sat Carl between the girls, and he joked that Carl was even luckier than the groom since he got the double date.

The youngest sister, Cecilia, was the most beautiful of the three, Carl thought – thin-boned, unlike most of the Swedish girls, with high cheekbones, and shy, which made her even more enigmatic. Or maybe she was just reserved like him. She didn't speak much but when she did, he could see she was a passionate and independent thinker. Carl liked that in people – freedom, originality, quirkiness. Sometimes he wished that hedge funds excited him as much as Cecilia's studies of the behaviour of dust particles in a vacuum did her.

He had never doubted that finance was the right choice for him. It gave him money, prestige, social standing, everything he thought he wanted, everything he would never get in Sweden. He felt he fitted into the existence he had built for himself. And it wasn't devoid of life, as the Swedish girl had said today. She probably grew up in a wealthy Stockholm neighbourhood with her life neatly planned by her parents. What did she know?

Carl returned to his desk and worked for some hours until his stomach began to rumble. In the fridge, he found leftovers from yesterday's dinner. Fried potatoes soaked overnight in parsley and garlic butter and they tasted even better, he discovered, than the night before. He forked a piece of fillet steak from a tray – even cold it melted in his mouth. He took his plate to the couch.

The death toll continues to rise as the horrifying pictures of the extent of the damage emerge. More than eleven thousand people are thought to have been killed in South East Asia.

The BBC was broadcasting from the Indonesian province of Aceh, the worst-hit area, interspersing the report with short clips from the rest of the region. Video footage was showing something that had previously been a shoreline but now showed no boundary between land and sea. Buildings had been stripped of their facades and concrete walls joined the rush of debris along with the remains of buses, cars, trees, and random figures that popped up above the muddy water, arms stretched into the air.

Carl stopped chewing and put his fork on the plate.

"At least three hundred have been killed in southern Thailand," the reporter said, "including a large number of tourists, and hundreds of people are reported missing." There was footage of two adults and seven or eight children huddled together on a large floating object he couldn't identify. The picture shook for several seconds, showing blue sky, and when it came back on, there was only one adult left on the makeshift raft.

He muted the television and dialled a phone number he knew by heart.

"*Hej*, Goran."

He tried to sound light and cheerful. He had called Kristoffer's parents on Christmas night and wished them compliments of the season, and now he was thinking how to begin the conversation without causing needless worry.

"Carl, we can't reach Kristoffer."

A cold tendril worked its way along his spine, and Carl slowly breathed out.

"I'm sure he's alright," he said in an even voice. He hoped he sounded confident. He wanted to be confident. "I heard communication is almost impossible."

"His phone is off. We have been calling him from this morning." Goran let out a little sob. "The hotel lines are down too."

"It still doesn't mean that something bad happened to Kristoffer."

But all he heard was Goran's heavy breathing, interrupted by a series of sharp sniffs, then nothing.

Kristoffer's mum took the phone. "Carl, what do we do?"

"I'm going to keep trying. I'll call you. What's the name of the hotel?"

Carl wrote on the corner of a newspaper, '*Golden Buddha Bch Res*'. His fingers trembled and the pen fell soundlessly to the carpet. He held his head in his hands. His heart was thumping in his chest.

He dialled the Kristoffer's number for the tenth time.

"Hi, it's Kristoffer. Please, leave a message."

He sounded so close. Carl was about to leave another

message when the call dropped. The phone lay ominously silent in his hand.

Carl darted to his computer. The resort was on an island he never heard of, Koh Phra Thong, north of Phuket, almost at the border with Burma. The red dot on a Google map indicated the hotel on the western side of the island. It was the only resort on a deserted beach, twelve kilometres long according to the resort's website. It appeared to be isolated from the mainland infrastructure and hard to access – from Phuket it was two hours by car and another one and a half by longtail boat. '*Pristine beach away from the crowd.*' Put like that, it sounded menacing.

Carl dialled one of the numbers for the resort. First there was a long silence, then the call dropped. He tried several more numbers, with the same result. He called and called … and called. He called the Swedish Embassy in Thailand. He called the Thai authorities. Nothing. He couldn't reach anyone in Thailand. The panic inside of him grew but at the same time he comforted himself with the thought that phone lines were jammed for the entire country.

In the end, Carl managed to get through to the Swedish Ministry for Foreign Affairs but got only their voicemail. He called the mobile numbers the ministry posted online for emergencies, but still had no luck getting an actual person on the line. That was strange at the very least. How come nobody responded to a 24-hour line? Also, there was no announcement from the Swedish foreign minister – that was more than strange, as Thailand was a favourite destination for Swedish families in winter. Perhaps, as usual, the calamity had been exaggerated by the media and that was why all was quiet.

No. He knew from the news that at least eleven countries in the region were impacted. Tourists from Europe,

America, Australia had been caught in the wave. Dozens of people were blogging from the affected areas but the words 'tsunami', 'casualties' and 'Golden Buddha' didn't produce the information he was looking for.

Then his eyes lit on a link to the resort's own blog: *Golden Buddha Beach Resort hit. All but obliterated.*

Heat rushed to his face.

He pressed the link.

The post was five sentences, a seven-line message by the resort's general manager, Lucas Reedley, who said he was on a waiting list for a plane to Bangkok from Sydney. He wrote that there was no connection with the island, that he had received several alarming calls earlier from his staff, and that the resort was destroyed with a large number of people missing, presumed dead. '*We are calling everyone we know, plus rescue services there and elsewhere to try and mobilise a helicopter, so far without success.*'

Carl read the last sentence aloud. Twice.

He shut his eyes and pressed on them with his fingers until the blackness turned into webs of lights. Fatalities. Destruction. His thoughts were rushing in all directions but nothing was making sense.

Carl grabbed his phone and dialled Lucas's number. No answer.

He sagged into the chair, staring at the screen. The message has been posted at 4 p.m. Thailand time. More than twelve hours ago. And still no news. How come they still couldn't reach the island? How come nobody was sending help?

His senses were drowning in panic.

He rocked back and forth. Okay, so the wave had hit the resort but there was no way something could happen to Kristoffer in the water. Not to him. He was a great swimmer. He could have competed at international level if he'd wanted.

In fact, he had been approached twice by the Swedish Swimming Federation.

Carl glanced at the rusted frame. The same year that photo was taken, two weeks before graduation at the end of an unusually hot Swedish summer, he had gone to Hjo to visit Kristoffer. When he arrived Kristoffer wasn't home. His mother said he was still at the local Olympic swimming pool.

Carl found him sitting up on the lifeguard chair, looking down at the pool. His shift was over but he had stayed on. The sun was playing on the water's surface. A group of boys, not more than ten or eleven, stood in a line on the edge, listening to a coach's instructions. There was a whistle and the kids dived into the water as one.

"I'd like to be a coach." Kristoffer lifted his water cup and with the back of his hand he wiped the sweat from his forehead. "It must feel so rewarding to work with kids, see their excitement, their progress. What could be better?"

Carl shrugged.

Both their dads were coaches at local football teams. Carl's dad spent every weekend at the stadium, everyone knew him in his home town and Carl was proud to be his son. He loved to play football. But he had no urge to get involved in coaching. That was the difference between him and Kristoffer – Carl didn't have time for all of that; he still had to climb a hundred steps before he could become who he always wanted to be.

"I'm watching that boy in the second lane." Kristoffer pointed. "He's really good. Remarkably more advanced in his swimming than the rest."

The boy glided through the water, effortlessly cutting the surface with his arms.

Carl remembered saying, "Can you swim faster than him?" He intended it to sound funny. He knew the answer.

24

Of course he could. Kristoffer was the best swimmer he had ever met.

Carl switched off his computer. There was nothing more he could do here and now, in the middle of the night. His taxi was at 6 a.m. and he had to get some sleep.

He walked to his bedroom and mechanically threw clothes on the bed – socks, sweaters, ski suit still in a plastic bag from the dry cleaners. When he was packed he stretched out on the bed, turned off the light, put earplugs in his ears and closed his eyes. He lay still for a long while, maybe an hour or more, unable to sleep, heart thumping behind his closed eyes, thoughts rushing in all directions, an uneasy feeling in his gut. He repeated to himself several times that there was nothing more he could do at this moment.

Then, almost instantly, merciful darkness.

No air. The wave was tossing Carl around like a grain of sand. The current dragged him on his back over the stony seabed. He heard a cracking sound in his neck, and the next wave hit him on the back of the head with his board and spat him out on the beach. Exhausted, he lay in the surf choking, clearing his mouth of sand.

Two whole days like this and Carl still couldn't surf to save his life.

"Dude, you need to paddle faster." Kristoffer bent over him. "Girls fancy hot guys *on* surfboards, not under them."

"That wouldn't be me then."

Carl turned his head to the left and then slowly to the right. It obeyed and there was no pain. He rubbed a swelling above his left temple. The whole business of surfing was turning out to be more challenging than he had initially thought when the two of them showed up on Waikiki beach with their well-waxed, shiny rental boards. Neither of them had surfed before, but both were as excited as kids at the prospect. Of course, Kristoffer rode a wave at the first attempt.

"Water doesn't like fear. You have to feel the flow. Embrace it with your heart, with every cell of your body – be a part of it." Kristoffer reached out a hand. "You must go with it. Not against it."

In the afternoon they drove to the North Shore of Oahu, the place with the most astonishing waves in the world, where surfing without experience was suicide. When they pulled up in the jeep they paused to survey the action. The ocean was the arena and the beach always gathered spectators, who watched with amazement the displays of wild seas and courageous men.

"Raw athleticism," said Kristoffer.

"Crass stupidity," murmured Carl.

But Kristoffer wasn't listening. "Look at that," he said. His eyes lit up as he watched the massive white waves crashing over the reef. He slammed the door of the jeep and rushed down the beach. Carl followed, but halfway down he felt a pain in his stomach. Probably all the salty water he had swallowed in the morning. He stopped and dropped his bag on the sand.

"I'll be there one day," Kristoffer yelled over his shoulder. He was pointing at a colossal wave rising from the depths, and he took up a surfing pose, balancing atop an imaginary crest. Carl laughed. He couldn't hear anything else Kristoffer shouted – the wind was swallowing his words. Carl lay back on his elbows and dug his toes into the warm sand. He wondered if Kristoffer knew that he was afraid. He hoped he didn't.

He got out a can of cool beer from his bag, lifted the ring and took two large gulps as he watched Kristoffer mingle with the surfers as if he had always been one of them. Sometimes he looked over at Carl and shouted something or pointed, but

Carl didn't catch a word. Bizarrely, though, amidst the roar of the ocean and the whistling of the wind he could distinguish Kristoffer's laugh. It seemed that nothing could ever hold it back. It came from the bottom of his lungs and the depths of his heart: deep, confident, free. Its power triumphed over everything. His laugh was as contagious as life itself.

Carl's eyes followed a gutsy surfer gliding across the face of a splendid deep blue wave as it mounted more than five metres in the air and began curling into a perfect tube. The man disappeared into a phalanx of raging white foam. Carl stood up, peering into the spot where the man had gone. A minute later, the surfer slipped free from the jaws of Poseidon, effortlessly balancing on his board behind a magnificent rainbow of salty spray.

It was mesmerising to watch the sublime dance of man and ocean. One moment it seemed as though the surfers were riders of wild giants, the next mere random dancers, as small as grains of sand, in the hands of an untameable force. Why did they take such risks? To make the impossible possible? What made them surf to the edge of life and death?

"When you're surfing on the crest it's like being kissed by God."

Carl turned, and there was a white-haired man behind him, his nut-coloured skin shrunk like on an old apple, his muscles wiry and tight. He rested his hand was on the bony shoulder of a boy no older than twelve. Both of them had boards.

"The rest is dust," the man said, gazing into the hazy distance, his large grey eyes serene.

Carl woke up and sat bolt upright, staring at the blue light from the digital clock. 04:10. He had had that dream many times over the years. Every time, the story unfolded with such precision, word for word, that he found it hard to believe he was dreaming. He didn't remember that day as reality anymore; certainly, he didn't remember the old surfer. He had fashioned a memory out of a dream. He always felt empty when he woke up, lost, as if he had failed to understand an important message. Carl ran his fingers along his forehead, pressed lightly above the left temple. It felt tender.

He lay down and closed his eyes. There was another hour before his alarm. He tossed and turned but couldn't get back to sleep. His mind refused to be still. It would soon be midday in Thailand.

Carl got up and went to his office, turned on his computer. What yesterday was shocking news today became an overwhelming reality all over the world. Skipping though web pages with images of destruction and despair, he turned to the latest post on the resort's blog:

At roughly 10.30 a.m. on 26 December, a tsunami hit Golden Buddha Beach Resort in three successive waves. There is severe devastation on the island and fatalities among the guests and employees. Many people made their way to one of the two hills above the resort, where they stayed the rest of the day and through the night. On the morning of 27 December, a relay of helicopters took survivors from Golden Buddha Beach to various locations on the mainland – Kuraburi, Phuket and others. Many are already on their way to Bangkok. Some of the injured have been taken to hospitals in Ranong and Phuket. As of now, three-quarters of the missing have been accounted for. Six people confirmed dead. With so many rumours and conflicting reports, this can only be a rough outline of what happened.

Carl scanned a list of sixty-eight names of people known to be alive.

Nothing.

He leaned closer to the screen, tracing each name with his finger, whispering as he read. The names were written randomly, some without the last name or the first, some in couples or family sets. But no 'Kristoffer' or 'Eva'.

He sat for a while. Waiting. Hoping that somebody was still compiling the list and that it would update. That their names would appear on the screen at any moment. The hum from the computer was growing louder. He felt blood hammering in his temples.

Carl took the phone and dialled Lucas Reedley's number. Nobody picked up.

Then a thought struck him. Maybe they hadn't stayed at the hotel that day. Maybe they were already in Bangkok. He smacked his hand to his forehead. Of course! Kristoffer's parents were expecting them to come to Hjo for New Year. They could even have checked out early. Maybe they didn't like the hotel and found something else. Carl fidgeted in his chair. Let out a short laugh. Of course, they were not there.

He dialled the number again.

"Lucas Reedley."

Somebody finally responding took him by surprise.

"Hi," Carl said, getting his thoughts together. "I have friends staying at your resort, a Swedish couple Kristoffer and Eva Berg. We can't get in contact with them." He felt his throat tightening. "Do you have any information about them?"

"Give me a minute."

The connection was poor. With every crackle his heart missed a beat. A part of him wanted to hang up, for things to be as they used to be. A layer of sweat formed between his hand and the receiver.

"According to our records, Mr and Mrs Berg are missing."

"Missing?"

"Yes, I'm afraid we still have some guests and members

of staff missing. Searching continues on the island and I'm waiting to hear more. Please, don't lose hope, stories of people surviving the tsunami are coming in all the t—"

"Missing?"

"Be patient and pray for your friends. I'll come back to you once we have any information. It'd be helpful if you notify the Swedish Embassy. Sorry, I must go now."

Reedley hung up and Carl stood in the middle of the room, dazed, holding the phone next to his ear, listening to the long beeps. He absently put his thumb on the red button. His hand weakened its grasp and the phone fell to the floor.

"Missing?" he said, unaware he was speaking, unaware he was weeping. He knelt. He had to. The room was reeling, filled with snatches of news, Lucas's words, people's voices, the processor's ominous hum. He squeezed his ears with his hands and clenched his teeth. A feeling of helplessness overcame him and he leaned forward until his head touched the floor.

"You look rough," Ralf said.

Carl blankly stared at him.

"What did you end up doing last night?"

Carl rubbed his face. It felt numb. He looked around, as if realising where he was for the first time. It was quiet – nobody there yet apart from him and Ralf. There was something to be said for private jet terminal lounges.

"You look sick. I've told you often enough, you drink too much."

"I didn't drink."

"Bullshit. I know you."

"My friend and his wife have gone missing in the tsunami."

"What? Who?"

"Kristoffer."

"The Asian guy? The one who came to the office party?"

"Yes. He is Korean."

"How come he spoke Swedish?"

"He was adopted when he was a year old."

"I watched the news. Unbelievable. But hopefully your friend is fine. Give it a few days."

Ralf tore the top from a sugar stick, tipped it into his coffee, and stirred. The spoon clanked on the sides of the cup. He sipped noisily and smacked his lips. Carl recoiled. He felt the room was shrinking around him.

"They are still clearing the runway of snow, apparently. Can you imagine that in Sweden? A snowflake, and the airport is paralysed. Every year the same. Do they really expect they can skip a winter or two? But don't worry, my pilot says we should be in the air in two hours."

Ralf stretched his legs forward, threw his arms back and clenched them behind his head, yawning.

"There in time for lunch. I booked a table on a terrace of La Maison. Then we ski down and have après-ski at The Golden Pine with Mike Clifford from CDF. If these guys invest in our fund, it'll be at least a hundred million. We need them and their deep pockets."

Carl felt as if a steel vice was squeezing his chest.

"Mike is very keen to meet you. I bet he'll sign before the New Year." Ralf slapped his newspaper on Carl's knee.

Carl nodded and cleared his throat.

"I can't go with you," he said.

"What?"

"I can't go with you."

"Reason?"

"I must fly to Thailand."

"Because of your friend?" Ralf said, putting a little laugh on the last word.

"Yes."

"Missing only means they don't know where they are."

"What if something happened to them?"

"Carl, you can't be serious. It doesn't make any sense for you to fly there. What do you imagine you can do? Haven't you read the news? The whole place is a mess."

"I don't care."

"Well, I care. Because I need you here. We launch a new fund in a week. It's your fund. You worked on it for nearly two years. And we are meeting the key investor." Ralf gave a humourless smirk. "Well, it's good that I have Luka. He'll grab the opportunity immediately. You know that."

Carl lifted his shoulders in a tiny shrug.

"Carl, you need to chill and think about the consequences of your decision. And not play the hero."

"I can't leave Kristoffer behind. It's not who I am."

"Who you are is an idiot," Ralf shouted. "What are you going to do there? Volunteer to dig with your bare hands in the rubble? Do me a favour, Carl. I do know *that's* not who you are."

Carl stared at him, bewildered and angry. He had stood behind Ralf when the company almost collapsed under the weight of financial penalties and Ralf had split from his business partners. He had helped him to hide his financial assets when his ex-wife's lawyers were sniffing through the company accounts. He never said anything when Ralf flirted with Natalie. Ralf knew that Carl was in love with her, and yet there he was, seducing her with his wealth, and rubbing Carl's nose in it to boot. And Carl … well, he thought she'd be happier with him and stepped back.

Now he felt Ralf didn't know him at all. No, he wouldn't go to search in the ruins. But he wouldn't leave Kristoffer alone. That was the difference between him and Ralf.

"What would you do if it was your best friend?"

Ralf gave him a sidelong glance. "I definitely would not fly there, only to get in the way of the rescue teams on the ground. It's the tropics, Carl. And with the heat and, dare I say it, decomposing bodies, there's a high risk of infection and disease. To go there is stupid. Ridiculous. If you want to help your friend, you can do so from here rather than risk your own life. We have money, we can hire a search team. We get in touch with the Swedish Embassy, for a start." He leaned in close and whispered: "I have high-ranking friends in Thailand—"

Of course that was what Ralf would do, why had Carl even bothered to ask him? He turned away to the huge windows overlooking the airfield; it was getting light out there.

"Carl, look at me."

Ralf came so close that Carl couldn't see anything but blackheads and clogged pores on his flabby skin. He was breathing heavily through wide nostrils. "I'm telling you as your friend, not your boss. I'm not a heartless ass who wants only money. I do care about you, your wellbeing and our work together. You're like a son to me, and you know that." His voice had a metallic edge. "You do know that?"

"I do." It was a lie, and Carl forced a weak smile.

"I gave you your first proper job in London. I always believed in you, and that was the reason I hired you. Because I saw a man with great potential. You grew in front of me, from a provincial boy who didn't know what he wanted in life into a successful man."

The more he spoke, the less Carl wanted to hear. But a part of him knew that Ralf was right. Flying to Thailand was pointless. Worse, it was irresponsible – towards himself and his family, towards the fund, even towards Ralf. What *could* he do? Where would he even go when he got there?

But something inside blinded him to all reason.

Every day, Carl followed the logical path, weighed every decision. He did what was expected of him. What he believed to be right. He was always afraid he might take a wrong step. Now, there was no fear, no hesitation. Now, he felt liberated. He felt that for the first time in his thirty-two-years on this Earth he was making a decision that really mattered.

Two

Before

Eva squeezed Kristoffer's hand and felt the warmth of his skin.

A crimson sun dipped its lower rim into the sea on the horizon, and the boundless water's surface was mirror smooth. They were squelching in bare feet along the tideline, breaking the breathless stillness as the island sank into the night.

"Not many places like this beach left," Kristoffer said. "We must have been walking for an hour and look: no one trying to sell us anything, no reps, no boats overloaded with noisy tourists. It's an untouched, forgotten coast. Well, unknown anyway."

He squatted and picked up a seashell half-buried in the sand. He rinsed it in the water and ran his fingers along its smooth pearlesque inner surface.

"Throw or keep?"

Eva took the shell from his open palm and turned it in her hands. "Not the tiniest blemish. Keep."

"I certainly like that there's no phone connection," she said. "Imagine my boss calling every other day, reminding me about unfinished projects."

"You know I found a bit of reception?"

"Where?"

"On that hill. The Hornbill Hill, they call it." He waved to a rocky hillock, shaped like a thrown cape, falling to the sea at the end of the beach, just beyond the resort's clubhouse. "I climbed it early this morning to see the view. You were still asleep. It's steeper than it looks – I only got up to where that scrawny tree is leaning over the rocks. And then *ping*, my phone began to receive every message from the last two days. I only replied to Mum and Dad. And Carl. Anyway, everyone knows we are on honeymoon – they won't be offended if I ignore them for once."

"You didn't waken me?"

"Didn't like to. And I'm certainly not suggesting you go up there for a signal. Why don't you put your phone in the clubhouse safe, with our rings? Otherwise your boss will be your well-deserved karma."

"Too late. It so happens I also briefly got a signal – at the yoga *sala*. It's just patchy."

Eva bent and dug out a large seashell with a giraffe-like pattern. It was heavier than an empty shell should be. She turned it over and a pair of brown claws protruded from the opening. When she gently placed it on the wet sand, a pair of eyes followed the claws and the shell began to move towards the water.

"I don't think it will stay like that long," she said.

"The hermit crab?"

"No, this virgin beach. Some big chain will come and build a massive resort on the island."

"I thought Golden Buddha owned this beach."

"The big guys will offer them a price they can't refuse. You know how it works. Money rules the world."

"Love rules the world," Kristoffer said.

He hugged her from behind, placing his hands on her stomach. It was still flat, but they both knew it wouldn't be for long. She leaned her head back on his shoulder, and he put his chin against hers, their cheeks touching. She inhaled his skin scent and the warm, spicy aroma of the sandalwood fragrance he had been using since she first bought it for him. They were breathing in the same rhythm, watching the sun disappear into the ocean. The cicada chorus ceased as the last rays began to fade.

"In places like this you feel eternity in a single moment." Kristoffer whispered into her ear and goosebumps ran along her skin.

"And a single moment turns into eternity."

On the western horizon, shades of violet slipped gradually into palest lilac. The sea reflected the sky and intensified the colours, making them richer and deeper. The surface of the water was milky cream touched with rose powder, and the sand was momentarily aflame. The whole island seemed wrapped with the finest transparent silk, and the world became a pink mirage.

Eva stretched her arms into the air as if trying to hug the sky.

Kristoffer scooped her in his arms, lifting her in the air and spinning around. In his strong arms she felt safe, she trusted him with her life – he was her fortress. He kept whirling her until they fell together to the sand, laughing. She felt dizzy with joy, as if she had woken from a sublime dream in time to see the first stars light up the night sky.

It was fully dark when they got back to the resort. A huge, almost full moon rose above the palm trees. The night air was crystal clear, and on the moon's surface Eva thought she could see craters and lunar seas. She felt that if she could climb Hornbill Hill she might trace its edges with the tips of her fingers. She lingered for a moment, mesmerised, breathing in the humid, salty air laced with the honey aroma of a flower she didn't know the name of, tucked behind an elephant statue covered with moss. Then she followed Kristoffer along the sandy path between two rows of burning garden fire torches, to the clubhouse.

A collection of flip-flops and sandals lay at the bottom of the stairs to the lower stilted deck. Eva wondered who wore shoes here, because five days after arriving on the island she hadn't unpacked hers. She brushed off the sand from her feet and tiptoed up the weathered stairs. Jack, who seemed to live on the island all year around, had said that during the tropical monsoon the ocean was nothing like the tamed azure waters of the tourist season, and that waves would wash up over the lower deck of the clubhouse – that was why all the shoreline bungalows were built on high stilts.

The lantern-lit deck was like a beehive, crowded with resort guests and buzzing with a dozen languages. Looking for Kristoffer, Eva glanced around the bar area with its gold-painted statue of a smiling, rather than a contemplative, Buddha, his expression encouraging guests to order more drinks and have a laugh instead of inspiring a serene detachment from life's goodies. By now, she knew at least a third of the holidaymakers. It was impossible not to because the clubhouse was the only shared space at the resort, where everyone gathered for meals and drinks. It held the heartbeat of the resort, probably in the chubby torso of the happy Buddha, Eva thought.

She stopped to chat with Julia, an eccentric Australian woman with short grey hair which she didn't care to colour. She wore the funkiest bright shirts every night, but not tonight – it was the first time Eva had seen her in a plain linen shirt and she almost didn't recognise her until she grabbed her by the elbow.

"Do you want to join us for a cooking class tomorrow?"

"You are asking the wrong person. In our family, it's Kristoffer who is the chef."

"Oh, how Swedish," Julia said, pushing her lips forward and extending the '*sh*' so that it sounded distinctly French.

Jose had overheard the conversation. He raised an eyebrow and looked sideways at his partner Jonas.

"Swedish guys are the best."

Jose was the epitome of Spanish beauty, Eva thought, with his dark, intense, almond-shaped eyes under long lashes. He spoke like a male version of Penelope Cruz when she wasn't hiding her accent, and his lips were just as sensual. Jonas, who like Eva was born and raised in Lund, was his perfect blond counterpart, with a lighter tan and pale blue eyes, and no accent whatever language he happened to be speaking. They were like salt and pepper. They were travelling the world, Jonas donning his crisp white apron everywhere from high-tech kitchens in Tokyo to an open fire in Morocco, and Jose with his camera. They had published several hugely successful books on cooking. Kristoffer had said he had two of Jonas' books on a kitchen shelf; indeed that one of Eva's favourite dishes, salmon with ginger and shiitake, was Jonas' recipe.

Yesterday, listening to the pair's travel adventures, Eva wondered whether becoming a human rights lawyer had been the right choice of career. She had always wanted to fight for the rights of those who had no voice – it wasn't just her job, it was her life. But it was a burden because at times she found it hard to separate the two. The whole summer she had worked on filing an appeal to the International Court of Justice at the UN, to return ancestral land to the Sami – the indigenous people of northern Sweden. She and Kristoffer had postponed their honeymoon until Christmas because of unexpected delays with the case. Why couldn't she just devote her time to flowers rather than to injustice towards people? Why couldn't she sleep soundly at night, and travel the world taking pictures of gardens instead of fighting oppression? Flowers made people happier more often than the ugly truth. In the next life, she would become a gardener.

"Are you going to pay a celebrity visit to the kitchen?" she said.

"In fact, yes," Jonas said. "I don't know if you noticed, but everywhere you go you get a slightly different *tom yum* soup. Just as there are no two similar tiramisus in Italy, there's no one way to cook *tom yum*. I'm kind of looking for my perfect blend of lemongrass and chilli, so to say, and I like it more with coconut milk – here in Thailand they mostly do a clear version which is sourer than I prefer."

As he spoke, Jonas gestured with long, neatly manicured fingers. He held his back straight and his chin up, so that she thought he might start singing or dancing at any minute.

"How come you still don't have a TV show?"

"It's on its way, my dear. This summer we filmed the first season in Italy. It's released on the first of Jan. And once the holidays are over, we start shooting the second season in Thailand."

"Any episode from the Golden Buddha kitchen?"

"Quite possibly." Jonas stirred his drink – iced water with mint leaves – with a straw.

"Jose? Is that you?" A brunet pranced through the crowd, her strapless black dress with large printed poppies accentuating her curves.

Everyone turned to look at Jose, including people at the bar.

"Carmen!"

"Jose."

She threw her hands around his neck. As she moved her long hair away from her shoulders, the flowery scent of expensive perfume exploded in the air, masking the citronella smell of mosquito repellent the rest of them were wearing. She kissed his cheek, leaving a print of her red lipstick on his skin, like a little poppy. Eva couldn't take her eyes off them; they were like a Hispanic version of Barbie and Ken – thin and stunning.

Eva had never thought of herself as beautiful like her two sisters, even though Kristoffer always said she was the most beautiful woman he had ever met. She spent little time in front of the mirror, looking instead for beauty elsewhere – in the endlessly changing natural world, in books and art and music, above all in the souls of people whose beauty was on the inside. When she had learned that she was pregnant, Kristoffer asked whom among his friends they should choose as godfather, and she immediately said, "Carl – who else?". Carl was beautiful inside and out, even though he wasn't aware of it.

"Everyone, it's Carmen," Jose finally said when they ended their embrace. "I haven't seen you for, how long … ten years?"

Eva sneaked a glance at Jonas, who was still monotonously stirring the melting ice in his glass.

"Of all places on Earth," Carmen said, "we meet on this speck of sand in the sea. What a coincidence."

"It's because you never come to Barcelona anymore. Rumour has it you are dating an Italian?"

"Wrong." She flashed her ring finger. "We are engaged."

"Of all nationalities, you go Italian. A Spanish woman with an Italian man. You break my heart."

"What is this drama with Italians?" Julia whispered to Eva. She nudged Jonas. "Who doesn't love Italians?"

"Exactly. I think it's a Spanish conspiracy." Jonas finally pushed his glass away and folded his arms. "So, Carmen, how do you like the resort?"

"It's very rustic, with plenty of monkeys and bugs. I wish our bungalow had glass windows instead of bamboo shutters. I prefer protected places with air conditioning. But Georgiou loves it." She opened her purse, revealing three mobile phones and two lipsticks – unusual contents for the island life. "Do they have any reception on the island?"

"In the yoga *sala* occasionally," Eva said.

"Wonderful, I like yoga. Where is it?"

"It's dark there, princess," said Jose. "And more mosquitos than your skin can handle … Come, let's find your Italian fiancé. Where would he be?"

"With Jack. We are visiting him. Do you know Jack?"

"Everyone knows Jack."

"He's like an older brother to Georgiou."

"And where is your Swedish man tonight?" Julia said to Eva.

"On the deck. At the pool table." Eva could see Kristoffer applying chalk to his cue. He looked lost in thought, but she knew he was concentrating.

"I played him yesterday," Jonas said. "No chance for me."

Linda, the only person at yoga who could do a head stand, was navigating her way from the bar towards the pool table, with half a dozen cans of Chang beer on a tray.

"I think my husband has a chance tonight," she said, her arms trembling under the load.

"I want to see that," Jonas said and went after her, followed by Eva and Julia. Kristoffer was bent over the table, his index finger curled around the shaft of the cue, his eyes locked on the yellow ball at the edge of the corner pocket. Linda's husband Peter was leaning with both hands on the table, his thick ginger brows drawn together. A little knot of people stood watching. Since arriving, Kristoffer hadn't lost a game.

Eva squeezed into the space next to Jack and was immediately aware of the smell of strong cigarettes.

"Tricky shot," he whispered, and tucked his unruly black curls behind his ears. He motioned for her to move in front of him for a better view; he was tall enough to see above everyone's heads.

Eva knew that Kristoffer had to shoot the cue ball with no angle and no top, bottom or side spin, in such a way that there would be no energy remaining to carry the cue ball. She'd never be able to do such a shot.

Kristoffer took his shot and the yellow ball was in the pocket, the cue ball dead at the edge.

"You are just a lucky bastard," Peter said. He took off his glasses and wiped his whole face with the bottom of his linen shirt.

"There is no luck in pool," Kristoffer said.

"Not for me anyway. At least not good luck. My last shots were impossible."

"It's not bad luck. It's the laws of physics."

"It's chaos."

"Which is one of the laws of physics."

"You are a lawyer, not a physicist."

"Let's say I like laws full stop," Kristoffer said, and smiled.

"Okay, how do you explain that I obviously had an advantage for most of the game and then my last ball got sandwiched between your balls until your last shot?"

"You took the easiest balls too early."

Peter puffed. "Tomorrow. Same place, same time." He threw Kristoffer a beer from the tray.

Eva was leaning with her back to the railing, next to Jack and Linda. They were chatting to Nora, a German woman who had arrived the day before and was staying with her daughters in a bungalow not far from Kristoffer and Eva. A little girl with a lollypop behind her cheek and wheat-coloured hair pulled into a pair of thin ponytails knelt between Nora's feet, playing with a string of coral beads. Eva had seen her and her older sister that morning, collecting fallen flowers from the garden and putting them in a bucket. According to Nora they had been coming here every Christmas since Zoe was born, and the older girl had already picked up some Thai.

"When your husband arrives, we can finalise all the details. And the bungalow is yours," Jack said. "Though it's booked the whole of January, in theory. I might be able to move some reservations around, we'll see."

"Marcus texted that his flight was finally about to take off. He thinks with delays he will only make it to the resort at lunchtime."

"These guys are buying one of Jack's bungalows," Linda said to Eva.

"Baan Thursday, Nora? Where you're staying just now?"

"No," said Jack. "The seven-day bungalows are not for sale." He popped a ring-pull with his finger. There was a word tattooed on his inner forearm, beginning with a highly decorative 'B', the rest was concealed behind a row of braided bracelets, beads and silver charms around this his thick wrist. B for … what? Boundless?

"I'm confused," Eva said. "Do you own the resort?"

"No," Jack said.

"Yes," Linda said.

"I only own a third of the bungalows."

"But fifty percent of the land," Linda said. "He's a local mogul."

"I was the first to come here when nobody believed that people would travel so far for Robinson Crusoe shacks without air con and internet, swimming pools and attentive waiters, and yet pay good money."

"He's a *visionary* mogul," Peter said. "The rest, like us and Julia, own one or two of the bungalows, which are managed by the resort staff."

"And nobody apart from me and a handful of staff are here to get soaking here in the monsoon."

"It's part of the island's rugged appeal, no?" Peter winked. "We soft souls like it when the sun is shining and the sea is calm – or even better, we just collect high season rent at Christmastime, as we've done for the last four years, and go to cold, grey Scotland to visit family."

"Your boys look like they grew up here." Eva watched as a pair of redheaded twins climbed the column behind Linda and chased a gecko hiding between the roof tiles. Suddenly she wanted to fast-forward, to come back to the island with their own kids when it was freezing and dark in Sweden. She could see a boy looking like Kristoffer and a blonde girl in a linen dress joining the other kids on their hunts for lizards and crabs. They would speak English and Thai and pick up Italian and French from their partners in crime. She would do yoga with her daughter and maybe the boys would eventually join them. She thought perhaps they could check if there were more houses for sale. If there was nothing now, they could leave a note for the resort management to contact them if anything became available. She might research the Moken people, the stateless sea gypsies who lived along the Thai and Burmese coast – that would be one justification for time spent on the island. She would organise everyone to clear plastic, not only in front of the resort but all along the shore and on the islands nearby. And of course, she would learn to dive and join Kristoffer.

"Boys are like that. They don't care where they are, they just need the freedom to explore, to conquer," Linda said, and then added more quietly, "But I think Jack is hiding here …"

Jack's expression remained unchanged but he laughed – trying hard, Eva thought, to sound casual.

"From the tax man?" Kristoffer said.

"Worse," Linda whispered. "A woman."

A smile slid across his mouth, almost invisible, and the laugh lines around his eyes went momentarily deeper. He reached into his chest pocket and pulled out a cigar tube.

"Do you mind?" He addressed nobody in particular. He rubbed the cigar in his hands and it gave a soft crackle. He pressed it to his nostrils, savouring the woody aroma of its tightly rolled tobacco leaves. He offered another to Peter, and when he shook his head, he offered it to Kristoffer.

"I'll have it after the dinner if the offer stands," Kristoffer said. "Perhaps with a glass of cognac."

"Oh, you know how to appreciate the good things in life." Jack bit the head of his cigar and spat it over the rail. "I have some excellent XO in my bungalow."

Eva smiled. It was Carl who taught Kristoffer to drink cognac after dinner. But she knew he always had a headache in the morning.

Jack lit a long match and slowly rotated the end of the cigar, burning it equally, gently puffing until the end went from ashen to glowing and back.

"You see, I'm not just on the island to *hide*," he said, mimicking Linda's tone and disappearing in the dense smoke that hung like a cloud around him.

Was it the name of a woman, Eva thought? Bridgett? Beatrice?

But out loud she said, "Why did you call your bungalows after the weekdays?"

"Are you staying in Baan Saturday?"

"Yes, with a Buddha statue at the bottom of the stairs."

"All seven have Buddha statues. They are there for protection. But Baan Saturday is my favourite."

"Why?"

"Because it was a day when God had his most brilliant idea – to create a man. And a woman, to whom he gave a name like yours – Eva. I'm sure she was as beautiful as you are." Jack bowed his head and then glanced at Kristoffer. "If you don't mind me giving a compliment to your wife."

"So, on the seventh day God rested from all the work he had done and blessed the day and made it holy," Eva said. "That is why you live in Baan Sunday?"

"Absolutely." Jack let the thick smoke out. "But I like the Buddhist story better. They say that Buddha achieved the enlightened state as he sat under a tree for seven days in deep meditation. The Buddha's statue in my garden represents the seventh day, after the Buddha had realised enlightenment. All seven bungalows, '*baan*' in Thai, are built in Buddhist Thai style, and yet each house has a distinctive design and a different Buddha statue in the garden. Thai people usually know which day of the week they are born, as particular styles and attributes of Buddha have been attributed to the days of the week."

Could it be 'Buddha', then? '*Baan*' was too ordinary unless it meant 'home' to him. Or perhaps 'Be' – simple but powerful?

Suddenly she thought of something. "You know, I was born on a Saturday."

"Destiny," Jack said.

Eva loved little coincidences. Amulets, charms, symbols – she wanted to see the meaning behind ordinary things. A meaningless world would be such a boring place. There had to be some purpose in life if the meaning behind things was ascertainable. 'Believe' started with B …

"What does it mean, do you think? We were destined to come to the island … for what? To meet you? But why?"

Jack held his breath and frowned. Everyone looked at him as though expecting him to have an answer. Eva knew her question was silly and didn't deserve an answer. She blushed and for some reason she felt a strange trembling in her chest. As if she was swimming, and she wanted to put her feet down on something solid, but the water was deeper than she thought and there was nothing there. Maybe some questions should not be asked, she thought. Maybe some questions couldn't be answered.

Three

Powdery snow overnight had turned to slush by morning. Carl rested his head against the aircraft's window and stared down at the runway. The plane should have taken off an hour ago – they had closed the doors and disconnected from the bridge – but the twin Pratt & Whitneys still lay silent. Back in the departure hall he had seen that more than half the flights had been cancelled and the rest delayed. Long-haul flights were usually the last to cancel, and the fact that their boarding was completed was promising. He watched as swollen rain droplets trickled down the window, blurring even more an already grey day.

He turned around and stretched his neck. The plane was only a third full – quite unusual for the Christmas season – and a bizarre steely silence hovered in the air. Everyone knew what had happened but seemed to be pretending it was just another flight to Thailand – Land of a Thousand Smiles. An elegant Thai flight attendant walked along the aisle, making a final check.

Carl pressed into his seat back and fastened his seat belt. He had a connecting flight to Phuket in Bangkok. If they delayed another fifteen minutes, he wouldn't make it. He mindlessly tapped his foot on the floor. There were Thai Airways flights every two hours to Phuket, a flight attendant had told him reassuringly; but he didn't have an extra two hours.

He had called Goran on his way to Heathrow. They already knew that Kristoffer was missing – someone from the hotel had called them. They still hadn't got in contact with the Swedish Ministry for Foreign Affairs, and like Carl they had left a voicemail. Carl repeated to Goran several times that there was nothing final about the word 'missing' – it meant just what it said. Carl felt he may have given Goran hope by booking a flight to Thailand. A hope he was thirsty for himself.

Goran's last words were still echoing in his mind. *Please find my boy.*

"I'll do my best, although I'm not sure if …" A doubt crept in and sat heavily on his chest, making it hard to breathe.

Kristoffer had said that Goran needed heart surgery because of his atherosclerosis. He was on medication and a strict diet, and of course his doctor had recommended avoiding stress. His heavy breathing, almost panting, on the phone wasn't a good sign. Kristoffer always said his parents worried about him more than they should. How could they not? his mum once said. They adopted him quite late, and he was their only child – they would have nobody if something happened to him. But most of the time Carl didn't see their worries; instead he saw how proud they were that Kristoffer had grown into an excellent student and a good man, how excited they were that he had found a great girl, and how much they enjoyed their growing family.

Last time Carl had seen Goran was at the wedding. He was full of energy, drinking champagne and dancing with Kristoffer's mum, with Eva, Eva's mum, Eva's sisters. In his seventies and carrying too much weight, he was still active. He played golf and coached kids' football. Often, he had more whisky than he should, but who didn't? He liked to drink with

Carl. Kristoffer wasn't a big drinker – probably, he always said, because he had an inherited deficiency in one of the enzymes involved in the breakdown of alcohol. He would be the first to pass out, and in that sense he wasn't a good Swede ... Goran's favourite gin martini, the traditional welcoming cocktail in the Berg household, was a killer even for Carl. Two drops of vermouth in a large glass of gin.

During university Carl often went with Kristoffer to visit his parents in Hjo, and in summer he would stay several weeks. He immediately fell in love with the town and its wooden houses, lush gardens with fragrant jasmine blossom and the hum of bees, cobbled streets, cafés with open verandas, heavy wooden tables in the harbour, smoked mackerel with potatoes, salad and beer, tourists walking the long lane beside Vattern Lake.

The lake. Its water never got warm, apart from the very surface, even in summer. Carl would be chilled through within seconds, but he still swam with Kristoffer. The farther from shore they swam, the better the view of the line of blue, red, yellow, green and orange houses nestled neatly above the water, behind a fringe of lilac bushes and apple trees. Some houses were two storeys with large windows and balconies, and some had steps to the water.

Ever since Carl's first visit, the friends had played a silly game, choosing the house they would buy when they had enough money. Carl's favourite was a ginger house with a simple jetty where they could moor Kristoffer's wooden boat. The uprights were covered in thick green moss and the walkway was missing two planks, but that would be easy to repair, Kristoffer said. But what Carl liked most about his ginger house was the large terrace in front, with its intricate iron railings partly covered with a creeper which in autumn turned bright red. He would replace the white plastic table with the massive oak dining table he had seen in an antique shop in town. In summer, he would host his friends every weekend and cook fillet of venison or pulled pork on a simple barbeque in the shade of a lime tree which, for a short period in July, was covered in yellow blossom.

"Do you need anything, sir?"

A Thai stewardess turned off the call light above Carl's head. Petite, her face covered in a thick layer of white powder, her lips the same lilac colour as her uniform, she resembled a doll, with a perfect smile to match.

"Some whisky with ice?"

"Sir, we'll serve alcoholic drinks as soon as we're in the air. Can I offer you water or juice instead?"

"Water, please." Carl tried to return her smile, failed badly and turned his face to the window.

The engines started and the air was filled with the contained roar of twin turbines under load. Carl breathed a sigh of relief.

As they accelerated down the runaway, his body trembled with the vibration of the aircraft and the water in his glass splashed over the rim and onto his hand. He heard clunk of the wing flaps and moments later they were in the air.

He wished he had sent Kristoffer's mum a message before taking off. Kristoffer always did that when he boarded a plane. Carl knew she worried most about Kristoffer when he flew. She believed it was the only time man had little control over his destiny. "Man is not supposed to fly," she had said many times over the years, as they embarked on transatlantic and European flights without number. Flying was something that her generation didn't take for granted. She trusted the land. The water.

The seat next to him was empty. It felt as if this emptiness had a physical shape, pressing upon him with its cold presence.

He leaned forward, resting his forehead against the back of the seat in front, clasping his hands between his knees.

In his heart, Carl felt nothing could happen to Kristoffer. There were things in life that were beyond imagining. He couldn't imagine Kristoffer being a random victim. He couldn't imagine he would never speak to him. He couldn't imagine his world without him.

He knew that going to Thailand wasn't one of his wisest decisions, but something stronger than himself was dragging him there, defying all reason.

He didn't believe in God, so prayer was not an option. He believed in common sense and statistical likelihood. He tried to calculate the probability of Kristoffer's death, and decided it was minimal, impossible really. But a cold iron claw was squeezing his throat, making it hard to swallow, and memories were rolling over one another like pebbles in a stream.

No. At worst, Kristoffer was in a hospital and had no means of contacting his family. Any number of things could have happened. Of course they were still alive. Why would they be on the wrong side of statistical probability?

Antibiotics, torch … Carl went again through everything he would need. He certainly needed a more powerful torch, like the one Kristoffer had on his boat in Hjo. It used to be one of Kristoffer's few concessions to technology when he was sailing. Carl thought of a midsummer's night, when the saturated colours of late afternoon were toned down and the air was touched with pink, and the water's salmon surface reflected the clouds and the steam that hugged the lake. The wind had ceased playing in the sails and the boat drifted only with the flow, the mast occasionally groaning in its housing. Kristoffer was plucking strings on his guitar, one at a time, and listening to the distant twang that echoed back. The fog became denser, and the shoreline faded away.

"Take to the oars, sailor," Kristoffer commanded.

Most of Kristoffer's friends had installed small outboards on their boats, but he still clung to tradition. It was more romantic, he said, and Carl thought so too – even if he struggled to stroke rhythmically and his palms became blistered within minutes.

"My turn."

While Kristoffer rowed, Carl sat at the bow peering into the fog which, like a goose down cloud, wrapped around them. It felt like he could gather it in his hands and roll it into a fog ball.

"How do we get home?" He knew Kristoffer had a compass on the boat, but he had never seen him use it.

"I know where home is."

Four

Before

Kristoffer was watching tiny waves purposelessly tossing sand over his toes. Long shadows slowly shrank away as the sun rose behind the palms. A crab was burrowing a hole at the edge of the water, pushing sand balls away from the entrance with great persistence, creating mysterious patterns. The beach around was covered with an intricate galaxy-like array of tiny sculptures – and his own haphazard footprints. He fixed his eyes on the horizon, where the water changed from turquoise to cobalt blue, and he took a long breath of the clean, salty tang of the sea, feeling his lungs expand to the size of the ocean.

He had fallen in love with swimming quite late in life. It wasn't a swimming pool or Hjo's lake that had created the spark. It was when he had seen the sea for the first time, with its fluorescent azure shades; when he had inhaled its hitherto unknown, invigorating smell; when his heart had thumped a little bit faster because he couldn't see the ocean's end. In this instant he saw his nine-year-old self, standing at the edge of the water, squinting through glistering sunrays and watching the waves rolling in, curling upwards as though in suspended animation before crashing into dazzling foam that pulled a thousand pebbles in and out to sea. The waves were almost as high as he was, but when they came close they dissolved, gently licking his toes, tickling the soles of his feet. His father stood behind him and asked if he was scared. He wasn't scared; he was enchanted. He wanted to wade in deep and become friends, but he knew he had to earn the respect of nature, to let the sea watch *him*, to taste what he was made of. And so, he stood admiring the waves, feeling their pulse, until his dad turned away and called for him over his shoulder. Later, he returned and ran straight into the water, crashing and jumping through the surf, rolling in the sandy shallows, scratching his skin on broken shells, his eyes burning from salt.

Kristoffer threw his towel on the sand and after three long strides into the sea, he dove. Gliding through beams of sunlight, he swept his hands from his head to his hips, slowly, rhythmically, feeling the velvety touch of the water running along his skin. He swam until he knew he was deep enough that his toes wouldn't touch the seabed. Otherwise, he felt restricted, and the sea was a place of ultimate freedom. His ears began to ring, and he let his body float towards the light.

He swam until the island became a thin line. He felt a strong current against his stomach, and the water grew dark sapphire. He spread his arms and his legs and let the sea carry him, and he watched as two seagulls circled above, gliding with the airflows, looking at one with their environment, ultimately in control. He never felt equal to the sea, to nature, not even close, but he thought he knew his share in the game. He knew his limits.

Before going up the stairs of their bungalow, Kristoffer stood and studied their Saturday Buddha. He sat in a full lotus position in meditation, atop the coiled body of a snake whose seven-headed body rose from behind the figure as if making a shelter with its hoods against the rain or the sea. On the sand in front of the statue, a dragonfly with radiant aquamarine wings landed on a fresh offering of orange flowers and palm leaves woven into a tiny basket containing a part-burned incense stick.

Kristoffer carefully pushed the bungalow door, which grated on its rusted hinges, and poked his head into the gloom. Eva was in bed with her eyes closed. She had asked him to wake her so she could go with him to the beach, but he knew she needed her morning rest. He pushed the door a little bit more, clenching his teeth and squinting as if that might help to silence its groans, and squeezed his body through. The bungalow was quite new and stylishly done out with rough wood, stone and bamboo. It was in perfect harmony with its remote location, but the humidity was taking its toll. No wonder, he thought – with heavy rains from May to October the resort required constant repair and maintenance. He loved the thought of returning to the island, maybe more than once if it stayed as pristine as it was now; but to buy a bungalow as Eva suggested would be irrational. The maintenance costs would eat all the rent and give them too much hassle. It was wiser to rent.

He began tiptoeing towards the open-air shower patio behind the bed, but the boards creaked under his every step. Eva turned onto her back and threw her arm above her head on the pillow, giving a soft moan as she exhaled. The blanket slid below her pubic bone, until just the hem concealed her clitoris. Her breasts, which he could usually cup with his hands, were swollen now, her nipples a deep chestnut-brown.

A burning sensation spread through his body. Holding his breath, he stepped forward and moved the veil of thin mosquito net wrapped around the bed frame. How many times had he woken early and gazed at her peaceful face, the sharp line of her jaw, her delicate neck and collarbones, the curve of her shoulders. Her skin, normally milky white, was a pale shade of peach. His married friends had said that passion would fade with marriage. He had never felt its fading. Every time he looked at her he felt a tingling in his chest, just as when he had seen her for the first time, walking down the stairs of the university building. The wind had gusted from behind her as if pushing her towards him, throwing her hair over her face, wrapping her dress around her curves, lifting it above her knees. She clasped a fluttering pile of papers to her chest and held her skirt with her free hand. But one page escaped and flew over his head. She rushed down the stairs and passed by him, her shoulder brushing against his, and he felt an electric shock run through his bones. He turned, following her with his eyes, breathless. A denim-clad student at the bottom of the stairs caught the flying page and handed it to her. Kristoffer watched as she thanked him, playing with her hair as they chatted. He cursed the wind, stung with envy for the fellow's luck, regretting that he hadn't jumped to catch that page, and filled with an urgent desire to know her name.

Eva opened her sleep-swollen eyes, the colour of cornflowers, framed in the wheat of her hair spread on the pillow, and slowly fixed her gaze on him.

"Hi, baby," she whispered, and smiled.

He sat on the bed and kissed her parted lips.

"You taste of salt," she said.

With the tip of his tongue, he traced from her chin down to her breasts, around the line of her taut nipples.

"You taste of heaven." Kristoffer slid his hands along the curve of her waist, tracing the line of her hips and buttocks. He firmly pushed her legs apart and stared at her wet opening.

She arched her body. He entered her.

"To shave or not to shave?"

Kristoffer rubbed his stubble. He liked how it looked on Jack – rough, manly, adding to his rebellious charm. Carl's was more designer stubble. Everything, in fact, was polished about Carl these days – the expensive shirts, the slick haircut, the whole city lifestyle. Kristoffer leaned over the black stone sink towards the mirror. He, on the contrary, looked like an unshaved man on holiday, which he was, of course. But his beard was sparse, and that looked distinctly unattractive to him. He glanced at Eva sitting on the bench in the shade of the patio wall, gently using a stick to push a tiny green frog from the edge of the granite vase of water lilies into the water.

"To shave or not to shave, babe?"

"You asked that yesterday," Eva said, not looking at him. The frog was immovable, as if made of plastic. She took it between her two fingers and placed it on a lily leaf. "And the day before yesterday."

"I think it just doesn't get any better."

She walked to him and hugged him from behind. Resting her chin on his shoulder, she looked at him in the mirror.

"I'm dressed and ready to leave, and you are still on your existential dilemma."

Suddenly, the floor trembled. To steady himself, Kristoffer grabbed the sink's edge, but that was trembling too. Their toothbrushes clinked in a glass, and one of the wooden beams supporting the bungalow's roof gave a long, thin squeal. His eyes snapped to Eva's pale reflection in the mirror. He heard her gasp and felt her nails pierce his skin.

"What was that?"

"An earthquake?" Kristoffer said.

"Did you see our reflection? It was like ripples on the water."

"No, I didn't." He was lying. He turned to face her. Little bits of straw from the roof dusted her head and shoulders. She

59

was trembling. He pulled her to him and held her for a long time, until her breathing calmed down.

Shafts of sunlight cut across the deck like piano keys. Kristoffer liked the clubhouse in the morning; the ocean view was breathtaking and there were fewer people around.

He poured himself a cup of coffee and brought it up to his nose. Like every morning, it smelled of burnt beans. There was nobody around who could possibly understand his frustration with bad coffee. Only Carl understood. He couldn't remember if they had bonded over coffee or football, but he knew that if he mentioned to Carl they made terrible coffee, he would never come to the resort if it was the last paradise on Earth. He added some milk to mask the flavour and sipped the thin liquid with great reluctance. He rubbed his lips with his knuckles as if it would clear the taste from his mouth, put his cup away and poured himself some iced coffee. Low temperature softens unpleasant tastes, Carl always said – or was that about cheap wine?

With his plate of sliced fruit he joined Eva at the long communal table. He sat across from her, next to a man in a faded grey T-shirt with thinning greasy hair pulled together in a kind of bun.

"How are you this morning?" Kristoffer said. He couldn't remember seeing the man before.

The man either didn't notice his question or preferred to focus on his plate of fried eggs and rice. A woman with a face covered in large freckles, sitting on the other side of him, answered instead.

"It's still fresh before the day's heat, isn't it?"

She wore a similar grey T-shirt, though not as shabby. She was too young to be his partner, Kristoffer thought; more likely his daughter.

Kristoffer tried again. "Nice eggs they make here."

The man lifted his eyes from the plate and, still chewing, nodded half-heartedly. He was sweating profusely and his glasses had begun to slide down his nose. He pushed them up with his thumb and returned to his food.

A blond, Nordic type stopped beside the table. He was holding the hand of a tall woman with sunburned nose and cheeks. In his other hand he had an iced coffee.

"Guys, did you also feel a tremble? Was it an earthquake?"

A grey-haired man – Chinese or perhaps Japanese, Kristoffer thought – who was sitting next to Eva, beamed and giggled.

"Yes, an earthquake. Nothing. Very small."

His wife giggled too, covering her mouth with a childlike hand. Eva looked askance. Kristoffer guessed that she was probably thinking the same as he was – that in Japan earthquakes were an everyday occurrence. Not so in Sweden; none of them had ever experienced anything like it, and it was a big deal for them.

"We from Japan," the man said.

"Any damage anywhere around the resort?"

"No damage, no damage." The Japanese man giggled again and drank the rest of his mango juice. He nodded to his wife and they got up together and glided away from the table, like a pair of dancers leaving the floor.

"Can we sit here?" the tall woman said. "I'm Emma. This is my husband, Lars."

"Sure, please. Eva."

"Anyone know where the epicentre was?"

"We don't have earthquakes in Thailand," said the man in the grey T-shirt. He wiped his lips with a napkin. Probably couldn't do two things at once, thought Kristoffer. He glanced at the man's empty plate, so clean he might have licked it. "It could have happened in Burma. Or more likely near Sumatra, and we got the tail."

"Sumatra is quite a distance isn't it?" Eva said.

"Yes and no. It's a huge island, the size of Thailand. The north tip is maybe 500 km away." The man folded his napkin into a small square and put it in the middle of his plate. "All I know is that there are a lot of earthquakes in the Indonesian region and I'm speculating that it might have been a strong one given that we felt it even here."

It made sense, but Kristoffer couldn't get his head around how big an earthquake had to be to travel so far. "And of course, there's not even a radio on the island to know what happened," he said.

"I have a radio, but I'm on a different package," the man said. "You guys are paying to be cut off from civilisation, the news."

"And you?"

"I'm a scientist, a biologist. I'm working for Naucrates, a marine conservation centre." Only now did Kristoffer notice the man's T-shirt had a logo, though it was barely visible on the washed-out fabric.

"Are you studying sea turtles?" Eva leaned over the table towards him. They had a pet turtle in her office called Judge, about whom Kristoffer had heard a great deal. She loved to watch Judge moving about, chewing unhurriedly on a cabbage leaf, enchanting her with his meditative slowness. But she always felt the poor chap was lonely. "We were told this beach is one of the best in Thailand to watch turtles hatching," she said.

"Yes, three out of four marine turtles recorded in Thailand regularly show up on this beach. Catch Jenny, my volunteer assistant, anytime." He glanced at the girl next to him. "She can tell you more about turtles. Now, we have to go to the mangrove creek." He stood up as if he was on a mission and looked expectantly at Jenny, who looked less than enthusiastic about the invitation.

"I've been on the island for a month and have spent most of my time soaking in that stinking creek," she said. "I'm sick of smelling like a rotten egg."

"It's not my fault the turtles are late this year." The scientist shrugged his shoulders with exaggerated feeling. "Have you all checked to the mangrove creek yet?" He was addressing the table.

"We kayaked there yesterday," Emma said.

"Isn't it the most special place on the island?"

Emma tilted her head to one side and chewed on her lower lip before answering.

"Yes, it's interesting. Nice to go once."

"Interesting?" The scientist puffed, his glasses slid down his nose, and he looked over their heads into the middle distance. "It's a planet within a planet there. Mangroves are very advanced plant life. They have ultra-efficient filtration to keep much of the salt out and a complex root system that allows them to survive in the intertidal zone. Do you know how many rare birds there are?"

"We both prefer diving." Emma pressed her lips together.

Her diplomatic answer may have been a disappointment to the scientist, but Kristoffer couldn't agree more. He watched the man walk away with Jenny trailing behind, then said to Emma, "Have you been to the Richelieu Rock?"

"Yes, last year, but from Phuket," Emma said. "Then we learnt that Golden Buddha is the closest point to the Surin Islands. That's why we thought it'd be perfect for our honeymoon adventure. But the resort boat is full for the next two days – that's how we ended up in the mangrove creek." She laughed.

"You're on honeymoon?" Kristoffer said.

"Yes. We got married in Copenhagen last Sunday."

"We are on honeymoon too!" Kristoffer and Eva spoke together.

"We must have a honeymoon kayak race, Sweden against Denmark." Lars thumped two massive fists on the table and it shook as if another earthquake had struck. Kristoffer never said no to a fun challenge, but he wasn't sure if they had any chance against these two Vikings. They looked like they rowed their kayaks every weekend in the Oresund Strait.

"Just tell us when." Eva shot it out before he had time to come up with an alternative they'd be more likely to survive.

Five

"Would you like chicken with noodles, or fish with rice?"

The stewardess' voice shook Carl out of a fretful sleep.

"Chicken, please."

"Another drink?"

"Yes, please."

She dropped two ice cubes in a glass, poured more whisky than she would normally, and handed it to him.

"Thanks."

"Do you need an immigration landing form?"

"Yes, please."

"Where are you going in Thailand?"

"Koh Phra Thong," Carl said. It came out as a question. He glanced down. He didn't know where he would go when the plane landed. He had a plan, and he hadn't.

He looked up at the stewardess. "It's an island."

She shrugged her shoulders. "I haven't heard of it. Is it beautiful?"

Beautiful? Carl stared at the pearly white string of perfect teeth, the lilac lips spread into a wide smile. She slightly tilted her head, waiting for an answer.

"I don't know." He rubbed the back of his head. He supposed it must be but somehow he couldn't imagine it so.

"Where is this island?"

"It's on the northwest coast, close to Burma."

The stewardess still looked puzzled, and shook her head. She smiled and moved on with her trolley.

"Anyway, I'm going there," Carl said quietly. He opened the in-flight magazine and carelessly skipped through glossy pages with stunning images of sandy beaches and luxury resorts. At the last spread he paused, scrutinising a map of Thailand. The island was not marked. Carl pressed with his finger at an invisible spot close to the northernmost tip of Thailand. It was there. He knew it. It was just too small and anonymous, even for a travel magazine. He lifted his finger and the glossy paper retained his fingerprint for a few moments, before shedding it like the island.

"Excuse me, do you know how bad the devastation is in Phuket?"

The high-pitched voice came from two seats ahead of him. A manicured hand with orange nail varnish gesticulated to the stewardess. "We were looking forward to our holiday so much that we decided not to cancel our plans."

"I haven't been back since the tsunami, but from what I heard it's pretty bad."

The stewardess passed two trays with food to the woman and her companion.

"Oh, really? We called our hotel, and they said there's no damage to our hotel, and they're looking forward to welcoming us. They offered us two hours of free massage each. They are so nice, aren't they?"

"You're very lucky, madam," the stewardess murmured.

"Can we have some more champagne, please? It's our first trip to Asia, and we're very excited."

"I hope you enjoy it, madam."

The woman lowered her voice. "Isn't the plane a little empty?"

66

"Many people had to cancel their plans, unfortunately."

"Oh, that is sad. Still, you know how the news exaggerates everything. Anything to keep you glued to the screen – it's all about advertising revenue."

"Don't worry, if your hotel says you can come then you will be alright."

Carl fidgeted in his seat. How could these people be so oblivious? And yet a flicker of hope trembled in his chest. Even as the death toll for the tsunami-affected area grew, the latest from Thailand was that only three hundred and fifty people were confirmed dead. Three-fifty, including Thais, along the entire coast from Burma to Malaysia, a stretch of more than a thousand kilometres. There was no way Kristoffer and Eva were among them.

Carl scanned the immigration form on both sides. He dragged his backpack closer and pulled a pen from a frayed side pocket. He began filling in the form, but then stopped and stared at the pen. With the tips of his fingers, he slowly rolled it in his hands. The red lettering had almost faded away, but he still could still make out the words.

'*Red Tulip Hotel*'.

He had kept it as a souvenir from his trip to Amsterdam with Kristoffer a few years after they graduated. He remembered walking in the red light district, more out of curiosity than anything, and a prostitute, likely younger than eighteen with bright red lipstick, in a black latex skirt and a lace bra over her tiny breasts, asking Kristoffer to come in, and Kristoffer politely refusing.

"So, you don't like sex?" she said. Kristoffer had laughed. He had turned to Carl and said, almost pleadingly, "What can I say to that?"

Carl felt a tightness in his chest. He took a gulp from his glass, held the whisky in his mouth for a moment and then slowly swallowed. He clasped the strap of his backpack and drew it closer. The threadbare strap felt familiar, like the hand of an old friend. Its khaki colour had faded a long time ago, and the base had turned a dirty brown from countless floors in third-class trains, long-distance trucks and bone-rattling buses. It had gathered dust for years at the bottom of his storage closet, under a pile of classy Louis Vuitton bags. He had got rid of most of his old belongings when he moved to his new flat, but the worn-out backpack had a life behind it, and he had been unable to throw it out.

Perhaps when he discarded his old gear he had given up on his dreams to change the world. Or perhaps he had done that naturally, just by growing older.

"It doesn't look like you are going on vacation."

A man in the same row was leaning across the aisle towards Carl. He wore a brown checked shirt and a mustard-coloured jacket, his face was flabby and slack, and he spoke with a northern regional accent. He held a full glass in his hand, certainly not his first.

"No," Carl said curtly.

"You lose someone? In the tsunami?"

Carl winced.

"No." He dug his teeth into his lower lip until he felt the pain. "But I learned that my best friend and his wife are missing." He didn't want to continue the conversation and turned to his window.

"Do you have any information where they might be?"

"No."

"So how will you find them?"

"I just will," Carl said quietly to his reflection.

"I received a call last night that my daughter is at Phuket's hospital. Unconscious, with bad head injuries. They identified her by a metal badge she was wearing. She has diabetes …"

Carl reluctantly turned his head and the man continued, clearly eager to talk.

"Maybe you will receive some more news about your friends too?"

"Maybe."

"It's strange." The man lowered his voice and leaned closer to Carl. His breath had a strong odour, and Carl recoiled a little. "When I first heard the tsunami news, it didn't cross my mind that she could be in danger. Even when they said that the Thailand coast received waves too. But now I feel quite guilty about it, to be honest."

Carl sipped from his glass and nodded.

"Nowadays," the man went on, "there are just too many catastrophes broadcast from everywhere in the world. Do you remember the earthquake in southern Iran, with tens of thousands dead, just last December?"

Carl didn't remember the earthquake, but the man was looking expectantly at him, and Carl nodded.

"Well, I don't," the man said. "Because there were a dozen large earthquakes that year in every part of the world. Almost every day, believe it or not, there's an earthquake somewhere, but that was a bad year. The Earth's crust is in constant movement, which of course we don't notice. If we didn't have TV, we'd never hear of any about half those quakes."

Carl found it difficult to understand everything the man said. The lengthened vowels distorted some words. It reminded him of the way some of the Manchester United players from their native city spoke, though this man was more coherent. After his years in London, Carl still didn't feel comfortable with accents from outside central London.

"The Sumatra earthquake wasn't any more remarkable to me at first than that December one in Iran. There was other big news, like SARS in Hong Kong or the most recent storm in the Philippines. I've stopped paying attention to most of it. It's just news, someone else's stories. I could never have imagined that my girl would be caught in one of them. A tsunami? In the safe haven of Thailand? And who'd even heard of really *bad* tsunamis?"

Carl listened to the man quietly, almost distantly. He thought of how it had crept up on him that Kristoffer might have been affected by the tsunami. The first news carried images from Aceh, where there were a thousand dead. But how could that be even distantly connected with his best friend's honeymoon? Then the reports extended to Sri Lanka, with some referring to casualties in Thailand. Only when Luka said that his brother had got to the hospital had he thought about Kristoffer, but he still didn't feel that the Sumatran earthquake had any bearing on his own life, or on him personally. Until he learned that Kristoffer was missing.

"What I don't understand," Carl said. "Is that the tsunami flooded Aceh fifteen minutes after the earthquake. The waves reached Phuket nearly two hours later. That would be enough time to evacuate everyone, surely? I remember in Hawaii there was lots of information on what to do if a tsunami was imminent."

"That's because most of the tsunamis in this century occurred in the Pacific Ocean where a chain of faults has long set the stage for earthquakes and volcanic eruptions. Anytime there's a quake in the Pacific Ocean higher than six on the Richter scale, the Pacific Tsunami Warning Centre goes into action. But no such warning system was set up in the Indian Ocean. Historically there were fewer earthquakes, and I'm not sure if any had created a tsunami before."

The man took *The Guardian* from the seat pocket in front of him and pointed to the headline.

"Look." He got his glasses from a case with one hand. "It says that this quake in the Indian Ocean was 8.9 on the Richter scale. The only quakes bigger were in Chile in 1960, at 9.5, and in Alaska in 1964 – that one was 9.2. But what they don't say or explain," – he looked at Carl over his glasses – "is that with each number on the Richter scale, the wave amplitude is ten times greater, and the amount of energy released increases thirty-two times. A level seven earthquake is ten times greater than a level six earthquake. And level nine earthquakes are one thousand times stronger than level six. The energy increase is even greater. A level nine 'quake releases thirty-two times more energy than a level eight, more than a thousand times more than a level seven, and thirty-two thousand more than a level six. And a level—"

"I didn't know any of that," Carl said.

"Do you know how much energy a level nine earthquake releases?"

"No."

"It's 475 megatons. Which is about twenty-three thousand Hiroshima-sized atom bombs."

Carl said nothing, reflecting on what the man had just told him. Twenty-three thousand atom bombs. What would *that* mushroom cloud look like? The blood in his veins turned cold. In the case of the Indian Ocean, the shifting of the tectonic plates happened under the seabed, and all that energy was released into the ocean instead of the air. The whole body of water, the volume of the ocean, expanded, creating the wave. The monstrous wave. He jerked up in his seat; there were many more fatalities than they knew about. There had to be. He had an irrational impulse to scream to the people to run. But it was too late.

"You like your numbers," he said, his lips barely moving.

"I do." The man looked smug. "I teach history at Oxford but I find it fascinating that people often don't understand what is actually behind the numbers—"

Carl was looking at the man but didn't hear him anymore. The image of a wave carrying a rural bus overloaded with people, their belongings tied to the roof, flickered in his consciousness. The bus was half-submerged under the brown water; men were stretching their arms from windows, their mouths gaping open, eyes black with terror. A woman was holding an infant with both her arms above her head, the water up to her chin.

"What do you do?" the man asked.

"Hedge fund manager."

"In that case I would think you would be better with numbers than me."

Carl smirked. Funnily enough he was, and not because he worked for one of the biggest hedge fund firms in London. He recalled a day when they were driving to their summer house, and his father asked him what he was doing because he had been quiet for so long, staring through the window. To Carl, the answer should have been obvious. What else was he going to do on a day-long drive? Nothing was happening. The view was an endless forest, sometimes lakes, birch trees, pine trees, birch trees again.

"I'm adding up the numbers on car plates."

"What do you mean adding up numbers, you haven't started school yet?" His dad stared at him in the rear-view mirror. "You mean you're counting number plates?"

"No, I'm adding the three numbers written on the plates."

"You mean, like, three plus one plus six?" His mum had turned to look at him. She had a funny look on her face, her eyes looked like a frog's, but she didn't laugh the way she did when she was making faces.

"No. I mean like 316 plus 316."

"And how much would that be?"

"632," Carl said, his eyes following a car turning into a side road.

"How do you do that?" The words came out as a croak. There was no indication that she was playing with him.

"I don't know."

His dad slowed down and stopped on the side of the road.

"What about that white car, STH 267?" He pointed through the windscreen to a Toyota that was overtaking them.

Carl leaned forward between his parents' seats and said, "534."

"How long you have been doing it?"

"I don't know. Always."

A stewardess announced that passengers should fasten their seat belts as the plane was entering turbulence. The man folded his table. He rolled his glass in his hands, then took a large gulp. He grimaced and wiped his lips with his hand.

"In my day it was honourable to be a teacher, a doctor. Now everyone wants to be in finance, to run a hedge fund, to make big bucks."

"My parents are teachers."

"And you? How come you chose such a lucrative profession?"

"Why lucrative?"

"There's no other meaning in what you do."

Carl sniffed. "Today, even those who choose to become doctors are more often than not seduced by the steady income. As you say, times have changed."

The man pushed back strands of white hair that had stuck to his sweaty forehead, in an effort to cover the balding top of his head.

"Where are you from?" he said.

"I'm Swedish."

"You don't look Swedish."

Carl blinked and took a moment, even though he was used to raised eyebrows when he said he was Swedish. He was one of those people who felt awkward when he saw his own reflection.

"I am Swedish," he repeated firmly.

"I thought maybe … I don't know – not Swedish anyway."

No matter how much you wash you'll always be dirty. For a moment Carl was back in the changing room at uni, laughter coming from behind his back. His smile was fading, replaced by tightly clenched teeth. He was walking through the football club shower room and his head was up, but his fingers were curled into tight fists. He turned on the shower in his cubicle and stood under the stream. He hung his head, his chin trembling.

"Here, filthy Turk." A piece of soap hit the back of his head and plopped down at his feet. He stared at it, curling his toes. Last time it was mud. In his face. In front of the whole stadium. His heart thudded dully in his chest. He wished he could disappear. Forever.

"He's as Swedish as you, loser," Kristoffer shouted from his shower. "The only difference is he plays better football."

"Shut up, Chink!"

"First, you don't swear here. Secondly, I am Korean."

The sound of running water shut out the voices behind. Carl closed his eyes. For as long as he could remember he had been taunted. He never took off his shirt, even on the hottest day. Not even on a beach. His skin was darker than any children he had met and exposed to the sun it turned a deep bronze. But he couldn't hide his face, his hands; he couldn't hide from the scorn of his peers. Children could be so cruel. Way more than adults. Adults learned to control their worst impulses, though he saw the confusion in their eyes when they looked at him. It was bizarre, especially when his parents, both respected teachers at the local school, were well known in the neighbourhood. People's ignorance was never far below the surface.

In his facial features, Carl looked a lot like his dad, an average Swede born in an average Swedish village near Ostersund. They shared a low forehead and an aquiline nose slightly shifted to the left.

His sister's skin was lighter than his, though still a shade darker than that of her classmates, and she had inherited their mother's blue eyes. Everyone else in the family had dark, straight hair but Carl's was coarser and denser and turned into curls if it was allowed to grow, accentuating his unusual appearance for a Swedish boy.

He had once asked his parents if he was adopted. They said he wasn't, and he used to wonder whether he had been swapped with their son when he was born.

Pushing back tears and trying to stay invisible, Carl learned very early that the world didn't care to see inside him, that it didn't care about his hopes and dreams or the anguish buried deep inside. It saw only his skin colour. As he grew older, he learned to hide everything behind an impenetrable mask. With time he couldn't distinguish what was him and what wasn't. At times he felt a numbness in his chest, as if the cold breath of his own shadow was passing over him.

"Why don't you get a genome test? Those tests are so advanced these days," Luka once said to him.

Carl merely replied, "What will it change for me?"

When an English voice intruded on his thoughts, Carl almost jumped.

"I read that today, Sweden takes in more immigrants relative to its population than any other country in the world, is that true?" The Englishman was staring into his empty glass. "They say every fifth person in Sweden can be classified as of non-Swedish origin." He reached up and pressed the service button above his head.

"Sweden would never be where it is now without immigrant workers. It's a big country with a small population." Card paused. "It's important that we help those who are in need. They are refugees from Syria, Iraq, the Balkans, from countries where war touches every individual's life. I don't think they would choose to leave their homelands if they could stay."

During school holidays, he had worked on Sundays at a grocery shop belonging to an Iraqi Kurd named Amir. He had long dark curls under which he hid the scars on his neck from when a mine exploded as he walked his son to school. His boy had died at the spot, in his arms. Amir's father was a retired army officer and using his connections he fled Iraq, taking the whole family. They had spent their first Swedish winter in a cramped apartment provided by the state, and Amir's father had passed away six months after their arrival.

Sometimes after closing, Amir would invite Carl to share tea, and if there had been a delivery from the Middle East he would serve the sweetest dates Carl had ever tasted. Amir would often sing in his native language. A man never forgets the songs of his homeland, he used to say. He said he missed the torrid midday sun, late afternoons when the heat faded, the warm evenings. He missed loud markets and people chatting their days away smoking *shisha*, he missed melons that were sweeter than honey and the smell of sand in the wind when it blew off the desert. Listening to Amir, at times Carl felt envious of him, envious of his love for a land that didn't love him back. He wished he had a fraction of that admiration for Sweden. Too often, in an outburst of emotion, he wished he had been born somewhere else, someone else.

He felt an outsider in his own country. He knew he bore

more resemblance to Amir than to his school friends. He wanted to go to university, to leave Finspång and its small town mentality, where he was too different to be accepted. But Malmo and later Stockholm turned out to be even more hostile. It was a decade when the country experienced a remarkable increase in crime, much of which was rightly or wrongly attributed to immigrants from the Islamic world. The capital had a vast population of immigrants in its suburbs, and he was automatically taken to be a Turkish or Iranian refugee – even with his distinctive Swedish name and indigenous accent. It was different with some less ignorant, more enlightened Swedes, but too often he was treated with ill-concealed suspicion.

"It's not easy for immigrants to integrate and become a part of society, is it?" Carl had said.

Amir had mastered spoken Swedish quite well. On his arrival he diligently attended the language courses the government provided. He worked hard, first as a handyman, then finally opening his little shop in partnership with another Kurd, at the end of Carl's street.

Carl grew fond of Amir. Apart from helping at the shop, he did his accounts. When Carl read in the newspapers that the Swedish bank sector didn't have enough jobs, he thought about studying finance. It was Amir who planted the seed in his mind to study law. You have a pure heart that naturally seeks justice, and a sharp mind, Amir had said as he poured tea into Carl's glass. It was a summer evening and they were sitting with their legs crossed on the steps outside the shop. "Just don't let your mind corrupt your heart." Amir had squinted as he blew away steam from his tea. Something shivered in Carl's chest under the intense gaze of his friend – he didn't know whether he truly understood what the man had said.

Amir died during Carl's third year at Lund University, and two years later Carl graduated with two degrees – in law and finance.

"… and I was surprised to hear an Iraqi student of mine, who grew up in Malmo, say that Sweden is a racist country." The man pressed the service button above his head several more times. "He said he felt more accepted as a foreign student in London than he ever did growing up in Sweden. I suppose he quite enjoyed being Iraqi and had little desire to become a Swede so this wasn't a problem for him. But he said the feeling of permanent exclusion was a serious problem for those Iraqis who did want to assimilate. I was surprised, I must say. I always had an image of the Swedes as one of the most open, tolerant and equal societies."

"It's true that Swedes in general pride themselves on their tolerance," Carl said. But many found these feelings tested when actually confronted with immigrants of vastly different backgrounds, values and beliefs, so in due course the kind of ethnocentric, xenophobic behaviour so often criticised in other countries surfaced in Sweden. Our government is very progressive with immigration policy. The liberal elite, the politicians and media may love – or pretend to love – the new multiculturalism but I think they have struggled to get ordinary Swedes to accept immigrants who have not integrated."

Because in truth, most of the immigrants Carl saw were not like Amir. Often hostile to their adopted country, they lacked basic cultural awareness, staying in closed communities in the suburbs, some hardly speaking Swedish even into the second generation. Under the Swedish welfare system, people could live comfortably even if they were not employed, and too few immigrants were willing to accept low-paying or disagreeable work, preferring to live on welfare and in time becoming trapped in permanent exclusion from the labour market and, by extension, from society. In segregated neighbourhoods, not working eventually became the norm through social osmosis, creating a vicious cycle that carried on into the next generation.

"If it doesn't work in tolerant and generous Sweden, where could it work?" the man said.

"Canada seems to be doing pretty well. And Australia?"

The stewardess filled the man's glass and turned to Carl. He had to admit he did crave another drink, but he passed.

"A long day tomorrow," he said, and handed back his empty glass.

"Most countries in Europe," said the man, "face difficulties keeping their multiracial populations happy. But you know what I think, my finance friend? I think this so-called multiculturalism itself is an even bigger impediment to integration. It teaches that natives have no moral right to impose their culture on immigrants. Instead, immigrants are encouraged to cling to the culture of their home country. And this approach impedes integration. In fact, it arguably privileges third world over Western cultures."

"And I believe," he continued, "that a large part of Europe's immigration problem can be found in its colonial past. Western civilisation is being held to account for historical crimes – colonialism and racism. The problem with this is not that the West is innocent; it's certainly not. The problem is that the blame-the-West interpretation of world history fosters an us-and-them mentality that makes integration harder. Immigrants discover, and often assume, the mantle of victimhood, which breeds hostility towards the host society."

"But Sweden doesn't have that colonial past," said Carl. "Perhaps it was simply never a particularly well-chosen testing ground for the multicultural experiment. The country was linguistically and ethnically homogenous for centuries.

It's not an easy country to integrate into culturally. We have a complex cultural structure, full of subtle rules and opaque codes of conduct. And Swedes tend to be reticent, solitary and reserved. They are conformist and quite intolerant of deviation from group norms, whether it's immigrants or Swedes who break with protocol."

"That's why Canada and America are doing better – they're countries of immigrants."

"Not sure about America," said Carl. "The race issue seems as raw as ever."

"Nonsense, there's no racism in America anymore."

"That is what every white Anglo-Saxon says – from a position of privilege and power. They don't recognise racism because they never experienced it. Ask the average black citizen."

The man began to say something but Carl interrupted him.

"It's depends whose truth you want to know," he said.

It was a line Kristoffer often used. Carl's eyelids were heavy and he couldn't be bothered being polite anymore. He opened a pack with eye mask and ear plugs. The last thing he saw was a stewardess serving the man another glass of whisky.

Six

Before

Nora stretched on a bamboo daybed on the upper terrace of her bungalow, immersed in a book.

The whirr of the fan above her head eased her, little by little, into a doze, and when she could no longer focus on the page, she leaned her head back on the silk cushion, close to sleep.

Suddenly she opened her eyes wide.

Why had the birds gone silent?

The jungle, always filled with tweeting and chirping, frogs croaking and insects abuzz, was unusually still. It normally happened only at the sundown. The sun, still not at its zenith, splintered through the canopy of the palm leaves, spreading an energy-sapping heat.

She sat up straight, listening hard.

Only the ceiling fan's hum. Odd. Not even the whisper of the waves from the beach.

She got up and leaned over the terrace's wooden railing, looking out over the lush hibiscus bush. Their three towels were neatly spread out on the sand, already half in the shade from the tall casuarinas, but she couldn't see her daughters, only their pink flip-flops piled next to Zoe's inflated pool ring.

They would never go into the water without her permission. She paced along the railing, peering through the shrubbery to the garden below.

"Kat? Zoe? Where are you hiding?"

Bound to be under the blossoming Chinese rose bush in front of the stairs to the terrace, she thought. Where else? They had set up their new doll's house under its low branches that morning before breakfast. "There are tiny fairies living in its flowers, Mummy," Kat had whispered, her large eyes larger than ever as she shared her secret. "They like to drink tea with our dolls on their pink balcony." The doll's house had been the girls' Christmas present. A pile of torn wrapping paper was still on the floor, removed only as far as the corner. Nora smiled. There were three presents still waiting for her husband to open. The largest, in the red paper, was from Kat. She had drawn a painting of the blue sky and the azure sea. Only two colours. Like Rothko.

The sea.

She shuddered. It was not there.

She stared into the empty bay. There, several hundred metres away, she saw her daughters, one sitting cross-legged on the naked seafloor, the other bending down and collecting something – shells probably – which she was placing into a little red bucket.

She couldn't remember seeing such a low tide on the island. Was it normal?

Her heart thumped.

Nora rushed down the stairs. Striding through the garden she heard her phone ring in her room. She slowed down and half-turned back. Probably her husband – he was supposed to land in Phuket any time now. She would call him back. She marched across the foreshore, the ringtone fading behind her, and began jogging when she reached the sand.

There was something distorting and blurring the horizon line but she couldn't yet tell what it was. She stopped for a moment, screwed up her eyes and peered into the haze, far beyond the girls. As she stared, she began distinguishing the sea line from what appeared to be a rising mist immediately above, forming into a diaphanous wall of milky white.

She broke into a run.

"Nora, stop!"

She looked over her shoulder, slowing down just a little. Jack was running along the beach waving his arms in the air. She couldn't make out what he was yelling. There was an odd sound in the air, of wind and something else, as if the seafloor was slightly trembling.

"My girls!" Nora shouted, and pointed over her shoulder.

When she turned to the sea again, she saw her daughters running towards her. The older girl was dragging her sister behind her, holding onto the front of her dress, the little girl's skinny arms flailing in the air and her legs windmilling as she to catch up with her sister.

The mounting wall of water was behind them.

Seven

'Welcome to Phuket Airport. It's thirty-two degrees Celsius and a clear sky. We hope you enjoy your stay in Thailand. Thank you for flying Thai Airways.'

Carl unfastened his seat belt. The view from the window, just as the plane began descending, had dazzled him. Dozens of limestone formations like enormous mushrooms fringed a dizzying array of offshore islands. It was serene, enchanting – the perfect holiday postcard.

The newspaper pictures told a different story, a story of coastal devastation. At least six hundred people were confirmed dead in Thailand.

He hitched his backpack onto his shoulder and strode to immigration, overtaking most of the other passengers. There was no line at passport control and he got his stamp, thanked the officer and marched through the baggage reclaim area to the glass exit doors.

The doors slid apart.

Carl took two steps forward and met a solid wall of people. Men, women, children, old people were standing, sitting, lying, crying and shouting everywhere he looked around the vast hall. In an instant, his shirt clung to his back and he joined hundreds of others in the fight for a gulp of heavy, humid air. The atmosphere was thick with sweat and anxiety.

A group of fellow passengers walked through the sliding door and almost collided with him. As more people emerged from the baggage reclaim area, he felt in danger of being lost in the crush.

"Oh Jesus," a woman said behind him.

"Excuse me." A guy in a Yankees cap shoved him to the side and began dodging and weaving through the crowd, the woman following him. Carl swung his backpack to the front, grasped it tight and trailed after them.

Before he reached the exit he smelt the exhaust fumes from the street. Then from the babel behind him he heard someone yell, "Carl!"

His heart missed a beat and he whirled round.

A woman in a filthy T-shirt, with bruises all over her face, staggered amongst people sitting on the floor next to their bags, holding above her head a sheet of A4 black with a black and white photograph of a boy's face.

"Have you seen this boy?" the woman cried. She leaned with her back against a column, her eyes wide open, scanning the crowd frantically as if she had just lost the boy moments before.

"Carl!"

The column was covered in sheets of paper, each bearing an image, a name and a phone number. Carl glanced at the glass exit glass doors. What looked at first like advertising posters were in fact photographs of the missing – some handwritten, some printed, some without even an image, just a name and a phone number. He scanned the hall. Every column was covered in posters. Tens of columns. Hundreds of posters. He felt his pulse pounding in his temples, his wrist, his neck.

He rushed outside.

Eight

Before

Julia blew the steam away and sipped from her spoon.

"Do you see the difference?" Jonas played with a lemongrass stalk between his fingers.

"Not yet."

She tried *tom yam* from everyone's plate but they were all the same to her, apart from Antoine's which lacked something, she couldn't tell what. Or maybe it was because she didn't like his I'm-French-so-I-know-food attitude. By now her tongue was burning so much from chilli that she couldn't tell the difference between sugar and salt.

"Which do you like the most?" said Jonas.

"Your version, with coconut milk." She wiped sweat from around her nose with the corner of her apron.

"Do you know why?"

Everyone was looking at her. This didn't feel like a tasting session – it felt like being back at school. What did he say about it before …?

"The creamy texture. It softens the sourness and the chilli doesn't burn immediately."

"Exactly. It balances the spiciness and brings the fragrances together," Jonas said. And Julia breathed a sigh of relief. "Who else prefers it with coconut milk?"

Suddenly, the door to the kitchen swung open against the wall with a bang.

"The sea." Dang, the skinny barman, caught his breath. His eyes seemed to goggle out from their sockets. "Come to the terrace, quickly!"

Outside, Julia pushed her way through the staff crowded on the deck, but was still unable to see much of the sea because of the guests standing against the rails.

"Oh gosh, oh gosh," Jonas kept saying. He was standing behind her and was two heads taller.

"What? What do you see?"

"*Stor vag*," he muttered.

"What?" she said. Then suddenly, she caught a glimpse of the shoreline through the crowd, and didn't need a translation. A wave. It was approaching with the speed of a train.

"I'm sure it will break on the beach," said a man and put his cigarette out in an ashtray he had placed neatly on the rail. Beside it was a coffee cup and Julia was sure she could hear the surfaces clinking together. Was the floor trembling?

"Jack, there's Jack. What's he yelling?"

Julia couldn't hear above the noise in the air – not just voices but a hiss and rumble, as of storm clouds building up. Jack began to run up the dunes towards the clubhouse, shouting, waving his arms in the air. Other people from the beach followed behind.

"Tsunami," Jonas whispered. "He's yelling, tsunami."

Nine

"The Swedish temporary consulate is located in our largest bungalow with a sea view."

The receptionist accompanied Carl through the Perl Village Hotel grounds.

It struck him as peculiar that she should mention the sea view. He glanced at the water as it revealed itself between the palm trees along the beach. It was flat calm, and the beach seemed relatively intact – no rubble, only lots of debris, broken branches and plastic scattered on the sand. His taxi driver had said that not all the beaches were damaged. Kata beach, where he had breakfast that morning, had suffered little impact, whereas Patong beach north from Kata had seen severe destruction. He said a lot depended on the angle of shoreline to wave. Carl asked him if he knew how Golden Buddha Beach ranked in that respect, but the driver hadn't heard of it.

"Here we are." The receptionist gestured towards a bungalow where a group of people had gathered outside.

"Do you know how things are at Koh Phra Thong Island?"

"No, sir, I'm sorry. I'm from north Thailand I don't know the islands around here well."

She headed back in the direction of the main hotel, and Carl walked towards the bungalow, where people were sitting in the porch and on the outside steps. Four backpackers sat in the shade of the bungalow wall, speaking in hushed tones, and next to them an older woman was lying on the grass with a magazine under her head.

"Are you all queueing to get inside?" Carl said.

"Yes, there's no space left," said a woman who was sitting on the topmost step. She had two deep cuts on her face and her arms were criss-crossed with scratches.

"Are those people waiting too?" There were more people by the hotel swimming pool, sitting fully dressed on bamboo loungers beneath parasols that afforded partial shade.

"I think they've been inside already and are waiting for temporary documents."

"They're very slow," said a man who was leaning against a pillar on the porch. His arm was in a sling and he had a patch of dried blood above one ear. "Only two women dealing with enquiries and a senior official who seems to do not much else."

A heavily pregnant woman sat on the floor next to him, her legs dangling down between the uprights of the porch balustrade. "If you need food, clothes, to call your family or print anything," she said, "you better go to Phuket City Hall. They set up an emergency help centre there – officials from more than twenty countries, and more temporary embassies."

"We've been here since yesterday," the woman on the stairs said. "We slept here because there's nowhere else to go. Our hotel is destroyed, we don't have passports, money, phones. Nothing. Just what we're wearing." She pulled her stripy sleeveless top down to her chest, revealing swimwear underneath.

"I bet we sleep here tonight again," someone said.

"So, who is the last? Where do I start queueing?" Carl said, and glanced at his watch. It was almost eleven.

"Who is the last?" the woman on the stairs shouted.

"Us." A high-pitched voice came from somewhere behind. Carl turned around but couldn't see who had spoken.

"Over here." A woman in a yellow T-shirt stood up, shooting her arm into the air. She was with two small children in the partial shade of a palm tree. It was a little too far from the bungalow entrance, but it was the nearest shade available.

"Who is before you?"

"That woman with the red umbrella."

A woman waved. She wore a clean white dress that oddly stuck out amongst the mass of torn and dirty clothes on everyone else.

"How many people ahead of you?" Carl wiped his forehead. The blue sky stood tall and clear, the sun like a branding iron pressed to the back of his neck.

"Maybe fifteen."

"How long you have been standing here?"

"Half hour, forty minutes," she said, and lifted her umbrella, inviting Carl into the shade.

"Anna is an angel," said another woman. "She turned her villa into a refuge for those who have no place to stay. Last night it was thirty-two of us, and she fed us, found taxis, gave us money, clothes. My husband is at the hospital and I don't know how long I can stay at the villa. I can't leave without him though."

"You can stay as long as you need to," Anna said, and asked Carl to hold her umbrella. She opened a bottle of water and offered it to a teenage girl standing motionless next to her, dressed in an oversized Rambo T-shirt which looked like a dress on her, reaching halfway to her knees. The girl didn't react to the offer of water and kept her eyes fixed on the ground. Anna put the bottle into the girl's hand and, supporting it with her own hand, brought it to her mouth.

When the water touched her lips, she took a small sip and then pulled back.

"Somebody brought her to us this morning. She was wandering amongst the wreckage in North Kao Lak," Anna said.

Carl did a double-take. It took him a moment to register what she had said. Koh Phra Thong was just beyond Kao Lak.

"I heard there's nothing left of that beach," someone said.

"Yes, my husband went there this morning. He said the area received the worst hit on that stretch of coast. Three-storey hotels reduced to rubble …"

As Anna continued, Carl saw her lips move but he didn't hear her anymore. His heart was pounding in his ears.

"Have … have you heard anything about Koh Phra Thong Island?"

"Where is it?"

"It's just north of Kao Lak."

Anna frowned. "I don't know it."

Didn't *anyone* know the place? Carl left the shade of the umbrella and hopped up onto the bungalow steps.

"Is there anyone here from Koh Phra Thong?" he shouted. He repeated the question, louder. He hoped the people by the swimming pool could hear him too. "Golden Buddha Resort. North of Kao Lak."

The man leaning against the pillar shook his head. "Kao Lak. There's nothing left."

Carl felt the skin tightening on his face; he felt goosebumps, even in the heat.

"I know. That doesn't really help me." He tried another tack. "Anyone met Kristoffer Berg? Or his wife, Eva? They have been missing since the tsunami."

There was a murmur, but he saw only shaking heads.

He took a deep breath. "Young couple. He's a tall Korean guy. She's average build … blonde. Swedish."

"Don't worry, you'll find them," a man in a baseball cap behind him said. "You know there's such a mess everywhere. The first day there was no reception. And half of the people lost their phones. Give it time. Don't panic."

"It has been two days," Carl said.

"We were in Kao Lak. My three sons and wife gone missing. I found my wife yesterday morning at an emergency centre. She also thought I was dead. Then together we went round the hospitals; we found our oldest at one hospital and later that night the youngest in another. Now we have only one boy to find." As the man spoke, he stared at his toes, which curled in and out, in and out of his flip-flops. "But he's a big boy. I'm sure he's fine. It's a mess. It takes time. Keep looking. Keep looking."

"I heard them say two thousand Swedes are missing," the man at the pillar said.

"Can't be two thousand. It's because of people like my wife and me writing both our names," the man in the baseball cap said.

"Call it a thousand, it's still a lot."

"I don't get why there are no more officials then?" Carl said. "In the last ten minutes nobody has come out of that door."

A man lying on his back immediately outside the door, cuddling a little girl with a bandaged head who was asleep on his chest, said: "That's because our government are still in their pyjamas, unpacking Christmas presents. Switched off their mobiles for the holidays and popped off to the theatre. You're in charge of a country, I say, not a village shop. You have TV, for God's sake, a radio."

In the taxi from the airport, Carl had called Kristoffer's parents. It was still early, but he knew they'd be awake. He hoped that Kristoffer had got in touch with them, but the only progress was that they'd got hold of the Swedish Ministry for Foreign Affairs the previous night and registered them both as missing. They said every Swedish newspaper was full of questions as to why Prime Minister Göran Persson hadn't come back from his holiday retreat, and why Laila Freivalds, the foreign minister, went to the theatre the night of the catastrophe.

Now, when he thought about it, it made sense that nobody had got much out of the Ministry for Foreign Affairs, why there were so few consular officials on site, and why no one had even mentioned repatriation flights.

"Even the next day Laila Freivalds didn't rush to her office," the woman on the steps said. "My son lives in the block next to the ministry, and he was there from early morning because he couldn't get hold of us. She finally showed up at ten thirty."

"They should resign, the lot of them!" A wave of angry voices rose from all directions.

"Lottie Knutsson for prime minister!"

"Yes, Lottie!"

"Who's she?" Carl asked the man by the pillar.

"She's from the Fritidsresor travel company. She began contacting people, hotels, hospitals the same day and arranging lists of people to travel back. It's only thanks to her that people can return at all. She chartered two flights yesterday."

"Unless they need travel documents, like us," the woman on the steps said. "Then they have no choice but to wait for Laila to finish her breakfast before she gets round to sending more officials."

The woman with kids, who was just before Carl in the queue, gave up waiting and left. At one point he too wondered if there was any point spending his time waiting, instead of actually doing something. But it was logical to begin the search by establishing contact with the temporary consulate.

He hoped that they would have information from hospitals or the local authorities.

Several people came out in the space of a few minutes, and Carl followed Anna and her teenage charge inside. The air was stale with sweat. The half-lit room was cramped – a small couch and a row of chairs were placed along the wall, but most people were standing. There was an anxious buzz.

Only one representative was sitting behind the table, a woman with a soft roundness about her, probably in her mid-twenties, with piles of documents and a computer. A man was speaking to her, raising his voice as he leaned over the table, his nose and left eye bruised and swollen and his lips twisted in anger and frustration. She'd look up at him, nervously biting her lower lip and nodding, then making some notes. It didn't appear that she was helping him or, for that matter, that she could. When he asked her something she would shrink behind her stack of papers, shrugging her shoulders. The tension was high, not just at the table but also among the weary people still in the queue. Because of the hum, Carl couldn't hear what the man was saying.

He felt sorry for the young woman – she looked entirely unprepared for dealing with desperate people. It wasn't her fault that her colleagues were on holiday back in Sweden and the Ministry for Foreign Affairs hadn't sent more officials. She was probably a trainee.

"His daughter is in intensive care," Anna said. "I met him yesterday in one of the hospitals. She requires complex surgery for which they don't have facilities here in Phuket. He needs a medically equipped plane to take her to Bangkok. Some Swedish officials promised him a plane yesterday, but nothing happened."

"Why is only one person serving?" Carl said.

"There were three, and I think the other two went to

arrange a bigger space in the hotel's lobby. They finally realised that this room is too small and that there are more people than they can handle. It's cruel to keep people outside in the heat."

The representative spoke with someone on her mobile and passed it to the man with the broken nose. He held the receiver to his ear, tightly pressed against the other with the heel of his hand and walked outside.

Anna stepped up to the desk, gently pushing the teenager in front of her. She rested her hands on the girl's shoulders.

"I spoke with her grandparents in Stockholm; they'll meet her at Arlanda."

"What's your name?" the representative asked.

The girl stood still, as if she hadn't heard the question.

"Where are your parents?"

She blinked but remained mute. She was staring blankly into the space in front of her.

Anna lowered her voice. "She's in shock. She doesn't speak. She wrote her name."

"We need some proof of her identity. We can't just assume that she's –" she glanced at the paper Anna placed on the desk – "Ulrika Gustafsson. If she would speak …"

"I did find the right family. Her grandparents described her. Look, she has a birthmark under her lower lip and a double piercing in her right ear."

Anna pulled back the girl's hair to expose two little star earrings, and Carl recoiled. Her neck had a deep, ragged cut, and strands of hair were glued to her scalp behind the ear by coagulated blood.

"We'll double-check the information to the extent we can, and arrange a flight to Stockholm." The representative flipped through some documents. Trying, it seemed to Carl, to give the appearance that she was doing something. "Can she stay with you meantime? Maybe a day or two? We have nowhere to accommodate her."

"Didn't you hear me? She lost her parents and her siblings, and she's alone. She has to fly home as soon as possible to her family. To the rest of her family. Of course I can take care of her. But the girl is in shock – the longer she stays here, the worse the consequences will be."

"I understand."

"No, you don't." Anna kept her voice very even. "Can I speak to someone more senior? Can you connect me with the Swedish ambassador in Thailand? I can't reach him."

"You'll have to wait."

Anna shook her head.

A man sitting on one of the chairs against the wall began manoeuvring his crutches to stand up. "My sister is on a charter flight tomorrow," he said, "and she has children the same age. Surely we can get the girl on the same flight."

"We can't just put her on a flight with anyone," the representative replied. "We have to consider child trafficking laws."

"Oh for God's sake, just do something. Something useful. Send one of your staff with her," said Anna.

"We'll do everything possible. Thank you for taking care of her in the meantime. If you want to speak to someone senior you'll have to wait," the representative said and motioned Carl forward with her hand. He looked at Anna, uncomfortable about taking her place. She shook her head, leaned forward to whisper something to the girl, and stepped back.

"Useless," she whispered.

"My two friends are missing."

"Are you Swedish, or looking for Swedish citizens?"

Carl recognised the doubtful glance.

"I am Swedish," he said firmly. "And I'm looking for two Swedish people."

"What are their names?"

"Eva and Kristoffer Berg."

"Age? Where were they staying?" The representative was writing notes on a sheet of A4.

"Thank you." She put the paper onto the pile and gestured to the person behind Carl in the queue.

"Wait, that is all? Can you check your system to see if there is any information about them? Anything from a hospital? Maybe an entry from someone on a noticeboard, a forum or something?"

"We haven't synchronised the information we have yet." To give her credit, she looked embarrassed. "If we find out something, we'll contact you at the number you gave me."

"What is the point of you even being here?"

"We're working hard here to help Swedish nationals in a time of crisis." A lanky man had appeared beside the woman, dressed in a white short-sleeve shirt. He had a long neck punctuated by a protruding Adam's apple.

"Help?" Carl leaned on his hands on the edge of the desk. He squinted and read the name tag on the pocket of the man's shirt. *Fredrik Svensson.* His thinly veiled condescension, his superiority and his false authority irritated Carl. "How? I haven't seen you help anyone else in this line."

"We do what we can, given the situation. We already have a thousand missing in our register—"

"I don't care about your register. How can you help me? How can you help the woman just before me? The man whose daughter's life depends on your unfulfilled promises."

"We're not all-powerful. I understand your frustration. Start with hospitals in Phuket town. Here's a list of phone numbers and addresses." He handled Carl a printout.

"That is it?"

"For now, yes. We're expecting more staff to arrive. Please don't hold up the queue."

"Leave them." Anna grabbed Carl by the elbow. "There's obviously no coordination with the hospitals. It looks to me like there's no coordination with the Ministry for Foreign Affairs either."

Carl looked at the sheet of paper. His hands were trembling. Did he just spend two hours in line to get a list of hospitals?

"There are nine hospitals on this list. Can there be so many in Phuket?"

"No, there are three major hospitals, forget the rest," Anna said.

"How far are they from here?"

"The other side of the island, in the southeast. An hour from here. But they are next to each other."

"Nothing closer?"

"There's Thalang hospital thirty minutes away in the direction you need to go. But it's a small public hospital. Usually, foreigners are sent to private hospitals with English speaking staff and better facilities. I'd skip it for now and return there later if necessary."

"What if Kristoffer is unable to get in touch because he's in a small hospital where nobody speaks English?"

"Yes, but start with the big hospitals where there's more likelihood of finding him."

"Try Vachira Hospital," said a woman in the queue. "This morning, I found my son there." A tear ran down her cheek. She wiped it away and, embarrassed, added quietly, "I feel so lucky. So lucky. I saw a lot of Swedes in the hospital beds. Some unconscious, some without limbs … some so …" The woman closed her eyes and more tears came. She breathed in deeply and got hold of herself. "Registers in reception areas are unreliable. Go to the nursing stations and the wards, go among the beds."

"Okay, thank you. Vachira."

Anna pointed to the list. "It's the largest of the government hospitals. It's next to the two large private ones. Start with any of the three."

"They flew me to Vachira Hospital from Phi Phi Island," the man on crutches said. "Doctors were great. But God, it's such a mess there."

"My wife is at Bangkok Hospital," a man said. His jaw seemed to be pinned and every word was an effort for him. "A Thai guy found her the morning after the tsunami. Under the wreckage of our hotel in Kao Lak. Miracle."

A disembodied voice came from the crowd. "My daughter is at the International Phuket Hospital."

"They took me to the International Phuket Hospital too."

"I found my mother at the Bangkok."

Carl's ears began to ring with the clamour of distressed voices, of cries and of intermittent tears. Suddenly, he was shoved roughly from behind. He staggered, and grabbed Anna's arm to stop himself falling.

There was a brief hum of indignation, and then everyone became quiet.

The man with the broken nose burst in, breathing hoarsely, little flecks of saliva in the corners of his mouth. His eyes were wild. With anger or despair, Carl couldn't decide. Perhaps both.

"They said they can't do anything." The man threw the phone onto the desk. "Anything at all. To hell with them." He reeled away, sobbing violently, pushing people aside to get to the door.

"Next," the representative said. She rested the fingers of one hand on her brow, as though hiding her eyes.

Ten

Before

Linda was meditating in the yoga *sala*. She had been late for the early morning group class – her jet lag was stronger than her discipline. And now, seated in a lotus position with her eyes closed, she still couldn't let go of her thoughts. How come the tide was so low today? The image of the retreating sea bothered her. She wouldn't be surprised to see it in the much shallower Bay Beach lagoon; at low tide the water could go out behind Pling Islands. But here, at the Sea Beach, the seabed was steep and the water would go out two, maybe five metres. In all the years of coming to the island, she had never seen anything like this. Could climate change create such a drastic drop in water level? Surely not. Anyway, it wouldn't happen overnight. These things happened gradually. Or not?

She slowly exhaled, counting to ten.

Fragments of people's voices coming from the beach were getting louder and she opened her eyes.

There were men, women, kids, hotel staff all gathered on the dunes. Some were taking pictures, others stood shading their eyes from the sun. A few, including an American couple they had met yesterday, walked the naked seabed, picking things up from the sand. She saw Peter strolling from the clubhouse, Shaun and Jude circling in excitement around him with their *National Geographic* binoculars. A surfer with a board under his arm caught up with them and they exchanged a few words before the chap ran down the beach. Did he really expect to ride a wave on Koh Phra Thong?

Linda peered into the hazy distance. Two or three kilometres away a misty line was forming across the horizon from south to north. She shifted onto her knees and began rolling up her mat. There'd be no excuses tomorrow. She'd be at the *sala* at sunrise.

When she stood up, she had the feeling the sea had come closer. She could distinguish a rising mist over the white horizon line. Was it breaking that deep?

"It's coming back," a woman shouted, peering into her camcorder as she walked towards the sea.

"The sea is returning," someone said.

Linda saw Jack running along the tree line, waving his arms in the air, screaming something to the people on the beach, but he was too far away to be heard. She saw a few people begin heading towards Hornbill Hill. She saw Peter nudging the twins to follow them. She felt her pulse quicken. Something was wrong.

She glanced at the sea; the wave was less than half a mile away. It began climbing in the air, developing a foaming lip.

"Peter—" She tried to yell but instead only a squeak came out. Her throat was tight. She wanted to run to Hornbill Hill but her legs turned steel heavy. As though in a dream, she couldn't make herself move and the air was too thick to breathe. She stood as if rooted, mute, as she watched her boys climb the hill. Peter was running towards her.

The floor beneath her feet began trembling. The beams above her head creaked.

She dashed to Peter.

Eleven

The siren grew louder, and hospital staff moved people to the side to let an ambulance park in front of the entrance. Others lifted a motionless woman from a stretcher that had been laid on the asphalt, and placed her on a trolley. Her hair and face were covered in dry blood and mud, her eyes closed, grimy arms spread, dangling. Carl couldn't tell if the woman was alive; there was no sign she was breathing, but she probably was because on another trolley they had placed a body covered with a white sheet. He glanced inside the ambulance, where another much smaller body was wrapped in a sheet from head to toe. People were pushing from behind to get closer and Carl was thrust against the second trolley. He stumbled forward and found himself almost leaning over the corpse. His nostrils filled with a sickening smell. He grabbed one of the rails and pushed back.

A woman from behind pushed Carl aside and tore the sheet from the head.

"I have to see."

Opaque blue eyes were wide open, unmoving, sand under the lids. The mouth was twisted in a scream or a gulp of air. A swollen black tongue stuck out. Carl retreated, stepping on people's feet. He had never seen a dead body before. Or maybe he had, but not so close, and the corpse would be neatly arranged, giving the impression of deep sleep. But it wasn't the death that shocked him, it was the agony of the last moments imprinted on the bloated face.

A medic put his hands on the woman's shoulders and pulled her away. "No," he said firmly.

Her face twisted. "My husband … I'm just looking …" She dropped to her knees. She rocked backwards and forwards, hitting the dusty ground with her forehead, howling.

People moved away from her – not scattering, but as if there was nothing unusual in her behaviour. At first, Carl too had the urge to walk away. He felt sick from the smell, but he stood for another moment and then squatted down next to the crying woman. He patted her back and spoke quietly to her, but she didn't respond. He put his hand under her elbow and tried to help her up, but she was unresponsive, heavy. She turned her face to him.

"Why? Why?" she said through the dirt and tears. The words pierced his heart.

"Lift under her armpits," Anna said, and together they dragged her into the hospital lobby where it was cooler and dropped her into a chair. She didn't look at them and continued sobbing. Anna left them for a moment and returned with a glass of water and tissues. The woman didn't acknowledge either and Anna put them on the floor next to her.

"I guess we can't do any more for her," she said, and looked at Carl. "Are you okay?"

"I'm fine." He rubbed his face vigorously. He was finding it hard to think through the sounds that were all around – sirens in the distance, the rattle of trolleys, weeping, agitated voices.

"For the first two days people were quieter. Most were probably overwhelmed by shock and could only go through

103

the mechanics, writing down the names of their missing. Lists of survivors became an obsession. People wandering between hospitals and emergency centres, desperate for news. I thought by now the situation would have improved. Everyone thought so …"

Carl looked around the lobby area. The woman they had helped was just one of many here. The seating area was full of desperate faces, hollowed eyes and stifled cries. Anxiety hung in the air like dense, suffocating smoke.

"The number of people searching did not come down," Anna said. "Just what they were searching for. They had to face the reality that it was bodies. They don't really bring injured anymore. That woman on the stretcher was an exception."

Anna led Carl to a noticeboard with so many photos that they overlapped and stuck out over the edge. "Start here," she said. "All from the morgue. This way, you eliminate the worst possible outcome straight away."

Carl hastily glanced at the photos and then at a list of sixteen known names of deceased.

"They aren't here."

"You have to focus on each photo. People look different when … you know …"

"I'd recognise them from a million photos." Carl dug his fists under his armpits. The dead blue eyes from the trolley came to his mind. He didn't even know whether it was a man or a woman. But he was still sure he'd recognise the two familiar faces. If he had to.

"They are not dead," he said.

Anna looked at him, and a feeble smile touched the corners of her lips. She probably wanted to say something consoling, but she didn't. He felt doubt in her eyes. But she wasn't to know that Kristoffer couldn't drown. He just couldn't.

"I'll go to check the noticeboards with the hospital's patients," he said.

"I'll be at the help centre, in the lobby behind the seating area. Ulrika's grandparents sent me pictures of her parents and sister – I'll make a missing poster. Do you want to make one of your friends?"

"Yes." He shifted on his feet. "I'll come after I've checked the board."

"Here's my phone number, in case we get separated."

"Where I can buy a SIM card and a phone?"

"7-Eleven. It's outside, just across the road. They probably sell phones."

There were four people in front of one of the noticeboards. One man was broad-shouldered and took almost as much space as the others. The printing on the lists was small and Carl couldn't see it from behind them. He noticed a couple leaving from another board and dashed over to take their place.

There were eight sheets of paper in English. The lists were obviously intended to be in alphabetical order, but they weren't. One page with names starting 'A' was between pages with K and L, and one page had names written in seemingly random order. Sometimes just the first name, and almost none with any additional information. *'Henri.'* Carl raised his eyebrows. No nationality or even an approximate age. And was Henri a French guy, or Swedish or German with a missing *k*? Or simply English with a misplaced *i*? How many Henris might there be amongst the missing? Was he a man or a child? To add to the confusion, Henri came up several times in different lists, including a register of discharged people.

A man in a soiled vest top, leaning on a crutch, stood so

105

close to Carl that he detected the smell from his armpits. He shifted a foot to the side. When the man brushed his sweaty shoulder against his bare arm, Carl flinched.

"Sorry," the man said. "These lists are rubbish. This guy, Timothy Barlow? He was discharged along with me yesterday morning. They don't update it." He turned to a petite Asian woman next to him. "Do you read Thai?"

"No, I'm Japanese," she said, and her hand went involuntarily to her face.

"Oh, sorry," he muttered. He winked at Carl and mouthed the words, '*How would I know?*'

Carl didn't react. Could Kristoffer be mistaken for a Thai? He was taller, was Carl's first thought, and most people would know the difference between a Thai and a Korean. He looked again at the Japanese woman. Her skin was dark for a Japanese and the eye shape was a bit different. He wouldn't like to guess where she was from, but his first guess wouldn't have been Thai. Or maybe that was because he had heard her say she was Japanese. Would he see the difference in a hurry if she had wounds or was unconscious? Or, worse, dead?

"Excuse me, are you Thai?" the man said to a woman in red-framed glasses.

"Yes."

"Can you check the register for the name John Stuart? Or just John?" He pointed at the register in the Thai language.

"You need to check English language register."

"I did that already. In this hospital, only a few doctors speak English, trust me. Sometimes foreign names are written in Thai."

"Ooh," she said. She spoke in singsong Thai to her friend in a flowery blouse.

"Look over there." Her friend first pointed to the English

106

registers and then to the man, and then she put her hand on her chest and pointed to the Thai lists.

"I know, you're right. But I looked there already. Please, can you search for John Stuart in the lists that are in Thai?"

The woman in the glasses stepped closer to the Thai register. The woman in the flowery blouse stood behind her and spoke to her in Thai.

"Jo Stuwa, Jo Stuwa."

There were six or seven lists written in Thai. As this was a government hospital, nearly everything in the building was written in Thai, apart from the green EXIT sign.

"Can you please check for Jo Stuwa as well, the way your friend says it?"

"I'm checking, I'm checking," the woman said.

The man bent towards her. "I meant, check Jo Stuwa *too*. Please."

She fixed her glasses on her nose and said something in Thai to her friend, and both wrinkled their noses. The woman in the flowery blouse walked away to where bikes were parked in front of the entrance.

Carl turned his attention to the patient register in English. On the last page, he spotted the name 'Christopher'. No surname, but the nationality was given as Swedish. His pulse quickened. Could it be Kristoffer? Was he in such a bad state that he could only say his name, and not spell it out?

"Jo Stuwa." The woman pointed to a name written in Thai.

"I knew it! Does it have any more information?"

"No."

"Can you write me the way it's written on the list – here?" He handed her a pen. The grip of envy clutched Carl's heart. He followed the man with his eyes as he limped on his crutch into the main hospital lobby.

Carl wondered for a moment if he should go and enquire first about 'Christopher' but he turned to the Thai woman and said, "Can you look for Kristoffer Berg and Eva Berg?"

"Kristof Beg and Ev Beg." She sighed, fixed her glasses and returned to the lists.

"And Jean and Pierre Dubois please?" A woman with frizzy hair rose up on her tiptoes behind the Thai woman.

The Thai woman turned to Carl.

"Sorry, I forgot the name."

"Kristoffer Berg."

"And yours was Zan … what?"

"Jean Dubois," the French woman said.

She turned to Carl. Her left eye was red and there was a purple bruise on her temple.

"I jumped the queue. I'm sorry. I checked every hospital in Phuket. My sons just disappeared. One moment we were in the swimming pool and then …" She covered her mouth and gave a long sob.

"No Kristof Beg." The Thai woman shook her head.

Carl pulled a folded list with hospital names from his pocket. He turned it over and handed it to her. "Can you please write Kristoffer and Eva Berg in Thai?"

Carl strode to the lobby, to the long tables where hospital staff were helping with enquiries. He found an available chair across from a Thai woman in a T-shirt with a ballerina design, a hospital badge pinned to her right side.

"I found my friend's name on the list of hospital patients. Christopher. Where is he? Can I see him?"

The woman scanned her printed register of hospital patients.

"No Christopher name here."

"But it's there on the noticeboards."

"Maybe he left already."

"Don't you have lists of discharged people?" Carl knew that if Kristoffer had been discharged he'd have contacted his family immediately. And that would mean it was the wrong Christopher.

She took a pile of sheets stapled together and went through a much longer list of discharged people. Carl looked around the lobby for Anna but couldn't see her.

"No." The attendant shook her head.

"That means that he could be still inside the hospital, doesn't it?"

"No. He is not here." She tapped the register of patients.

"But he's in the register on the noticeboard which means he was registered at some point at the hospital."

"Yes," she said, and looked at Carl blankly.

"Can you request more information? If a person was here, he couldn't just vanish."

She half-turned to a woman in a nurse's uniform sitting next to her, and they looked at the register together.

"Sorry," Carl said to a man with red hair next to him, whom the nurse had been assisting. His arms were blistered from sunburn.

"That's okay, I'm not in a hurry."

"They don't speak good English here."

"That's good enough English, trust me. The woman serving you is a volunteer and was accepted because of her language skills. The nurses speak very little English." He had a definite Scottish accent. "My wife is here in the hospital. Yesterday they moved her to another ward but didn't record it. They told me she had left the hospital. Both her legs were broken. I explained to them there was no way she could have left. It took me three hours to find her."

"And how did you?"

"I went through the wards, one by one."

Shrill voices came from near the lift, and Carl and the man turned together.

"Not allowed inside. Not allowed!"

Two hospital staff were pushing a man with a professional video camera over his shoulder from the lift. He was two heads taller than them and quite bulky, unless he went willingly they weren't going to get very far.

He held onto his camera with one hand and lifted the other into the air.

"Alright, alright! I'm leaving." He shook them off.

"They're like vultures," the Scottish man said. "They're everywhere – in hospitals, hotel ruins, at the City Hall. I have a feeling they're the only ones who truly rushed to the tsunami-affected areas. Not government agents, not doctors, but reporters. Such a self-sacrificing profession."

"Maybe it's not such a bad thing. At least journalists report on what happens here. Otherwise, how would any of us know anything?"

"They're too intrusive. They show up in hospital rooms, where people are in physical and emotional distress. They thrust cameras in people's faces ask how they're doing. I refused an interview, but they still filmed me, and my wife was lying right there, unconscious."

"Discharged," the nurse said to Carl.

"Does it actually say that?"

The women looked at him in confusion.

"How do you know he was discharged?"

"Ask them to take you to intensive care," the man whispered to him. "That's where patients with serious conditions are, many of them unconscious."

"Can you take me to the intensive care unit?"

"No, can't. Friend not there."

"How do you know?"

"Not in the register."

The man leaned into Carl's ear. "Wait for me at the glass door and I'll tell you how to get there. If anyone asks you where you're going, say you're visiting Linda Brown."

Twelve

Before

Carmen was snoozing on Georgiou's shoulder in their bed.

She would have got up hours ago but his deep, even breath was lulling her. They rarely had a chance to stay in bed late together – he would always run to the office or the gym. Mornings were short in Rome. Even on holiday his phone would always ring, there would be friends to catch up with, things to do. She enjoyed having him all to herself. She had begun to like their remote escape.

Carmen dreamt she was walking up some airplane steps, alone. The sound of the plane's engine was deafening; then through the din she began to distinguish the sound of screams.

She opened her eyes and lifted her head. All the shutters in the bungalow were open, the curtains were moving in the breeze, and occasional beams of light stole in. She thought she saw a long shadow pass by the window. She pushed herself off the bed, took three steps and looked out. There was nothing but a column of raging brown water. As if in slow motion, a torrent swept away the sun chairs and umbrellas from their terrace like they were made of paper, and smashed into the pillars supporting the roof of the bungalow, breaking them like matchsticks. A second later, water rushed into the bedroom, instantly filling it.

Her feet left the floor and she felt suddenly disorientated, weightless … breathless.

Thirteen

Carl passed his sheaf of printouts to and fro from one hand to the other as he stood in front of the long wooden noticeboard with posters of the missing. His clothes held the faint smell of disinfectant. He hadn't allowed himself to stop after checking every face in the intensive care unit; he had worked his way through every floor in the hospital, every bed. Nobody had heard of Kristoffer, nobody was from Golden Buddha resort, nobody knew about Koh Phra Thong.

He studied the images on the board. A little girl laughing as she rode a big dog out of the water. A man with a golden haired boy on his shoulders, standing against the sunset. A woman on a swing, her bright red hair flying in the wind. An old couple tenderly embracing each other. A crawling baby girl smiling a toothless smile. How would a baby survive in the water? Did her parents still hold hope to find her?

These posters were everywhere – on the columns inside the hospital, on the walls outside, on the sliding doors of the entrance, pinned to trees next to a taxi rank, on a lamppost near the 7-Eleven. The shop assistant who helped him to top up his mobile had a picture of her son pinned to the front of her T-shirt.

What was most unsettling about these photos was that they were of happy, smiling people, full of life and energy. All the pictures were taken by family or friends, on holidays, celebrating birthdays, weddings and other occasions. They all captured lives. They were images of people the way we always want to remember them – happy.

Carl looked at the photo in his hand, his heart drumming in his chest. It had originally been of three of them at the pre-wedding dinner. It was the only one he had of Kristoffer and Eva together, without sunglasses, both looking into a camera. He didn't want to use it – it felt too brutal – but he had no choice. He had cut himself out of the photo, but his left arm was still there, around Kristoffer's shoulder.

Eva was in a linen strapless dress with a turquoise necklace, leaning in towards Kristoffer, her hand in his, strands of wheat-coloured hair falling over her delicate shoulders. Carl smiled. There was a mark left by a piece of chocolate cake on Kristoffer's white shirt, which he had tried to clean without much success. Kristoffer was the only person he knew who was clumsier than he was.

After dinner, he had walked with Kristoffer to the edge of the cliff, where they sat on a wooden bench. The sea was calm and the gentlest breeze flapped Kristoffer's tie. The sun had hidden beyond the horizon, but the sky was still the colour of ripe cherry. The waves were breaking over the smooth rocks, lifting into the air, and then retreating, shushing and returning as foam. Cranes gave a long bugle call that echoed in the distance.

They sat in silence. Not because they had nothing to say but because they didn't have to say anything. They understood each other, and silence between them was the measure of the depth of their friendship. He saw so much of himself in

Kristoffer. And maybe he loved his friend all more for those qualities he longed to see in himself.

Carl pulled himself straighter and gazed at the boards. The word 'missing' on each poster stood in sad counterpoint to the images themselves. However, he thought, the word 'missing' applied just as much to a person in an unknown location as to someone assumed to be dead. For each of these individuals there was someone desperately hoping to bring those happy moments with loved ones into their tomorrows. The boards were a reflection of the human capacity for unconditional hope.

And who could blame someone for wanting a miracle?

Carl tacked his poster to the board, stepped back and looked at it once again. He strained to remain composed, but inside a burning bubble of dread was filling his chest.

He turned and walked away.

Fourteen

Before

Above the shoreline, Kristoffer shielded his eyes from the sun. The shallow Bay Beach lagoon was calm and he could see the rollers around Pling Islands where the water changed colour to dark blue. A longtail boat with resort guests grounded in the shallows and two Thai staff helped to drag it into ankle-deep water. Kristoffer recognised the boatman, a skinny chap with two prominent front teeth; the same man had brought them to the island five days ago. His name was Aod – which Kristoffer would have forgotten had he not explained that the name meant 'tadpole'. Kristoffer and Eva had found it amusing that the boatman was so proud of it, particularly as he did indeed look like a tadpole, his head too large for his body, his long mouth too big for his head. Aod claimed it was very good luck to have a name like his – he was protected on sea and land. Kristoffer told him that his own last name meant 'mountain', and Aod said that was good luck too – which did make more sense to Kristoffer.

Aod passed suitcases to the staff who carried them on their shoulders to the dry sand. He noticed Kristoffer and waved to him; Kristoffer saluted back.

"It's so peaceful. Paradise on Earth," Kristoffer heard a woman say. He remembered Eva saying the same; he smiled and glanced at her over his shoulder. She stood in the shade, putting sun cream on her shoulders, watching the boat, probably thinking the same.

"Let's hurry while the tide is up," Lars shouted. He had his kayak over his shoulder. His arms were twice as thick as his, it occurred to Kristoffer, so his and Emma's body weight together would be at least a thirty-kilo handicap, which he hoped would slow down their kayak a little.

Bill, the owner of the diving shop, was dragging the second kayak through the grass. "You have time, guys. Just use hats and creams, the sun is very strong today."

"How far are those islands?" Kristoffer said. "Can we land and have a picnic?"

Lars dropped his kayak into the water.

"Only after the race."

"We call them islands," Bill said, "but they are really twin rock formations overgrown with vegetation. The smaller, the closest to us, is about five hundred metres from here, the bigger seven hundred. You can't see it from here, but on both there are tiny sandy beaches where you can take your kayak out. And it's cool to snorkel between the islands."

"What will we see, do you reckon?" Kristoffer held his kayak steady while Eva climbed in. He passed her a paddle and two bottles of water.

"It's not Richelieu Rock with its manta rays, right enough, but there are several anemones, clownfish and the other usual shallow water suspects."

Manta rays. Kristoffer had seen them only once, when he was with Carl in Hawaii. Their gliding silhouettes against the bottomless blue were far away but still impressive. Jack had said he saw a whale shark at the Richelieu Rock a month ago – with overfishing they had become a huge rarity. And an Australian guest had said he saw it again only a week before. When they booked their honeymoon Kristoffer had reserved their places on the resort diving boat for today and tomorrow. Now, with Eva pregnant, she couldn't go diving, and to be on a boat on a hot day would probably make her seasick. Even the ride to the resort in a longtail from Kuraburi had been uncomfortable – they had hugged the shore to avoid the choppy sea. She had urged Kristoffer to go alone – she would be fine. What could happen to her? She would lounge on their bungalow terrace with her book or hang out at the clubhouse. But he hadn't felt comfortable about leaving her, even for a day. He had cancelled their places two days ago. Richelieu Rock would be always there, they would chase sharks and manta rays somewhere else, they had a long life ahead of them.

"Quick final brief." Lars fixed his cap. "We go round the islands clockwise, returning to this exact spot at the mouth of the mangrove creek. Bill is the referee. Losers buy the drinks tonight."

"Are you sure you don't want lifejackets?" Bill said.

All four of them glanced at the pile of deeply pleated lifejackets on the grass and shook their heads. "It's too hot to wear those," Emma said.

Kristoffer leaned into Eva's ear. "Let's stay to the right of them. The water is calmer in the lagoon. And don't try to overtake them, at least until we get round the islands. We have to use our energy wisely."

She looked above her sunglasses and winked.

They were in the middle of the lagoon when Kristoffer noticed that his paddle was getting heavier. It was becoming harder to keep the kayak going straight to the islands, as if some undercurrent was sucking them towards the sea. He knew it would be more difficult to paddle in choppy water – that was why the longtails arrived at the shallow Bay Beach lagoon instead of the more open Sea Beach in front of the clubhouse – and the constant bumping wasn't good for Eva's pregnancy. He dug deeper, trying to stay in the bay.

"Is it just me or is the water leaving the bay and taking us with it?" Eva shouted over her shoulder.

"I don't get it; Bill said low tide was at four something, right?"

The Danes' kayak was ahead of them, but it was getting closer to the open sea than to the islands. At first, Kristoffer thought it was part of their strategy, but then he noticed they were paddling only on the right, trying to steer inland.

Kristoffer glanced back towards the beach. The water was retreating as if someone had pulled a plug on the sea bed. It hadn't been so dramatic several days ago when they had walked in the lagoon at low water. If they didn't go back right now to shore, they would have to leave the kayaks at Pling Islands or go further out to the sea and around Hornbill Hill to come in in front of the clubhouse.

He saw Emma signalling with her arms, shouting something.

"See you at lunch!" was all Kristoffer could make out. The pair continued paddling rhythmically, but they were moving faster now towards open sea, as if carried by an invisible force.

"Eva, we're going back. Push only with your right paddle. Aim for the mouth of the mangrove." He could see that running water had cut a channel in the sand between the mangrove and the low water mark.

The kayak's hull grated along the seafloor and stopped, still some way from the beach. Without saying a word, Kristoffer hopped out and offered Eva his hand. The Bay Beach lagoon was empty. The blue line of the water's edge appeared to be miles away. They could have walked to the Pling Islands without getting their feet wet. On the sand at the bigger of the islands, a fisherman took his sails down and jumped out of his boat. The longtail that Kristoffer had watched a few minutes before, had made it only to the middle of the bay. Aod, loaded with two suitcases on his skinny shoulders, was plodding back to the beach, and the Japanese couple they had met at breakfast were tottering after him.

"How strange. It does seem nobody knew about this." Kristoffer noticed a little school of stripy fish caught in the shallow strip of water formed by the grounding of the kayak.

"There's still water in the mangrove creek," Eva said.

Kristoffer looked into the channel meandering between the mangrove trees, whose branches came together above it like a tent. It seemed a serene shelter, away from the unfolding day's intense heat, the bright green foliage pierced with diffracted beams of sunlight.

Kristoffer couldn't shake off the sense that something was very wrong. He wondered fleetingly if the scientist would have had something to say about the early tide in the lagoon.

"Should we drag the kayak back to the dive shop or try sailing into the creek? It's just after ten."

Fifteen

"Which entrance do you need?"

The taxi driver had slowed down at a roundabout as he approached Bangkok Phuket Hospital.

"I don't know," Carl said. "Here is fine." He stared through his open window at the massive white buildings of the hospital, which stood in contrast to the slums that surrounded it. One block was at least eight floors – checking every room was going to take hours. After Vachira he had gone to the International Hospital and the smaller Mission Hospital where they had only two dozen patients. Bangkok Phuket was almost his last hope. There were several smaller government hospitals on his list but he understood it was highly unlikely Kristoffer or Eva would be there. If they were in a serious condition, which was the only explanation he could accept as to why they still hadn't contacted anybody, they'd be transferred to a larger facility.

He stepped out of the taxi and headed towards the entrance. Medical staff hurried in and out of the massive glass doors. Everything was bigger here – the lofty lobby, the crowds of people, even the noticeboards. There was more space for missing posters, and the lists of patients were lengthier but tidier, the list of the deceased longer.

"The morgue is full," he heard someone say. "They're no longer taking the corpses that the rescue teams are bringing. Nobody's equipped for such a large number of dead."

Carl caught the man's attention. "Do you know where they take them?"

"Sorry. No idea."

The morgue is full. He lingered a little longer in front of the board with photos of unidentified corpses.

"Have you seen my wife?" The husky voice came from behind.

A tall, balding man was standing so close behind him that Carl had to step away.

"Have you seen my wife?" The man was staring at him with dry red eyes. A sickening smell came from his mouth. Carl winced.

"No, I haven't."

The man stepped closer to him. "And my boy?" He was shedding patches of skin from his scalp, revealing raw pink flesh underneath.

Carl stepped back again.

"No." He glanced around, looking for a way out without being rude.

"Here's their picture."

The man took a crumpled photo from his pocket and thrust it into Carl's face. A woman with pale blue eyes held a boy with blond curly hair with one arm, a blonde girl of possibly seven or eight with the other.

"Are you from Sweden?" Carl said in Swedish.

The man's face flushed with hope.

"Eric," he said, and shook Carl's hand. He had fixed Carl with his inflamed eyes, waiting for him to say something, irrationally, desperately hopeful.

"I wasn't here. I just arrived this morning," Carl said.

Eric stood there as if thinking through what Carl had said. Then, without saying a word, he turned away and staggered towards the entrance of the hospital. Carl followed him with his eyes.

That woman in the picture … She reminded him of someone.

He followed after Eric, keeping a few paces behind.

The cavernous lobby, with its endless glass windows from floor to lofty ceiling, its crystal chandelier, deep-upholstered armchairs and intricate gold-coloured side tables, reminded Carl of an expensive hotel. A twittering came from above, and Carl threw his head back and looked up. A small bird was crossing to and fro from the chandelier to the top of a lavish Christmas tree in the middle of the lobby. The tree was decorated with big red bulbs and golden ribbons. Surely not, Carl thought. He glanced at the piles of boxes and bags around the base of the tree, and then it dawned on him. These weren't Santa's presents. These were charity donations from the island's citizens, boxes filled with T-shirts, flip-flops, toilet paper and necessities like toothpaste and tampons. Christmas was different this year.

He watched Eric talking to an Asian couple, showing them the crumpled photo. When they shook their heads, he walked up to a chubby man with a red suitcase.

Carl heard an articulate woman's voice coming from behind a little knot of people. There was the glow of lights and he worked his way closer.

"Guilt and anger tend to replace the initial shock. Then the third wave is the overwhelming feeling of loss that comes to those who are left alive. Finally, there is the long-term trauma that follows days, weeks or months later."

A woman with immaculate make-up and a doctor's coat draped over her shoulder stood in front of a camera. She noticed Eric standing not far from her, staring at the paper in his hands, and signalled the cameraman to focus on him.

Carl spotted a doctor accompanying a woman out of a room behind reception, her face swollen from crying. Carl strode towards him.

"Doctor, please." He grabbed the doctor's shoulder but quickly withdrew his hand when he realised that he was clinging to him. "I'm looking for my missing friends, but I can't find any information on the boards."

"Do you have any indication that they might be in our hospital?" the doctor said. From his accent, Carl guessed he might have been Dutch.

"No, I don't really."

The doctor raised his eyebrows. "Well, if reception have no information on them either maybe they're not here. We're not the only hospital on the island."

"I've tried the others. Everywhere I go, the registers are a mess. Nurses at the information desk referred me back to the notice boards. I thought, what if their names were misspelt?"

The doctor stared at him coolly.

"I'm tired of people complaining about messy registers," he said. "My medical staff are swamped. Yesterday was even worse. Do you realise that nurses were working non-stop for more than forty-eight hours, and they're still here? They were responding to a complete catastrophe, with no chance even to check what happened to their own families and villages."

Carl shifted from one foot to another. He hadn't thought about it that way, about the doctors, the nurses, all the Thai people being impacted. The television crews didn't mention them, they focused instead on the number of missing tourists, the Brits, Australians, Americans. He swallowed.

"It's unsurprising so many administrative problems are coming up now," the doctor said. "Many nurses, even at our hospital, speak very little English and so they would just write English names in Thai. No one cared about writing names properly and keeping the register clear – it wasn't the main task at hand. They had to save lives."

A nurse brought some papers for the doctor. He looked through them and hastily put his signature on the last one.

"This morning," the doctor said more quietly, "I asked my Thai assistant to go through all the names written in Thai in our register and within fifteen minutes he found ten foreign names. Now, I think there are more than fifty."

He fixed his glasses on his nose and stared at Carl. He had dark circles under his eyes. "You can come with me to my office where we are updating the lists, taking mistakes into consideration. You would be the first to see it. I'm afraid that's the best I can do."

"Dr Green, do you have any news for me?" Eric caught up with them as the doctor opened the door to his office. The low-ceilinged long room had bare white walls with only a portrait of the King in a gold leaf frame for decoration. In the middle of the room there was a long table with half a dozen staff in front of computers. Piles of papers, registers, photo printouts, missing posters were everywhere. A noisy air con blew cold air.

"Can you give me an updated register, please?"

Someone handed the doctor a batch of pages neatly stapled together, and he gave them to Carl. The first thing Carl noticed was that the names were in perfect alphabetical order.

"The body of a boy we feared might have been your son happens not to be." Eric seemed to stop breathing as he listened to the doctor, his face frozen. "Another couple identified him as their child."

"They told me the same yesterday," Eric said to Carl. "The bodies of two blond boys found in the area we were staying.

The ages and descriptions were close, but in the end neither of them turned out to be my son – I was able to describe a triangular birthmark on his left shoulder."

When Eric left the room, one of the staff said, "It's the fourth time he has come today already. With every corpse not identified as his son, his faith has been getting somehow stronger that his boy is alive. It's hardly rational but you can understand."

Dr Green slumped onto a plastic chair at a corner desk. A fan blew air onto Carl's face and ruffled the documents on the doctor's desk. "It's hard to blame him. He is in his own vacuum of all-embracing hope. We all cope differently with loss – it's part of our survival instinct. The real trauma will come when the inevitable is so obvious that he won't be able to escape it." He fixed his eyes on Carl, his expression filled with melancholy fatigue. Perhaps he too had lost someone he loved.

There was nothing in the register. Carl handed it back to the doctor.

"You don't believe that people can still be found alive, do you?"

"The general rule is that if survivors are not found within forty-eight hours, unfortunately it means they are probably lost. Unless …" – he was flipping through the updated list of hospital patients – "unless they're under the wrong name or in such a serious condition that they are unable to provide their names."

"People still find each other," Carl snapped.

"I'm not trying to console you here. I told you the reality."

"How many admissions have you had over the last two days?"

"Our capacity is two hundred beds and I think we have more than five hundred patients now." Dr Green leaned back on his chair, took off his glasses and rubbed the corners of his eyes. A stack of plastic cups from a coffee machine stood on his desk, and a bin on the floor was filled to the brim with more.

"The first day we didn't realise the scope of the calamity. No one did. We were just trying to cope with thousands of injured flooding non-stop into our hospital. We were dealing with injuries simple cuts and broken arms to life-threatening conditions. The first day we had people mainly from Phuket. Yesterday, rescue helicopters were bringing people from small islands and distant areas. Also, small hospitals along the coast ran out of supplies, not having the equipment and enough doctors to take care of severely injured patients, so they began sending them to us. Even we need more equipment urgently, more medication and in fact more doctors."

The doctor paused and in a softer tone said, "Where were your friends?"

"Koh Phra Thong Island."

"Where is it?"

Yet another person who didn't know where the island was. Carl had checked several times whether he was saying the name correctly. "After Kao Lak – closer to Burma."

"Haven't heard of it. But there are no big hospitals in that direction anyway. So, if your friends are in a serious condition, they're likely to be sent here or the International Hospital in Phuket. Leave your missing poster with us."

"Do you have any unidentified patients?" Carl said.

Dr Green picked up his phone. "Hi. Dr Green. Do we have any unidentified patients? In intensive care perhaps?"

He put the phone down.

"No," he said to Carl.

"What should I do? Where do I look now?"

"Maybe you should wait."

"For what?"

"For a miracle? There's nothing you can do."

Sixteen

Jack felt the roof of his parched mouth with his tongue. Sand was everywhere – on his teeth, on his lips – but not a drop of saliva. He coughed. It scratched his throat and brought more sand into his mouth. He tasted seaweed and blood.

He retched and tried to roll onto his side, but his lower body refused to obey and he only had time to turn his head before convulsing with vomit that flowed down his throat and filled his nose. A soup of brown water with lumps of yellow and blood clots. He wiped his lips and his cheeks with the back of his hand, unable to clear his nose of sand and puke. He breathed in deeply, and gagged.

He needed water.

Water.

The thought of it sent a rush of sheer desperation through his being.

The wave had crashed into him with such force that he had thought there would be no bones left intact. He had grabbed a pillar of the clubhouse terrace but the torrent had flung him off. It had dragged him across the floor, sucking him inside the building and smashing him into a wall. Furniture, stones, pans flew everywhere, striking his body like cannonballs.

He rubbed his eyes. He saw shades of blue and green

above him, his vision still blurred. He was in some kind of sandy ditch that felt more like a grave because it was a struggle to move. His lungs burned every time he breathed in, and he settled for small gulps of air, suppressing the urge to cough to try to ease the pain.

With an effort, he lifted himself up on his elbows. The pit's rim was beyond reach and a mass of naked roots stuck out from the sand on both sides. Far above, palm leaves seemed to float like angels, throwing a blessed shade across the construct of his grave.

He looked towards his feet. His stomach was covered in casuarina needles and the rest of his body was buried under a haphazard heap of trash and branches. He swiped at the leaves, but only the dry ones moved – the rest were glued with dirt and dried blood to raw wounds all over his skin. He tried to pull his legs from under the pile but something was holding them. He shifted back on his elbows, wiggling his hips slightly, but he was able to move only his left leg. He backed up an inch more, pulling on just his right leg, but a nerve-shattering pain went through him and he roared to the angels in agony.

He manoeuvred onto one elbow and began methodically removing branches, split boards, cans and cartons wrapped in seaweed, a dead crab and a tangle of vegetation and sand, until both legs were clear. He curled the toes of his right foot, slowly flexing his ankle, then his knee, and the pain became more intense, coming from low down on the back of his leg. He reached for his foot and with both hands began inching it closer.

There was a large side-to-side gash in his calf and the flesh around was red-black and swollen, almost indistinguishable from the sand and small debris that clung to it. He plucked out a jagged splinter of wood and some casuarina needles. At least, as far as he could tell, there was no fracture, and that gave him hope that he could walk or crawl to the resort for help. If the resort was still there. If, indeed, help was there. How many could have survived a tsunami of such ferocity?

He pushed his hair behind his ears and noticed a deep cut on his forearm, from the edge of his tattoo to the elbow. He was surprised the artery was intact. The bracelets were gone.

Jack slowly turned onto his knees and then slowly rose to his feet. Wavy lines and pinpricks of light floated in front of his eyes, and he staggered backwards.

Savannah? In a golden grass field in the distance, he recognised tall cajeput trees with their flaking bark. That meant he was at least half a kilometre away from the coast. Did the water carry him here? He stared at the gouges and craters in the soil around him, the debris dumped so far inland, the uprooted shrubs. Should he go back to the resort or cross the savannah to the east side of the island, to Tapa Yoi? The village faced the mainland and that, he reasoned, was where he'd most likely find help and water. He looked at the searing disc of the sun. It was past its zenith so it must be early afternoon. He tried to remember when the wave had hit. Was it around ten? The land towards the sea was a marsh. What if the water was still high closer to the coast? What if Tapa Yoi village got its share too? How big was the tsunami?

He saw a chunk of concrete bigger than himself, next to a round plastic table. There was no plastic furniture at the resort. Nothing there was built from concrete either, only the foundations. Perhaps this massive slab had come from somewhere else. But if the wave could uproot mature trees it could rip out concrete foundations just as easily. He remembered running up from the beach, the wave racing behind him, and thinking that it would surely break before the clubhouse, it would not reach the elevated deck.

Jack hobbled in the direction of the sea. He had to see what, or who, was left.

The wind brought the hiss of the sea. Of waves. Jack shuddered and stood still, listening hard. Every distant crash echoed in his head. Was it safe to go further? There could be another wave anytime. He turned around. No trees to climb, just a few palms. He couldn't go up a palm trunk, not with his wound. He couldn't run either.

The ditches became deeper, filled with water. They were harder to wade across without falling, or getting caught in branches and debris. The sand was soggy, and every few steps he plunged in knee-deep. He dragged his exhausted body out of the sinkholes with the same agonising difficulty it took to run in a dream. He was dizzy, breathing fast, wheezing as if something was obstructing his airway. But he didn't think about that and he ignored the pain in his shin, plodding on, focused only on the resort.

He spotted a body floating in a pool of water and stepped over the prow of a longtail boat to reach it. He turned the corpse face up. A Thai man he didn't recognise. He left him where he was. A few steps further on, he noticed another man half-buried in the sand, also Thai, with a huge open wound in his chest, around which flies were already gathering. He walked by without stopping.

At the base of a mound of wreckage he found a man sitting as though in repose, his head resting on an upturned pram.

"Hello," Jack said. He hesitated, unsure whether to approach, as though he would somehow be invading the man's space. His eyes were closed and blood had clotted around his mouth. The body of a small child lay a metre away, its head half-visible under a plank.

Dead. They were all fucking dead.

He stared at a dune which stood like a wall in front of

him. To his knowledge there were no such high dunes on the island, indeed there were no dunes at all in this part.

He began to climb, his feet sliding in the soft sand. He fell, gasping, coughing, his heart racing in his chest. To go around would take even more effort. He knew the sea was just behind the dune, he could taste the salt and he heard its hissing whisper. He wondered what was buried beneath these tonnes of sand – it could be half of Golden Buddha. He crawled to the top.

The shore came into the view.

Bay Beach. The Pling Islands. The mangrove creek. The sea was back in the lagoon but nothing was the same. The green and blue were gone, replaced by brown on the land and in the water, debris and wreckage everywhere. Brutal. Ugly.

Hornbill Hill and Monkey Mountain at the entrance to the creek were the only two natural elevations on the island. Their green caps appeared as a mirage, two ghosts from the past.

The shadow of Hornbill Hill covered most of Bay Beach. It was late afternoon, a time when the day's heat began to fade and Jack would leave his bungalow to water his orchard at the south end of the resort, further inland where the soil was more fertile.

Using a stick for support, Jack climbed over a carpet of broken boards to get to the ruins of the clubhouse, its sharp edges scraping over raw gashes on his legs. The entire resort frontage had been flattened – buildings, trees, everything. A dusty haze hovered over the wreckage. A huge industrial oven had been dumped upside down where the yoga *sala* used to be. Nothing remained of the *sala*. For the first time, images from the preceding hours or days began to form in his mind. He vaguely remembered seeing the *sala* roof floating in a narrow corridor between the palms, Aod and one of the gardeners holding onto the barge boards, only their heads above the water. For a short moment, while he struggled to stay above the surface, Jack thought they were lucky; then he saw the structure collide with a casurina tree and split into many pieces.

Jack stood listening, hoping he might catch a human voice, a moan perhaps. There had to be dozens of people buried under all this debris, but all he could hear were cracks and squeals, as if the wreckage itself was alive, breathing.

He began to lift planks where he calculated a storage room behind the kitchen used to be. If he was to survive to the end of the day, he needed fresh water. The wave had displaced everything, but he had to begin somewhere. He sat on a joist to catch his breath; all he saw was an orange, skewered incongruously on a butcher's hook. He dug his nails into its skin, tearing the fruit in two halves and sinking his teeth into the juicy flesh.

Through the haze, he saw a man trudging from Hornbill Hill. He didn't recognise him immediately. The man wore only shorts, and his torso was purple from sunburn.

"Jack, is that you?"

"Peter?"

"You look like you went through the meat grinder."

"You look like you were barbequed."

They stood staring at each other as if not believing their eyes, startled and relieved to find each other alive. Jack had so many questions, and no doubt Peter had too, but he suspected that neither of them wanted to hear the answers.

"Is there anyone else alive?" Jack said first. He didn't want to ask directly about the dead.

"Yes, my boys are alive, unscathed." Peter pulled a crooked smile. "They made it in good time to the hill, thanks to you."

"Good." Jack wanted to ask about Linda but didn't dare. He had seen her in the water, bouncing from tree to tree like a pinball, her face covered in blood.

"There are twenty-two people on the hill, ten of whom survived the wave and joined us a few hours ago," Peter said, and dropped his eyes. His hands began shaking. "I can't find Linda. I grabbed her arm before the wave hit us. And in the next second, she was yanked away."

There was a soft moan, weak, like a wind sighing in the wreckage. Jack glanced at Peter and they both darted over to a split tamarind tree.

Jack saw a grazed leg and flung up a sheet of thatching. It was a woman, one of the guests of the resort he had never spoken to. She had a slash along her neck, still bleeding, probably because she had begun to move, and her left eye was half out of its socket. He carefully lifted a bough which lay across her chest. The woman was naked, but curiously, because her skin was covered in mud and dried seaweed, her nudity wasn't obvious at first.

"Do you think you can move?" Jack said, carefully lifting the woman's head and then her shoulders.

The woman nodded and blinked. Her hand shot up to her injured eye and she tried to say something, but only a moan came out.

"Take it slowly, you'll be alright." Jack took a mucky sheet Peter had pulled from under some planks and wrapped it around the woman as best he could. He caught sight of Peter retreating, as if repulsed by the gruesomeness of her wounds, the smell of her faeces.

"Do you think we can get her up Hornbill Hill?"

Jack looked up at Peter's face and realised his disappointment at their discovery, the ache that it wasn't his wife. Despite himself, Jack too wished they'd found someone they knew, someone they cared for. He knew that of those twenty-two people on the hill there was nobody they were looking for, otherwise Peter would have mentioned them by name. Georgiou's face came into his mind; he hadn't seen him that morning, nor Carmen. They had been jet-lagged after their flight from Rome. When the wave hit they were still in their bungalow, which was right on the beach. But people had survived. Jack began to feel a glimmer of hope.

"I'll call and get help," Peter said.

"Why is nobody coming down?" Jack glared at the hill. "Why is nobody searching the ruins? There must be more people alive under the rubble."

"They are all afraid of a second wave."

"Injured and children, fair enough. The rest should come down. Apart from anything else, we need to find water to survive." He glanced at the woman's pale face. She looked as though she might die any moment. "We need to find a first aid kit too. All my bungalows have a basic kit in the bathroom."

Jack caught a glimpse of his shin. The wound looked angry, and blood was oozing out through small cracks in dried mud sculpted around his lower leg. He managed to push the pain out of his immediate thoughts, but it was still there, throbbing, demanding attention. He had seen too many people in tropical Asia develop gangrene within days from neglected wounds. He needed the medical kit from his own bungalow; it had everything – antiseptic, antibiotics, dressings, even skin sutures.

He gazed along the carpet of ruins and thought he could see at least a part of his bungalow in the distance. He frowned. It couldn't possibly have withstood the wave, he must be hallucinating.

"Jack, you are alive? Was that Peter you were talking to?"

Jonas was limping over the debris, his T-shirt shredded

into strips. A lanky man and a teenager followed him – other resort guests. Jack vaguely remembered them from the beach, watching the wave's approach. "Have you seen Jose?"

"No," Jack said, and faltered. "… And yes. I saw him when the wave hit. He was running up the stairs to the upper clubhouse terrace with Julia."

Jose nodded. "Carmen said she saw him in the water—"

"Carmen?"

"Yes, she's on the hill."

"Which hill?"

Jonas waved behind him. "Monkey Mountain."

"Is Georgiou there?"

"No."

"Who else is there?"

Jonas shrugged his shoulders.

"How many people are there?"

"Twenty-something, maybe thirty."

Jack tried to remember how many people were at the resort. Capacity was 102 people but he wasn't sure if the resort was full. And there were Thai employees too, maybe forty or more.

"A boat." The teenager pointed out to sea.

The four of them watched as a motorboat slowly came into view. It was heading towards the island.

"It's the diving boat that left this morning!" the teenager yelled, and started hopping over and between the wreckage to the shore. Jonas and the lanky man ran after him, and Jack hobbled behind.

A figure on Hornbill Hill was waving something white in the air. Two women descended the hill and ran to join Jose and the others near the water, waving as they went.

The boat was slowing down as it approached. Jack could see people's silhouettes against the sunlight. The sea was calm enough but choked with floating debris and planks, and the boat was painstakingly picking a pathway to the beach.

"Why has it stopped?" the lanky man said. He was holding a palm branch and began waving it faster.

"I think they are getting someone out of the water."

Jack stood a couple of metres behind the others and held both hands against his forehead to shield his eyes as he peered at the boat. Someone went into the water and returned to the boat with what appeared to be a child. Then Jack saw a person's head next to an orange buoy. Head and buoy edged closer to the boat as they watched. When the figure began climbing the rope ladder to the boat, Jack realised that it could be Julia. He wanted it to be Julia, but he couldn't be sure.

Ten minutes passed and the boat remained still. More people descended from Hornbill Hill; Jack recognised a French couple who were staying in his Baan Monday. A man with a beard came from the direction of Monkey Mountain and stood next to Jose. He didn't have any visible injuries, only his clothes were soiled. Jack remembered seeing him ordering a whisky at breakfast. Four Thai staff from the restaurant trotted over the debris. Dang, the resort driver, greeted Jack, smiling feebly, and stopped not far away on a patch of sand, clear of wreckage but dotted with dead fish. Jack looked him over. His cheek was scraped of skin and appeared almost black. Jack knew Dang didn't know how to swim. How had he survived?

Agitation on the beach was growing, but no one took their eyes from the boat, just as on the morning that all eyes were fixed on the approaching wave. Jack shivered.

The boat began slowly moving back into the sea and then turned south.

"Where's it going?" The man with the beard rushed headlong – and pointlessly – into the water.

"To Kao Lak," Jack said.

Everyone turned and looked at him as if he had just dropped a bomb.

"Didn't they see us?"

"Very well, I should think. But they can't come ashore because of all the obstacles. We should get ready for a night on the island."

The man began pushing the planks to the side with his hands and wading further into the sea.

"Come back!" He flung a piece of wood high into the air. "Come back!"

"We have one hour before it will be completely dark," Jack said. The boat was sharply silhouetted against the setting sun, and the water had turned a deep red. "Get everyone who is in a good condition from Monkey Mountain. We need water, food, mosquito nets, blankets, anything we can find."

Seventeen

"Can you take me to Kuraburi, please?" Carl flopped into a dusty taxi seat.

"Is it after Kao Lak?"

"Yes."

"It's at least four hours."

"I'll pay you."

"No, thank you. I drive in Phuket only."

Carl got out of the car and dragged out his backpack. There were several taxis behind and he hopped back to the next one.

He leaned through the open window. "Can you drive me to Kuraburi?"

"Where is it?"

"After Kao Lak."

"The road to Kao Lak is not good."

"How much do you want? I'll pay you well."

"Five thousand baht?" the driver said doubtfully.

Carl knew it was more than it should be but he couldn't bear to wait as the doctor had advised. Wait? This was the whole reason he had flown to Thailand – he couldn't just wait and do nothing. But he felt that time was slipping through his fingers and he was walking around in circles among the hospitals without getting any closer to discovering anything about Kristoffer and Eva. There was a message from Goran on his phone: *Any news?* He didn't know how to answer. He didn't have anything reassuring. With every hour passing his panic grew.

The taxi driver got out and spoke to the driver of the taxi behind. They were making a lot of 'Oooh!' sounds and indulging in too much head shaking. Carl moved impatiently from foot to foot, clasping his phone. Finally, the taxi driver waved to him.

"Do you know where in Kao Lak?"

"No, it's not Kao Lak, it's after Kao Lak. It's Kuraburi."

The second taxi driver spoke fast and loud, raising his arms above his head.

"He says the road is damaged in Kao Lak," Carl's taxi driver said. "You know tsunami?"

"Yes, tsunami. I'll pay you six thousand baht."

"No." The driver shook his head, though his eyes told Carl he wanted the job.

"Seven thousand baht."

"I can't. Dead bodies. The road is not good."

A taxi in the line behind beeped twice, and Carl's driver ran to his car and drove forward.

Frustrated, Carl marched to the next taxi and opened the passenger door.

"Kuraburi?"

The driver shook his head. "Too far. A lot of traffic."

"Six thousand baht."

"The road is bad."

Carl slammed the door and watched the last taxi drive away.

"Why do you need to go there?"

An Asian man was unlocking the chain that secured his motorbike to a street lamp in front of the entrance. His key stuck and he shook it vigorously, ash from the cigarette squeezed between his teeth powdering his hands. He growled with frustration and with the last twist unfastened the lock. He wasn't Thai, thought Carl, but he couldn't place his country of birth.

"I'm looking for my missing friends."

The man straightened up. His khaki shorts were festooned with bulging pockets. With a sooty hand, he took the half cigarette left from his mouth and straightened a leather cord and silver pendant that went under his linen shirt collar.

"Where's this Kuraburi?"

"It's after Kao Lak, towards Burma."

"I didn't know there was anything there. Were your friends backpackers?"

"No, it was their honeymoon."

"Oh. Doesn't sound like a happy start." He smirked and took a long draw from the last of his cigarette.

"No."

"And where were you?"

"I flew in today."

"To find them?"

"Yes."

"Admirable." He flicked his cigarette onto the ground next to the bin. "Where are you from?"

"I'm Swedish."

"You don't look Swedish."

Carl shrugged. "Do you know where I can find someone to drive me to Kuraburi?"

"Try a normal car, not a taxi – they might be more agreeable."

"Where do I find that?"

"There's a lot of them around usually."

"Is five thousand baht a good price?"

"One way?"

"Yes."

"It's two hundred Australian dollars. Very good."

Carl squatted down and pulled a map from the side pocket of his backpack. One of his missing posters, folded double, dropped to the ground.

The man picked it up from the asphalt.

"This Kristoffer Berg looks Korean," he said.

"He is, but he grew up in Sweden."

"I'm Korean too. But grew up in Australia." The man grinned.

How come Carl hadn't spotted that he was Korean? It was obvious now he said it.

"Kristoffer was adopted by a Swedish family."

"Then he might be more Swedish than I'm Australian." He handed the poster to Carl, and then said slowly, "Actually, can I keep it?"

"I don't have many. Why?"

"Maybe I can help you." The man reached for a small notepad from his shorts pocket and uncapped his pen. "How do you know Kristoffer Berg?"

"I met him at my university," Carl said, and the man made a note. Carl felt something was wrong about the guy.

"Who are you?"

"I'm a journalist with an Australian—"

"You should have told me that before asking your questions."

"Chill out. I can help you."

"No thanks, I can do without your help." Carl grabbed the notepad and tore off the top sheet. He lobbed the notepad to the man and strode back to the taxi rank.

"Kuraburi." Carl threw his backpack onto the seat and climbed into the taxi.

"No, too far."

"Okay, take me to the airport." Carl remembered there were more taxis and other vehicles and it was an hour closer to Kao Lak. He would definitely find someone there.

Through the window he saw Eric had joined the taxi line. He looked agitated.

"Where are you going?" Carl shouted.

"Swedish consulate."

"Jump in, I'm going in that direction." He opened the door.

"Papa. Papa!" A girl with blonde hair that looked like a bird's nest ran after Eric.

"Is it your daughter?"

It took a moment for Eric to answer, as if he really had to think about it.

"Yes. Margo. Can she come?"

"Of course."

The little girl sat between the two of them and immediately fastened her seat belt. Her knees were grazed and bruised and the skin on her arms and legs was scarlet from sunburn. She was no more than six. Carl knew that Eric was looking for his wife and son, but he hadn't mentioned a daughter. Was it four people in the picture that Eric thrust into his face earlier at the hospital? It did feel more as though the girl was following Eric than that he was looking after her.

"Pearl Village Resort. It's before the airport," Carl said to the driver.

"They called me, said they had identified my wife's body," Eric said. He was clasping his hands between his knees, tapping with both feet, his eyes moving erratically.

"I'm sorry to hear that," Carl said. The words felt bulky and useless in his mouth. He peered into Eric's face, not entirely sure if it was bad or good news. He didn't want to receive the same call himself; for once the unknown was more comforting.

"A guy called me. From Stockholm, I think. He said to go to the Swedish temporary embassy. I tried to call them but they don't pick up."

"Where is her body?"

"He said at the temporary embassy."

"Really? Why did nobody from the temporary embassy call you if they had the body and your phone number?" There was nowhere to store bodies either, Carl thought, but he didn't say it. There was hardly space for the living in that room, never mind the dead.

Eric shrugged.

"How do they know it's your wife?"

"The man said she was found under our hotel's rubble and she fits the description I left." Eric turned away to the window. "He said she was wearing a red cotton dress."

"And that's what your wife was wearing?"

"Yes …" It was the little girl, and she whispered the word. Eric didn't hear her.

"I don't remember," Eric said. He pressed his forehead against the window and shut his eyes. He took several deep breaths, holding each for a long time, before continuing with his eyes closed. "I remember everything about that morning. I remember where we sat at the restaurant. Outside under an umbrella. It had a hole that let the sun in. Burned my arm, here." He pressed his finger into his forearm. "Maria was across the table from me, her back to the sea. There were purple flowers in a small vase on our table. She had a cappuccino, cornflakes with soya milk and a teaspoon of honey, and sliced mango and pineapple. She insisted I try her mango; she did it every morning, and I always refused. I hate fruit and told her so, but she said that Thai mango was out of this world. She said it melts in your mouth … Or did she say it melts on your tongue? No, I think mouth, she said mouth."

Eric pressed his fists into his eyes and a vein on his temple began pulsating. His jaw trembled and he screamed, "Mouth! She definitely said Thai mango melts in your mouth."

He opened his eyes and stared at Carl.

"She still had two slices of mango on her plate when the wall of water rose behind her. I should have seen it sooner, I should have warned her, but I was feeding my son; I had just squashed banana with a fork in a white teacup and added a bit of milk, he liked it better that way. I didn't see the wave. I put a small spoon of banana mash into Fredrik's mouth and was wiping his chin when I glanced at Maria because she asked me if I wanted more coffee …"

Eric's voice began to tremble. His forehead glistened with perspiration.

"There was a man in a T-shirt the colours of the Brazilian flag behind Maria. He scooped up a small girl with ponytails and a hairband with cherries on each side. Then I saw umbrellas falling, water rushing, everything crashing around and there were screams from everywhere, and in a split second I was underwater. Just like that. In less than a split second." He clicked his fingers. "But I don't remember what dress she wore. Strange, isn't it?"

"I suppose," Carl said, and glanced at the girl. Eric didn't mention her or look at her – it was as if she was a ghost. With the bottom of his T-shirt, Carl wiped the top of his water bottle and offered it to the girl. Not lifting her eyes or saying anything she clasped the bottle and drank until there was nothing left. He wished he had some food – cookies or sweets or something else child-friendly – but there were only energy bars in his backpack and he wasn't sure they would be good for her.

"I don't even remember the colour. Not even the colour."

"It doesn't matter really."

"It does. Maria always says I don't notice what she wears. She likes to dress well." He sighed. "How could I not remember?"

"Why don't you ask someone to take care of Margot while you look for your wife?" Carl said. She was still clasping the empty bottle. There was dirt under her nails, her face was unwashed. She was probably scared and it would be so easy for her to get lost.

"I don't think it's her."

"What?"

"I think it's not her body. I think she's alive." Eric's lips twisted into a crooked smile. "What do you think?"

"I don't know." Carl watched Eric's face drop. "Hopefully it isn't her."

"It can't be Maria. You know, I don't believe in God. But Maria did. She was a saint. God wouldn't allow this to happen to her. Never. Not at Christmas. Not when he was born."

What Eric was saying didn't make sense, but Carl nodded to comfort him.

"Where were you staying?"

"Phi Phi Island."

"Pee Pee? That's a name?"

"Yes, but it's written *phi*, so it doesn't mean pee," Eric said. "My son found it amusing though. Margot too. We all joked about it."

The girl glanced at him as he said her name but he didn't look at her and she dropped her eyes and sighed.

"Where's the island?"

"It's two hours from Phuket by boat. Haven't you seen the movie?"

"Which movie?"

"*Beach*, with DiCaprio."

"No."

"It was filmed on the island. There's a beach with limestone cliffs that are like gates to the most beautiful lagoon you can imagine, with calm turquoise water. It was just like it looked in the movie."

"What's it about?"

"A hidden paradise island. Then someone dies and things can't be the same." Eric swallowed. "Just like two days ago. Though in the movie only one man dies. It's the most beautiful beach I've ever seen. We arrived there early in the morning in a longtail, before the crowds. Took so many great pictures. Do you want to see it?" He tapped one of his pockets. "Oh, I lost my camera. You know there are moments I forget what happened. Or it seems to me I'm asleep and wake up and things will be normal again."

"I know," Carl said. He too felt he was caught in a horrible dream.

Eighteen

The temporary consulate had been relocated to the lobby in the main building. Six tables of volunteers were now dealing with enquiries, doing the same job as the single representative Carl had spoken to earlier. He asked again if anyone had a record of Kristoffer or Eva but, as before, the answer was no. He glued his missing poster near the entrance door, above a stack of boxes containing bottled water. Anyone who took a bottle would notice it. He attached a second poster to the toilet door.

Carl gave Anna's phone number to Eric and explained to him that she could take care of little Margo, but he got the feeling Eric didn't understand why Carl should want Margo left with someone she had never met when she had her mother and a little brother. Carl left him speaking to Fredrik, who had already said they didn't have Maria's body and didn't know anything about it. Carl wasn't surprised, but for Eric it was another confirmation that his wife wasn't among the dead.

Before leaving, Carl took Margot to a vending machine in the hotel lobby and asked her what she would like. She picked Oreo cookies and a pack of M&Ms. Carl wrote Anna's number on a piece of paper and said that if she got lost, she should ask an adult to call the number and someone very kind would come and pick her up. He slipped the folded paper into her skirt pocket and she tried to say thank you, but her mouth was full of Oreos.

He hurried outside. But even before the glass door had slid closed behind him, he realised his taxi wasn't there. The driver had dropped them off in front of the entrance and said he'd wait in the shade at the parking lot. The lot was empty. Carl strode out onto the road, looking left and right, hoping the car was still around. He had been away for longer than he initially said to the driver. Why on Earth had he prepaid? He stamped his foot and dust whirled around him.

"Are you always running away?"

Carl turned. First, he saw only her piercing blue eyes staring at him. No mascara, no liner, the turquoise sea behind her pale compared to the cobalt of her eyes. For a brief moment, all sounds around him ceased and everything went still.

Her long dark hair was pulled back into a tight ponytail, a line of perspiration traced the upper edge of her tall forehead, and small studs adorned her ears. She wore a loose white T-shirt tucked into jeans shorts and had rolled up the sleeves to reveal tanned and muscled upper arms. In the low V-cut neckline, a silver pendant in the form of a sea turtle with yin and yang on its shell hung down on a black string into her cleavage, where tiny droplets of sweat chased each other in a narrow line between her breasts.

"Carl, right?" She shielded her eyes against the sunlight, a seashell bracelet jangling on her wrist.

He stared at her for a long moment. Long enough to change the direction of the wind for the rest of his life.

"Liv? I don't believe it. Hi. I …" He tried to compose himself. Suddenly, he became acutely aware that he smelled of sweat, he wished he'd changed his T-shirt.

"Nor me." A touch of pink coloured her cheeks. "Luka said you were going skiing together."

"That was the plan." His tongue was stiff in his mouth.

"Why are you here?"

"My best friend and his wife are missing. They just got married in July. It was their honeymoon. She was pregnant." He suddenly felt he wanted to tell her everything. How the temporary embassy was useless. How he spent the day in hospitals. How he had no clue as to what to do next and how his taxi had disappeared. How much he wished she'd met Kristoffer. How much he wished she knew who Kristoffer was.

"I'm sorry," she said, and put her hand on his shoulder, squeezing it gently.

He clenched his teeth, resisting tears.

"The Thais have got hundreds of people searching. Countries from all over are sending rescue teams, representatives, medication. Give it time."

Time. Carl shook his head. Time had become a word of hope and yet the more it passed, the less hope there was.

Carl glanced down. Her trainers were covered in orange powder from the local sand and clay. How long had she been here?

"Are you working for the embassy?" He said it almost with a note of disappointment.

"No. I'm a teacher at Phuket International School."

A teacher? If she had asked him to guess he never would have.

"It's the school holidays here too. I was in London to see friends. And planned to go to Sweden for Christmas."

"Usually people do it the other way around."

"I often do things differently," Liv said. There was something enigmatic about her. In her gaze. In the words left unsaid. The slight hoarseness in her voice. It drew him in. Usually, Carl disliked vagueness, but with Liv, it was an invitation to find out more. An invitation he didn't want to accept.

"Did you know Luka's brother is in a hospital in Phuket?" she said.

"Yes, he told me."

"I went to see him this morning. He isn't getting any better, unfortunately. And there's still no news about Achara."

"Achara?"

"His fiancée."

"How do you know Luka by the way?" Carl said.

"I met him and his brother here in Phuket some years ago. Their family bought a stunning villa on the hills above Surin Beach. I was brokering the purchase. They have a couple more properties on the island. It's a good investment."

Carl smiled inwardly. Brokering multi-million-pound property deals sounded more believable than the teaching job.

"Did you sleep with him?" He blurted it out and immediately regretted it. But he did not want, yet again, to be put in a position where he'd get interested in someone with whom Luka had had a one-night stand.

He watched her face, trying to read between confusion and pique, dreading her answer. He felt his heart pulsating behind his eyeballs.

"Rather a blunt question." Liv glared at him, leaned back and crossed her arms in front of her chest.

Incredibly, he heard himself say, "Well, did you?"

"No, I didn't. You're terrible. Why on Earth—?"

"Luka is handsome, is he not? Successful. Rich. Everything a girl wants."

Liv smiled with just the corner of her mouth and gave a little snort.

"He is not my type."

There was a long pause. Carl feared she might turn and go. He wanted to say something. Something easy, maybe funny, to defuse the awkwardness between, them but there were no words. He wished she would speak again. He liked her silvery voice, the way her lips moved as if she was kissing the air. And he wished she would say what *was* her type.

"Were your friends in Phuket?" she said finally.

"No, they were north from here, on an island."

"Similan Islands?"

"No, Koh Phra Thong."

"It's off Kuraburi, isn't it?"

"Yes. At last, someone who knows the place!"

"I haven't been to the island, but I passed it in a boat on my way to Similan Islands from Kuraburi pier. Stayed near Kuraburi a couple of times. I was backpacking around Asia for two years after my first year in university. There's a land border with Burma and it was open for tourists for several years. We used to go in and out, to get a fresh three months' stamp for Thailand."

She craned her head back, exposing her long neck to a random breeze from the sea. She had a delicate jawline and her skin was smooth, almost velvety. She wiped sweat from the back of her neck with her hand and lifted up her thick hair in the breeze. Her breasts lifted slightly as she breathed in. Carl couldn't imagine her with a large backpack in soiled clothes in a herd of filthy youths. He could, however, imagine her without any clothes at all.

"Two years backpacking?"

"Well, it was four years and two months to be exact. But usually, I say a year or two. To not shock people." Liv shrugged.

"Most people give four years to university."

"Do you want to be like most people?"

153

He felt his cheeks redden; he certainly didn't want her to see him as most people.

"You're the teacher. What do you tell your students?"

"I say that you don't learn about life at university."

"Strange that the school hasn't sacked you for your unorthodox views."

She raised her eyebrows, then her mouth slowly widened into a smile and she burst out laughing, and he laughed with her even though he tried not to. There was a surprising and immediate intimacy in laughing together. For that short moment, Carl forgot where he was and why. For that moment he felt at ease with her, not worrying about what to say to impress her, not trying to read between the lines, not trying to analyse her.

"At university you set yourself up for a career – that is why most people go there," he said, his face still relaxed and warm from laughing.

"I guess you never tried to do things differently?" Her eyes twinkled and when they locked their gaze he felt an enervating warmth spread through his body.

"Liv?" Fredrik, the embassy guy, strode over. He glanced at Carl dismissively and then stepped between him and Liv. He wrapped his arm around her shoulder and led her aside. He had long bony fingers with messy nails.

"If this guy bothers you, let me know," Carl heard him whisper in her ear. Blood rushed to his temples.

"No, no." She shook her head.

"Can you come inside? I'd like you to look at something." He cast a look at Carl and said loudly, "It's great that most people appreciate what we're trying to do."

"Okay, but I don't have much time." She followed him.

She looked over her shoulder at Carl. "Can you wait for me for five minutes?"

He nodded.

The glass doors slid closed behind them and Carl could no longer hear what they said. He watched as Fredrik told her something, gesticulating, sometimes touching her arm. When he leaned in to her ear again, she smiled and put her hand on his shoulder.

Carl turned away.

In the sparse shade from casuarinas trees, a handful of people sat on their towels, a pile of broken chairs and umbrellas not far behind them. A little girl in a pink swimsuit with an inflatable ring around her waist was pulling her mother's arm, asking her to get up and walk with her to the sea. They both ran to the water, skipping over piles of seaweed and plastic. There was nobody else in the sea. Carl was surprised to see anyone at all getting in the water. But it was calm and inviting. The girl picked a soaked soft toy from the water and showed it to her mother. The woman shrugged her shoulders.

"Pineapple, watermelon, papaya?" A fruit seller stopped his bicycle cart in front of Carl. Carl stepped into the shadow of the cart's umbrella and glanced at the fruits laid in rows on crushed ice. In a lower section were whole fruits, and in the section above the peeled variety. Was the fruit washed at all? Carl was hungry but was reluctant to choose from the cart.

"Two bottles of water please."

"I have cold beer also."

"No, no, thank you. Just water." Carl gave him a hundred baht.

He watched the vendor fumbling in his pocket for a change. What was Liv doing with this embassy guy? She couldn't possibly be interested in him. At the very least he would have to cut his nails and wash his hands before touching her skin. Her skin. It had the same scent of jasmine as when she had sat in his car in London. Or did he imagine it?

He glanced at the glass door again but couldn't see them anymore. He shifted on his feet. What was the point in waiting?

A rusted pickup truck without glass in the doors parked on the roadside. A guy in a faded basketball top jumped out from the passenger side, took some crumpled banknotes from his shorts pocket and handed them to the driver. He went around and pulled his filthy backpack from the cargo bed. As he passed by Carl on his way to the hotel entrance, the musky smell hit him – authentic backpacker sweat.

The driver started the engine. Carl didn't have five minutes to wait for her. That was not what he came here for.

"Wait," he shouted, and ran to the pickup.

PART II

—

The Island

Nineteen

Carl stared at the traffic. The air was filled with exhaust fumes and a suffocating cacophony of engines and car horns. Trucks were attempting to pass buses, cars to pass trucks and endless scooters to pass and squeeze between every vehicle on the road.

"When do we get to Kuraburi?"

"I don't know. Usually, it'd take three hours," the driver said.

"But not today." Carl ran his forearm over his wet hairline. The windows were open but the hot, dusty air that occasionally blew through was a poor escape from the day's heat. Perfume from a garland of fresh flowers hanging from the front mirror cut through the fumes from time to time, and the effect was intoxicating, almost dizzying.

"Is there another road?"

The driver was silent, as if he hadn't heard. Carl looked sideways at him. He had heard him. And he did speak English. In fact, he spoke decent English, thank God.

"Can we take another road?"

"No," the driver said indifferently.

Carl fidgeted in his well-worn seat. The road was getting narrower, only one lane in each direction. Their rattletrap puttered along, the speedometer's red arrow close to zero. Carl unfolded the map on his knees. The road they were driving followed the line of the coast up to Burma's border. It was in yellow, indicating a national highway. A two-lane national highway? It didn't make any sense.

"Look, there are lots of roads." He showed his map to the driver. "They're smaller along the coast … We could take this one farther inland?"

"This's the only way."

"I don't want to be stuck here the whole day. We are not getting anywhere, don't you see?" Carl waved his hand in front of the driver's eyes. "Do you even know how to read a map?"

"I do," the driver said. "I drive these roads every day. But this's the shortest way, trust me."

"If it's about money, tell me how much more you want?"

"Your money won't help you to get there faster." The driver tossed a roll of notes onto the dashboard. "If you are not happy you can go."

"Sure, like where?"

"You have your map." The driver smirked and, for the first time, turned his face towards Carl. His grin wasn't mean, it was bitter, his bleary eyes filled with sadness. Carl felt uncomfortable under his gaze.

"I'm sorry," he said, and dropped his eyes. He tried to remember his driver's name but couldn't.

"What's your name again?"

"Nok."

"My name is Carl."

"I remember."

"Nok, I really need to get to Kuraburi as soon as possible. My friend is missing. I have to find him."

"On this road, everyone lost someone," Nok said in a

thin voice. His lower lip trembled. He clasped the steering wheel with bandaged hands. "We are descending hills of the National Park and, here, the road is above sea level but a mile further down it was badly damaged by the water. They did some repairs and the flow is good today." He glanced at Carl. "All the small roads along the coast are destroyed, and to go inland around the hills would take us a day."

"But we are not moving."

"We are. Once we pass the temples and Takuapa Hospital the road will be clear."

Takuapa? Why did nobody mention that one before? He opened his map. The hospital was closer to Koh Phra Thong than to Phuket.

"Is it a government hospital?"

"Yes."

"Big?"

"Sizeable."

"Do you know if they have any foreigners?"

"Of course, hundreds."

"Hundreds?"

"Where else you think they'd take them?"

"I was told to go to private hospitals."

"Private hospitals are only in Phuket. But wounded people are everywhere."

Carl glanced at his watch; it was almost 4 p.m. He wanted to get to Kuraburi as soon as possible and speak to Lucas, the hotel manager, who would certainly be more helpful than the Swedish temporary embassy in giving him leads. The heavy traffic had already messed up his plans and if he stopped at the hospital it would take him at least an extra hour.

"Do you know if the doctors speak English at the hospital?"

"How would I know?"

The hospital was so close to the island. It would make

sense to take the injured to a regional hospital, especially as the main highway was damaged by the wave. If Kristoffer was in a serious condition, unable to speak, they would think he was Thai and wouldn't reach out to Phuket hospitals. There seemed to be little contact between the embassy and the hospitals – and the hospitals probably hadn't had time to coordinate their efforts. Kristoffer and Eva might be at Takuapa but unable to communicate. Carl tapped the floor restlessly with his foot. He would go to Kuraburi first and then return to Takuapa Hospital and spend as much time there as he had to, ask Nok to speak Thai to the hospital staff, go from ward to ward as he did at Vachira Hospital.

The shrubs and elegant palm trees along the road gave way to desolation. A vast dumping ground extended on all sides, an unending ugly mass of wreckage, pieces of furniture, heaps of broken trees and branches. Buildings that hadn't entirely collapsed stood with no windows and scalped walls. Fragments of concrete were everywhere. Tangled electrical cables. A row of collapsed telegraph poles. Carl shrivelled in his seat. He wished that Nok had taken a wrong turn but he knew it was their road. A cold sweat formed on his brow.

"How far are we from the sea?" Carl poked his head out the window, scanning a line of three-storey buildings missing two floors, their concrete walls with yawning holes.

They passed entire blocks that had been reduced to rubble. Foundations rose from the ground as a reminder of buildings, cafés or small shops. A concrete post with a sign saying "7-Eleven" stood forlorn, with no reference to the store's existence. A haze of dust hovered over.

"A kilometre or less," Nok said. "This part of the coast was completely flattened. The water rushed two kilometres inland, flooding everything."

"And people?"

"Nowhere to run. It's Khao Lak, man," he said, it as if announcing a death sentence.

"Impossible …" Carl whispered the word through numbed lips.

"Yes. Impossible to survive."

Two monks, their orange robes fluttering in the breeze, ambled through the rubble. They looked surreal in this wasteland.

"Where were you when the wave hit?"

"I was in this pickup, in this seat," he said, and began to rock back and forth, at first gently, then faster. He told Carl that most of the day he'd driven workers from nearby villages to hotels in Kao Lak. His sister was a cleaner at the Sofitel Hotel and early that morning he had driven her, his aunt and other men and women from his village. His father had had the day off – he was a builder, and was working at the site of a new five-star hotel in Khao Lak.

"We went together to a local market, bought bok choi and herbs and a small chicken for that night's dinner. My dad insisted we buy two bags of rice. I told him we still had half a bag at home. But he had received his Christmas bonus and wanted to celebrate. We went to a road café at the corner of the market. I had an iced coffee with caramel topping and my dad had a beer."

Nok paused and took a deep breath before continuing.

"The reason I wanted to go to that café was to introduce him to Aeh, the girl I like. She's usually busy serving tables but at that time there weren't many people and she sat with us and we spoke. When we left, my dad said I should ask the girl for a date. He said she reminded him of my mother when she was young. I don't remember her, she died giving birth to my sister."

Carl was watching Nok as he spoke. His thin voice

trembled and he swallowed hard before continuing his story. His faded T-shirt, once probably purple, hung on his narrow shoulders like a rag on a hook. There were pimples on his forehead and no sign of him ever having shaved. Carl wouldn't have given him more than eighteen, but for his eyes – the sadness they hid, the tiredness they held. Or had he grown old over the last couple of days? He glanced at Nok's arms, at the inflamed cuts, at his bandaged hands.

"We went to see my brother in Nam Khem harbour. But there was no sea, the bay was empty – it was bizarre, the boats were resting on the sand. My father asked fishermen about my brother and they said he was still at sea. They said they had never seen such a low tide before." Sweat formed on Nok's forehead and he wiped it with the back of his hand. He said a fisherman asked if they could drive him and his fish to a hotel in South Kao Lak. Nok's father helped to load baskets with fish and sat with the fisherman on the flatbed as they drove, chatting.

"We got to the end of the village and were about to turn to the right when they started banging on the back window of the cab, and yelling. My father was shouting something but I couldn't hear the words, the engine's a bit loud as you can see." Nok sucked in his breath; his jaw trembled.

"I looked in the side mirror and I saw brown water rushing after us. It was crushing everything in its path – houses, telegraph poles, trees. I floored it …" He was gasping now. "But my truck was already floating." He let out a long, wheezy cry. "The water was up to my knees and then the truck seemed to tilt up … I couldn't hear them shouting anymore … only breaking, bending, twisting noises… the water filled everything inside." Nok stumbled over his words and tears ran down his cheeks.

Carl put his hand on the man's shoulder.

"Your father? Did he—"

Nok shook his head.

"Your sister, at the hotel?"

He shook his head again.

"But at least I found her body and she can be buried properly."

"Where did you find her?"

"I went with a search team that worked on the rubble of the Sofitel Hotel. We were collecting human remains. There were as many as shells on the beach after a storm. Corpses were everywhere – stretched on the sand, floating in the shallows, sticking out from under the rubble, hanging from trees, sunk at the bottom of the water pools the wave created. And the hotel swimming pools … Oh, there were so many children at the bottom."

Carl pressed his back against his seat. He felt sick, his stomach was burning.

"This morning we pumped water from the hotel's basement and found it was filled with bodies of Thai staff. My sister and my aunt … they must have tried to escape. They were doomed when they went to the basement."

"I'm sorry," Carl said, but Nok didn't hear him. Carl regretted asking him to recall that morning. But would he ever forget anyway?

"I think I transported more than thirty bodies in my pickup, from that place alone."

"So many?"

"So few. My cargo bed is too small and I had to go back and forward three times. My friend Adit has a bigger pickup and he was able to carry at least twenty bodies in one go."

Carl still couldn't take in the numbers. Nok was surely exaggerating, maybe unwillingly but he was exaggerating.

"Where did you take corpses?"

"To Wat Bang Muang. It's a temple down the road."

"Why there?"

"Somebody told us to bring bodies there," Nok said, then looked at Carl and whispered as though afraid to hear the words himself. "There are already hundreds of bodies stored. No, more. Probably a thousand."

Carl rubbed his face with his hands. "They don't tell you that on the news, or at the embassies or the hospitals," he said. Before leaving Bangkok Hospital he caught sight of a TV screen in the lobby. The Thai authorities acknowledged that the scope of the disaster was much worse than reported in the first two days, but they were still estimating a thousand missing and a likely death toll above five hundred.

"You don't believe me?"

"I do, but—"

"You think the authorities know better?"

"Well, they have resources, people …" He didn't finish. His eyes were glued to a pickup truck, twisted as if made from paper, that had been hurled onto the second floor of a building whose roof teetered above, balanced on two supporting pillars that were all that was left of the second storey. "I'm trying to picture … Can you imagine what it would mean if there were dozens of people on one beach when … when …"

"Imagine? I don't have to. I know what it means."

For a few minutes they drove in silence. Carl didn't know if he believed Nok about the numbers. He didn't want it to be true. Nok was scared and overwhelmed, which was understandable, but his calculations were surely wrong. He glanced through the window on Nok's side, and it was the same there – a vast dumping ground with unending ugly masses of wreckage. Carl used his T-shirt to wipe the sweat from his face. Nok had to be mistaken.

"Did you find the girl you like, from the café?" Carl said.

"Yes. But I don't know if she will live."

"Is she in a hospital?"

"Yes, but they care only about foreigners."

"Nonsense. You can't prioritise foreigners in your own country."

"They can in Thailand." Nok's lower jaw began trembling.

"Maybe if you go to a private hospital there might be different attitude? I don't know how it works here …" Carl's voice faltered and he stopped to let Nok speak.

"As soon as I could get my truck out of the ditch I went looking for my father. I had lost sight of him as soon as the truck was carried off the road. Traffic was choking the highway in all directions. I went to Takuapa Hospital, hoping somebody might have brought him there." Nok tapped his thumbs on the wheel. "Wounded Thai people were everywhere, laying on the lawn in front of the hospital, on the entrance steps, in the entrance hall, in corridors in every direction. And then I saw Aeh – she was lying on the floor next to the reception desk and there was a trickle of blood coming from her mouth.

"I called her but she didn't respond. I think she was conscious but she wasn't there. There was a woman sitting at the doors to the emergency room with an old man in her lap who was foaming from his mouth, and she said she had been waiting for more than an hour. I lifted Aeh up and rushed to find a doctor. The emergency room was full of foreigners with cuts and fractures and most of them were able to stand but they were all demanding the only two doctors' attention because the nurses didn't speak any English. A woman was standing over the shoulder of one of the doctor, demanding that he contact her embassy because she'd lost her phone."

"What did you do?"

"I pushed my way through the crowd of white people. They were unhappy, shouting. I didn't care. A woman was being helped off a bed and I rushed forward and laid Aeh on the bed before it was taken. A man began remonstrating with me. He pushed me out of the emergency room, but he didn't dare disturb Aeh because the blood was flowing freely from her mouth by now. But you know what he did? As soon as the doctor began to examine Aeh, the man demanded information about the antibiotics he had been given. He had a bandaged arm and a few scratches, that's all."

An entitled white European, Carl thought. He felt a pang of vicarious shame. He knew Nok wasn't exaggerating.

"How is she feeling now?"

"She's very weak. She's asleep most of the time. Sometimes she wakes up but she doesn't recognise me. She coughs saliva mixed with blood and sand and little splintered twigs. From those, I expect." Nok waved at a casuarina tree on the roadside. "The doctor said she needs a machine to clear her lungs of debris."

"Bronchoscope?"

"Yes, that's what he called it. Unfortunately, they have only three of these machines in the hospital. She is still waiting her turn."

"I don't understand why Thais were so neglected."

"Thais don't know how to stand up for themselves."

"But the doctors and nurses are Thai, right?"

"The senior physician told me he knew that when everything was over his hospital would get complaints from foreigners and Thais alike, saying that doctors didn't care. The region depends on tourists and the hospital would be slated for neglecting people with private insurance. Whatever the hospitals did was going to hurt the country's reputation. His emergency plan was to serve foreigners first, as they were making more noise than Thais, then to discharge them or send them to Phuket and give beds to Thai people. Unfortunately, the numbers were unmanageable – they ran out of antibiotics and bandages in the afternoon and many Thais died on the steps of the hospital before doctors could look at them."

For the last ten minutes, the car hadn't moved an inch. Nok turned off the engine.

"I'll go check on the traffic."

The pickup was an oven and Carl opened his door and stepped out. He pulled out his shirt, allowing air between his body and the fabric. He bent forward and touched his toes, stretching his stiff legs. In the sand on the roadside near a pile of litter, he spotted a trashed passport. He squatted, wiped it on his shorts; the photo ID page was soaked and blurred, and the name couldn't be read. At first, Carl thought to take it back to Phuket City Hall, but then he noticed another red passport under a plastic bag. He opened it. The water had spoiled the first page entirely. He dropped both books on the ground. If their owners were alive, they'd get new passports.

He peered into the deep ditch beside the road. Filthy clothes were tangled in branches and electrical cable, along with plastic cups, soaked magazines and a mangled suitcase. A broken vase half-covered a dead fish covered in flies. Stinking puddles had become mosquito and bug breeding places. The smell scratched the back of his throat.

Carl walked back and sat on a wooden plank in the pickup's narrow shade. He pulled his phone from his pocket but there was no network. He wished he had Liv's number, then immediately pushed the thought away.

Four years backpacking … It was a privilege for those who had means and the time, or rebellious souls. He didn't belong in either camp but she probably fitted both.

Do you want to be most people?

Her words had touched a nerve. Scrapping university in favour of years of backpacking simply wasn't his way of putting his stamp on the world. Besides, his savings at that time would be enough only for the return ticket. He couldn't ask his parents for the money – it wasn't in his upbringing, and anyway he knew they hadn't much in the way of savings. Certainly not for their son's irresponsible travel bug.

Of four people from his town who went backpacking, one returned with a severe tropical infection, another was beaten in Cambodia and the third came home with a pregnant Thai girlfriend. The odds of misfortune were too high, Carl had thought. He loved to travel, especially now that he was making good money, to stay in hotels with clean sheets and eat in places where the cutlery was cleaned after the previous customer – but that was different. Backpacking was just an invitation to trouble. Kristoffer had gone for nine months around Asia, he said it was the best way to see the world and his place in it, to make up his mind about what he wanted to do. Carl, on the other hand, felt that his rigorous studying helped him to fit into the world he wanted to be a part of. Kristoffer met his first girlfriend, Astrid, in Kathmandu. They had travelled back to Sweden together and Kristoffer had gone to Umea University because her home town was nearby. The relationship didn't last and Kristoffer managed to transfer to Lund University for the second year of his law degree – where he had wanted to study in the first place. So, in a way, backpacking had diverted him from his original goal. But Kristoffer often said, "We need to make a mess of things in order to find out who we are." He was good at making sense out of nonsense.

"It's going to be at least an hour," Nok said, and squatted by the pickup next to Carl. "When the wave went over the motorway, it undermined a rocky hill formation on the other side, overgrown with scrubs. Now, a mile ahead, there's been a rock fall. Two scooters buried underneath apparently."

Carl shut his eyes and buried his head between his knees. Would he even get to Kuraburi by nightfall?

"On this side of the road was a school with a football pitch." Nok said. "When I wasn't driving on Sunday mornings I would come to play here with kids from the school."

Carl looked in the direction Nok pointed. There were only a few random palm trees sticking out in the yellowish morass of scarred and water-laden ground. He remembered seeing a football in the ditch.

At the far end of the field, men gathered around something that looked something like a swamp. A bulldozer was slowly edging its way across ditches to the site. A large diesel pump on a trailer hitched to an ancient tractor followed behind, every few metres getting bogged down in wet sand. People were heading over there from different directions.

"What are they doing there?"

"Fishing out corpses." Nok spat in front of him. He watched the sputum soak into the sand and then scuffed it with his shoe. "The wave created these hollows in the ground and they turned into basket-like swamps that amassed corpses. There are three like that in Nam Khem."

The province needed dozens of pumps in every coastal village to drain these cemeteries but, Nok said, the available machines were sent to large hotels in tourist areas. This was the first pump to arrive in the area – enough to drain one watery cemetery in a day. But the whole of Kao Lak was a fetid swamp.

"How do they know there are bodies?"

"They stink." Nok wrinkled his nose. "The very distinctive odour of decomposing corpses. You recognise it instantly."

He said the smell had begun to spread by the end of the second day. It came from rubble heaps and piles of debris. It was a cocktail of washed-up seaweed, rotting fish and animals,

171

food and decaying human bodies. After days heated by the sun, the swamps were emitting the acrid stench of death.

A scream came from the direction of the traffic ahead.

Carl strained his ears. At first unclear, the noise grew louder and more distinct. More people were screaming. Someone shouted in a megaphone. Nok's face convulsed with horror.

They both sprang up.

A Thai in a dark blue police shirt was riding on a motorbike towards them, weaving through the traffic. Clutching the megaphone in his free hand, he was repeating the same words over and over. A man in a pickup in front of them jumped out from his cab and darted away, yelling something at the top of his voice, the driver's door left open. He flung what looked like a half-eaten sandwich into the ditch. Everywhere, people were abandoning their vehicles, scurrying inland. The crowd near the bulldozer began to run through the field towards hills in the distance.

Before Nok said anything, Carl knew. The wave.

"Run …" Nok spoke very quietly, standing as if rooted, his body trembling, breathing in short, shallow gasps.

"Come on then. Move!" Carl pushed him in the direction everyone was running.

"No." Nok walked to his pickup and pulled Carl's backpack out through the passenger window. "Follow me," he said.

Nok scurried along the road, fending off people who were crossing his path to head inland.

Carl didn't move. There was nobody else going that direction. There, the road turned towards the sea.

Nok looked back.

"Follow me!"

Carl stared along the emptying road. The last man rushed by him, following the others. He tumbled across a gulley on the side of the road, got up, ran a short stretch and fell on his face in the damp sand. People were stumbling on the churned-up ground, falling into ditches, crawling in the mud. The air was filled with wails, howls of hysteria. The hills, and safety, were a mile away.

Much too far.

"Follow me!"

Carl dashed after Nok.

They ran in silence past abandoned vehicles, people's voices growing distant behind them. In two or three minutes, as they rounded a bend in the road, Carl saw a lone hill off to the left, a short way from the road. Several people were climbing its steep sides. The hill had two levels, the first not more than ten metres above the ground, where a cluster of people were already jostling for space. The upper level, twenty metres higher, appeared expansive and relatively flat, but it looked impossible to climb there from the lower level. On the other side of the road, the roof of a three-storey building hung precariously from three pillars, and on the second floor a woman and a monk were holding on to what was left of the outer wall. The structure didn't look as though it would survive another wave.

"Where are we going?" Carl shouted.

Nok didn't stop, didn't answer but sprinted faster.

"Did the policeman say how far the wave is?"

"He said the sea had begun to withdraw. It means it'll return. Ten minutes. Maybe five. We must get to the hill."

"What hill?"

Carl tripped over a chunk of concrete and landed on his knees, his backpack hitting the back of his head and almost smashing his face into the asphalt. He pushed himself up. Nok had disappeared from the road. Carl should have run with the others over the field. He glanced back at the three-storey building. The monk was climbing to the third floor. He looked over and pointed towards the hill. Carl followed his finger and spotted Nok's head bobbing up from behind a pile of debris just off the road. He ran in his direction, along a narrow passage formed by two great banks of timber.

When he caught up with him, he stayed close.

"Watch out for bare cables," Nok said. He skipped over a telegraph pole wires sticking out in all directions.

When the piles of timber tapered off, it was blocks of concrete that blocked their path. Under a mound of rubble, Carl distinguished the remains of clay-tiled floors, the footprints of rooms without walls, sliced off at ground level.

Nok climbed up onto the unstable barricade. Under his weight, a large fragment of steel-reinforced concrete broke off, landing next to Carl's foot.

"Why do you never find the easy road?" said Carl.

"It doesn't exist." Nok's voice came from behind the rubble.

As Carl clambered over, something caught his attention. At first he thought it was a piece of fabric stuck between two rocks, but then he distinguished human fingers the colour of concrete. He recoiled, scrambling down the other side of the pile, uncaring where his feet landed.

He caught up with Nok at the base of the hill, where the steep rocky slope was dotted with sparse vegetation.

"We climb here," Nok said.

"It's too steep."

Nok snatched Carl's backpack and slung it behind his back. "We don't have time to go around."

He proceeded on all fours, like a lizard, quickly climbing up through the shrubs. Gravel and sand from under his shoes spit into Carl's face. He wiped the dirt from his eyes. There was no choice. No time. He had to go at least halfway up.

Carl gripped a branch above his head and pulled up. Immediately, he felt his body weight pull him down. His feet began scrabbling on the rock face. He grabbed a long root.

"Reach for ledge just above – it's solid," Nok yelled. "I'll help you."

"Can you see the wave?" A rock slipped away from under Carl's foot and for a second he hung on only by the root. He held his body close to the rock face. Scarcely daring to breathe, he craned his neck and looked back. It was too high to survive a fall but still too low to be safe from the wave.

"Take my hand."

Nok pulled him up.

"The wave … Do you see it?" Carl fell flat on his stomach on the ledge.

"It was a false alarm."

"What?"

"There's no wave. The sea is calm."

"But what about the policeman with his bloody megaphone?" Carl rolled onto his back. He covered his face with his arms, his hands still trembling, still burning from clutching sharp rocks and thorny branches. He felt stupid. Embarrassed. For his fear. For his panic. For the run.

"The first day there were two warnings. We all ran. Both times it was false alarms."

Nok sat next to him. He drew his knees to his chest and hugged them, his shoulders slouched over.

"It's my first time … But you? Why did you believe it? Why didn't you stop and think?"

Nok didn't look at him. "Would you risk it? What if there had been a wave?"

Carl felt a fool. But Nok was right. He wouldn't take the risk. There were too many warnings about potential after-quakes, everyone was talking about it, everyone was afraid of it.

"Who spreads these stupid rumours?"

Nok shrugged.

"It's enough for one person to panic and run. A hundred will follow." Nok dug out a stone, brushed off the dirt and threw it. It bounced off the hillside and rolled down, dislodging smaller pieces as it went. "At Takuapa Hospital, at the second warning, they evacuated everyone who could walk to the top floors. It was already dark and nobody could see anything. It was terrifying. More so than the wave probably. In the dark everything seems bigger, worse."

Carl shielded his eyes and looked towards the horizon over a calm, shimmering sea. And then in the haze of dust and sunbeams, the devastation came into view. From the shore to the base of the hill, as far as he could see to left and right, the earth had been brutally stripped and vandalised. Raped. In some places, the sea cut deep into the land creating ugly lagoons. Jungle was flattened as if by a gigantic roller. Only the black stripe of the road, random roofless houses, lone trees were left. It was a cataclysmic battlefield without victors.

Carl rose slowly to his feet. He hadn't given much thought to how the coastline had been impacted. The scope of the tragedy had so far been beyond his comprehension. Yes, he had seen destruction along the road, had run through the wreckage, listened to Nok's story and spoken to people at the hospitals, but his mind had been assembling only fragments, without grasping the whole picture. How could anyone?

His heart was thumping in his chest, echoing in his ears like a distant drumbeat in a hollow valley.

The top of the hill wasn't higher than a four-storey building, but there was nothing taller in any direction. The people who had run through the fields would never make it to the hills in the distance if there was another wave. Anyone anywhere near sea level would be engulfed.

He remembered an old woman at the embassy who said she climbed a palm tree to the top. She didn't know how she had done it and called it a miracle. Looking around, Carl thought that the miracle was that she had found a tree still standing.

He glanced at Nok. He felt lucky that he followed him. It would have been so easy to take a wrong turn. Strangely, he already felt like a survivor. Carl wanted to hug Nok, to thank him, to console him, to tell him that his life would soon return to normal. But that would be a lie. Nothing would be the same. He would never be the same. It was Carl who needed to hear those words, that reassurance. He felt that somehow he, at least, still had that chance.

Farther inland, where the tsunami's destructive power had weakened, the wave had dumped sinuous banks of debris at the edge of the jungle, and atop the wreckage a steel-hulled boat, perhaps twenty metres in length, lay on its side like a grey ghost. He narrowed his eyes and just was able to read the word police written in white letters on the side.

"Was that boat there before?"

"Of course not. The wave carried it over the beach, past the hotels and the road and abandoned it there."

"It's so big …"

"It's a patrol boat. It was guarding the King's grandson as he jet-skied in front of La Flora Hotel. Yesterday they found the prince's body. He was only twenty-one." Nok grew much quieter, and Carl had to lean forward to hear his words. "The wave knew no distinctions. The tsunami made everyone equal in the face of death: Thais and foreigners, royalty and the ordinary man."

Carl lifted his head and stared out into the hazy endlessness of the sublime but indifferent ocean. A vile feeling in his gut told him that this was only the beginning.

They walked between peeling gold gates decorated with dragons, into the grounds of Ban Muang temple. Weeds grew against the surrounding stone wall, screening cracked white paint and competing with thirsty rose bushes. The sun was almost gone behind the tall trees and long shadows crept over patches of withered grass.

"Why do they bring bodies to temples?"

"Bodies are safe here," Nok said. He was stepping cautiously, as if afraid of something, his head hanging down. "The first day, villagers from the coast rushed to the temple for safety or to find missing relatives. Then everyone wanted to speak to the monks or to 'make merit', *tham bun* in Thai, by making donations to the temple. Those who survived believed it was because they had *bun* that they had collected over many lifetimes."

Carl left the path and headed for the shade of the trees, away from the blinding sun. He had been preoccupied for some time, nagged by the thought of something he should have seen or anticipated. The thought, half-submerged, chimed with what Nok was saying about the villagers' beliefs – the balance between bad deeds and *bun*, the merits that can be earned by good works.

Then he saw the bodies. He stopped as if rooted. His eyes passed slowly over the dead in their hundreds, lying in rows in the gloom of the trees. Naked, bloated corpses were caked with sand mixed with dried blood, some with dirty clothes stretched over ballooned stomachs. Some were in plastic bags with only the gaping and contorted faces sticking out. There were little cocoons with children's bodies. Large chunks of dry ice were scattered among them at random, and a bluish fog spread above the decomposing corpses. The mist created the illusion of bodies hovering as though in transit within a low cloud. It was surreal and petrifying at the same time.

Carl stepped closer, burying his face in the crook of his

elbow. The stench was choking him, seizing his throat. He held his nose and mouth tight shut as long as he could, and swallowed back the impulse to vomit. It was a huge effort to breathe in the presence of death.

"This may help." Nok handed him a piece of cloth soaked in sweet-smelling oil.

"Thanks. And you?"

"I got used to it. You will too."

Carl shook his head, pressing the cloth over his nose.

"There's a simple trick," said Nok. "Go over there, into the middle, and take a few deep breaths."

"Maybe not," Carl said. He stared down at the body of a woman nor a man – he couldn't tell which. Where there was supposed to be a chest, ribs jutted out from the flesh. The legs and arms had already turned dark and the swollen tongue looked anything but human. Flies were swarming around the eye sockets.

There was another smell in the air. Carl lifted his head. A column of black smoke hovered above trees. A frightening thought came to him, and he shivered.

"Are they burning bodies?"

Before Nok had time to reply, Carl darted in the direction of the smoke.

Behind the main temple, a group of monks in orange robes were gathered around a cremation oven. Corpses were neatly arranged in a long line. A monk with a birthmark at the back of his shaved scalp knelt over the last body in the row, dripping fragrant water onto the head. Another near the oven pulled open an iron door to reveal the thunderous red-blue blaze within, and sparks rushed high into the air.

Carl retreated. The smell was of burning human flesh.

"Do you know who they are?" he yelled at two monks who were lifting a body from the row.

They were silent. Neither of them raised their eyes to him, as though deaf to human misery. With dull monotony they lifted the corpse and carried it to the oven.

Carl clasped the wrist of a monk who was standing at the side, clutching a *sutra*.

"Do you hear me?"

But the monk only cast a blank and silent glance his way.

Someone grabbed Carl by the shoulder.

"You can't speak that way to the monks."

The man wore a blue face mask and cap and had a cellophane gown over his clothes. Carl could see only dark, slanted eyes piercing him from under thick eyebrows touched with grey. Was he giving the orders here?

"You can't just burn the bodies like that …" Carl began. His voice sounded scratchy.

"They're Thai. It's our tradition—"

"How can you be sure who they are?"

"They are Thai victims who have been identified by family members. We don't cremate white people. Go and check for your missing ones on the boards. They aren't here."

Carl clenched his teeth and tried to stay calm.

"My friend is Korean. His skin is like yours."

He rushed back to the oven but the body with the contorted face had disappeared. The monks were approaching the next one in line.

He turned to the man in the mask, who was watching with his hands clasped together in front of him, as if he knew there was nothing Carl could do.

"You must stop this now. How many did you burn already?"

"This cremation oven has been working for more than twenty-four hours non-stop."

"That's criminal! I'll call the newspapers. International institutions!"

The man's eyes remained as calm as the faces of the monks. "Good," he said. "We need help with the bodies we have on the ground."

Carl paused; he felt sure cremation at this stage was a disastrous approach which would lead to irreversible consequences, but perhaps he was missing something.

"Nearly every Western person who comes here complains about something. You have an interesting attitude to life. As if life owes you something. As if we, the host country, owe you something."

"I didn't mean that …" Carl said, grasping for words. There was a minute of silence. The man turned away and strode to the temple.

Carl followed him. "How many bodies are here on the ground?"

"Our guess, nearly two thousand."

Nok was wrong. It wasn't a thousand. It was twice that. And that was just here at this temple. For a brief moment, Carl felt the ground was giving way under his feet.

"And how many have you cremated? Do you keep a record?"

"Of course we keep records, including buried corpses."

"Buried?"

"The identification procedures for Asian people and Caucasians are slightly different. The first thing we did was to separate the Thai victims from the foreigners."

The man explained that he was a forensic pathologist, and had come to Phuket from Bangkok with a team of eight people six hours after the tsunami. He and his assistant had arrived at Kao Lak to investigate equipped only with a laptop and two cameras.

"Most of the bodies brought here in the first two days were soaked in the warm ocean or, worse, in trenches filled with water and blew up to twice their size. The tropical environment along with constant temperatures above 30°C, together with high humidity, leads to very fast autolysis. Covering the cadavers with dry ice hasn't prevented the process of decomposition; the bodies are now in an advanced state of decay. And every hour they are bringing more."

They walked to a tarpaulin tent which had been the doctor's office for the last two days. There was a plastic table loaded with papers and snapshots, two stools, a lamp bulb hanging low on a long cord above the table and a large bottle of water, half empty. The doctor turned on the fan and it squeaked into life, rotating slowly at first, then faster and faster, blowing dusty air around the tent.

"Bodies identified as Thai are released to relatives but most of them have nowhere to take them, nor means to arrange a separate cremation ceremony. And often they have to deal with not one body but five or more. They leave the corpses here and the monks take care of the cremation. We decided that the best way to prevent the unidentified corpses from reaching an advanced stage of autolysis too soon was to wrap them in separate plastic bags, place them in trenches a metre deep and cover them with dry ice until we got organised and proper refrigeration facilities arrived." The doctor lifted his hat and wiped his high forehead. His hair was greying, his eyes were on the sandy side of brown and his strong jawline and broad shoulders seemed unusual for a Thai.

"So, you bury anyone who looks like a Thai – anyone with an Asian look – in mass graves. What if there was a Korean? Could you tell the difference?"

"Unlikely."

Carl clutched his hands around his shoulders, his nails piercing into his skin. "There must be another solution."

"Have you seen where the ground is covered in bodies?" the doctor said. "We'd have twice as many corpses without these arrangements. They may seem radical to you but they're necessary. The situation is chaotic, we are terribly understaffed with only four qualified personnel on site and no equipment. Nobody from the international community has sent forensic teams or any other help. We are alone. We do what we can."

We do what we can. Carl had heard it so many times today. In hospitals. In the Swedish temporary embassy.

"We don't even have one camera to take good quality photos." The doctor opened a folder with pictures and put them on the table in front of Carl. He picked out a few especially blurry images and threw them into a bucket that was already half-full of prints. "These are from cheap disposable cameras some villagers gave us."

"What other ways are there to identify the bodies?"

"As we suspect them to be Thais, we take fingerprints because prints are routinely recorded by the Thai authorities when identity cards are issued. Also, we take photos of the corpses with numbered tags."

Carl sensed that there was more to it than the doctor was telling him.

"But?"

"But we are facing huge problems finding a way to mark the bodies so they're traceable. Not only those that we bury but also the ones on the ground. We didn't have purpose-made tags so we made up paper tags and added identification numbers and basic info in indelible ink. The tags were tied with twine to the wrist of each corpse, and photographs were taken. But already this morning we have found that the paper has absorbed fluids from the bodies and the ink has become blurred. So now we are sealing the tags into plastic envelopes. Waiting for microchips to arrive soon."

The doctor paused to read a yellow Post-It on his desk.

From among his documents he took out a sheet of paper with handwritten information, and fastened the Post-It and three printouts to it with a stapler.

"I'll take you to the boards," he said, and switched off the fan. "And by the way, to add a note of complicity, in the first days after the tsunami there was no single official in charge of coordinating the collection and disposal of bodies. The recovery of corpses was conducted by the military, local governments, police headquarters and volunteer rescue teams from charity foundations. At first, most of the search teams did not label bodies, nor keep maps of the locations where the bodies were found – which, trust me, will cause difficulties in tracking the bodies later. Collected corpses were transferred to temporary morgues, mostly in Buddhist temples. We know that in Phang-Nga Province there are at least five sites with piles of bodies, two of them – Wat Bang Muang and Wat Yan Yao – located in Takuapa district."

A young Thai, who had nodded off on a stool under a beach umbrella, sprung up when he heard the doctor's voice, offered a polite folded hands gesture and spoke fast in Thai, his voice sounding sincere, almost apologetic. The doctor gave him the papers and he rushed to stick them with tape to the noticeboard.

"I'll leave you here," the doctor said to Carl. "Good luck."

He walked away, puffs of dust whirling behind him.

Carl scanned the boards. The pictures were displayed in sets – two or three snapshots of face, cadaver and any distinguishing marks that might make the grisly forms identifiable to someone who knew them. A little written information alongside gave no names and scant information beyond tag number and approximate height.

There were a handful of people scrutinising the boards, among them Nok.

"Did you find anything?" Carl said.

"Not yet."

He peered at the images. They were all the same. Repulsive. Grotesque. These boards were different from the ones in Phuket. They didn't offer any hope – most of the bodies were unrecognisable. The faces and lips were horribly swollen and the tongues protruded, making visual identification unreliable or even impossible. In many cases the epidermis was partly detached, leaving the unpigmented dermis exposed, so that even the cadavers of dark-skinned individuals were pallid and colourless. If Kristoffer was dead and his body had been taken to a place like this, he would never find him, Carl thought.

"It's getting dark," Nok said

"Let's go to Kuraburi. We won't find here anything."

They walked in silence. The dusk washed the sandy paths in red, as if not enough blood had been spilled on the earth already. Random people were wandering amongst the piles of bodies, peering through the cold fog, trying to recognise faces they used to know. In the half-dark, the endless rows of human remains looked even more hideous. Some corpses had their arms reaching into the air, the fingers crooked as though in final prayer to a deaf and careless god.

Crooked fingers.

"Those are the Shades," Eva had said, pointing to the top of the monument. "The souls of the damned standing at the entrance to Hell."

Carl remembered how it felt – as though the Shades were gazing down at them from The Gates of Hell. He had shrunk back.

"Rodin set them in this bizarrely twisted pose, like the Adam sculpture we saw in the garden. It gave their bodies a highly expressive force, revealing extremes of physical torment and suffering."

"Why don't the Shades have hands?" Carl had said, peering at the truncated wrists, as though the hands had been made of wax and had melted or were never there.

"They're too close to the fires of Hell," Eva said, almost whispering. "The tongues of flame have consumed the hands." Her breath appeared as a white cloud in front of her. The air was still crisp from the night's cold. Kristoffer hugged her from behind, resting his chin on her shoulder.

He had called Carl a week before to suggest the visit to Paris, where Eva was working on a law case. Carl hadn't seen the pair since they had started dating, and Kristoffer had proposed the day before Carl arrived. The three of them had celebrated at the Jules Verne restaurant on Tour Eiffel. As night fell, the brown wrought iron lattice had turned to luminous gold lace and it felt magical to be inside the tower's iconic web, drinking champagne and waiting for the lights to flash at the top of the hour. It felt like travelling at high speed through the night sky. When he found the perfect person, Carl thought, he would propose to her there.

"Dante had described the figures as pointing to the inscription, '*Abandon hope, all ye who enter here*'," Eva said. "But for his sculpture Rodin replaced the inscription with The Thinker, at the centre of the tympanum."

Carl tilted his head to the side, staring at the eternally closed doors. The figures seemed chaotic at first but soon became distinct, human forms emerging from the abyss. Grimacing faces. Open mouths. Wrung hands.

Crooked fingers.

"Paola and Francesca." Eva indicated the two strained bodies combined in one perfect movement on the right-hand door panel. The morning sun reflected off the male figure who fought to reach the female, slipping out of his hands, leaving without a last goodbye. So much tension, thought Carl, so much despair in every line in his body, his face. The stone became alive to show death.

Carl watched Eva as she spoke, following the movement of her delicate hand. He had always thought she had something of the Parisian in her – in the way she gesticulated, how she spoke, the way her lips formed around even the harsher Swedish sounds, softened them to a melodic murmur. She was arty, deep, thoughtful – all the qualities Kristoffer loved about her most, at least to the extent that he could articulate why she was special to him. He had a keen interest in art and literature but Eva gave it another dimension.

Carl could see that Kristoffer was happy with her. She gave him wings and grounded him at the same time. And yet somehow it seemed too soon, too dangerous, to make a life commitment.

"It's said that The Thinker could be Dante, or even Rodin himself," Eva said as they walked away. The Rue de Bourgoyne was covered with a carpet of fallen leaves – red, yellow, brown – that rustled under their feet, and the birds were silent as so often in autumn. "In most art, we see the opposition between man and God. Here Rodin dared to depict a man contemplating his own existence. The most powerful opposition of all: a man facing himself."

Muddy gravel scrunched under the wheels as Nok slowed down and parked on the side of the road. The golden carved roof of the temple rose above the trees, dully gleaming in the moonlight.

Man facing himself.

Carl shuddered.

Twenty

Lucas, the manager of the Golden Buddha, was sitting in a café on a side road to the left of the Kuraburi temple. There were six empty tables under a tarpaulin stretched on poles, and the pungent smell of burnt garlic wafted from a cardboard shanty behind, which served as a kitchen.

"I will be with you in a minute," Lucas said, staring at the screen of his laptop. His glasses had slid down his thin nose and his bony fingers were moving fast across the keyboard. He had olive skin and a short, jet-black beard; his thinning hair was pulled together in a man bun.

A waitress, a teenager with half her hair dyed pink, brought him fried rice and chicken satay. Without lifting his head, Lucas moved a pile of documents aside, clearing a space for the food.

"Are you hungry?" he said, picking a plastic fork from a jar in the middle of the table.

Carl hadn't eaten since he had landed in Phuket. Nausea was choking his hunger; the smell of rotten corpses lingered in his sinuses.

"Do you think it's safe to eat here?" He glanced askance at the greasy stains on the table with bits of tissues stuck to them.

"I eat here all the time. Still alive." Lucas mumbled

through a mouthful of rice. "This's the only country in the world where you rarely get sick from street food."

Carl turned a laminated menu in his hands.

"Green chicken curry, please?" he said to the waitress, without looking at the list of dishes. It was Kristoffer's favourite dish – he always ordered it at any Thai restaurant. There was a small place in Lund, their favourite since student days, on a side street near the train station. It was run by an old Thai lady and her blind daughter, and the last time he was in Lund he had been devastated to find it had closed down.

"No, sorry."

"I thought it was always on a Thai menu?"

"Not tonight, *ka*."

"Then chicken satay and rice, please. And a cold beer."

"Bring me another portion of chicken satay," Lucas said, and pushed an empty plate towards her.

Carl placed his elbows on the table and leaned forward. "Were you on the island when the tsunami hit?"

"No, I wasn't. I arrived at Kuraburi yesterday."

"So, you never met Kristoffer? You don't know what happened at the resort?"

"No." Lucas pressed his lips together. "I run my business from Sydney."

The waitress returned with two plates. Carl forked his rice; it was cold and dry at the edges. Kristoffer would have found it annoying and he'd have leaned towards him and said so. Carl nibbled on the chicken – only a touch warmer but tender and aromatic, just the way they both liked it. He poured his beer into a plastic cup and emptied the cup in four big gulps.

"Today, our search team combed through the clubhouse ruins and nearby mangroves at the bottom of Monkey Mountain. We found a man trapped in mangrove roots at

189

the entrance to a creek. It took us an hour and a half to free him …"

Lucas launched into a long account of the situation on the island, and it felt to Carl as if he was not telling the story for the first time. His voice was monotonous and Carl had to make an effort to stick with him. The image of the hand sticking out between blocks of concrete came into his mind. What if Kristoffer was trapped somewhere, perhaps even under the ruins of the clubhouse? The people Lucas had assembled to do the search were local villagers – they certainly weren't the professional rescue teams Carl had envisioned.

He stopped Lucas mid-sentence. "Why can't you get professional searchers? I can chip in if you need money."

"The Thai Army doesn't have anyone available to send here. We are an island, and not exactly well known." Lucas wiped the corners of his mouth with a paper napkin. "The locals know the mangroves, they know what to look for. Don't underestimate them."

"How many people are still missing?"

"Eight, including your friends. Tomorrow a team of volunteers go to—"

"I want to go."

"You're most welcome. A boat leaves from Kuraburi pier at dawn to avoid the midday heat. We're meeting here and taking a truck to the pier. Come to the café at 6 o'clock."

"Do you think it's possible that they left the island somehow? Maybe a boat fished them out, or—"

"Everything is possible." Lucas fixed his glasses. "Yesterday, my list of missing was almost thirty, now it's shortened to eight names. That happened because some people left the island before helicopters arrived, and got to hospitals and embassies themselves. It may happen that suddenly they'll be found in good health. I just got news about a couple of Germans who were thought missing. We contacted their family in Berlin and they said they were already home."

A moth burned its wings on the light bulb and fell on the empty satay plate, wriggling. Carl watched it crawl out. If Kristoffer was conscious and had access to a phone he'd have contacted his parents. The silence meant he wasn't able to do that, for whatever reason.

"What about Takuapa Hospital?"

"I was told they discharged the last foreigner today. Badly injured were transferred to Phuket hospitals." Lucas scratched his beard. "It might be worth checking Ranong Hospital. One of our guests found his wife there today. A Thai villager saved her and brought her there. It's the closest hospital to Kuraburi."

"Do you think I can go tonight?"

"It's not far, about an hour's drive up to the Burmese border. Traffic isn't as congested in that direction."

Carl stood up.

"You didn't eat your rice," Lucas said.

"I'm not hungry."

Carl walked to Wat Pasan. A bone-white moon hung above the trees, casting an even light over the grand concrete arch and the people sleeping in its shadow. The square around it was swamped with Thais from the island villages and the coastal area who had been living there for the last two days. A group was sitting in a circle around a fire, and the flame occasionally cast a warm light on their shattered faces. Dull silence and an unbearable tension had settled over them. A child was clinging to his mother, and followed Carl with eyes full of fear.

"Carl?" A hoarse voice came from the dark, from the trees.

Carl turned. A man was staggering towards him, limping on his left leg.

"I'm Jack," he said, holding an unlit cigarette in the corner of his mouth. He reached out an arm covered in cuts. He had a tattoo on the inside of his wrist where the skin was much paler, from wearing a watch probably – intricately written letters in dark blue ink, a tangled yarn which Carl could not read.

"Lucas said you're a friend of Kristoffer?"

"Yes."

"They are still among the missing. Sorry."

"Were you on the island when the tsunami happened?"

"Yes, but I was one of the lucky ones." Jack fumbled in his pocket and took out a black bic lighter. He put his thumbnail on the little wheel and flicked it down. The flame lit up his unshaven face. A man of fifty or so, Carl reckoned, with a life intensely lived to judge by his wrinkles and the sparkle in his eyes. He was looking straight at Carl as if checking what he was made of.

Carl immediately liked him. He didn't know why but he felt he could rely on him. There was no bullshit about the man.

"Did you see Kristoffer that morning?"

"At breakfast," Jack said. "Bill, who has the island dive shop, saw him and Eva kayaking into the mangrove creek minutes before the wave."

"They were in a kayak?" Carl felt a fluttering in his chest. "Do you think the wave could have taken them away from the island?"

"Hopefully." Jack screwed up his face. "A Danish couple they were kayaking with ended up further up the north coast, almost at Ranong, when the water receded."

"Where are they, can I speak to them?"

"Not here. Back home, I guess. Bill said that before the wave they were taken by the ebb tide into the open sea. That's what saved them." Jack took a long draw from his cigarette. "Kristoffer and Eva stayed in Beach Bay and went into the mangroves. More likely than not they are still there."

"Alive, right? You mean they got lost in the mangroves?"

"No, I meant … Sorry."

"Lucas said they checked the mangroves."

"We checked only behind the hotel, whatever we were able to access. The creek meanders through the mangroves for miles inland. Half the island is a mangrove swamp." Jack blew some smoke. "Do you know what a mangrove forest looks like?"

"I think so."

"It's a trap. It looks like a dense, gigantic spider's web." He stared at Carl with his black eyes, and the crease between his heavy brows went deeper for a moment. "If they were in the mangroves, they had little chance to get out. And it's … Well, forgive me, but it's unlikely their bodies will be ever found."

Carl's heart gave a sick lurch.

"Kristoffer is a professional swimmer."

"Yes, I often saw him swimming. But I was in that water too, and it was not about skills."

"But you survived."

"It was a miracle. I can't recall everything, but I reckon the flow forced me to one of the basement offices at the back of the clubhouse. I was trapped. The room was filling with water and I couldn't find a door, a window, any means of escape. Then something hit my head and I just remember coughing and spluttering. I was done."

"So how did you …?"

"The ceiling caved in. And then the same force thrust me to the surface." Jack threw his glowing stub on the ground and crushed it with his shoe. "I don't know why destiny changed its mind."

He pushed his unruly black curls behind his ear, revealing a roughly stitched cut from the middle of his forehead to the base of his brow. "You know your friends stayed in one of my bungalows? Right on the beach, nothing between the house and the sea. And it withstood the wave. Can you believe it?"

"What do you mean? I thought the whole resort was destroyed."

"Yes, the resort is a pile of rubble but a few bungalows remain, mainly those at the back, near the jungle. But on the beach …"

Carl had to clear his throat before he was able to speak.

"Do you mean if they had been inside, they would be safe?"

"It's a big if." Jack clenched his jaw. "I don't know. When the wave hit, my friend Georgiou was sleeping in his bungalow, less than ten metres from Kristoffer's. It was swept away as if it was never there. Even the concrete foundations were swallowed."

"And Georgiou?"

"He is in the ice." Jack pointed to the lines of plywood coffins set under a tarpaulin stretched on poles to the north side of the temple walls. "I found him in the morning in the shallow water in front of the clubhouse. The waves probably brought his body back during the night because he wasn't there the night before. His fiancée, who is a poor swimmer, survived even though the odds were not in her favour."

Carl walked over to the tarpaulin. Most of the coffins were raised on low wooden benches but some were merely standing on the ground, stacked two high. Each box had a number and name in large letters scrawled in black paint on the side. Some were open. The bodies were covered in dry ice, waiting for embassy representatives to pick them up and arrange transport to their home countries. According to Jack, the dry ice had to be topped up every few hours during the heat of the day. So far, none of the coffins had been collected and the line was gradually growing.

Body fluids were dripping from the coffins' bottoms and trickling down in narrow streams to form small, stinking puddles. Dozens of incense sticks had been placed strategically around the makeshift morgue, the fragrance intended to fight the all-penetrating smell of death.

"Do you see that woman near this end of the line?"

Someone sat on a chair beside the last but one coffin. It was covered with faded flowers and dying candles, and on the side were the words, '*# 26. Camilla. 6 y/o*'.

"She and her husband went diving that morning … As they had done each of the previous two days. Only this time they didn't take their daughter with them because it was supposed to be a very hot day … I can't stop thinking about how random life is, how casual circumstances define one's life. Or death. How all of us …" There was a black abyss in his eyes that swallowed all the questions and released no answers.

Carl hid his trembling hands in his shorts pockets, squeezing them into fists.

"If the wave washed them offshore from the island where would they go with the kayak?"

"Anywhere. There are two large islands, to north and south of Koh Phra Thong, each separated from it by a narrow channel. Both are covered in ancient jungle and pretty much uninhabited apart from seasonal sea gypsies' settlements. About sixty kilometres to the northwest there's the cluster of Surin Islands. And about a hundred kilometres north is Burma and the Mergui Archipelago."

"That's a large radius of search."

"Begin with Koh Phra Thong. It'll strip you of any desire to go island hopping."

"Why?" Carl said, yet he knew the answer.

"You will see. Are you coming tomorrow?"

"Definitely."

"That's good. Most people are afraid to go there."

"Why?"

"Everyone is paranoid about another wave." He sniffed. "Also, locals are afraid of *phi.*"

"*Phi*?"

"The spirits, the benevolent and malevolent ghosts inhabiting Thailand."

"Really?"

"Look, Westerners are afraid of zombies, Thais of spirits. Nobody is comfortable with the dead."

Jack took another cigarette from a scratched and battered cigarette case and lit it, exhaling through his nose.

"Maybe you noticed how everywhere around the country, especially in temples but also in forests, some trees are wrapped with a cloth or tied around with multicoloured silk? It signifies that a spirit resides there. A tree should not be cut without warning the spirit to let him find another tree. After the devastation, of course, many spirits were left homeless and are furiously scouring the deserted island. Not to mention the souls of those who died violently in the tsunami – without a proper ceremony they can't go away in peace and will remain here around us, living, waiting to be released—"

"Jack, did you hear?" A man with wavy hair, his face and arms covered with large freckles, appeared beside them. "Lucas said he won't pay for additional helpers to go to the island tomorrow. How are we going to continue the search?"

"We have enough people. Carl is joining us. Jonas is still searching for Jose. There's you. Lucas. Chaow and Dang are coming."

"It's not enough. We'll need an army to search that damn island." The man was talking fast, his whole body in a state of animation. "Help me find people. You speak Thai. I will pay myself."

"It's not about the money. Locals don't want to go to the island, you saw that today. Did you find anyone in Phuket?"

"They're clearing up in Phuket now. They've begun sending people to Kao Lak. They say it was hit the worst."

"I was there," Carl said. "They already have two thousand corpses at Wat Bang Muang."

"Jesus."

"This is Marcus, by the way," Jack said. "Marcus – Carl."

Marcus said he had landed in Phuket at 10.15 a.m. on the day of the disaster, just at the time the wave was flooding the island. As his plane cruised above the island, before going in for the final descent, Marcus had watched the bay empty of water. He had known full well what was going to happen. Before they touched down, he tried to call his wife Nora at the Golden Buddha. He called and called. If only she'd picked up her phone. On the final approach he saw the sea rush inland, he saw the island shrink, the landing strip blurring and disappearing beneath brown water. The wave collapsed over Koh Phra Thong's beach ten minutes later.

Marcus clasped Jack's arm. "What about Moken, can we hire them?"

"The sea gypsies? They're lazy."

"But they know the sea like nobody else."

"They're a strange lot, living in their own world," Jack said. "I don't think they give a damn about us. They don't like people from the mainland. Thais have been fighting to civilise them for decades now. But they don't live in captivity. They are nomads. They stop on the islands only during the monsoons."

197

"Did you hear that they took to their boats and went far out into the open sea during the tsunami?" Marcus said. "As if they knew it was coming? Our boatman told me they have legends, passed to each other through the generations, about the sea withdrawing. They knew they'd have to leave the land because of a big wave. They knew. That's why they may know where to look for those who were taken by the sea. Maybe they have shamans who can see things we can't see?"

"I know you want a miracle. We all want one." Jack put a hand on Marcus' shoulder. "How is Nora?"

Tears blazed in Marcus's eyes. "Still in a coma. They say she has no chance."

"Are you sure you want to continue the search for little Kat? You can really only hope to find … you know …"

"I'm not interested in hopes," he said, turning to leave. "I have to *know*! I'm going to find help – whether you think it's worth it or not!"

A truck covered with a tarpaulin drove off the main road into the square and stopped under the trees. Instantly a mute crowd rushed forward, surrounding the vehicle. A Thai in relief worker's clothes climbed from the truck and announced something using a megaphone.

"What is he saying?" Carl said.

"He's giving the location where they collected bodies," Jack said. "For the last two days, every few hours a pickup with corpses has driven into the square in front of Wat Pasan temple. Mainly Thais from the coastal villages and islands nearby."

"Didn't he say Koh Phra Thong?"

"Yes, Pak Chok village. It's on the north tip of the island. Well, it was. Now it's a long empty dune, not even wreckage left. Most of the houses were built a stone's throw away from the water, made from wood and thatch – they dissolved like soap bubbles. I heard they were using fishing nets to pull bodies from the water off the north tip of Koh Phra Thong."

"But what if someone's body from Golden Buddha was carried up there?"

"They brought us the body of a woman yesterday. Jenny. She was a researcher at the turtle conservation centre at the resort."

"Kristoffer is Asian looking." A muscle ticked in Carl's jaw.

"I know. It would certainly complicate identifying his body – assuming the worst."

They walked to the truck. The crowd was hushed, no one speaking above a whisper. Immediately, the smell of rotten flesh burned Carl's throat. Nok was wrong – he would not become accustomed to it, nor to the sight of deformed remains, some of which hung down from the flatbed. At least not yet. He felt the little food he'd just had rise in his throat. He leaned back, clamping his hand over his mouth. Jack gave him a pat on the back and pushed him forward through the crowd.

Two relief workers in dark blue suits, only one of whom wore rubber gloves, climbed into the truck, placing their feet in the little space left between the bodies. They lifted a woman, her face sculpted grey with clay and dried blood, her hair as stiff as a scrubbing brush, and flung her to a man on the ground. He caught her by the legs, which were tied together by a strip of filthy material, but her head tipped back into the dust, her eyes bulging from their sockets, brown fluid oozing from her open mouth. The worker in the gloves hopped down and lifted her head with both hands, and together they manoeuvred her onto a long wooden table.

Monks came holding lanterns and stood still behind

the table, motionlessly watching, witnessing. Do they feel anything in their inscrutability, thought Carl, or only bloody peace?

Suddenly the silence was shattered by a woman's harrowing cry. She collapsed sobbing over the dead woman's body, kissing her lifeless hand, caressing the deformed face. Her tears fell on the cheek of the corpse, leaving a wet mark on the dry clay as if the dead were crying too. Carl's stomach dropped and tightened on a curdling mix of nausea and pity.

"Very unusual public display of grief," Jack whispered. "Thais are very composed. Even in such tragedy."

The workers carried another body wrapped in a plastic bag. They shoved the sobbing woman aside and placed it next to the first corpse as if there was limited space on the long table, as if they knew they would fill it all. The bag flopped like a wet thing and a medic tore the plastic open and pushed a torch into the face. Carl snapped his gaze away.

The next corpse was much bigger than the previous two. One of the workers' knees buckled under its weight and he leaned against the truck side to keep from falling. Two men from the crowd stepped forward and helped to place the body on the table.

A police officer ran his torch over the bloated stomach covered with oozing blisters. There were almost no clothes left, only torn and filthy bits of material that hung around the hips. Someone measured the body's length and took a picture of the face. At first Carl thought it was a man, but there was an earring in one ear that looked distinctly feminine. The man with the torch was making notes on a pad. He tightened a string around the cadaver's wrist with a number written on a piece of cardboard roughly torn from a packaging box.

"That won't last a night," Carl whispered to Jack.

"No?"

"It'll soak in the body fluids."

Jack looked horrified. "They have been marking all the bodies that way here."

Carl pointed to a woman's body. Her hands were held in front of her face as though for protection. "Do you think she's Western?"

He had been watching the policeman taking height measurements. He was careless, he could easily lose or add ten centimetres.

"You think it might be Eva?"

"No, no, she has short hair. But the skin is white."

"It's grey to me." Jack shrugged. "They all look grey to me. The colour of the skin seems to depend on where the body was found."

"We're here," Nok said.

Carl opened his eyes. They were in the front of a three-storey concrete building with very few lights in the windows.

"Ranong Hospital."

"Thanks for bringing me here. I know how much you wanted to see Aeh."

"I can't help her anymore. For now, she has to fight for her life alone."

Carl walked to the glass doors. It was different from the overcrowded hospitals in Phuket – there were only a few cars in the car park and no people. It looked abandoned, as if the wave had washed through the whole site. The doors squeaked as they slid apart. He crossed the lobby, his steps echoing through the empty space.

A nurse was resting her head on her arm, leaning over the information desk. He touched her shoulder. She jerked up and began to speak rapidly in Thai.

Carl stopped her. "Do you speak English?"

201

She nodded fast.

"I'm looking for my friends, Eva and Kristoffer Berg."

She nodded. Smiled.

"Can you check if they might be at the hospital?"

She blinked, still smiling.

"Do you understand me?"

She nodded.

Carl rubbed the back of his neck. "You don't understand me, do you?"

She nodded again.

He glanced around hopelessly. There was nobody. Not a sound. Only a blur of blazing white overhead fluorescence. It felt weird, as if the whole hospital was dead.

The nurse touched his arm and pointed to the elevators, then stepped out from behind the desk and motioned him to follow her.

She went past the elevators and continued to an inner hall. There was no furniture and only posters on the walls. They walked through a chain of poorly lit corridors. Carl felt a light touch on his hip and a waft of air. Did someone just pass by? He looked back over his shoulder, waiting for his eyes to adjust to the dimness. Ahead of him, he could only distinguish the nurse's cap silhouette against the light at the end of the corridor. He reached for the wall with one hand, staggered forward and stumbled over something on the floor, tumbling down and landing on a figure lying against the wall. A man moaned.

"Sorry." Carl began to make out the shapes of more people leaning against the wall. "Sorry," he whispered, getting up. Nobody said a word.

The nurse opened the door to a staircase and began to descend. The musty air hit Carl in the face. The ceiling was low and he stooped to avoiding swathes of dusty cobwebs. He wished they could go back.

Two flights of stairs down and they continued into a narrow corridor with a metallic door at the end with blue lights above it. A rat darted from under his feet and Carl recoiled, ending up against the wall. It was cold, mouldy and somehow cloying.

"Damn." He hissed through his clenched teeth, cleaning his hands on his shorts.

Suddenly, it dawned on Carl where the nurse had brought him. His heart sunk.

"Wait, you didn't understand me." He grabbed the woman's arm. She nodded, smiling, and with her free hand she knocked on the heavy metal door of the morgue. The sound echoed in the emptiness.

A long moment passed.

The door clanked and a Thai man with a dark-stained white coat peered out. The nurse said something to him.

"Wait for me here," the man said, and disappeared behind the door.

The nurse bowed to Carl and headed back along the corridor. Carl stood alone, watching her little shape vanishing in the darkness. Soon the clicking of her heels on the tiles faded away too. He began feeling cold. He clasped his hands around his arms, rubbing his numb skin. The absolute silence was disturbed only by the *click, click* of a broken, blinking blue light bulb.

The door clanked again, a harsh, malevolent echo in the emptiness around.

"I'm Doctor Tan. I was updating my files." The doctor took off his mask and put it in his coat pocket. "The nurse said she thought you were looking for someone? Let's go upstairs."

The ceiling fan in the doctor's office almost touched the top of Carl's head. The room had cream-coloured walls with chunks of plaster missing, and a line of dark grey mould ran along the top of a panel of waist-high tiles that might have once been white. Carl sat in an armchair. Foam stuck out from tears in the upholstery. The doctor's chair looked a little newer, but behind him was a nearly empty medicine cupboard, one of its doors missing a hinge and hanging forlornly down.

"We discharged the few Westerners we had," the doctor said, looking at his register. He couldn't recall anyone with the characteristics of Carl's friends. He said they hadn't had many foreigners to start with – the north part of the province was far from being a primary tourist destination.

"Those who required further treatment were sent today to Phuket. Apart …" – the doctor paused and looked at Carl – "… apart from one man. He keeps asking if we found a woman. I think he called her Eva. She was in the water next to him. He thinks she drowned."

Carl flinched as if he had been slapped.

"Kristoffer!" he sprung up.

"I don't think so. This man is English."

"I want to meet him anyway."

"I may have confused the names or it may not be the woman you're looking for. Would you like to follow me?"

Carl felt his heartbeat in his throat.

The doctor took him to the floor above his office. He opened the door to a dimly lit room choked with beds. The air was stale and thick – the smell of medicine mixed with urine. A Thai man rose from his pillow, squinting against the light from the corridor.

The doctor pointed to a bed next to the window.

"Be gentle with him. He's unwell."

The man lay still, covered with a crumpled sheet up to his stomach, his hands in tight fists along his body. Carl leaned over and peered into a stranger's face, his eyebrows almost joined together above his closed eyes, his long, thin hair stuck with sweat to his bony jaw. His pupils were frantically moving under his eyelids. His lips twitched and he moaned.

'*Naucrates*', Carl read on the chest of his tattered grey T-shirt.

He shifted from foot to foot. He stretched out his hand and touched the man's shoulder.

The man sat bolt upright on the bed with his mouth wide open, gasping for breath. Carl took a step back. The man was shivering, clasping his sheet to his chest. His goggle eyes rolled around the room until they fixed on Carl.

"Who are you?" he croaked.

"My name is Carl."

He wanted to say more but couldn't find the words. He felt a numbness spread across his face.

"How long have I been here?"

"Probably two days. It's December the twenty-eighth."

The man fell back on his pillows and stared at the ceiling.

"It seems like much longer," he said, his eyes blank. "Do you know if they found the body of that woman?"

Carl licked his lips. "Which woman?"

"The woman … the woman next to me in the water." He sucked in his breath and let it out in a long, hoarse cry. "She was begging me to save her … She was so scared …" The man was sobbing between words. "It was impossible … When the wave hit, she clung to me in the water, but I couldn't … I couldn't do anything." He choked a little. "Anything at all …"

A clock on the wall was ticking loudly. Carl could hardly hear what the man was saying. The noises were getting louder. The noises in his head.

"She was pregnant …"

"Where were you?"

"Eh?" The man stopped sobbing, and blinked.

"Where were you? Which hotel?"

He drew his sheet to his chin.

"Golden Buddha."

"What happened to the woman?"

"I don't know. I never saw her again."

"Why you didn't do anything?"

"The water was coming from everywhere. I didn't understand what was happening … I couldn't breathe … I was drowning. I thought I was going to die …"

"But you didn't. And you let her drown."

"Yes. Yes! God help me, I prised her arms from around my neck—"

"You let her drown!" Carl was shouting now.

"She would have drowned us both." The man's fevered cheeks were covered in tears, and saliva drooled from his mouth. "We would both have drowned. Both. Do you understand?"

Carl said nothing.

The man fell on his bed, buried his head in his pillow.

"I had to save my life."

Carl leaned against the wall next to the bed. Here was a man who could have saved Eva and he hadn't. She had had a chance. And he didn't help her. He clasped his hands behind his head, pulling his hair.

The man began speaking again. Maybe to himself, maybe to Carl. "I see her face every time I close my eyes. It haunts me whenever I fall asleep. I couldn't do anything. I had to survive …" He paused for a moment and seemed to be looking into the distance. "She was such a beautiful woman. I remember her arriving at Golden Buddha a couple of days before, with her husband. I sat next to him at breakfast that morning. I can't recall his name now. It was their honeymoon …"

Silence. Only the clock ticking.

"Kristoffer. His name is Kristoffer." Carl stared at the floor. "He's my friend."

"Did he survive?"

"I don't know."

He pushed himself away from the wall and stood swaying, his head spinning. He walked unsteadily away and the man's voice faded behind him.

When Carl got back to the car, he found Nok with his head tilted back onto the neck support, his mouth open, gently snoring. Carl waited. The road was pitch dark – there were only three street lamps in front of the hospital. It was close to midnight.

Shoulders hunched, he walked behind the pickup and climbed up onto the flatbed. He collapsed on the hard floor, curled into the foetal position.

"Eva is alive," Carl muttered. The man was wrong. He was out of his mind. He mixed things up. He was confusing her with someone else. Kristoffer would never let her go. If she had fallen in the water, he would have dived after her.

In any case, Eva was agile, she would have the strength to stay afloat on her own. She was a good swimmer, a great runner. She was strong.

Carl was neither awake nor asleep. He tossed and turned on the rough floor, his heart dully drumming in his chest, echoing in his ears. He pressed his hands against his ears to stop the echo but it only grew stronger.

Jack had said a Burmese man had been washed up on the beach of Golden Buddha the day after, clinging to a log. He had spent almost twenty-four hours in the sea before drifting to the island. Kristoffer and Eva were in a kayak. The current could have taken them anywhere, to the islands around them. To Burma.

They were both alive. Maybe still drifting. Maybe lost in the mangroves. Maybe injured. But alive. He just needed time to find them. He needed time.

Time. Black spots were moving in front of Carl's eyes.

He was in a maze. It was murky. He could hear Kristoffer's voice calling him but couldn't tell from which direction. The maze was filled with water up to his knees. The walls were close on all sides. He had no sense of direction. Kristoffer's voice was getting weaker. The maze was turning darker and darker. Carl began to run.

Darkness turned to blazing light, and Carl saw Kristoffer sitting in his lifeguard's chair, facing the swimming pool. The sun was playing on the water's surface. A group of boys stood in a line on the edge, listening to the coach's commands. There was a whistle. Kids dived into the water and began splashing around.

"I'd like to be a coach."

Kristoffer lifted his cup and with the back of his hand, he wiped the sweat from his forehead. Suddenly the wind got stronger. Carl couldn't hear his words anymore; he saw his lips move but couldn't hear his voice. The sun disappeared behind dark clouds. Everything was flying around, spinning. Sand was slapping into his face, blinding his eyes. He was shaking from cold, from fear.

The swimming pool became a gigantic whirlpool, sucking children into it as if someone had pulled a cork from the bottom. The wind was hissing with evil intensity.

Carl looked for Kristoffer, but he was gone. Everyone had gone – the coach, the parents, the pool and the building containing it, the people from the streets outside. Only wreckage, leaves and dust whirled in the air.

Carl felt utterly alone. Afraid. Paralysed. At once he saw himself naked, stripped of his clothes by the wind. He screamed, but his voice had gone too.

He opened his eyes, his pulse racing, hands in tight fists. He rubbed his sweating face, wiping off sand blown up from the floor of the pickup.

The cargo bed smelled of death. It smelled of the bodies that Nok had been carrying for the last two days.

Sickened, he crawled out and went down on all fours, leaning forwards and pressing his forehead into the ground, gasping for air.

"Mangrove creek," Carl whispered. "I start there."

It was still dark but he already felt the freshness of the coming dawn. A bird gave up its early morning song. He stood up, swaying slightly on his feet. Nok was still sleeping, resting his head on his arm in the car's open window.

He shuffled over to the hospital, quietly passing by the sleeping nurse on his way to the restroom beside the lift. He turned on a tap covered in lime crust. The water was cold, refreshing. He stuck his head under the flow.

When he returned to the lobby the nurse was awake, flipping through papers. He indicated the coffee vending machine and pulled a hundred baht note from his pocket. She smiled and gave him four ten-baht coins but didn't take the note. He slipped it under her papers.

With two cups of coffee, he returned to the pickup. Nok was still sleeping.

"Wake up." Carl shook his shoulder. "We have to go back to Kuraburi."

The sky was lightening. Fresh air blew on Carl's face through the open windows. He watched the empty road in silence.

There were only a few cars but Nok was reluctant to drive too fast. He slowed down as they passed by random settlements in palm groves, dogs walking on the road, chickens nibbling grass at the edges, a little group of barefoot children kicking a deflated football on the roadside. A woman with an infant wrapped tight to her chest rode a rusted bicycle, with two large baskets containing fruits and herbs balanced behind her. Nok stopped the car to let a huge brown ox hitched to a basket-shaped cart mounted on two wooden steel-rimmed wheels cross the road to the banana plantation on the other side. Sitting on the ox's yoke with his legs dangling free and smoking his *beedi*, a peasant gave them a toothless smile. These people didn't even know about the tsunami, Carl thought. For a moment the nightmare of the last day felt like a bad dream.

His phone rang.

"Is that Carl?" a thin female voice. Carl plugged the other ear with his finger.

"Speaking."

"Are you looking for Ef Beg?"

Carl sat up in his seat. "Yes, Eva Berg."

"She's in our hospital."

"Which hospital?"

"Bangkok Hospital in Phuket."

Carl felt the skin tighten around his skull. He didn't dare to believe.

"Who are you?"

"A nurse from the hospital."

"Is she alright?" Then another thought came into his mind. "Is Eva … alive?"

"Yes. She's alive."

Alive. The air around him vibrated with the word.

"How do you know it's Eva? Can she speak?"

"No, she's in intensive care."

"How do you know it's her?"

The nurse didn't say anything, and he realised he had confused her with the question. He thought he could hear her speaking in Thai to someone else. He pressed the phone tighter to his ear.

"How do you know it's Eva?" he said again, dreading her answer.

"Dr Green told me to call you."

Carl rang off, his heart hammering in his ears.

"I knew it!" he screamed, his face transforming, for the first time in days, into something like a smile.

"I knew Eva was alive!" he shouted to Nok. He shouted it to himself. He shouted it to the world of chaos around him.

Nok grinned with genuine pleasure.

Carl sagged down into his seat, warmth growing in his chest.

When they got to a fork in the road, he told Nok to take him directly to Phuket, leaving Kuraburi behind.

He closed his eyes and slipped into sleep, fanned by the breeze.

Twenty-one

"I met someone."

Kristoffer was beaming and Carl was glad to see him excited about someone again. Six months before, Kristoffer had found out that his girlfriend of four years, with whom he worked in the Frankfurt office, had been cheating on him with an office colleague whom he had thought of as a friend. The betrayal had hit him hard. He took a six-week break from work and returned to Stockholm. For the first time in his life, he was unsure about things. He had questioned friendship, relationships, truth.

Carl had flown in from London and Kristoffer had met him at the airport. Kristoffer took Carl's suitcase and walked ahead of him. "Why so heavy?"

"Two bottles of excellent red. To celebrate."

"Good, perfect timing. French?"

"Yes, Burgundy."

"Is that where we drove along the river to a chateau?"

"No, we went to Burgundy just before you relocated to Amsterdam. Remember that family-owned winery? And the tiny hotel we stayed at in Beaune, with the restaurant at the back?"

But Carl could see that Kristoffer's mind was somewhere else.

"So, tell me about her," Carl said. "She's not French, is she?"

Kristoffer beamed. "She is not." He pointed at a grey Toyota in the car park. "My new car. Well, technically second-hand, but new to me."

"Did I miss something? Are you settling down in Stockholm?"

"Maybe. We'll see how things go."

"I thought you were considering moving to London?"

"Well, until last week I was."

They climbed in and Carl said, "So, who is she?"

Kristoffer took hold of the wheel and stared straight ahead. "It's Eva."

"Eva?"

"Yes."

"Eva Andersson?"

"Yes."

"From the students' library?"

"For God's sake Carl, yes!"

"I thought you said last year she was dating that geeky guy from the Ministry of Defence?"

Kristoffer's usually pale cheeks flushed. "Not any more. I met her by chance last Sunday at a friend's house. She's single and I think she likes me. And she's so beautiful."

Everyone at Lund University knew Eva, mainly because she had worked part-time at the law library. Carl had only ever chatted with her in the library.

"She asked me how your forehead is doing."

"My forehead?"

Kristoffer pressed his thumb against the scar above Carl's left eye.

"She still remembers? How embarrassing."

"She said you are a sweetheart."

"A sweetheart …"

The scar. He had gone to the library to pick up a book on corporate law and planned to have a short chat with Eva, maybe share a joke, as Kristoffer often did. It always amazed him how at ease Kristoffer was with girls. He had a way of making them laugh without appearing a clown. He was confident in his settled way, comfortable in his own skin. Carl had prepared a joke, as spontaneity wasn't his strong suit. He remembered standing in front of Eva's desk, clasping the book in his sweating hands, his tongue dry, unable to say a word. There were two girls from his class behind him so it was now or never.

"Do you have a book on how to chat up a beautiful woman?" he finally muttered, avoiding her eyes.

"Say again?"

Carl could hardly move a muscle.

"A book on how to chat up a woman."

This time his voice sounded too loud; he knew that the whole library could hear him. The girls behind him giggled. He died inside. He was sure they'd gossip about him.

Eva laughed. But it wasn't mean, she wasn't laughing at him. Not like the girls behind. Her voice softened. "Wrong library, my friend."

"Oh, really?" he mumbled, his face burning. He turned to walk away, and crashed into the corner of a bookshelf. He heard the crack, unsure if it was the shelf or his forehead, and everything turned dark for a moment. He came to on the floor, looking sideways at Strömholm's *Introduction to Swedish Law*, Volumes 1 and 2.

That was the day she called him 'sweetheart' for the first time, as she bandaged his head while Kristoffer distracted her with his chat. Every time she laughed she had to start again. Eva had probably liked Kristoffer already by then, but she was a year older, very popular and dating a hockey star from the university team. Kristoffer didn't have much of a chance.

Carl was fingering his scar as the nurse pressed the call button of the lift for the third time. On the digital screen above the door, the arrow was pointing down. *10 … 9 … 8…* The lift stopped on the fourth floor. A minute passed and it didn't move. Of the three lifts, one was out of service and another was just for medical personnel. People had begun to gather behind him.

According to the nurse, Dr Green had said that Eva was transferred from Takuapa Hospital the previous afternoon. She had needed an urgent blood transfusion, which she had received on arrival. She was conscious and her condition was gradually improving, so they had moved her from intensive care into a side ward.

Carl still didn't know what he would say to Eva when she asked about Kristoffer. He knew it would be her first question. He had to say something hopeful, to give her a reason to recover. He had to say that Kristoffer was alive. He would say that he was in a local hospital in Burma, and that that would be the reason he was unable to call her.

His body suddenly shivered. It started in the pit of his stomach and then exploded into every part of his body. A surge of hope that Kristoffer really was alive spread like a light into his every cell. Like everything in life, it was about those tiny chances, those moments, the apparent coincidences that in the end wove events into a coherent story. It was what Kristoffer had always said; it was just that while Carl had liked the sound of it, he hadn't been able to bring himself to see things the same way. But now he did. He felt in his bones that this tsunami horror would be soon be in the past, like the nightmare he had had last night. Look at Eva – she was on the same road at the same time, but she was going to Phuket and he was heading in the opposite direction, to Kuraburi. They had probably passed within feet of each other.

The arrow pointed up and the lift began to ascend. *5 … 6 … 7…* It stopped on the eighth floor and then kept going.

"Can we use the stairs?"

The nurse shook her head.

"Which floor is it?"

The nurse said something in Thai and showed four fingers.

"Then of course we can take the stairs. Where are they, can you show me?"

Once on the fourth floor, the nurse led him into a room softly lit through closed window blinds, with a row of beds on both sides. The air con above the door gently blew cool air. Immediately, Carl realised how lucky Eva was to be in a hospital with walls and without cobwebs and handfuls of dust under the beds; with more than one bronchoscope and antibiotics delivered by the Red Cross before they could run out.

The nurse, still out of breath, pointed Carl to the first bed on the right. As he approached, he could see strands of blonde hair sticking out from under a disposable head cap. Her chest rose and fell to the rhythm of a hissing oxygen tank, and her nose and mouth were covered with a mask. Her thin arms, criss-crossed by raised and livid weals, lay at her sides, and there were tubes connected to drop counters on both sides of the bed.

According to the nurse, Eva had sustained a severe spinal injury and might never walk again. Carl knew she would walk. She had survived the tsunami and she would walk again – with Kristoffer to help her. As he looked at her lying helpless, he knew he couldn't lie. He would come clean. He would tell her that he had no way of knowing whether Kristoffer was alive, and that he was still looking for him.

Carl stepped along the bed. His feet felt distant and heavy, as though the blood had drained from his legs. He stared at the grey face of a woman through the tangle of gleaming plastic tubes and lines. He leaned closer. Even with her face swollen and bruised she was beautiful. Her features were delicate, and her freckled forehead was covered with tiny drops of sweat. She looked so much like Eva. So much. But it wasn't her.

The walls shifted closer.

Carl wanted to scream. He closed his eyes and pressed hard against them with the palms of his hands; blood thundered in his temples. He crossed the room, rushed down the stairs, marched through the crowded foyer and ran out of the hospital. Tears were burning his eyes.

He strode to the hospital parking lot. The pickup was empty. He jerked the door but it was locked. He looked around for Nok but couldn't see him. The sun was searing his eyes. The prospect of another half-day cooking in the car was unbearable. He'd made his way to Phuket for nothing. Nothing! The boat from Kuraburi had already left – he had missed his chance to go to the island just to be caught in this stupid confusion.

"Fuck." Carl kicked the front tyre with his foot. He kicked it again, harder, barely aware that he had hurt himself.

"Fucking fuck." He collapsed on the truck's bonnet, thumping it with both hands.

He pulled out his phone and dialled Jack. Then Lucas. He couldn't connect to either. He dialled Nok but he didn't pick up. He stared at his text to Goran, in which he had said he was on his way back to Phuket because they had someone like Eva. He wished he hadn't sent it. Maybe Goran hadn't read it yet. He began typing. It was the middle of the night in Sweden, and he hoped that both messages would be read at the same time. His fingers trembled and he kept pressing the wrong button. A drop of sweat fell on his phone's screen. It was half past ten but the sun was already high and Carl felt breathless in the humid heat.

In his peripheral vision he noticed a slender woman parking her scooter two rows away. She took her helmet off and her thick dark hair fell on her tanned shoulders. She had a tattoo on her left shoulder blade, half-visible under a strap of her crop top. She squatted to chain her bike to a pole.

Liv. He wasn't sure why, but Carl slid behind the pickup. Why was he bumping into her everywhere? Through the glassless window of the cab, he saw her take a package from her scooter and walk towards the hospital, her silk wrap trousers draping around her hips, underlining her curves. She had a light gait with large steps, and her hips swung rhythmically side to side. It was the walk of someone used to people staring at them, and she was clearly at ease with it.

He leaned against the pickup door, arms folded, staring at the second hand slowly moving around his watch face. He wanted to go to the hospital bathroom and clean his teeth, wash his face. They probably had a shower there too. He wanted to get coffee, food and more water. But he didn't want to miss Nok – he had probably gone to get something to eat or maybe to the toilet, and would be back any minute. He didn't want to speak to Dr Green. He didn't want to meet Liv. He just wanted to get to the island as soon as possible. If they left now and the traffic was the same as yesterday, they'd be at the Kuraburi pier by 3 p.m. No time to go to the island but he might meet Lucas and Jack at the pier. There was no point going alone in the night to Koh Phra Thong, and he began to doubt whether he should rush to Kuraburi at all. Lucas was short of trained search and rescue personnel and

Carl wondered if he could look for people to hire here in Phuket, perhaps ask at the Swedish temporary embassy. Or perhaps not – having seen what he'd seen there, he knew that they wouldn't be very helpful. Maybe he could go to Phuket City Hall and try his luck there, but he knew if there were available search teams they'd be sent to Kao Lak and it was not about the money. He wondered for a second if it was worth a call to Ralf but immediately knew the futility of any efforts in that direction.

It was the day of the meeting with investors that he had been working on the entire year, but instead he was getting fried in a dusty car park. Still, it felt truer to himself to be here, sticky with sweat and hungry rather than skiing through powdery snow. Part of him had begun to admit that Ralf was right, that he couldn't do anything here, couldn't help to find Kristoffer and Eva, but he wasn't ready to accept it yet.

He caught the *slap-slap* of someone walking fast towards him in sandals, and before he could lift his eyes he heard his name.

"Hi, Carl."

"Hi, Liv."

She stood in front of him with both hands on her hips.

"We're bumping into each other with remarkable regularity," she said, and he wondered if by now she'd rather not see him either.

"True." He tried to force a smile. "What are you doing here?"

"I went to see Luka's brother. Brought him stuff he needed."

"How is he?"

"Stable apparently, but he needs complex surgery which they can't do here. So, Luka is arranging a private medical plane to take him to Singapore."

"Good."

"How do you think he pulled that one off?"

"What?"

"A private medical plane," Liv said. "There are more important people in the hospital who'd do it if they could because of their political or celebrity status. It's not about the money – many have the means and everyone is scrambling to get medical flights. I've had several people call me – even the Swedish temporary embassy asked me if I could help find a plane. But I can't. Nobody can. So, who is helping Luka?"

She was staring at him, expecting an answer – and he knew the answer but just shrugged. He wondered whether he had made the right choice in saying no to Ralf. Would he be able to get a professional search team to go to the island? How fast he could manage it?

"It's pretty impressive, I'm telling you," she said.

Carl wished that the woman who looked like Eva was Eva. He'd sell his soul to the devil to put her on that plane, of course, if the devil was still up for the trade. He looked through the iron fence of the hospital car park, towards the main road, watching scooters weave in and out of a line of stationary cars.

"Can you drive me to Kuraburi on your scooter?"

He was surprised to hear himself say it. He saw her turning her eyes away and biting on her lower lip, and for a moment he thought she was searching for a polite way to excuse herself. He immediately felt stupid asking her at all.

"I think my Yamaha is too small for that length of journey." She tapped her watch. "It'll take too long—"

"That's fine. It was silly of me to ask you that, sorry. The road is really bad in that direction. It took us more than four hours from Perl Village yesterday. And you need to go there and get back, which is at least half a day. You must have better things to do. I'll wait for my driver; he should be here any minute."

She tried to interrupt him but couldn't get a word in – he was talking too fast. When he had finally finished she said, "But what we can do … My friend has a garage, not far from here. I can ask him to lend me his motorcycle. With that we could be in Kuraburi in two hours."

"Really?"

"Yes."

"Thank you so much. You'll have saved my day." He had hoped that something less banal might come out.

"Then let's hurry." She clapped her hands together. "I don't have a helmet for you now but it's only five minutes' drive and I can borrow one from my friend."

"Wait a moment."

Carl pulled his pen from a pocket of his backpack. He scribbled a message on the back of a receipt and rolled a couple of one thousand baht notes into a bundle. He leaned in through the driver's window and pushed the roll into a hole in the upholstery of the driver's seat.

Liv had already retrieved her scooter and was waiting by the pickup.

"I hope nobody finds that," she said.

"I'll call him later. He's a very nice guy." Carl felt a twinge of sadness for not saying goodbye to Nok.

He hopped on the scooter behind Liv and instantly took in the intoxicating scent of jasmine. He stared at the tiny droplets of perspiration on the smooth skin between her shoulder blades. He felt almost dizzy, not from her sweet, rich smell but from being so close to her. He wanted to trace with his fingers the lines of her back, her shoulders and her exquisitely long neck. He wanted to know every inch of her body.

"Where do I put my feet?" Carl moved back from her as much as the seat allowed and grabbed the handles at the back.

"Behind mine. But keep them on your toes. There isn't much space for two."

Liv turned the ignition key and edged forward, and he felt the scooter struggle under their combined weight.

She drove through the car park, and before turning onto the road she slowed down and stopped, both feet on the ground, waiting for the right time to get into the flow of traffic.

"Keep your knees tight around me otherwise you are going to scratch yourself on something."

"I didn't want to make you feel uncomfortable."

"If you bash your knee, that would be uncomfortable."

He pressed his knees against her thighs. At that moment, his desire was so intense that his groin ached.

"Lean a bit closer – you and your backpack create too much weight at the back," Liv shouted as she steered into the traffic flow. Hot, dusty air rushed into his face and as she accelerated, his T-shirt flapped in the wind and the sweat dried from his body.

Liv navigated between lines of cars waiting for a green light, but when the lights changed most of the motorcycles and scooters overtook her and they were left behind. She turned into a narrow side street between mouldy concrete walls and reeking gutters, rats scattering from under the wheels.

They emerged onto a three-lane highway full of exhaust fumes, but Carl preferred it to the stench from the gutters, which reminded him of the acrid smell of decomposing flesh. They passed a line of small shops that had seen better days, then a Shell petrol station, and Liv stopped in front of a two-storey motorcycle shop with windows so covered by promotional and marketing posters that it was impossible to see inside. She said something in Thai to a man washing the forecourt.

"This is my friend's place," she said.

She drove through the half-open iron gates and parked the scooter in the shade of a lush bush with clusters of flowers the colour of strawberry jam. In the centre of the yard there was a low fountain with a half-filled basin of water containing a little carpet of floating pistia, which Carl used to grow unsuccessfully under a desk lamp in his fish tank in Finspång. A rusted pipe hung over the centre of the basin.

The garage was much deeper than it seemed from outside. The ceiling was high, with five large round lamps hanging on cords from the middle joist. A row of motorcycles half-covered with tarpaulins stood along the back wall, and the three remaining walls were covered with steel shelves holding an apparently random assortment of spare parts and bits of engine.

There was a retro-style red cabriolet in the middle of the floor with a man's hairy legs sticking from under the body. A Thai with a lotus tattoo on the back of his shaven head was rummaging through a box of tools beside him.

Liv tiptoed closer, got the attention of the Thai worker and put her finger to her lips.

"Where is Marco? It's time to pay his debt," she said in a deep voice. The Thai covered his mouth with both hands and his skinny body shook.

"Only in exchange for your soul, Liv," a gravelly voice answered from under the cabriolet. A man with broad shoulders and a triangular sweat patch above his ripped and filthy T-shirt, slid from under the car. He had dark hair and long curved brows which accentuated his almond-shaped black eyes. He was like something from *Men's Health*, and for a brief moment Carl felt a twinge of jealousy as Liv smiled at him, her eyes sparkling.

"How did you guess it was me?"

"Oh, it was hard," he said, wiping his hands on a grimy cloth and glancing at Carl.

"Hello." Carl put out his hand.

Marco simply nodded, rubbing the cloth around the tip of his index finger and then his thumb, black with oil. Liv squatted beside him and leaned forward, bringing her lips very close to his cheek but leaving the kiss in the air.

"I really need one of your motorcycles," she said, in the voice she clearly reserved for asking a big favour.

"*Really* need it? Why?"

"I need to drive my friend to Kuraburi as soon as possible. I'll bring it back to you tonight. I'll leave my Yamaha as a guarantee."

"That rattle bucket?" Marco stood and reached out an arm to help her up. He took her shoulders in his hands and, with the genuine care of a true friend – which Carl immediately liked about him – said, "The road is not in a good state through Kao Lak. Stones, debris, ditches that weren't even there before. You can't go at any speed. It's dangerous."

"I'll be very careful," she said, more quietly than usual.

Marco brought his face closer to hers. "Can you handle it?"

"Of course."

He sighed. "Which one do you want?"

"The Kawasaki, like last time?" She pointed at a shiny grey motorcycle with a slick line on the engine casing and a wolf's head on the tank. It looked like one of the racing beasts that Carl and Luka used to watch outside London. Carl wished he'd waited longer for Nok.

"No. Last time you scratched it. It's too heavy for you, I told you that. Plus, you haven't driven it with a pillion passenger, which is even trickier. Trust me."

"I'm sure I'll figure it out. Please?"

"No," he said firmly, and Carl felt relieved. "You can take my old Suzuki."

Liv rolled her eyes and crossed her arms.

Marco walked to the far corner of the garage and lifted the cover from another machine. The headlights were shaped like the devil eyes of Japanese cartoons. He fired it up and made a circle around them. The Suzuki had a larger seat and fuel tank but didn't look any safer than the Kawasaki that Liv had wanted. Carl wondered why Marco referred to it as 'old' – was something wrong with it?

"It's a bit lighter and has excellent rider control. You'll like it better." Marco pushed down the side stand and stood away from the bike.

"But the Kawasaki is faster," Liv said.

"You don't need a powerhouse engine. It won't make you fly. The road is bad. Don't mess with it." He pointed into her face, then took a cloth and wiped the instruments, windscreen and seat. "Come, try it. It has a four-cylinder, sixteen-valve engine."

Carl cleared his throat. "How fast is it?"

"Nought to sixty in four seconds and two hundred in twelve," Marco said.

Carl gasped with genuine surprise. "And the Kawasaki?"

"Nought to two hundred in 8.2 seconds," Liv said quickly, with a degree of excitement that Carl couldn't share.

"Do you have insurance?" he said.

"I do. But it won't cover you."

"Are you sure your Yamaha won't do?"

Liv arched an eyebrow. He saw surprise on her face, and something else he wasn't sure of. Was it disappointment? Carl felt a weakness in his knees.

Liv walked to the bike, threw a leg over the seat and gently landed in a riding position. Her face lit up as she leaned closer to the instrument panel, listening to Marco's explanations. Carl watched the curve of her back against the hazy sunlight coming through the garage door. He couldn't help but admire her slim silhouette, the curve of her breasts, her long neck, the delicate contours of her face. She tucked a strand of hair behind her ear and played with the clutch. It occurred to Carl that she looked … fragile. Why did she choose to stay in Thailand?

"Speedy, go fill the tank at the Shell and give her a test run on one of those bumpy side roads," Marco said.

"Can I borrow a full-face helmet for Carl?"

"I'll find something for him while you are away."

"Do you think Tanawat would make me one of his iced coffees?" She pulled a cream linen shirt from her bag and slipped into it. It was a size or two big for her and the sleeves reached down to her knuckles. Carl wondered whose it was.

She looked at Carl. "Do you have a long-sleeve shirt? The sun is very strong. On the bike, you'll burn quickly."

"I do."

"Long trousers?"

"Jeans. But it'll be too hot."

"Okay, put this sun protection on your legs and neck." She threw him the tube.

Carl bent to his backpack and rummaged for his shirt. He took off his grimy top and rubbed it under his armpits; it stank. He glanced around the garage, wondering if there was a basin – he could freshen up a bit before putting on the shirt, maybe even clean his teeth.

"Marco, do you have a bathroom I can use?"

"Nice six-pack, mate. Oh, wait … eight." Marco whistled. "Ripped."

"Thanks," Carl said, and blushed a little, not because he

hadn't been told that before but because he knew Liv was looking at him. He felt a light tingling in his chest which spread to the lower part of his body. He tensed his stomach muscles.

"There's a shower and basin outside. No roof but there's a screen. The tap requires a bit of patience." Marco grinned and waved towards the sunlit forecourt.

Tanawat was bustling around by a two-burner stove against the concrete wall as Carl passed, stirring something fragrant in a wok. He nodded to Carl through a cloud of steam, then turned down the gas under a large aluminium pan and began chopping leafy vegetables. There were two bowls of rice on a round plastic table under a patched umbrella. Carl felt a rumbling in his stomach and hoped that they could buy a sandwich on the way.

In the shower cubicle, Carl hung his shirt on a long nail and turned on the tap. Nothing happened and he stared at the copper pipe, waiting for water. A blob of bird poo landed on his shoulder and dripped down towards his elbow. He smiled. Kristoffer always said that to be hit by bird poo was as a sign of good luck.

A trickle of warm, rust-coloured water came from the tap and Carl scooped it into his palms and splashed it over the bird mess before giving himself a thorough wash. The flow increased and he wondered whether good things were beginning to happen.

Kristoffer would certainly say so.

"I thought you'd like one." Marco handed Carl a tall glass of iced coffee. On the plastic table were three glasses of water, slices of mango and pineapple on a plate, and something deep-fried in a bowl.

"Thanks." Carl flopped into a plastic chair in the shade of the umbrella. He was about to ask where they got the water to make the coffee but noticed a gallon container next to a fridge. A large metal bowl with cutlery sat on top, clanging every time the fridge's compressor cut in. He took a small sip of coffee. It was made with milk, something Carl wouldn't normally do, and was sweeter than he was used to.

"There's cold beer in there." Marco pointed at the fridge.

"I'm fine, thanks. Is Liv back?"

"No, but she will be soon."

"I have to ask – does she know what she's doing?"

Marco didn't answer straight away. He half-smiled and raised his eyebrows.

"You'll be fine. Just listen to her and you'll be fine."

"How do you two know each other?"

"Everyone knows Liv. She's a great gal."

Carl didn't know what he had expected to hear. Perhaps that she wasn't a kamikaze biker.

As if reading his mind Marco said, "You'll be safe with her, don't worry. She'll get you to Kuraburi in one piece. Here, try this fried banana." He picked a deep-fried piece from the bowl and held it out for Carl. "I like it with coffee, like a croissant. Tanawat is excellent at making it just so."

Carl bit a small piece. It was crunchy but soft inside, and sweet. "It's good."

"Have more."

Carl hesitated and then took another slice. Marco moved the whole bowl over.

"You don't trust easily," he said, leaning back in his chair crossing his legs in front of him.

"Meaning?"

"You don't even trust the coffee."

"What?"

"Look how you're sipping it. Like you're not sure if it's going to bite you."

"An interesting observation," Carl said, and cleared his throat.

"And true?"

"Yes, probably." Carl took a mouthful of coffee and was surprised to find that he liked the taste.

They heard the motorcycle and moments later Liv drove into the garage. She dismounted and strode over to the table, breathing fast, some stray hairs stuck to her forehead and tiny droplets of sweat reflecting off the sensual curve of her upper lip.

"Great bike," she said, and grabbed a glass of water from the table. "Oh, fried bananas, my favourite. Can I take a couple?" She picked up two at once. "You're the best, Tanawat. Carl, let's go."

"Slow down, girl," Marco said, and winked at Carl.

Carl wondered if Marco knew that he liked Liv. He was startled and a little confused to discover it himself. Maybe it wasn't what he wanted. It was the wrong place. It was the wrong time. And definitely the wrong girl.

"Have you done this before?" Marco said.

The three of them stood beside the motorcycle.

"Between the hospital and here," Carl said. "Apart from that, no. But how hard can it be?"

"It's not. But you need to know a few things," Marco said. "Liv, which side do you prefer him to get on?"

"Left."

"Okay, come here." Marco led Carl to the left side of the bike. "The sudden weight transfer can pull the bike to one side and onto the ground. Before getting on or off the bike, make sure that Liv is aware that you are about to do so. And always do it from and to the left side. She's the first to get on the bike and the last to get off."

Liv threw her leg over the seat but kept her feet on the ground. Even while he should have been concentrating on Marco's instructions, Carl couldn't help but notice she had beautiful feet and delicate ankle bones. He wondered how she would drive in sandals but he knew there was no point in asking.

"Do the same," Marco said, holding onto the bike to provide extra support. "And try to concentrate on the job in hand." He winked at Carl for the second time. "Now. Put your feet on these footpegs. Avoid touching the exhaust. It can get very hot."

"She should be able to support the bike without your help, so keep your feet on the footpegs when she stops – at a traffic light, for example. Don't be startled if the bike leans into the turn. It's supposed to do that. Lean into the turn with the bike, but not too much, don't push it. Your body will instinctively lean to the side at just the right angle."

"Where do I hold on?" Carl said.

"It's better if you hold around my waist at least with one hand," Liv said. "Put the other hand on the grab handle behind your seat. That way if I brake too abruptly you won't slide into me. We'll start slow, there're a lot of cars and traffic lights. When I drive between the cars keep your knees tight to my thighs. When we get to the main road I'll accelerate—"

"Let's not go too fast, please," Carl said.

"She won't have a chance to use all six gears, don't worry," Marco said.

Liv adjusted her helmet and turned on the engine. He felt a slight tremble in his body from the engine and wiped his palms on his shorts.

"When we're going faster, I won't be able to hear you," she shouted as they drove out of the garage. "If you want me to slow down, tap with your hand on my stomach. If you want me to stop, for any reason, tap me twice."

Carl wrapped his arm around her waist, as instructed. She was so slim he could have held her between thumb and index finger. He felt her tense her abdomen when he placed his hand on her stomach.

She manoeuvred the bike along the clay road, weaving between the dried-out gutter on one side and the ruts and potholes in the middle. He was surprised at how effortlessly she kept the bike upright, and slowly he eased his grip on the grab handle behind him.

Later he would remember it as the moment when, for the first time, he trusted his life to her against all his reason.

"One hour thirty-two minutes."

Liv pulled her helmet off and her hair tumbled out. She was going up and down on tiptoes, unable to contain her excitement. There was something adorable about her joie de vivre, even if it bordered on craziness.

"I'm impressed. Thank you so much," Carl said. He was gazing at her, grinning with his entire face.

She lifted the bike onto its main stand, beside one of the wooden pillars that supported the pier's corrugated iron roof. There was a strong fish smell in the air. The long shelves covered with shimmering scales were empty of fish and there was nobody around but a handful of kids sitting on a bench playing cards. When they noticed the new arrivals, they scampered away. Carl looked along the deserted jetty. There were two rows of fishermen's boats anchored in the bay, but they were all abandoned, the longtails anchored for the duration.

"So, what now? How do you get to the island?"

"I need a boat," Carl said.

"Definitely loads of boats – but no boatmen."

"Do you know how to sail a boat?"

Liv looked at him sideways.

"I guess I could figure it out," she said. "Do you suggest we hijack a boat?"

Did she mean to be so flippant? For her it was an adventure, but for him it was life and death. It irritated him. The elation he had felt on getting there so fast was subsiding, and all he saw was another wall in front of him.

Liv headed to the jetty and Carl walked among the deserted stalls towards the end of the pier, hoping to find someone. All was eerily quiet, but for the cracking of wooden planks under his feet and the rhythmic whoosh of water against the pillars.

Carl noticed a dog, black with white ears and showing its ribs, watching him from behind a bench. The dog began trotting towards him and he stepped back without taking his eyes off it. Two more came into view, as gaunt as the first, and headed towards him. He looked around quickly, but there was nothing to hurl at them.

He jumped up on a bench beside one of the stalls. "Go away!"

The first dog stopped and snarled, revealing yellow teeth, then began barking. The other two showed no intention of stopping. Carl climbed up onto the roof of the stall and stomped with his feet. The dogs began circling the stall, and a fourth dog joined them. It was the biggest – its ribs protruded under thin, patchy fur and two rows of stretched and empty teets hung low to the ground, swinging to the sides as it moved.

From his vantage point, Carl saw a man sitting on a stool against the door of what looked like a stockroom. His skin was the colour of rusted metal and he blended into the surroundings – if he hadn't moved Carl wouldn't have spotted him. He was untangling seaweed from his nets, but when Carl again yelled at the dogs, he lifted his eyes.

Carl jumped down and made a dash for the man, who rose unhurriedly from his chair and tapped on the door, indicating for Carl to stand next to him. He spoke Thai and smiled with his four remaining teeth, which were the colour of his skin.

The man stepped forward and flung his net in the direction of the dogs, cursing in Thai. They stopped and looked at him. He hurled a wooden bucket. The black dog with white ears licked his snout, then settled on the decking and put his head on his front paws, keeping his eyes on them. The other three turned away and slouched in the direction they came from.

The man pulled up his tattered shorts, pointed at the dogs and cackled, tapping his dry hand on Carl's shoulder.

"Thank you," Carl said.

The man nodded.

"I need a boat to go to Koh Phra Thong," Carl said. "Boat. Koh Phra Thong." He pointed out to sea.

The man shook his head and said something in Thai which sounded a lot like the curse he had thrown at the dogs.

"I don't understand you at all," Carl said, partly to himself. It was clear there would be no meaningful conversation between them. With some force, the man stamped one foot on the floor and yelled, gesticulating with both hands above his head. Carl guessed he was swearing about the tsunami. What else? As he walked away, the man was still scolding, shaking his net in front of him.

On the jetty, Liv was leaning on her knees talking to a man in a longtail who was pulling his handmade anchor from the water. As Carl came closer, he could tell she was speaking Thai but not, it seemed, with any success because the man repeatedly shook his head. He made to start the boat's engine.

"He doesn't want to go to the sea. He said his village elder had a vision last night of another, bigger wave."

"But where is he going?"

"He says he wants to get his boat out of the water. Last time many boats were damaged at the pier."

They heard voices and saw some men further down the bay, dragging a boat over the sand and then through knee-high grass, away from the water.

"Do you think there will be another wave?" Liv said, and for the first time he heard doubt in her voice.

"They say there's a possibility."

"Do you swim well?"

Carl guessed she was trying to make a joke, and attempted to reply in kind.

"I float," he said.

"I think it's crazy to go to the island."

She grabbed his arm with both hands, and now there was real fear in her eyes.

He half-smiled. "Crazy is going too fast into a tight curve. On a motorbike. With a pillion passenger."

"I knew what I was doing."

"I think I know what I'm doing too."

"No you don't." Liv swallowed hard and her words tumbled out. "These islands are overgrown with mangroves. Look, they start from this bay. What you see in the distance is not Koh Phra Thong, it's a mangrove belt around the island. What if there is a new wave? If you get trapped in the mangroves you are gone. If—"

"Kristoffer and Eva were last seen in their kayak, heading into the mangrove inlet."

"You are planning to go into mangroves and look for them, aren't you?"

"Of course."

"You definitely don't know what you are doing."

"Come with me?" For a brief, irrational moment, he hoped she'd say yes. He felt stronger next to her.

"No, it's too risky."

"I thought you didn't understand the meaning of risky."

"Okay, what about pointless? It's pointless."

"What is? To look for my friends?"

"No, to go to the bloody island three days later. You won't find them alive there, you do understand that?"

"So what do you suggest?"

"Perhaps just wait?"

"For what?"

She shrugged, and he shook his head and began to march away.

"Where are you going?"

"To wait. To wait for a boat. In the shade."

He sat on a bench on the pier, leaning with his back against a stall, and peered into the pale green line between sky and sea that was the island. Jack and Lucas would return sooner or later. He would take their boat.

Liv flung one leg over the bench and sat facing him.

"You know if we did hijack – let's say borrow – a boat, the challenge wouldn't be in using the engine and steering and all that stuff, it would be in navigating the shallow estuary waters between the mainland and the island."

"Maybe it's better that we don't *borrow* the boat."

She began plaiting her hair and when she had finished, she said, "So how do you know your Kristoffer?"

"I met him at uni." He glanced at her. "A place you think is a waste of time."

She laughed and slapped his shoulder. The plait fell apart and her hair swung with the motion of her head. Again he noticed her jasmine scent.

"I thought that you were going to say he was someone you grew up with. That you took your first steps together and went to school on the same day."

"Why?"

"Well, because there is so much dedication in your heart. It's obvious. You would sacrifice everything for him."

"Do you think friendship is measured in years?"

Liv shook her head and half-smiled.

He traced with his finger around a split in the wood on the bench between them. The wood was dry and dark – the rain and sun had both played with it. There was an ovate black seed in the crack, just bigger than the grains of sand next to it. He wanted to pick it up and throw it in the grass over the road to give it a chance. But he didn't. The wind knew better where to blow it.

"Do you think we choose friends," Liv said, "or do we find them? I mean at what point do we decide that someone is a friend?"

"Kristoffer used to say that we choose our friends. He said we don't choose our family or whom we fall in love with – all that happens randomly, on the throw of the dice – but we do choose our friends."

"Do you think it's so?"

"Friendship is about the choices we make about our lives, what kind of human beings we wish to be, and what we value the most. And so, in that sense, it's a choice."

"Or do we recognise something in certain others? Like a missing part, something we wish to have or to be, some indefinable quality that would be hard to describe even after many years? Are we drawn to people who live out something that we carry within us in embryonic form? Because a vibrant friendship connects you to your aliveness and reconnects you to your hopes and dreams and ties them all together in the most unexpected ways."

He nodded, staring at the feather-like swirls in the wood. Wood patterns were never the same, like fingerprints, like people. Like that day at university.

"Kristoffer asked me if I wanted to have a beer after a football game. To be honest, I hesitated. I didn't even know his name. Someone had said he recently got transferred from Umea University. And I had seen him play several times and recognised his skills. But I didn't seek to know any more about him, and I was surprised to receive his invitation. Then, before we even ordered our first beer, I somehow knew we would discover parallels in our lives, shared experiences, hopes and aspirations, and something else – something in the delicate play of mirrors that would make it easy to become friends."

A droplet fell on the wood and intensified the pattern of the grain. He didn't realise he had been crying. He cleared his throat. He wanted to say that their friendship wasn't conditioned by the past, it wasn't about where they had been and what they had done – it was about what was next, what was still to be accomplished. It was about sharing the future. He pressed his fingers into the corner of his eyes.

"You know," he continued, "university was my first grown-up choice, where for the first time I chose to spend time with likeminded people who shared the same life goals. If you think about it, we are born in some random area of town we may like or dislike, and we become friends with our neighbours' kids or our parents' friends' kids. Then we go to the local school and make a few friends there. But can we say it was really our choice to become a friend of John's, or Joanna's, or Josephine's, or was it more about the limited choice of playmates and a basic need to socialise?"

"I have a close friend from the age of three," Liv said. "Don't dismiss childhood friends."

"She gives you a certain comfort, right?"

"Yes, she knew me even before I remember myself."

"But does she really know who you are now?"

She shrugged and threw her head back. "I'm not sure I know myself."

"I have a childhood friend like that too. Most of us do. I think the critical thing is whether you make a positive decision to stay friends with them twenty years later, right? I'm sure you had more than one friend as a child but how many remained friends you actively seek to be with? For me, university was a place where I learned about grown-up friendships. You don't focus on similarities from the past – you search for shared space in the future."

"I did go to university you know," Liv said. "But I dropped out after a year. I just didn't feel I needed it."

Carl opened a bottle of water and drank until its thin plastic sides drew in, then he let it go and it crackled, searching for its original shape.

"I think, in true friendship, we are more ourselves than at any other time," Liv said. "There is no concern about whether love is returned, there's more space, more freedom."

She moved her fingers in the air as if tapping the keys of an imaginary piano, then glanced at Carl, smiling only with the corners of her eyes.

"Do you think," Carl said, "that love is the opposite of friendship?"

He almost choked as he spoke the word. He looked away. Why would he ask that? Why would he ask *her*? But he had asked her, and he wanted her answer. He felt her eyes on him but couldn't bring himself to look at her and continued staring into the distance, his heart pounding so hard that he could barely breathe.

"Nothing is the opposite of love," she said finally, and then added with slow deliberation, "Except common sense."

A Thai man rode up on a bicycle, left it on the pier near Liv's motorcycle and descended the wooden steps to the water's edge. He began pulling in an inflatable boat that was tied by rope to the stair rail.

They rushed down the steps and Carl said, without introduction, "I need to go to Koh Phra Thong. Can you get me there? I can pay well."

"No, no, no." The man shook his head and waved them away.

"Ten thousand baht," Carl said.

The man's face tightened. He looked furtively to left and right, and then slowly headed up the steps. It seemed to Carl that if he and Liv hadn't been blocking his escape, he would have run for his bicycle. The man cursed and turned his narrow back to them, balancing on the edge of the steps. Carl wondered if he might jump into the water.

Liv stepped around Carl and spoke in Thai to the man. He ignored her, silently unwinding his rope from around the rail. After a while, he started responding to her, at first in short lines and then in a long monologue in high-pitched tones, but he never took his eyes from Carl. Carl watched them, all the while knowing that the man wouldn't take him to the island.

"He is sure that you are an evil spirit who tried to seduce him with big money, to take him to the bottom of the sea," Liv said as the man stepped into the dinghy and pushed off.

"Are you serious? Their superstitions are out of this world. Literally."

"They're all terrified. He said there are hundreds of dead floating around Koh Phra Thong."

Carl sighed. "Sooner or later there'll be a sane boatman to take me to the island."

"Carl …"

Liv stepped closer, filling his field of vision, her silhouette framed by the sun and the shimmering sea behind her.

"I need to go." She rubbed her arms. "Sorry. I have to leave you alone, waiting for your lucky boat."

He felt a sudden prickling in the middle of his chest.

"Of course, you should go. Thank you for driving me here."

"You're welcome." She was gazing steadily at him. The intense blue around her pupils, a cobalt blue he had only ever seen in the depths of steaming geyser pools in Iceland, was magnetic, enchanting. She squinted slightly, fingering the sandalwood beads on her bracelet as if wanting to say something more. He ached to know what she was thinking. A breeze from the sea blew her hair onto her face and she tucked the strands back behind her ears.

"Do you think there is any reception on the island?" she said, and looked away.

"Not sure. The two guys from the hotel, who went to the island this morning, their phones are off."

"So how do I find you if you don't come back?" She gave a close-lipped smile that quickly dimmed, and the blue in her eyes went darker.

His heart was somersaulting in his chest, his mind empty of words. He craved seeing her again and wished that he didn't. It was too painful.

She pulled a black marker from her bag, took his wrist and began writing her phone number on his arm. He watched as the skin absorbed the ink.

"It should stay on even if you're in the water – for whatever reason," she said. "Promise to call me when you come off the island?"

"I promise."

"You are crazy," Liv said. And for a moment he wondered if she was right.

She stepped forward and hugged him but didn't withdraw straight away. Instead she pressed her body against his and leaned her head on his shoulder. He felt her heartbeat, and the ground shifted under his feet.

Twenty-two

Carl met Paola at a conference in Berlin. They had seats next to each other and naturally began chatting. She had an MBA from Harvard, had just arrived in London from Madrid and was a junior at Goldman Sachs. He put a reminder on his phone and called her ten days later, suggesting a date at his favourite Spanish restaurant on the Old Brompton Road.

Carl thought she was a perfect match. He liked how people looked their way when he was with her. He liked how her presence reflected on him. She laughed at his jokes, played golf, ran marathons, thought the Picasso market would crash and knew more about wine than any woman he had ever dated – though he sensed that had more to do with intelligence and general knowledge than palate.

"She is predictable," Kristoffer said after the three of them had met for afternoon tea at The Wolseley. "She is too diligent."

"What's wrong with that?"

"She is too perfect."

"Come on. You're saying it like that's a negative thing."

"She speaks English with an English accent."

"I like that."

"Wouldn't you like it more if she'd kept her Spanish accent?"

"I don't mind perfect English. I wish I could do it. She works very hard to speak the language so well."

"Exactly, she works too hard. Don't you want her to have a flaw or two? To be real?"

"What you're saying doesn't make any sense."

"What I'm telling you is that you are going for the perfect, but cardboard, image of what you think you want," Kristoffer said. "Does she make your heart stop when she enters the room?"

Carl shrugged.

"If she is not turning your world upside down from the beginning it's not worth it."

Carl sat staring after the bike long after it had disappeared in a cloud of dust on the sandy road that meandered through the trees. He hoped that Liv would drive safely and that nothing would befall her on the road. She had a thick scar from her wrist to her elbow. She said it was from a 'small' accident last year when a Swedish tourist had cut her off on a motorway and she had hit the crash barrier. She said she had not been speeding – the tourist was driving dangerously, drunk or high on something. What Carl found peculiar that she called the Swedish guy a tourist. Was he also just another tourist to her, a Swedish tourist who came to Thailand and left a week later? He remembered how familiar she was with Marco and felt jealous of their closeness. She said they were just friends and Carl believed her, but he could see that Marco harboured a secret hope for more. Who wouldn't?

A striking girl like Liv couldn't *not* date anyone. It was impossible. He didn't dare ask and she didn't give anything away, but he was happy just not to know about that side of her past. All he did know was that there would be a long line of men waiting for her nod, and that it would be Liv who chose. Immediately, he felt a sharp pang behind his ribcage. In London, he was a catch; here, it didn't matter. It definitely didn't matter for her.

On the motorway earlier, Liv had accelerated to overtake a line of lorries, and instinctively he had pressed his body to hers and gripped with his legs for stability. Now, he felt a tremor inside, remembering not the sudden bolt of speed but the burning in his crotch when he had fitted himself against her, their bodies so close it felt as though they were carved from the same stone.

Carl sprung up from the bench, embarrassed by his thoughts, and marched backwards and forwards rubbing his temples with his fingertips. How could he possibly think about anyone but Kristoffer?

He checked the time, drank some water and pulled his phone from his backpack pocket as if miraculously he might have reception. Then he grabbed a bag with fried bananas Liv had left for him, and began monotonously chewing one by one, staring at the thick black lines on his forearm. By now he could recite her phone number backwards and forwards, find the square root and multiply it by the same number.

Liv had said she was not planning to return to Europe any time soon. He definitely was not coming back to Thailand. What was the point of even thinking about her? They were living on different sides of the planet and had nothing in common.

A distinctive clattering *chuff-chuff* came into his consciousness and grew stronger. Carl stood up and searched the sky for a helicopter. A huge military rotorcraft was climbing into the air from beyond the corrugated roof of the pier. It hovered for a minute or two above the pier with a deafening blade-slapping sound and then slowly disappeared inland.

Jack had said that two military helicopters arrived on the island the day after the tsunami, around midday, by which time many of the survivors were beside themselves with fear and despair. Jack said they didn't know what had happened. There were two dry and functioning phones between them, but the batteries died before they were able to reach someone who could tell them any news. Lines were jammed and friends and parents hadn't picked up because it was the middle of the night in Europe. They knew it was a tsunami but that was it. They didn't know what had caused it, whether it was local or the result of a meteorite strike, whether they might even be the planet's last survivors. One American was sure that it was the Russians, the shock wave from a nuclear bomb in the Indian Ocean, and that soon they would all die from radiation. The fears were absurd but it was the reality of that moment. They were in a surreal information vacuum; they only knew what they saw – the wave, the devastation, the dead, the pain. Most people were missing someone – friend, husband, mother, child. There were six people in a serious condition and one man died before sunrise. Hardly anyone had slept that night, surrounded in the dark by unfamiliar, bleak and echoing noises. Cracks and splits and the whistle of the wind created the illusion that the island was alive, breathing, moaning. They waited without knowing what for. Time became a vague concept. The time was now. Yesterday never existed. And to think about tomorrow was even more terrifying than to stay in today. It had seemed that there was nowhere to go.

By the time a motorboat pulled up at the far end of the jetty, Carl was already there, striding back and forth, the planks of the walkway rumbling dully under his feet. He had first noticed it as a white speck against the hazy line of the mangroves, and soon after that he caught the engine sound on the wind coming off the sea. He had watched as the boat approached the bay at a low speed.

He hoped it was the boat from Golden Buddha, but he dreaded knowing what they might be bringing back. It was just after three thirty. Why were they returning early? Did they find all the missing bodies? Or were they empty-handed and had given up searching?

A Thai in a straw hat jumped out of the boat first and fastened the mooring line to the pier. Jack followed. Then Carl's heart gave a sickening lurch. Lucas and Marcus were manoeuvring a grey plastic body bag onto the gunwhale. Carl stepped forward to help, and he and Jack took the body bag and placed it carefully on the walkway. A tall blond man with a diamond earring picked up another, smaller, bag from the bottom of the boat and passed it to Jack.

Jack saw the look on Carl's face and said, "It's not Kristoffer. His name is Jose, he's one of the guests on the missing list. Another strong man who didn't survive the wave. Jonas found him three kilometres down the beach, half-buried in sand. We enlarged the search perimeter today."

"Whose is the second body?"

"Thai, probably from Pak Chok village. We found him in the same area, where the undergrowth is less deep."

Carl relaxed a little. This news gave him hope. Jack caught his look and gave a grim smile, didn't say anything, just gently clapped his shoulder. Carl felt stupid. What had Dr Green said? *We tend to grab anything that may give us the hope we're so desperate for. It's in our nature.*

"Jack, I want to go to the island. Can I take your boat?"

"Now?"

"Yes."

"This boat goes back to Phuket," Lucas said.

"Can it drop me on the island first?"

"No, it has to be in Phuket Marina before dark."

"That's plenty of time, isn't it?"

"Sunset is at 18.40 tonight. It takes three and a half hours," Lucas said.

Carl glowered at Jack.

"Don't worry; we can go tomorrow." Jack grabbed the end of the mooring rope and began winding it around his bent elbow into a loose coil.

"Actually …" Lucas's eyes rested on Carl in a flat, unblinking stare. "I decided that we wouldn't send a boat to the island again. We searched pretty methodically around the perimeter of the resort and found most of the missing. It's only three people now" – his voice fell to a whisper – "Marcus's daughter and Mr and Mrs Berg. We don't have the resources to continue the search."

"You can't possibly leave the island until everyone is found." Carl felt a rush of heat to his face.

Lucas sniffed and adjusted his Yankee baseball cap. "It's the third day after the tsunami. We cannot be certain that their bodies are even on the island. Perhaps they are somewhere else. Have you considered that?"

"I have. But I first want to make sure they haven't been left behind on the island."

Lucas threw his bag over his shoulder, took a rusted spade in his free hand. "It's up to individual volunteers to continue the search," he said. He turned his back and walked after Jonas.

Carl grabbed Marcus by his elbow. "We can go together. I have some experience with boats. If we can find—"

"I don't want to go back. I give up."

"You can't."

"I can. I've got Nora … I mean, I have her body, to take care of."

Carl glanced at Jack.

"Nora died this morning."

"Marcus, I'm so sorry. But your daughter – surely …" Carl turned to Jack. "I must go. Today. Please help me find a boat."

"What's the point? By the time you arrive you'll have only two hours of daylight left."

"I know. I know. But I still need to go." Carl brushed his hand through his hair, digging the nails into his skull. "I can't find a boat. Offered money, my watch. Nothing works."

"I told you, nobody wants to go to sea." Jack put the rope coil over his shoulder.

"So, what do I do?"

"Listen, Lucas is not just some asshole who doesn't want to help. We have gone to the island two days in a row. You should have come with us this morning. You'd understand what he means. Nobody can check the whole island. Nobody."

Carl was staring into the misty distance towards Koh Phra Thong, his legs dangling from the pier. The island seemed entirely out of reach. What could one person do? He had been naïve to fly to Thailand. He bowed his head and peered into the black water, between the iridescent patches formed by fuel leaks and discarded engine oil. Fragments of people's lives floated slowly by – a satin ponytail scrunchie, a yellow Crocs shoe with a Mickey Mouse pin, a plastic teat, a pair of black Calvin Klein briefs. He stared at the waistband logo. Could they be from Kristoffer's suitcase, carried here by the current? They both wore CK underwear, but Kristoffer preferred black and Carl wore mostly white. Back at uni they had made the waistband visible above low-hung jeans, but had long since grown out of the habit. The most popular underwear of all time, launched into immortality by the iconic Bruce Weber campaign shot of Olympian Tomás Hintnaus lying on a hot roof. He blinked. No, they couldn't be Kristoffer's. And even if they were it didn't mean anything, only that his suitcase had gone with the wave.

Maybe Liv was right. What was the point of going to the bloody island three days after the tsunami?

He heard Jack calling his name from near the bench where he had sat with Liv.

"I've found you a boat," Jack said, and pointed to the jetty, where an old man stood beside a longtail boat. Carl had been so caught up, he hadn't even noticed their arrival.

"Come on. He's Burmese, very familiar with these waters. He has agreed to drop you on Koh Phra Thong and pick you up by sunset."

Carl followed Jack over to where the old man waited.

"Saya, here's your passenger." Jack bowed and his hands met in front of his chest and Carl repeated the greeting. "Saya means 'teacher', by the way. It's a way of addressing an older, respected person."

Carl smiled at the man. "How much do I pay you?"

"No payment."

"I need to give you something."

Jack said, "How about five hundred baht at the end?"

The old man didn't answer and invited Carl onto the boat, making an open gesture with his bony hands. A linen robe was wrapped around his shrunken body and tied with a rope around his waist. His lips were dry and almost invisible on his tanned and deeply wrinkled face, and his dark eyes gazed out from under heavy lids, radiating blissful peace.

"The boat is old," Carl said.

Whole sections of the top strakes had turned to dry sponge, the paint peeled off. Red, blue and white chiffon scarves had been wrapped around the prow and seemed to serve to hold it together rather than to protect against the perils of the sea.

"You'll be fine. He knows what he's doing – he's been at it long enough." Jack fumbled in his pocket for a pack of cigarettes. "Beats swimming anyway."

"Thank you for finding him." Carl offered his hand.

"Stay safe." Jack ignored his hand and hugged him. Something in Jack reminded Carl of Kristoffer – the way he cared about strangers, his way of being. Above all, how much he missed his friend. He blinked back a tear.

"I don't understand why, if people saw the wave coming, they didn't run," he said.

"It was the opposite. Yes, we saw the wave but there was no comprehension of what was going to happen next. People were like moths to a flame. The pull of the unknown overcame all caution. Besides, waves always stopped before they reached the beach, even the biggest. Why wouldn't they now?"

Carl threw his backpack into the boat.

"How long will it take us to get to the island?" Carl sat on a plank in the bow, trying to keep his feet out of the water that sloshed between the wooden beams.

"We won't go fast," Saya said, perching himself on a wooden seat beside the motor.

"Why?" Carl held onto the gunwhale, steadying himself against the rocking motion.

"You will see."

The old man turned on the engine, using his bare feet to control the long lever that held the propeller under the water. The boat began slowly sliding away, and in just a few minutes the bay and the pier were a narrow line.

"What is your name?"

"Carl."

"Carl, why do you go to the island?"

"I'm looking for my friend. He was there when the tsunami hit."

"Do you not know that everyone left the island? That they have collected all the bodies already?" Saya spoke in a soft voice. His English was good but he tended to lengthen his vowels, which made it difficult to follow him.

"That's what they tell me," Carl said. "But his body has still not been found."

"And you think you will find him?"

"Yes."

"Why?"

"Because that's what I came here for."

"It may happen that his body will never be found. That's the sea."

"Why do you tell me that?" Carl took off his sunglasses and looked into Saya's face. It was expressionless. He gazed straight ahead, and Carl felt goosebumps on his skin despite the heat. He had an uneasy feeling, a tremble in his stomach.

"Because the sea gives and takes."

"And?"

"Nobody can fight the sea. It would be like fighting the wind. Or destiny."

"I don't believe in destiny. I don't believe what I can't see."

"But you believe in the wind even if you don't see it."

"I feel it."

"Don't you feel destiny's touch sometimes?"

"No."

"What do you believe in then?"

"I don't believe it was my friends' destiny to die in the tsunami."

"But what do you believe in?"

"I believe in facts. Raw facts. I believe in probabilities. The tsunami was a natural disaster which will happen again and again. Eruptions and earthquakes have been forming and reforming the Earth for millions of years—"

"So, there was a purpose to this tsunami?"

"No." Carl shook his head. "My friends were very unlucky to be on the island, to be caught in the wave. Things are the way they are and not the way we want them to be in order to feel comforted. I count on my common sense instead of dwelling in illusions."

Saya smiled. "Common sense tells us the Earth is flat."

Carl rolled his eyes.

"The judgement of the intellect might be only half of the truth," Saya said.

"Maybe. What does it change?"

"You're young. But time slips by faster than water. One day you'll look back at your life and see a chain of events. You will ask who composed that chain."

"Tell me, then. Who?" Carl said flatly. The wind picked up his shirt.

"Your whole life is composed of the will that is within you." Saya touched Carl's chest with the tips of his fingers. Carl shivered.

"What did you like about your friend?"

"Everything. He was the best among us."

Carl had raised a toast to his friends. All his close friends, he said, were better people than himself, they all had virtues he would wish for. Kristoffer vehemently disagreed – he didn't like that Carl even considered that anyone else might be better than him. But for Carl, it made sense that he chose to be with people who had more humanity than he did, so that eventually he could learn from them. He had never seen Kristoffer so cross.

"My grandfather was a fisherman," Saya said. "We lived in a small village on the Burma coast. When I was a small boy, he often took me to sea with him. I loved it. I loved him. He always told me stories that he learned from his own grandfather, about the sea, about what lay behind the ordinary appearance of things. One morning he went to sea and never came back. We never knew what happened to him and his boat was never found."

They were heading into the bottleneck channel between the two islands. Inhabited Koh Ra was to the right, a long, narrow island of rocky hills overgrown with jungle. To the left was low-lying Koh Phra Thong, almost split in two by a channel and its dozens of tributaries that weaved through the mangrove forest on its eastern shore. The bright green mangrove trees stretched far into the shallow estuary.

A deserted dune at the north end of the island was slowly coming into view. Was that where Pak Chok village used to be? The more Carl had asked for a boat to the island at the pier, the more bizarre were the stories he heard in response. Someone said he saw a body covered in crabs at low water; another fisherman said that he saw a gigantic, man-size crab near the mangroves; and someone else that the crab had tried to overturn his boat. By such means are legends born, thought Carl.

"Now, every time I go to sea, I feel like I have found my grandfather. When I sail, I feel I am in his hands."

Saya reduced speed and Carl tensed. It was low tide and the water was particularly shallow in the channel. At one point he thought he felt the boat scratch the bottom. But Saya didn't notice anything or simply didn't show it, calmly steering through a raft of broken furniture.

"My grandfather is the sea. I told him all the suffering I had in my life on the Earth and he told me to leave it behind and stay in the sea to cure myself. There is something healing in the water. You can never step into the same water twice."

Now the channel was behind them. Saya explained that he couldn't stray too close to the island as it was near low water, and turned the boat towards the open sea.

"I went to sea for an answer and I found one. Have you ever been far out in the ocean, where you don't see land anymore? Where there's just an endless horizon line?"

Carl looked ahead at the rich, shimmering cobalt and nodded.

"The horizon is the illusion of sky touching sea. And it's everywhere. It's in front of you; it's behind you. It's where you came from and where you are going. You experience this meeting point with your eyes but you know that the horizon is not the end of things. You know that you can sail beyond. Beyond the visible world. Then you realise you are in a circle. The horizon around you is your personal boundary line, illusory but nevertheless real. There in the middle, between the sky and the sea, before and after, you see and feel yourself – whether a meaningless grain of sand or the master of the world. It's up to your perception. But whatever size you chose, you are at the centre of the world. You *are* the centre.

"People go to Jerusalem, walk to Mecca, search Tibet and climb Everest. They believe that is where to find God, the source of energy, the centre of the world. Not realising it is here" – he laid a hand on his chest – "inside themselves. It starts and ends here."

Wind and tide were by now against the boat, and the waves were growing stronger. The Burmese turned the throttle to maximum and the engine's roar forced him to shout.

"People run away from their homes, their countries, their relationships, hoping to find a new life, a better life. But they can't run away from themselves. They are the cradle and the limits of their world. They are the beginning of their sufferings and end of their happiness. The person next to them cannot help them to become whole, unless for a brief moment. Their new home will have the same holes, the same leaks. Unless, again, for a fleeting moment."

Seagulls were hovering above the boat, screeching into the wind.

"Imagine the sky as your spirit and the sea as your body, closed within the Earth's extent," Saya said. "The sky always finds its reflection in the sea. The sea intensifies the sky's colours, feelings, dreams. When the sky is crystal blue the sea is deep blue. When the sky is dark at night the sea is even darker. The moon pulls the tides in the sea and when it travels the sky its path is magically reflected. When the sun touches the sea in the west its colours are beyond imagination. When the atmosphere brings the wind, the sea becomes restless. No one ever touched the sky but everyone breathes it in. Only the sea touches the sky, and only at the horizon line. That is what my eye tells me here and now."

A wave crashed over the boat's side, hitting Carl in the face. He opened his eyes. He felt as though he had dozed for a while, lullabied by the sea's rocking. He pressed his eyes with his hands and shook the reverie away.

Saya was turning the boat, heading to the Sea Beach on Koh Phra Thong.

Carl shifted on his plank. A bare shore, broken and twisted tree trunks on the sand, came into view.

"Where do I start?"

"You should follow your heart."

"Great." Carl curled his lips. "Anything else?"

"That is enough." Saya said, calmly gazing at him. "The world is just a reflection. Remember, it's not the destination but the journey that counts."

"You don't think that in this case, it's actually the opposite?"

"You came from a personality-cult culture where too many people believe that the world revolves only because there is a handle on the top which they personally turn. And if they were to drop this handle for even a moment, it would be the end of the universe." He smiled. "This is not so."

Carl sighed. It was easy for the Burmese to say. His life was in this boat, the old robe was probably his only possession. It was easy to be a saint when you had nothing to lose.

"What do you have to lose?" Saya said, as if reading his mind.

Carl shrugged.

"It's not about the difficult road," Saya said. "It's about the little stone in your shoe."

"What is that stone?"

"Your fear." Saya dropped the anchor. "You will find out more as you go."

Saya again folded his hands, dry as leaves, in front of his chest.

The light framed the old man's silhouette and Carl narrowed his eyes against the sun, which didn't burn his skin anymore, rolling down to the horizon beyond.

"Thank you," he said. He folded his hands in like manner, swung his backpack onto his shoulder, jumped into the shallow water and splashed towards shore.

Twenty-three

Carl remembered from website images of the resort that at the end of the sand line there was a row of casuarina trees and clutches of elegant palms, with the wooden roofs and terraces of bungalows picked out against tropical greenery and lush hibiscus bushes. Now, the scene reminded him of the body of a man he had seen in the Ban Muang temple grounds. His head was thrown back and his mouth was wide open. All of the front teeth were gone, leaving traces of clotted blood where they had once been, and only two or three molars remained. There was a massive gap at the head of the beach where the front bungalows and the parade of flowers used to be. Only a few wrecked buildings peered out from the jungle beyond, with missing roofs and just the stumps of what had once been walls. Some trees had been snapped in two and others reached their gigantic roots into the air behind a barrier of palm branches and planks and bits of furniture, all covered in sand.

Carl pushed absently against a fallen casuarina tree. It stretched across the sand and into the water, a headless giant missing most of its branches. The trunk was so thick that Carl couldn't reach even halfway around it with both arms. Its roots, like the tentacles of a monstrous octopus, were exposed to the air, and a vast crater had been left in the sand beneath it. He wondered how old the tree was. Did it really matter?

Carl turned to the sea as if he had forgotten to say something to the Burmese. His heart hurled itself against the inside of his chest like a trapped bird. He was afraid. He was afraid to go to the island. He was afraid not to go. He was afraid of finding Kristoffer's body. Most of all, he was afraid he would never see him again. He had set out to find him alive and he was afraid he might fail.

He stood watching as the boat disappeared into the distance.

Suddenly, Carl felt a light tickling between his toes. He looked down into the crystal-clear water. A run of little grey-striped fish were playing around his feet, pinching his toes. He squatted and dipped his hands in the water, trying to catch them. They slipped between his fingers.

"Maybe everything will be alright," he said aloud, and splashed water on his face. He straightened up and walked towards the dunes.

Towards the north, to the left, the beach ended in a steep rocky hill, whose slopes ran like a cape into the sea.

"Hornbill Hill," he said.

He opened his map of the resort and the vicinity, which Jack had quickly drawn on a piece of paper at the pier. The sketch included the clubhouse near the hill and from there the two lines of bungalows – one along the beach and another behind, a little into the jungle. Although most of the houses no longer existed, Jack counted the spaces where they had once stood, marking them with dots on the map. With Jack's help he had put a thick circle to indicate Kristoffer and Eva's bungalow, right after Jack's, both still miraculously standing at the end of the beach.

Carl forced himself to lift his eyes from the piece of the paper in his hands and gaze along the shore. In the haze, the two houses rose as ghosts from the devastation that surrounded them. He felt a thickness in his throat and swallowed hard, returning to his map.

Little crosses indicated the spots where eleven bodies had been discovered in the course of the last three days. But Carl's thoughts were over there, at the far end of the beach. Why was Kristoffer's bungalow still standing? Was there such a thing as chance?

A year before Kristoffer met Eva, the two of them went to Egypt, got their PADI certification and for the last day of the stay booked a diving trip to Ras Mohammed National Marine Park. When they arrived at the marina in the morning, they were told there was no space for them on the diving boat. He remembered how frustrated they were, watching the boat depart.

The boat exploded only minutes later, before leaving the marina. Someone's unfinished cigarette had been left on the engine casing, and the vibration had caused it to fall off onto a row of fuel containers. The guy who cast the boat off said it wasn't their time.

How could it be Kristoffer's time now? Suddenly, Carl wanted to believe in tiny meaningful coincidences, in one chance against the odds, in destiny, whatever it meant. But why would they become casualties on their honeymoon, when Eva was pregnant, when they were both happy as never before? The choice of the moment couldn't be more cruelly orchestrated. That was not a destiny, it was crude randomness. Blunt and indifferent.

He couldn't take his eyes off the lonely bungalow. It was him and the house, staring at each other. The wind lifted his hair, and he shivered.

Jack had suggested that it would be worth exploring the creek deeper into the mangroves. The creek was hemmed in by dense forest and impassable shrubs far into the jungle, behind the resort, and then its various feeder streams continued into marsh and savannah further inland. The search team had checked only the accessible parts of the creek maze, abandoning the rest. Twice-daily high tides flooded the area, adding to the complexity and rendering the search both dangerous and ineffective.

Carl glanced along the line of the creek, overgrown with mangrove trees. From a distance, their crooked prop roots looked like an army of huge spiders marching on top of the water.

"It's like looking for a grain of sand in the ocean," Jack had said. But if Carl didn't go to that swamp no one else was ever going to go there.

Carl folded the map, put it into his pocket and headed to the mangrove creek. Marching by a mound of crushed concrete and rusted metal – what the map had indicated as the clubhouse – he spotted a yellow pool ball among shards of broken glass. He stared at it until he began to see double. Jack had said Kristoffer was the best player he knew.

Carl picked up the ball and wiped off the dust with his T-shirt. He remembered walking back late from a student party when they practically tripped over an old pool table thrown into a skip. Kristoffer had insisted they carry it to their flat in Lund, and Carl had agreed only because he was drunk … or maybe he didn't even agree. But they ended up with the table in the middle of their tiny living room. Kristoffer repaired two broken legs and repainted the frame but was never able to get rid of a wine stain beside the centre spot. They used the shape of the stain as the logo for a monthly pool tournament at the flat. Carl had been told that the table – and the tournament – outlived them in Lund at the student union bar, where the competitions had been held ever since they left.

Carl tossed the ball in his hand a few times, then squeezed it in his fist and hurled it across the clubhouse ruins into the jungle behind. A troop of macaques shrieked an alarm call and dispersed in panic somewhere high in the foliage. Carl ducked and grabbed a stone, but everything was quiet save for a light wind that hissed in the palms leaves above.

At Beach Bay, the shallows were jammed with floating wreckage and broken trees. Carl grabbed an aluminium pole from under a pile of wet palm leaves and trudged into the water. The entrance to the creek was no more than ten metres away, but the debris had cut off any access. With every tide, the pile must have mounted as more rubbish floated in from both directions. He leaned all his weight against two large branches in turn, but neither moved. He bent down and rolled a half-submerged tree trunk to the side, and it gained enough space for just two small steps. He glared at the barricade. It was pointless trying to get in this way. He hurled the pole away and trudged out.

On the other side of the creek stood Monkey Mountain, a long steep hill overgrown with banyan trees. The creek followed the contours of its lower edge, and Carl wondered if he could get to it further in, by coming at it from the direction of the hill.

He crossed the creek and grabbed a liana, pulling himself up far enough to get his foot onto a rock ledge. Then he reached for another liana, its sharp edges cutting his palms. The rocks were moss-covered and concealed by foliage, and it was hard to place his feet without sliding. His body trembled with the effort. He clutched a clump of thinner vines above his head but immediately jerked his hand away. A hirsute spider with a thick yellow body clung to a thorny tendril. He ducked and knelt down to take a rest. Jack had said that survivors got up the hill in less than a minute. Not from this point, Carl thought,

261

and wiped his face with the front of his T-shirt. The hill he had climbed in Kao Lak with Nok was certainly easier – but maybe it just felt so because his fear had given him a kick. Perhaps, indeed, that was what accounted for the speed of the survivors.

At the last stretch, the hill became too steep and Carl began to move sideways along the slope, parallel with the mangroves below, holding onto creepers above his head and placing his feet with care. The late afternoon sun had already abandoned the creek and the shadow of Monkey Mountain loomed over it, cloaking everything in semi-darkness.

He trod on a loose stone, lost his grip and sprawled face-down in the moss. Trying to stand up, he lost his footing again, leaving a long gouge in the wet earth between two mounds of moss. He tried to find a foothold, digging his toes in between small stones, but the soil kept falling away from under his feet. He flailed his arms, grabbing at thin roots and bits of foliage, pulling them out of the ground, the damp leaves cascading over him, but it was no use and he rolled the rest of the way down, coming to rest with his face in the marsh. The saltwater stank from decaying vegetation – the sulphorous smell of rotten eggs – and he retched with revulsion.

As his eyes adjusted to the dimness, he blinked hard in an attempt to still the swaying image. Twisted roots thronged around him – tentacles with wart-like sprouts that seemed to sway and undulate with a life and pulse of their own. He crawled backwards. His hands were sinking in the glutinous mud, and the trees' snorkel-like roots grew so densely that there was little room to move between them.

Carl reached above his head for a thick root covered in slimy, brownish moss and pulled himself upright, crying out in pain as the razor-sharp bark cut into his flesh. He tried to straighten up but there wasn't much room above his head, the branches forming a dense and tangled canopy. He could just make out the high water mark on the roots, roughly at the level of his neck, and an uneasy feeling sneaked in as his feet sank slowly into the mud. To get caught here at high tide here would be very dangerous, and he was still at the shallowest part of the creek. What was there ahead?

He narrowed his eyes, peering into the gloom. Anything further than two or three metres away was little more than a shapeless mass of vegetation. He glanced back towards the hill, and it flashed through his mind that he could still return, but he shook his head. He turned his back on the hill and faced the mangroves.

He double-knotted one end of the rope he had wrapped around his waist to a thick root and hung the rest of the hank on his shoulder. Whatever happened he could come back to this point and then up the hill and to the beach. He squatted low and began to work his way forwards, cautiously placing his feet between the roots that formed a tangled mat below the surface. His feet made a guttural, sucking sound every time he pulled them out of the mud to take a step.

There was no straight route through the thicket; the root system was too dense. He ducked and climbed and squeezed between the intermingled limbs and, pausing to look back, hardly recognised which direction he had come from. Behind, in front, to left and right, everything had become the same. The mangroves were a sentient, devious enemy and the creek water was a sleeping predator.

In the army he had been through several survival courses. One involved being taken to a virgin forest in northern Sweden, with no human habitation, just the wilderness on all sides. In a never-ending labyrinth of pines they had to orientate, to find food and water, to stay alive.

"I know what I'm doing," he said, and tugged on the rope one more time before tying the end to a branch well above the water. He wondered momentarily whether he had reached the point of no return.

After an hour and a half Carl emerged, waist-deep in water, into an oval-shaped basin about three hundred metres long, its far end snaking again into the mangroves. In the middle of the creek, the flow had kept the water clear of obstacles, forcing heaps of broken branches to the sides. The surface was murky but it looked possible to swim.

He waded into the channel until his feet left the bottom, then began a slow breaststroke, working hard to overcome the current. After a dozen strokes his stomach scraped against something and his legs became tangled in some unseen vegetation. It felt as though he was being dragged down and his heart battered in his chest. He thrashed his legs and arms, floundering on the spot, trying to reach the bottom with his feet. When he finally managed it, his feet inevitably began sinking in the mud. The water was up to his neck, almost his chin. Flailing with his arms below the surface, he touched something firm but slick. It was unstable but he managed to get one leg hooked over its rounded surface. Probably a tree trunk, he thought, but his mind was playing tricks. What if it was a sunken corpse? What if it was a hard, slick body, bloated, putrefied – even familiar? The blood froze in his veins at the thought. This part of the creek would never drain away on the tide, never divulge its secrets. It would be forever neither full nor empty, but always in between, in continuous silent movement.

He pushed off from the trunk and returned to the shallows he had started from. He gazed at the basin again. Now, it felt endless.

"Hello!" Carl shouted, and the emptiness returned the word with indifference.

Carl shuddered.

"Kristoffer!"

"… stoffer… fer …" This time the echo came back with the tones of a wounded animal.

To check every twist of the creek, he would have to spend days, even weeks in this never-ending swamp. He looked back. He'd hardly travelled a hundred metres from Monkey Mountain but it had taken him two hours. Two hours of struggle.

He stared at his lacerated hands. He clenched his teeth until he felt the pain in his jaw.

Dusk over the swamp was getting thicker. He must hurry back to the beach to meet the Burmese. He would return tomorrow, better equipped and with suitable footwear. He'd find volunteers to come with him or hire a search team if necessary, from Bangkok or even Sweden, no matter how long it took. There was nothing he could do in these mangroves alone. He found his rope and before following it though the thicket he glanced upstream again. A thin layer of mist had formed on the surface, as if the swamp was coming alive.

A chorus of cicadas filled the sultry air.

The sky melted into the sea. The island stood still in anticipation of black night. Carl sat on the sand, not far from the spot where Saya had left him. The sand was cool under his bare feet. The day's heat had gone and a gentle breeze was refreshing his shuttered face.

He stared towards the horizon. There was not a wave to break the mirror-like surface of the water. He was too late. The boatman had come and gone and there was little chance that anyone would pass by the island. Not this late. Carl threw his head back and let out a long sigh. How was he to get back? He had lost his phone in the mangroves, but he was certain it would have been rendered useless in any case.

He gazed at Hornbill Hill, silhouetted against the coral

red of the horizon. He would have to climb the hill before it got completely dark. It was too dangerous to stay at sea level.

Jack knew that he had gone to the island, but no one else was aware of his whereabouts. His parents, and Kristoffer's, knew he was in Thailand but that was it. Now he was just another missing person. Except, by his own hand.

Carl stared at Liv's phone number on his arm. He ran his fingers over the numbers, their edges barely blurred. Maybe they should use her pen to mark bodies at the temple.

"Don't create work for the rescue teams," Ralf had said.

"God, I'm such an idiot."

Carl clasped his face in his hands. It was sticky from sweat and cobwebs and he rubbed it vigorously.

His ankle was swollen and he pulled his foot closer, sweeping the sand away with his hand. The ankle was warm to the touch, and when he squeezed it he felt a sharp stab of pain. He must have twisted it getting through the swamp. Across the sole, there an open gash cut from heel to toe. He vaguely remembered stepping on something sharp.

Moaning, he flipped onto his knees, stood up and hobbled in the direction of Hornbill Hill.

Then he remembered his backpack. Before going into the creek, he had hooked it over the bough of a casuarina tree. He had everything in there: clothes, a thin warm blanket, energy bars, torch, a medical kit and a full bottle of Jonny Walker which he'd bought at Heathrow for a medical emergency or celebration, whichever came first. He had tied his sneakers to the bough next to it.

He circled among the trees in the darkness. He was certain he remembered the tree; it had a stump beside it on which he had stood to reach a higher branch. But in the twilight, all the trees looked the same and after some fruitless searching he gave up.

Jack had said looters were operating on the island – a number of things had gone missing from his own bungalow. So, not only was Carl stranded on the island; he had no phone, no passport, no ticket back home, no money, no shoes, nothing. His situation was close to ridiculous. He sat with his back against a tree, bowed his head and let out a long, low wail.

A half-moon had risen to the east, casting its bleached light over the foreshore.

Carl shuffled over to the clubhouse ruins. He rummaged amongst the wreckage for food. In the shadows cast by the moon, it was too dark to see much. He sat on a large chunk of cement, pulled his flask from his shorts pocket and drank the last of his water. A bat passed overhead, close enough to hear the dry rustle of its wings.

The top of Hornbill Hill was covered with sparse trees and tall grass. Carl wandered around, looking for a flat place to sleep, but everywhere was too rough or too steep. He climbed down to the lower ledge on the seaward side. It was a wide enough area, covered with polished stones. At some point in history it must have been at sea level. In a little scoop filled with sand, he found the remains of a fire and a pile of crumpled blankets.

Jack had described this place. It was the spot where he had spent the night after the tsunami with a small group, while the rest were on Monkey Mountain. They had kept the fire going all night, in case any survivors wandering in the dark should see it. They took it in turns to watch the sea; if it began to withdraw they would use the fire to try to warn the people on Monkey Mountain. Carl squatted and peered into a small hollow in the side of the hill. There was a lighter with very little gas left, an empty pack of Marlboro and a little green soldier.

Carl busied himself lighting the fire. The tropical night was pleasant but he felt chilled to the bone. He wrapped himself in a dirty blanket, tucking it under his feet. Every time he moved, the rough fabric chafed his wounded skin. He stretched his hands over the fire, as close as he could bear, but it didn't warm his body. He began shivering. His whole body ached, and a numb coldness was creeping into his heart. He curled up on his sandy perch, trembling with fever. He couldn't sleep and lay motionless, staring at a sky thick with stars like ice crystals, flashing and flickering. In another time, another place, it would have been sublime but now, the vastness was crushing. He had never felt so alone. So worthless. So irrelevant.

What was the point in being at the centre of the universe if you had no one to share it with? The sea, the stones, the stars, the whole world seemed neither benign nor hostile, merely indifferent.

In time, his eyelids became heavy and he fell into a shallow and troubled sleep, moaning frequently from the pain in his foot. A cold sweat broke on his forehead. The fever was getting stronger. The fire died and only random embers still held onto life, flaring occasionally in the breeze.

The cranes were calling.

In his sleep, Carl heard the familiar sound again, somewhere far in the distance. He forced himself to open his eyes and sit up. Light was already sloping in through the summer house windows – the gentle, soft light of a midsummer morning.

He fell back on his pillow, and the planks of his bed made a predictable creak. He closed his eyes, turning away from the window and drawing his knees up to his chest. He pulled up the covers and folded an arm under his head, breathing deeply and steadily.

Yet, he couldn't fall asleep again. Something within him was urging him from his bed and outside. It was very quiet, but in the silence he heard waves splashing on the bottom of a boat. Strange, he thought. In all his twelve years, he couldn't remember his grandpa leaving the boat on the water at night. Rubbing his eyes, he swung his legs off the bed.

Carl peered out the door. He couldn't see further than a few metres ahead – a pink-suffused fog was all around. He tottered down to the beach. The lake was still. Grandpa's boat was out of the water, on the sand. Carl stood there, bewildered. He could still hear waves tapping gently on the wooden hull of a boat, and the sound was very close.

"Carl."

He turned to the voice coming from the fog.

There was an old boat anchored just off the shore. Tiny waves were breaking against its sides. Kristoffer was walking around the boat, the water up to his knees. He squatted down, peering at a point in the hull where a section of planking was rotten or missing.

"I can't sail it anymore. Its time is over." He glanced at Carl.

Was it his boat? Carl gaped. He had never seen Kristoffer's boat in such a wretched state, the paint peeled off. He couldn't say what colour it was anymore.

"Kristoffer? What are you doing here?"

"I sailed here from Hjo." A broad grin spread across Kristoffer's face. His smile was so familiar but so special. Carl's heart lifted, as always.

"But it's too far!"

"In the fog, the distance disappears."

Carl kept staring, hesitating to come closer. Kristoffer was a boy, like him. His shoulders were still narrow and his frame skinny, like on the childhood pictures he had seen at his house in Hjo.

"But I thought we met in Lund, at the university?"

"We did indeed. But tonight, I missed you and couldn't wait until we grew up, so I sailed here."

"Good thought."

Carl sprung to Kristoffer and hugged him with all his might. They wrestled until both fell in the water, giggling and spraying each other with water.

"Let's repair your boat."

"It's beaten. We've travelled as far as we can together."

"We'll make it like new. You'll see."

Carl ran back to the house. He returned with a box of tools and a few new planks. Kristoffer already had a brush and was painting the boat in his favourite blue-green colour.

"How is your dad doing?" Carl said, and began to hammer a nail into a plank.

"He's good. But he's waiting for your call."

"Why?"

"I don't know. He wants to hear news from you."

"Hmm. Strange. Okay, I'll call him tomorrow."

Carl paused and listened to the morning silence. "Strange, there's no sound from my hammer."

Kristoffer shrugged his shoulders.

"Maybe it's a dream?" Carl looked around.

"Who cares? We're together."

"You're right," he said in a thin voice.

They tinkered for a bit longer, and soon the boat looked sailable again.

"See? I told you." Carl bounced his fist off Kristoffer's shoulder. He leaned over the side of the boat and toppled in.

"Come aboard, we need to get the sails up. We'll go around the world like we always dreamed."

Carl began baling out water from the bottom of the boat. Then suddenly he realised there was no mast.

"Where is the mast?"

A cold breath wafted through his hair.

Kristoffer dropped his eyes. A shadow ran across his face.

"Don't worry," Carl said. "We'll sail in mine."

Carl climbed out of the boat, took his friend by the shoulders and shook him.

"What's mine is yours, remember?"

Kristoffer nodded, but he didn't lift his eyes.

Together they pushed Carl's boat into the water and sailed into the fog. The beach disappeared in an instant and Carl couldn't see anything anymore.

"So where do we go now?"

"You choose, it's your boat."

"Kristoffer, it's our boat."

"Well, you are the captain and you have to choose your journey."

"How can I choose where to go if I can't see anything?"

"Trust your heart."

Carl stared into the gloom, turning his head in all directions. He couldn't even see the top of the mast.

"I can't see anything in the fog."

"The fog is not real."

"I don't understand …"

"Okay, close your eyes," Kristoffer said, and took hold of his forearms. Warmth spread from Kristoffer's hands through Carl's body, and he relaxed. "And now, with your eyes shut, tell me – do you see me?"

"Yes."

"Do you see the end of the mast?"

"Yes."

"Do you see the bay we left?"

"I do."

"Do you see the beautiful villas along the waterfront in Hjo?"

"Yes!"

"Do you see my old boat? Left at the edge of the water?"

"Yes, I see it. It's near a tree with huge roots. But wait. I never saw those trees before." Carl's teeth began to chatter, and he opened his eyes. "Kristoffer, we didn't tie it up. The waves took it."

"Don't worry, we'll find it."

"Together?"

"Of course."

Kristoffer untied the gaff and began to pull up the mainsail. "In every heart," he said, "there's a compass."

"That's how you found me last night?"

"Yes. You need to understand something. You can't get lost if you know who you are."

"Really?"

"Absolutely."

"Kristoffer, you are wearing your wedding ring."

Kristoffer looked at his left hand in amazement. A silver ring was around his finger, though it was too large for him.

"Who gave it to you?"

"It was always mine."

"Can I see it?"

Kristoffer carefully took the ring off his finger and put it in Carl's open palm.

"Eva's name is engraved inside – look."

"We always belonged to each other. Time can't touch us."

As he spoke, a wave came from nowhere. The boys didn't see it until it hit the hull with a crash. The boat tilted to one side and Kristoffer reeled, waving his arms in the air. He would have tumbled into the water but for Carl grabbing him by the shorts. The ring flew up in the air and fell into the lake. Carl froze and looked at Kristoffer.

Kristoffer went pale.

"I have to find it."

He peered into the water, and no reflection peered back.

"Please don't go. Don't leave me alone." Carl grabbed Kristoffer's wrist.

"Don't be afraid. I'll always be with you," he said, and gently hugged Carl.

"No, I want you to stay with me on the boat and sail back home. The water is too dark."

"I can't lose the ring. Otherwise, I'll never find Eva."

"But how are you going to find it?" Carl's voice was trembling.

"I'll go with the flow, wherever it takes me."

"But the lake is endless! The ring is too small."

"Nothing is endless and nothing is too small if you look with your heart," Kristoffer said, and plunged into the water.

Carl was alone on the boat. The fog grew denser. He sat there, numb, staring at the point where Kristoffer had dived. He held his breath. Tears were running down his cheeks.

"How will I find you?" he whispered into the fog.

Carl opened his eyes to a crystal blue sky. A fresh breeze blew in his face. He could hear waves crashing on rocks. He sighed, still caught in the web between dreams and reality.

His thirst was unbearable. He passed his fingers over his parched lips and glanced at the back of his hand. It was a man's hand. Time had touched the skin with a light web of wrinkles.

He heard the distant note of an engine, at first indistinguishable from the wind and the waves, then growing steadily louder. Carl raised himself on his elbows and stared at the great shimmering pearl of the sea. A small motorboat with a few people on board was passing by the island. He knew that if he stood up and waved, they would likely spot him. But he didn't move. He watched until the boat grew small and disappeared.

Carl's ankle had swollen more overnight and felt hard and hot. Gently, he wiggled his foot from side to side; it was flexible enough but painful. He stood up and gently put his weight on the foot. He yelped in agony and lifted it off the ground. Thoughts were flying through his head but he didn't want to think too much. He knew he was getting himself into trouble.

"The tide must be low now. Time to go."

He ripped a cotton sheet he had found into long strips and began bandaging his ankle, carefully applying layer after layer. From a flip-flop he'd dug from the sand, he tore off the Y-shaped strap and bound the sole to his foot, securing it by criss-crossing the remaining cotton strips across his foot and ankle.

With the rope – his only remaining possession but for the empty water flask tied to his belt – over his shoulder, Carl limped to the base of Monkey Mountain. His ankle seemed to ease a little with movement and he made good time to the top. Before going down into the creek marsh, he knew he had to locate the survivors' night camp, which Jack had described as being on the very crest of the hill. He hoped that something useful had been left behind – in particular, Jack had mentioned water. Carl passed his tongue over his rough lips.

The crest was between half a metre and two metres wide for most of its length, and he cautiously placed his feet on a carpet of stones and tree roots that moved under his weigh every time he took a step.

The camp area was a broadly rectangular patch halfway along the crest. The first thing he saw was a white five-litre water container. He lifted it and gave it a shake. Empty. He felt his head spinning and squatted. How was he going to survive on this bloody island? He could hardly go to the swamp without water. It would be suicide.

Why hadn't he waved at the motorboat? What made him so sure he would find water?

He hurled the container. It hit some lianas and ricocheted into the leaves in front of him.

There was a hissing sound, sudden and intense. He froze, staring at the swishing leaves. Of course, this island must be full of snakes, it was the tropics for God's sake. There were so many ways to die, and a tsunami was probably the least likely of them.

He stood still until the sound died away and his pulse calmed, then continued his search. Among the items of clothing and blankets scattered around, he spotted another water container. He nudged it with his foot and it gave a dull sound and moved only an inch. It was two-thirds full.

He picked up the bottle, unscrewed the cap and tilted it to his mouth. He choked at first, and water got into his nose and ran down his cheeks to his chest. He put the container aside and let out a great belch.

At the bottom of a banyan tree, he rummaged among aluminium pans, plastic bottles, empty cans and jars. In a carrier bag with used plastic cups and chocolate foil wrappers, he found an open pack of Oreos, the cookies were soggy and covered with ants. He brushed them off as best he could and stuffed them into his mouth two at a time, chewing like his life depended on it. Which, he reflected, it probably did. He chewed with his eyes closed, feeling something between pleasure and disgust. He knew from his army training that ants were rich in protein, and some of his army mates had even tried earthworms. He spotted a caterpillar on a stone and thought about it, but demurred.

He discovered a small can of tomatoes with a ring-pull top, and put it in his pocket. A second tin required a can opener. He held it up to his ear and shook it vigorously. Not liquid. Meat, possibly, or tuna. The surface was dotted with little dips as if someone had already tried to open it with a blunt object. In an otherwise empty first aid box he found a small pair of scissors of the kind used by nurses, with short blades and blunt ends. He stabbed the tin's surface close to the rim, denting it but failing to pierce it. His palms were sweating and the scissors kept slipping away and falling into the foliage. He gave up when the tin fell on the ground, rolled to the edge of the campsite and disappeared.

From among the strewn clothes, he pulled out a bedsheet. He snipped it with the scissors and tore it into four long strips, two of which he rolled up and stuffed into his shorts pockets. With the other two, he bandaged his hands and wrists. When he had finished, he brought his bandaged hands in front of his eyes, turning them from front to back.

He was ready for a fight.

Carl descended into the mangrove thicket. In the morning light, it was oddly peaceful. The bright green foliage above offered a soothing and shaded glow. He stood still and listened to the forest. It was silent but for buzzing insects and the scuttling of mud crabs through dry leaves.

Carl wriggled between the mangrove's stilted roots towards the open creek. With each step he cautiously twisted his feet in the mud to prevent them from sticking. His every movement through the watery maze was precise. He instinctively merged with nature as if he couldn't fight it otherwise. Today, the creek water was shallower and Carl was able to wade faster. He could tell from the glistening of the trunks above water level that the tide was still going out, so he had at least six hours before high tide.

On the other side of the central basin of water, where the mangrove bushes were lower, Carl fixed his eyes on a dry and skeletal tree. It was incongruous to see it dying, surrounded by water and lush greenery.

He worked his way methodically across the basin and when he pushed against the tree it stood firm. The trunk was hollow, so the tree was slowly dying from the inside. He grabbed a branch, pulled himself up, and placed his good foot into the first fork available, then climbed quickly up towards the naked canopy. Wrapping his arm around the trunk and standing with both feet on a thick branch, he looked around.

Near to the tree and over to his left the shrubs were low, not taller than himself. He peered into the bushes for signs of anything out of place. When the tide turned these shrubs would disappear under the water, so Carl decided to comb the area first, moving later to the huge banyan trees that framed the far end of the basin where the waterway narrowed.

He looked in the direction of the sea. At the mouth of the creek, the mangroves had been crushed and flattened, overtopped with wreckage. From the point of view of a proper search, this band of destruction presented an utterly hopeless obstacle, so far from heavy machinery and professional search teams. The only threat these trees had ever seen was the sea. It would take an army equipped with axes and chainsaws to make an impact on this accidental barricade and look beneath the branches.

The blue sky stood tall and far; the sun was on its way to the zenith. As Carl searched in a zigzag pattern amongst the low shrubs, there was neither shade nor breeze. Weak and lightheaded after his night fever, he found that the choking stench from the sun-warmed mud made it hard to breathe. He moved his tongue in his dry mouth, but no saliva formed to wet his throat. With shaking hand he turned the stopper of his flask and took a small sip of water. He didn't swallow but held it in his mouth. The flask was still almost full, and Carl didn't dare to drink more. With the tip of his tongue, he moistened his parched lips and closed the flask tight.

Carl hissed through his teeth and smacked his forehead. A tiny black trace was left on his palm. He had read about the sandflies, the curse of these saline swamps, that bred in their trillions in the windless habitat. He was their guest, and he couldn't run from them. They were biting his ears and cheeks, creeping into his nostrils, getting under his collar, even finding their way under his sweat-soaked shirt.

Were these the sandflies that caused leishmaniasis? He slapped the back of his neck. His neighbour in Finspång had spent a gap year in South East Asia, and his father had flown to one of the Indonesian islands to bring him home. Carl went to see him in hospital. Large ulcers seeping yellow ooze covered his face, arms and hands. The doctor had said that more than ten million people a year got infected in the tropics. But was leishmaniasis transmitted by black flies or sandflies? Or was it the black sandfly? Did the vaccination he got the morning before flying cover this kind of infection? He couldn't remember. His anti-malaria drugs had gone with his backpack – but would they help anyway?

Carl stared at the mud at his feet. His legs were covered up to the knees. It was the only part of his body that didn't burn from the bites. He dipped his arms into the glutinous mud and began spreading a thick layer of it up to his shoulders and under his shirt sleeves. He then applied it to his face, his neck and around his ears, leaving only his eyes and lips exposed.

He stood still for a moment, blissfully marinating in the decaying ooze, waiting for it to dry; and when it seemed to be working, he let out a howl of triumph.

The tide slowly turned and began filling the creek.

Carl slouched through the last few metres of low shrubs towards the half-drained basin of rust-coloured liquid in the middle of the creek. On the other side, enormous banyan trees with thick trunks towered above the water. He had to get there before the tide, while the water was still below his waist.

But the tide was running faster than he could walk, and with each step his body went deeper into the bronze-coloured water. He daren't look back.

He kept marching, grabbing branches ahead of him, pulling himself even as he was moving with the force of the water. The air was filled with the hiss of the incoming tide.

Before long, the tops of the bushes disappeared under the surface, and Carl was chest-deep in the stream. His legs were wobbling; the tide was strong and he kept leaving a foot behind in the oozy bottom, wrenching it free and falling forward, struggling to stay upright.

At one point, he glanced up at the trees. They were glorious in their calmness, their imperturbability. They were as high as Monkey Mountain behind them. They were the walls of a medieval castle, solid, immense, impregnable.

He swam, allowing the flow to take him.

Half-sunken branches clogged the way, and his legs kept getting entangled in an unseen mantrap of vegetation, the topmost boughs of the shrubs though which he had been walking minutes before. He thrashed with his arms, struggling to stay above the surface. He was in the middle of the largest part of the waterway. To get to the banyan trees, he had to swim righthanded, across the flow, but the current was stronger than he was and was carrying him inexorably towards the creek's bend, and what looked for all the world like a beaver dam – a great berm of branches and mud and foliage, in which he had no wish to become entangled.

Above his head, occasional vines hung down from the banyan trees, and with great effort he managed to grab one. But it slipped between his fingers and he collapsed back into the water.

Again and again he lunged for vines or branches, whichever presented themselves, and finally managed to hold onto one long enough to grab another, higher and thicker. Like a monkey, he swung from one branch to the next until he got amongst the roots and out of the water.

Carl flopped on his back, near exhaustion, making short, rasping gasps. He kept hearing the rushing water. His head spun and the creek, the trunks, the lianas, blurred into one. A woodpecker hammered somewhere high above, and soon all other sounds faded away. He lay amongst the roots and stared at the dense foliage above. Not a beam of sunlight came through.

Long, rope-like aerial roots hung down from branches, some reaching the ground and acting like props, others already matured into woody trunks that circled their ever-widening hosts. In some places, roots twice as thick as his body interlocked in a gigantic wickerwork that formed a vast and relatively safe platform above the water.

"I've never seen such giants before," Carl whispered, moving his dry tongue in his mouth. He felt like a Lilliputian, an inconsequential wanderer in the world he didn't know. He closed his eyes, his thoughts slipping away, and when he opened them again the tide had stopped running, the water was still, and the creek and its inhabitants had been plunged into a strange afternoon slumber, with only the chirping of unseen crickets and the occasional sound of a blue heron – a kind of music only found in the mangrove swamp – to break the silence.

He pulled the sodden bandage from his left hand. Mudlines followed the creases of his palm. The heel of his hand was the creek basin, the life line and others the narrow feeder channels further inland, and his fingers the giant trunks of the banyan trees. He blinked and the image faded.

"Sign of a long life," a gypsy had once told him when he saw his life line.

And where does my life go from here?

Carl winced; his foot was throbbing horribly. Every movement triggered spikes of pain and for a moment he wondered how to keep going. He unwound the dirty bandage to find that his foot was so swollen he could no longer distinguish the ankle bone. It was hot, an angry red colour and tender to touch.

Leaves on the water's surface started slowly floating in the direction of the sea. The tide began to leave the creek. It was late afternoon and the sun had already gone behind Monkey Mountain, leaving the swamp in lifeless monochrome. Carl took a wet but clean bandage from his pocket and began methodically binding his foot. Dusk would descend soon, much earlier than on the rest of the island.

When he was done, he took a closer look at the dam straddling the creek bend, at the wall of debris that had amassed on a bed of mangroves. He began crawling over the massive banyan tree roots towards the barrier. It reminded him of when his dad used to put him on his shoulders so that he could climb into the bowl of an old oak tree behind the house. Of the feeling, not that the oak tree was of unimaginable immensity, but that he himself had shrunk. He lay across the roots on his stomach and peered into the water. It was the colour of diluted coffee. He couldn't see into the depths but he did catch a glimpse of his own reflection, and was mildly surprised to find that he had grown a healthy stubble.

He edged closer to the dam. Bed sheets of an indeterminate

colour were tightly wound around branches and palm leaves, clothes were mixed with plastic bags, and a dead fish was lodged in the mesh of a sun umbrella's iron ribs. A red bikini top had hooked itself to the top of a mast and was flapping against the fibreglass in sync with the wavelets below.

"Kristoffer!"

All he heard in response was the whisper of the breeze in the banyan trees behind him.

Straddling two roots, Carl managed to stand up so that he could see over the dam. He hadn't realised it before, but the creek divided into three channels that disappeared inland in different directions. He climbed over the dam, taking care not to dislodge any branches, and managed to position himself at the point where the two narrower channels intersected with the widest of the three.

What now? He squeezed his eyes shut until zigzag lines flashed in the dark and his eyeballs began to ache. He glanced again at the crossing, spots and sparkles still floating in front of him.

He decided to follow the largest channel, stepping beneath and between the sculpted bridges formed by the enormous banyan roots. Now and then, there were still sidewaters veiled by lianas and adventitious aerial roots. It felt oddly peaceful, as though the tsunami had never reached here.

Pausing for a rest, Carl sat on a root the shape and texture of an elephant's trunk, with his legs dangling down, and peered straight down into the dark, almost black water. From this angle it appeared bottomless. He looked for his reflection but all he saw was Kristoffer, and all he could think about was how much he missed him.

A rhythmic slapping sound came from behind and he craned his neck to look. The forest was full of sounds – of rustling, of insects buzzing and strumming. He sat very still, listening, watching. A hornbill's call, for all the world like the bark of a dog, came from somewhere high in the canopy, and a smaller bird trilled in response. A toucan chanted. It was a full orchestra, with all the players hidden from view. He closed his eyes. Ants were swarming on dry leaves. A frog croaked, and he could hear the faint clicking of its sticky toe pads as it climbed a tree. He gazed in the direction of the slapping sound. The water was softly splashing against the roots as though against the sides of a boat.

There was a clearing among the trees where sunbeams were cutting through. He stood up. Was this the end of the channel? He dropped down into the water, and found it was knee-deep and the footing firm. He headed towards the light and emerged onto a wide shingle bank ringed with boulders, behind which was an impenetrable wall of jungle. Little waves lapped against broken planks in the shallows.

It was indeed the end of the channel. It had been a mistake to follow it. One down, two to go.

He was about to start back up the same channel, towards the dam, but instead he waited. Something was drawing him towards an old banyan tree to his left, and he took a step closer. The tree's branches were touching the water, like a massive portcullis protecting or imprisoning whatever lay in the shadows beyond.

A bird shrieked and flapped as if entangled. Carl shuddered.

He stepped carefully between the branches and entered a peaceful backwater overhung with a cascade of aerial roots. The water was perfectly still. Carl gazed around, and a cold voice in his blood told him to walk in further. He took two more reluctant steps. His knees buckled. He tried to take a breath and couldn't. He tried to blink and couldn't. All feeling left him and a steel hand seized his heart.

There, among the roots of the eternal tree, were two lifeless bodies, shoulder to shoulder, as though promised to each other for eternity.

Twenty-four

Carl was drifting in and out of sleep, in a room he didn't recognise. On the grey, chipped ceiling were a pair of striplights, one missing its cover and flickering continuously, and a squeaky plastic fan. The air was thick, stuffy, but he was shivering with cold. He tried to draw up the covers but his arms were too heavy to obey.

Someone came and stood next to him. He tried to lift his head but could only turn it to the side. It was a woman with dark hair, and she was saying something in a language he didn't understand. He wanted to ask her to give him water but could summon only rasping, half-formed words. She leaned towards him, put her hand on his forehead and gently pulled down on the skin below his eyes. The striplights were suddenly blindingly bright, but he couldn't see any better.

The woman adjusted something on his forearm. Normally, that area was ticklish but he didn't feel anything. Before he drifted off, he wondered if it was his arm at all.

He was in the creek water, fighting to swim against the tide, his body sluggish and numb. Banyan tree branches above him were within touching distance but he couldn't move his arms – they were not his. He tried kicking to lift himself out of the water, but his left leg was leaden and unresponsive, dragging him down. The flow pushed against his chest, making it hard to breathe. He held his breath and submerged. From the darkness he watched the branches gently moving with the breeze, and he heard the tune that Kristoffer always played on his guitar. Looking down, he realised his legs were entangled in mangrove roots. He must wait until the water receded – then he could breathe again.

He heard a voice but he couldn't make sense of the words, as if it travelled through the water, fragmented by the ripples.

"Carl."

He opened his eyes. Everything was floating. A man. A woman. A clock behind them on which the numbers fused into one.

His stomach heaved. He turned his head to one side and retched, but nothing came out, only air. He felt the taste of blood in his mouth, and rotten creek water. His stomach convulsed again.

"He's getting better," the man said in English. He was dressed in white and wore glasses. His face became sharper but Carl didn't recognise him.

"What happened?" Carl said, his tongue dry and uncooperative. A blurred image of a policeman, sitting on a coffin and filling out papers, floated into his mind. He was smoking a cigarette, holding it between his teeth in the corner of his mouth, and there was a dusting of ash the coffin. Carl told him to stand up.

"You were brought here last night with severe vomiting and a high fever. We—"

"Do I still have my leg?"

"Yes." The doctor sat on the side of his bed. "You are in one piece."

"Why don't I feel it?"

"You are still recovering from anaesthesia and we have given you morphine."

"Anaesthesia?"

"I operated on your left calf. You had a deep laceration in the muscle, and it was close to gangrenous. I tried to keep as much healthy tissue as possible so that you can walk again with the minimum of support."

Carl clasped the sheet in his fist.

"And will I?"

"I think so," the doctor said, rather uncertainly. "But I'm worried that the infection may have gone into the bloodstream given your high fever. We haven't been able to bring it down. Your blood tests will be ready tonight, though they will give us only basic information. You need more advanced blood and tissue tests which take longer, and there are no resources to do it in Phuket. For now, we have given you a tetanus jab and you are on intravenous antibiotics."

"Which hospital is this?"

"Takuapa. But we can transfer you to Phuket private hospital anytime you wish."

Carl looked around the room. Peach-coloured walls with a ribbon of dark mould running down one corner. Seven more beds, all close together. The man in the bed next to his wore an oxygen mask and had all sorts of plastic tubes and lines connected to a monitoring device. His left arm had been amputated at the shoulder. Carl couldn't make out the other occupants, but he guessed he was the only foreigner.

Still, he had no wish to go anywhere.

"How long do I have to stay in hospital?"

"Two days at least or until we see that your condition is improving – no fever and the wound looking nice and healthy. It's important I keep an eye on the progress of the infection."

The doctor had large hands with protruding veins, more

like a builder's than a surgeon's. Carl wondered how he was able to hold a scalpel or even scissors with his thick fingers. But he listened to him carefully, he felt he could trust him. He was like the huge bear his sister had been given for her sixth birthday and into whose arms he would sneakily cuddle when afraid.

"It's likely to be polymicrobial infection caused by bacteria, fungi or some kind of parasite. You have been exposed to seawater, sewage, mud, soil, sand, corals. Infection caused by waterborne and highly resistant pathogens can be very serious – it can affect the bones, even the brain, and is often life-threatening. Natural disasters produce odd combinations of pathogens with unexpected clinical implications for our bodies."

A Thai man went to the open window beside Carl's bed. He put his crutches against the bed rails and leaned on his elbows out of the window. He drew in mucus loudly and spat, then began coughing. The doctor cringed and stopped speaking. The man coughed again and again with great effort, spitting from the window until his clogged lungs were clear, then took his crutches and began swinging back to his bed. Only then did Carl notice that he was missing his foot from the ankle down. The air suddenly smelt like rotten ham.

"Everyone in this room initially had cuts or minor injuries which received rudimentary treatment on the first day, if at all," the doctor said. "Now, many are returning with severely infected wounds that require heavy antibiotic treatment and often surgery. Sadly, it happens particularly among Thais who, I understand, were for the most part neglected from the very beginning. And so, a new death wave is coming several days later."

"I wasn't caught in the tsunami."

The doctor raised his eyebrows. "So, how come you ended up in such a condition?"

Carl shrugged and shook his head. He had no wish to go there.

"Did you hear anything about a Swedish military plane landing this morning in Phuket?" Carl said. "I was told they were supposed to bring medical supplies. And to transport the bodies of the deceased to Sweden." Carl felt a lump in his throat.

The doctor shook his head. He said he had arrived with a team of German paramedics thirty-six hours ago and had gone straight into the longest shift of his life.

"It's good if the Swedes brought more medical supplies," he said. "More and more people are returning to the hospital. We are already running out of the medications my team brought." He stood up suddenly and adjusted his white coat, as if remembering that others needed him. Before walking away, he said, "None of us appreciated the scope of the calamity."

Carl wondered why the doctor had spent so much time talking to him. Was it because he was a foreigner and thus his life and comfort were a priority? Or did he feel the need to share, in a common language, his shock at the scope of the catastrophe?

The nurse changed his iv bag and reset the infusion pump.

"Do you have a Thai girl here?" Carl said. He had heard her speaking in broken English with the doctor. "Aeh. She used to be a waitress in the café down the road."

"*Mai kha*. How old? What she look like?"

"She is beautiful, so I hear," Carl said, repeating what Nok said to him. "And she desperately needed a bronchoscope."

"I'll check the register."

She said something else but he couldn't hear her anymore. He felt a surge of lightness sweep his body, and he closed his eyes. He was grateful to be kept in the half-world; unaware, untroubled.

"Hey, boy scout."

Only Kristoffer had ever called him that, whenever Carl had stuck his nose in someone else's business. He got the nickname after they were beaten by thugs in Lund when Carl walked up to a distraught-looking girl who turned out to be part of the gang, and asked her if she was okay.

Carl opened his eyes.

Jack sat on the side of his bed. The fan above his head was recycling stale air. The windows were open, letting in hot air mixed with traffic sounds and distant voices. The shorthand of the clock pointed to four. The long hand was missing.

"Boy scout," he repeated, and Carl wished he wouldn't because immediately he felt choked with tears. "Doc said you got yourself in deep shit."

"Thank you," he said in a thin voice, "for bringing me to the hospital."

"You look fresh compared to most of them." Jack scanned the room. "Sorry, this place probably doesn't meet your standards but I was worried that another two hours to Phuket was an unnecessary risk. They said they would transfer you tonight to the International Hospital so you can get better care, but you told them you wanted to stay here? Is that because it's close to Kuraburi?"

Carl took a moment to compose himself.

"Yes."

Carl stared at the two red string bracelets around the pale part of Jack's wrist, above his tattoo, just visible under his shirt cuff. They were new; the ends hadn't begun to fray. When Carl had first met him, Kristoffer had numerous string and bead bracelets around his wrists, which he had collected during his backpack year in Asia. With time, most of the bracelets failed, apart from one braided cotton string which lasted against all the odds. He noticed it when he helped Kristoffer with the cufflinks on his tuxedo before going to church on his wedding day. Was it around his wrist when he went to Thailand? The local doctor who examined the corpse didn't mention it in his record.

"I thought the mission was complete?" Jack said.

Carl shut his eyes and rubbed the middle of his forehead with his fingers. For a while, he thought so too.

"Did the van from the Swedish Rescue Services Agency pick up the coffins?"

"No. The bodies are still at Wat Pasan temple."

"What?" Carl propped himself on his elbows. "They said they would be using a refrigerated van to collect them last night and take them to the Swedish refrigerated containers in Kao Lak."

"I know. But nobody requested the coffins."

"Maybe the van came but they couldn't find anyone to release the bodies?"

"Carl …"

Carl leaned back on his pillow. "Do you remember I called twice yesterday while we were at the police station waiting for the death certificates, and they assured me that a van was on its way?"

"They will come tomorrow, or the day after. They'll come eventually."

Tomorrow or the day after? Carl was told that the undertaker would embalm the bodies before consigning them to the refrigerated containers. They had already decayed beyond recognition when he had found them two days ago. If he saw them in a row of corpses at Wat Bang Muang temple, he would never know them. In Kuraburi, the policeman who filled out the paperwork had asked him twice if he was certain that these were his friends' bodies, and Carl had followed Jack's advice and shown no doubt. Jack had also made a statement to the effect that they were the same people who had vacationed in his bungalow. New rules would come into effect from the first of January, Jack warned him, mandating forensic investigation of all tsunami victims prior to any bodies being taken out of the country.

Carl had convinced himself that it was Kristoffer and Eva. The bodies were male and female, they were the right height, and they had been found together in the mangroves behind the resort. But they had not been wearing wedding rings, which Carl found strange that the very least. Kristoffer always wore his ring.

"Has anyone found their rings?" Carl said. In his mind's eye he saw Kristoffer's bloated fingers, the nails almost disappearing into the flesh. It would have been impossible, at anything even close to that level of decay, to remove a ring without damaging a finger.

Carl had shared his doubts with Jack when they were loading the bodies into the boat to take them to the mainland, but Jack hadn't remembered seeing them wearing rings at all.

"Say again?"

"The bodies. They didn't have their wedding rings."

"Carl, nobody will look for the rings. Are you still thinking about that?"

"I had a dream about chasing a man on a bike. He was wearing Kristoffer's ring." He cleared his throat. "But when I looked at his face it had been eaten by worms. I didn't recognise the man."

"It was just a bad dream," Jack said. "Are you worried that the bodies might not be them?"

Carl half-shrugged.

"Did you ask for their dental records from Sweden?"

"I don't remember," Carl said. "I don't remember a lot of things from the last two or three days. I have been having all sorts of weird dreams. I often feel confused about what is true and what is not."

"You need to rest."

"And half of the time I forget that they are dead," Carl whispered, staring at the dirt under his nails, the dirt from the creek. Sometimes he thought it was he who had died. "I would take them myself to the Swedish containers, but I can't leave the hospital yet." He lifted his eyes. "I can't even go to the toilet on my own."

"No, you can't." Jack stood up. "And don't be crazy, it's not worth it. You found them, we did all the paperwork, so let things take their course."

"Can you bring them to Kao Lak?"

"Me? The police won't release them to me. They know me. They are quite strict about giving foreigners' bodies only to officials or relatives. They don't want problems."

"You mean even if I got out of the hospital, they would not release them to me? Even though they know I found them?"

"I think eventually we would persuade or bribe them, but you lost your passport and they would want to see that at the very least."

Carl lifted the bed sheet, rendered a faded grey from endless washing. He had on only disposable underwear. It was easy to forget that at this point he had literally nothing. He didn't have money to bribe anyone. He didn't have money to hire a truck. No money for a taxi to Phuket. No documents to receive a money transfer. No documents to leave Thailand.

"Jack, you do understand I can't just lie here and hope that their bodies will be picked up sooner or later. Not after everything I went through." Carl tried to keep his voice low, while everything inside him wanted to scream.

Jack walked to the window and peered through the dirty glass, covered in a thick layer of dried raindrops and dust.

"Accept it," he said, turning to Carl. "Accept that there are things beyond your control."

"If I listened to you and everyone else, I would be still waiting for an organised boat to go to the island."

"There's no doubt about it, you managed quite the feat. But you can't push any further. Not with the condition you're in. You know that a sip of water from that creek full of decaying shit contains more parasites and microbes than science knows. I'm frankly surprised that you are still full-on."

Carl clenched the bedsheet in his fists. He didn't feel full-on. He was in pain, he felt half-crippled and it scared him. Otherwise, he would already have found his way out of the hospital.

"Do you know any Swedes here?" Jack said.

Immediately Carl thought of Liv.

"No."

"You need someone with a Swedish passport so it's credible that they are a relative of Kristoffer or Eva. And of course, you need someone who would be comfortable to take responsibility for two bodies."

Liv.

Carl rubbed his neck. "I can't think of anyone."

"Anyway, Swedish Embassy representatives will eventually go and pick up the coffins. Stay and rest in the hospital until the doctor says it's safe to leave. I'm in the area – call me if you need me. Here is a phone. We should top it up if you want to call international, otherwise it won't last long."

"I don't have any money," Carl mumbled, feeling his cheeks burning.

Jack pulled cash from his back pocket and counted out four hundred-baht notes. "It's only about ten US dollars; sorry I can't give you more. Cash machines in the area are empty."

"Thank you," Carl said stiffly, and looked away.

"It's fine. Get in contact with your embassy."

Carl's eyes snapped back to Jack. "Wait. Do you think the coffins are safe near the temple?"

"Of course, why wouldn't they be? Nobody needs a dead body, there are plenty around."

"Thieves, maybe? Looking for anything valuable?"

"All the valuables were removed by police. Or stolen before."

"What if somebody goes there for a coffin? Drops the bodies in a ditch and takes the coffins? They are obviously in short supply."

"Now you're getting paranoid."

"I am. What if the monks decide the coffins smell too much and cremate them?"

"You know what? I guess yes, it's possible that something could happen to the coffins or the bodies. It's just that my brain is wired differently; I don't focus on what can go wrong. Maybe because I've seen the worst." Jack fixed his black eyes on Carl with the abyss of pain they harboured.

Carl recognised his pain. He had seen the worst too but he didn't know how to accept it, how to live with it. It was there in front of his eyes – the bodies of two people he loved, the flesh bloated, eaten by crabs and creek worms. He was at the bottom of the abyss and the light was too far away to see.

"Get some rest. I will keep an eye on your coffins."

Jack moved his hair back from his forehead. The long scar above his brow, which was raw when Carl had met him for the first time at Wat Pasan, had almost healed. Time had begun healing *his* wounds.

"Jack?"

Jack was already at the door. "What?"

"What is written on your tattoo?"

Jack brought his arm up and rotated his wrist slightly.

"Breathe," he said, as if reading it for the first time. "Breathe."

"Why's it written so that it's so hard to read?"

Jack gave a lopsided smile and ran his hands through his hair.

"Because sometimes it's so bloody hard to remember to breathe."

Carl drew the air into his lungs until his ribcage couldn't expand anymore. He felt lightheaded.

"Listen," he said. "Do you have a pickup or a small truck in Kuraburi I could use to transport the bodies? In case I find someone Swedish and crazy enough to bother with someone else's corpses."

"Maybe," Jack said, and walked away, limping slightly on his left leg.

Carl traced the well-worn outlines of the phone with his thumb. What was the point in calling Liv? He had managed not to think about her for the last two days. He didn't want to bring back that burning tension in his muscles when he was next to her. He didn't want that deep longing for something he had never had. But most of all, he didn't want to allow something that would never happen to linger between his thoughts. The only thing that mattered now was to take Kristoffer and Eva's bodies to Sweden as soon as possible. The refrigerated van would arrive today – may it already had. Carl wished he had a number to call them. He scrolled through the contacts on the phone, but only Jack's and Scott's names had been saved.

The nurse came in and adjusted his bedclothes. Without saying a word to him she wrapped a cuff around his upper arm and placed her stethoscope on the inside of his elbow.

Carl noticed her red, swollen eyes. She didn't look at him. He wanted to ask her if she had lost someone in the tsunami but decided not to ask the obvious. He looked at the bed next to his, at the man with the amputated forearm. He had no pillow and his top sheet was torn, and not for the first time Carl felt he was occupying a bed which could have been given to a Thai in greater need. Nobody in the room looked like they were here for just a day. He should move to the International Hospital. It was for unjustly privileged foreigners, but at least he would be freeing up a much-needed bed.

"Do you have a moment?" Carl said, when the nurse had written his blood pressure on an A4 sheet taped to the wall.

"Yes."

"Please, can you find me a phone number for the Swedish temporary embassy? Also, a pen and paper?"

"Of course. Anything else I can do for you?" A warm smile spread on her face, even though the corners of her eyes were still wet from tears. She was around the age of his mother, but her hair was still jet black and only the light web of wrinkles on her hands give away her age. She leaned forward and adjusted his pillow, then poured some water into his glass.

"Would you mind putting my phone on charge? Nothing else."

"There is a newspaper here. Your friend probably brought it for you." She picked up the *Bangkok Post* from the floor next to his bed. His eyes went to the front page headline: UN WARNS TSUNAMI DEATH TOLL LIKELY TO TOP 100,000.

"Do you want to read it now?"

"No." He closed his eyes and pressed his head against his pillow. He took a deep breath and let it out slowly.

"Sir, are you okay? Are you in pain?" The nurse felt his forehead and then lifted his wrist and pressed her fingers on the artery.

It took him a while to answer. "May I have more painkillers?"

"You've already received a lot today. I have to check with the doctor."

"Ask him, please ..." Carl kept his eyes tight shut. He knew that if he opened them the tears would flow.

"Where do you feel pain? Your leg?"

"Everywhere," he said through gritted teeth.

Carl heard a rhythmic tapping on the linoleum floor, alternating with the shuffle of a slipper. He opened his eyes. It was quite dark, only the broken striplight above his bed throwing its intermittent light. The ward was empty. Every bed had been left neatly made. The sound of the man hobbling on his crutch was fading away in the corridor. He knew it was the man missing a foot because he could hear him coughing and spitting, coughing and spitting. Soon all the sounds ceased and it became deadly quiet. Then the undulating, churring song of a nightjar, just as in the creek as the sun set, echoed through the empty building.

"Anybody?" Carl shouted.

"Body, body ..." came the echo. When the silence settled again, he distinguished the water's hiss. It grew louder and louder. He heard timber cracking, splitting, then the concrete wall crashing and the tortured sound of twisting steel.

He tried to sit up straight but realised he was cocooned by mangrove roots. He thrashed and wriggled but the roots tightened around him. He felt his ribs snapping one by one.

Carl woke up breathing hard, his heart drumming. The sheet he lay on was soaked with sweat. It smelled of decayed leaves. The amputee was sitting on his bed, the bedsprings squeaking every time his body convulsed with a new fit of coughing.

The light coming from the open window was pushing the darkness out of the room, the morning freshness obscuring the ammonic smell of urine. There was another odour in the room, very familiar, coming from the man in the bed next to his, and Carl wasn't sure what it was. The others in the room began to stir and cough, a few to moan. The man in the bed next to his was still.

The nurse came and asked Carl how he was today.

"I feel better." He propped himself up on one elbow. She handed him his phone. There were no new messages. Were the coffins still in Kuraburi?

"You don't have a fever today," the nurse said, filling in the chart.

Carl bent his legs slightly, then straightened them again. The left leg was heavy, bulky but he was glad to feel it, to move it. He slowly curled and stretched his toes, joyfully repeating the action several times.

When the nurse had removed the last layer of bandage, she soaked a piece of cloth in an antiseptic solution and began wiping the yellow crust from his calf, taking care where scabs had formed along the wound roughly stitched with black thread. The swelling and tenderness was now confined to the area of the sutures.

"Healing nicely," she said, though Carl was doubtful about the colour of the skin, which went from grey-green at the back of his knee to a weird blend of purple, yellow and green in the lower half of his calf.

"I do feel better. Can I speak to the doctor?"

"He will come soon," she said. "You are his number one patient."

Carl felt a reproach in her voice. Or maybe he imagined it. He hadn't seen anyone else in the room being attended by this or any other doctor.

A male nurse walked into the room and leaned over the man in the bed next to Carl's. He began methodically removing the plastic tubes and other lines. When he unplugged the heart monitoring device, Carl realised that it was already switched off, that he hadn't heard the rhythmic beeping since waking up, nor the hissing sound of the oxygen tank. The man's chest didn't rise and fall anymore.

Carl stared at his reflection in small area of mirror that had retained its silver backing. His thick black hair was streaked with grey and almost white at the temples. He ran his fingers over his dense stubble; he'd never allowed his beard to grow for so long. His black eyes were sunk into his head and the cheekbones were sharper, more defined. His lower ribs protruded and the hip bones stuck out, like the dogs on Kuraburi pier.

The grief had eaten half of his flesh.

He leaned over the sink, holding on with both hands, the toes of the healthy leg turning into the rubber mat as if holding on for dear life.

If Ralf could see where he had ended up just a week after they had last spoken, without means or clothing, almost minus his leg, he would laugh at him and call him plain stupid. He would ask whether it had all been worth it.

And Carl would say yes.

Holding on to the walls, Carl shuffled into the shower. Unable to work out how to get hot water, he stared at the taps, rough with limescale.

When the water came, the stream was cold and weak. Carl felt it numbly on his deadened skin. The only piece of soap kept slipping between his fingers, leaving no foam. He poured some kind of disinfectant wash into his hands and roughly rubbed his shoulder and chest.

"Can you help me, please?" he said.

The nurse was standing with her back to him a few metres away. He couldn't wipe himself dry with the towel, still less get dressed, and they didn't have any more crutches at the hospital, even for VIP patients like him.

The doctor had said a car from a Phuket private hospital would pick Carl up around midday.

A woman came on the line, her voice muffled as if she was speaking through a pillow.

"I don't have any record that our van is expected in Kuraburi," she said.

Carl felt his blood rising.

"Are you joking? One of your refrigerated vans was supposed to pick up the bodies of my friends on the evening of the thirty-first. Now you are telling me you have no record even of today's request for a car?"

He had spent the last hour calling between the Swedish temporary embassy and the Rescue Services Agency which was assigned to arrange victims' transportation and further assistance, but there was still no clarity as to when Kristoffer and Eva's would be taken to the refrigerated containers. He glanced at the screen of his phone. He had been on this call already for almost half an hour, mainly on hold, and wondered if there would be any credit left to make the next call.

"With whom did you speak?" the woman said.

"With Olaf, I don't remember his last name."

"Olaf is in Kao Lak today; I won't be able to get hold of him. But I wrote down your request and I will try to send our car to you as soon as it becomes available."

"Wait, you only have one car?"

"Of course not," the woman said sharply. "But only one in

your region. We will send it to you as soon as possible."

Carl stared at the ceiling. Before yesterday, when the death certificates were issued, he thought he had done everything he could and now it was the turn of the officials. He had handed them the bodies, for God's sake. Did he have to fly them to Sweden himself?

He turned on his side, facing the empty bed. His thoughts were sluggish, as if he was waking from a horrible dream. The few days since he left his flat in London felt like months. Here, time expanded in proportion to the wave and his life shrank in the opposite direction.

Carl lifted his phone, his hand trembling slightly. He dialled a number which by now had vanished from his arm but not from his memory.

Twenty-five

Carl heard the rhythmic squeak of Liv's shoes on the linoleum floor of the corridor long before she entered the ward.

He was sitting on the edge of his bed, trying to smooth out the creases on his T-shirt with his hand. It had come from the charity pile a truck had delivered earlier from Phuket. His shorts were XXL and hung below his knees. His shoes were big as well, but hadn't been worn. They couldn't find the clothes he arrived in but it didn't matter, since they didn't fit him either.

The sound of the steps stopped, and Carl looked up. Liv was leaning against the door frame, her arms folded. She wore an unbuttoned khaki shirt over a white tank top, and loose beige trousers with a brown leather belt.

"You didn't tell me you'd had surgery," she said, her brow creasing in a frown. "Was that because you knew that I wouldn't come to pick you up?"

"You see how well I know you," Carl said, forcing a smile.

"You lied to me."

He studied her face, looking for the moment when the left corner of her mouth would turn up first, unlocking beauty of a smile that seemed to radiate across her face to the tiny wrinkles at the corners of her eyes. What if she refused to take him with her? Fair enough, he thought. But he knew that she would go and pick up the bodies. That much he did know about her.

"I'm not that bad. I feel quite well today. The doctor said I can go, but I should complete the course of antibiotics."

"Okay, so let's go." She jerked her chin up. "Come over here."

He saw in her eyes that she knew he couldn't walk. She had probably spoken to his doctor already – and the doctor had not, in truth, advised him to leave the hospital. He had collected his antibiotics and painkillers from the doctor's office and had said that a friend would take him to Phuket International hospital. The doctor had clearly guessed that the hospital wouldn't be Carl's first destination, and had reminded him that even though the initial blood tests didn't show an obvious infection, he needed a number of further, more complex, blood tests since many waterborne illnesses took time to express themselves. The recovery he had been experiencing might not be the end of the story. Carl asked to take the results with him, but the printer was out of paper.

Carl got up from the bed, put all his weight on his right leg and dragged his left foot beside it. To take another step he would have to put his weight on his left leg, and he knew he couldn't. The leg felt numb, as though not his, and he knew that the only reason he didn't feel pain was that he was pumped up on morphine. He stared at a point on the floor between his feet. His right leg began to tremble with the effort. He knew he should not continue. He grabbed the rails on the bed.

"Come." Liv gestured again.

There were at least ten steps between them.

"I can't," he said, taking a breath. His head reeled.

"Why didn't you tell me to bring crutches from Phuket?"

"Because you would think twice about coming to pick me up." He lifted his eyes and then quickly looked away.

"That much you know about me."

"Liv, I'm sorry I misled you."

"I can't take responsibility for three bodies." There was a quiver in her voice.

"I can take care of myself. But please help me to take the coffins to Ban Muang."

She stood silent, gazing at him. Behind her, people were passing by in the corridor but their voices were muffled and the room became uncomfortably silent. The two men in the beds closest to the door, who would always murmur to each other, also fell quiet. Carl guessed that they too were waiting for her answer. He shifted back half a step and sat on the edge of his bed. He knew Liv was looking at him but he couldn't raise his eyes to her and he peered at the little bits of lint from the sheet that had appeared on his black T-shirt.

She walked to the empty bed next to his and sat facing him.

"I'm so sorry to hear that they are … gone," she said, and put her hand on his thigh.

Carl's throat swelled shut and he couldn't inhale. He groaned.

"Lean on me." Liv stepped forward, took his arm firmly and pulled him up. She wrapped one arm around his lower back. "Is it enough support?"

"Yes."

"Not to give you the wrong idea, but I would do the same."

This time she smiled.

He straightened up. How did she do it? How did she just blow the air into his lungs, his chest? How did she give strength to his aching muscles?

Carl shifted in his seat, trying to avoid the sun beating down through a rust-eaten hole in the roof of the pickup. Jack had told them the truck was borrowed from a friend in Kuraburi, but it looked as if he had found it in a ditch – there were no lights or indicators and one front wing was missing entirely.

As 'acting Swedish Embassy representative in Thailand', Liv had managed to convince the same policeman who issued death certificates earlier to release the bodies without further questions. He had even helped Jack and Liv to lift the coffins into the pickup, and it occurred to Carl that he must have been relieved to get rid of at least two coffins from the long line at Wat Pasan. As they left for Wat Bang Muang, he told them rather apologetically that they had run out of dry ice in the area.

"How close are we to the edge?" Liv said. The steering wheel pitched every time they hit a pothole, and her arms were shaking with the tension. She was manoeuvring the pickup along a narrow clay track between a ditch with a rusted pipe at the bottom and a row of vehicles parked on the other side, next to the temple wall.

Carl raised his hand. "Stop," he said. "We can't be more than two inches from the edge. Stones are rolling into the ditch – that's not good."

Liv slammed her hands on the wheel, reached out and pulled the wing mirror flat to the door. Just ahead of them, a construction lorry stuck out beyond the line of cars.

"I don't think I can get past this. And we can't reverse, it's too narrow."

"So, we're stuck?"

"No, we are parked. We are getting out here." Liv took out the ignition key. "Can you climb over to my side to get out?"

She pulled the handle of her door but nothing happened. She jiggled it and tried it again. The door refused to open.

"Rust bucket!"

"I guess now we really are stuck …"

Liv flopped into her seat and blew air up over her face.

"The door is stuck, not us."

Liv leaned out the pickup window, hitched an arm over the roof and swung her legs out onto the track. She put the key in the door from the outside but couldn't turn it. She wiped her hands on her shorts and tried again.

"I can wait for you in the car. Go on, don't waste your time."

"You will boil in there," she said. "Can you pass me my bag?"

She fished in her bag for her keys, and began removing a large paperclip from the bunch.

"You keep it on your key ring?"

"Why not?" Liv half-shrugged, unfolding the paper clip. She straightened it and inserted into the door lock, working it from side to side while her free hand gently wiggled the door. After barely a minute, the lock gave up.

"*Et voila!*" She flung open the door.

"Full of surprises, you …" Carl said, watching as she put the paperclip back on the key ring.

She helped him climb out of the pickup, then leaned him against the door before taking off her own shirt and throwing it through the window onto her seat. Her white top was completely soaked at the back, and strands of wet hair stuck to her forehead.

She glanced at Carl. "Are you okay? You look pale."

"I'm good," he said. In truth, the heat and the bumpy road had made him feel a little faint, and every movement produced a jolt of pain from his leg. "The doctor said I could take another painkiller after 2 p.m. I'll be fine."

"I'll take you back to the hospital once we've got the bodies organised. Agreed?"

Carl nodded.

"And don't try to run away." Liv gave a little giggle. Kristoffer always did that – he would say something and laugh, and others would join him. Carl wanted to laugh but his sense of humour had deserted him.

Ahead of them, the area in front of the temple was like the entrance to a bazaar, or some kind of street celebration. It swarmed with people, and there were carts selling food and chilled drinks. Wat Bang Muang was quite different from four days earlier. The deathly stillness had been replaced by construction noise, the sound of engines and honking horns, people talking different languages.

Liv stepped back and let a woman journalist with a shrill, commanding voice go ahead of them. She was followed by a cameraman and a Thai assistant carrying a large bag over her shoulder, a cooler box, cables and a white translucent umbrella.

They stopped in the shade at the gates. Liv leaned against the wall, breathing heavily, her cheeks red.

"Leave me here, I'll be fine," Carl said. He swiped grit from a granite block and lowered himself onto it, stretching his injured leg in front of him and checking that the bandages hadn't slipped. The Nikes he was given at the hospital were too big for him and small stones had got inside. He removed his right shoe, turned it upside down and tapped it on the wall.

When he looked up, Liv was staring at something, covering her mouth with both hands. He followed her gaze.

Off to the right, a group of men in white hazmat suits and rubber boots were lifting a long, dust-covered tarpaulin to expose a line of corpses tightly arranged along the temple wall. Two of them picked up the last body in the row, only a few metres away from where Liv stood. A female with long ginger hair coated in mud and grit. Her thin arms were folded around her head, as if she had tried to protect herself. When they placed the corpse on a small black tarpaulin that served as a stretcher, her head fell to the side to reveal eye sockets teeming with maggots. Dozens fell onto the tarpaulin, wriggling.

Liv gasped and stepped backwards. She tripped over Carl's outstretched leg but he grabbed her arm and she regained her balance.

"I won't be long," she said, and pulled a face mask from her bag.

Carl watched her as she stepped unsteadily along the passages cleared between rows of corpses. Many of the bodies were wrapped only in filthy sheets. Others, probably only brought in today, were lying naked under the scorching sun. The rows closest to the trees were the most organised – those bodies lay under blue poly tarps with huge chunks of dry ice on top, which were evaporating into a thick white fog that hovered low above the ground. Carl followed Liv with his eyes until she disappeared in the dry ice fog like a ghost. Or an angel.

"*Scheisse*."

A team of men in blue coveralls were working on Carl's left. One of the men removed his face mask and headgear. His hair was soaked, his face purple. He spoke fast and loud German and Carl could understand only snippets of what he said. They seemed to be trying to figure out how to lift an exceptionally large body which lay on its stomach, with legs akimbo. Excrement and body fluids had leaked out, and the ground around it was crawling with bugs.

Carl leaned against the wall by the gate, hiding in his pool of shade. He tweaked the neck of his damp T-shirt, letting in the air. It staggered him that these men were able to keep going in their coveralls in such heat.

311

Other teams in similar protective clothing, like something from a post-apocalyptic sci-fi movie, wandered amongst the dead, picking up bodies and carrying them into the white fog. One man in a hazmat suit with breathing gear and a tank behind his back, marched between the rows in rubber boots, spraying disinfectant. A few days ago, the idea of spraying formaldehyde so liberally would have repulsed Carl; now, he simply donned his mask.

Liv came and squatted next to him.

"They don't have refrigerated containers from Sweden here."

"What?"

"The Swedes didn't bring them."

Carl shook his head. "What about those?" he said. He pointed to four structures that looked like shipping containers, a hundred metres off to the left, where Thai workers were installing pipes in a trench between the containers and the temple wall. They didn't wear gloves, or even face masks, just peaked caps to keep the worst of the sun from their heads.

"Those are Germans."

"There *must* be Swedish containers somewhere here."

"If there were, they wouldn't be hard to spot," Liv said. "Is it possible you got confused about the location?"

Carl stared at her, doubting his sanity.

"I don't think … No, this morning I was told to go to Ban Muang temple, Kao Lak. I know this place. I was here before. No confusion on my side."

"Here are only Thai and German forensic teams operating. Nobody from the Swedish side, no officials, no forensic experts."

"No sign of a refrigerated van either," he whispered.

Liv looked over her shoulder at the rows of bodies.

"They told me they don't even know how many people they have here."

Carl could see goosebumps on her arms. "I …" – he cleared his throat – "I still can't believe they are dead."

She turned to him, her pupils still narrow from the sun. "Were their corpses as bad as this? She grimaced and immediately dropped her eyes.

"No." He shook his head. "And yes."

He was relieved she didn't say anything else, didn't ask anything else. No details about how and where he found the bodies. When others had asked, he had shrugged and said nothing. Death was a statement, final and brutal, with no need of details.

Carl pushed himself up until he was leaning against a large stone that protruded from the wall. "Can I have your phone to call the temporary embassy? We have to find those containers."

"Call them from the car," Liv said. "Somebody told me that we should check at Wat Yan Yao temple, which is a short drive from here. It is a smaller site but they are moving the main operations there because they have had some problems with power here. Apparently the Norwegian DVI are there, so hopefully the Swedes too."

They saw it at the same time probably – a long wet line on the ground under the pickup. Carl wondered how much ice had melted already, how much time they had before it was all gone. He knew that Liv would be thinking the same, but neither of them spoke. Liv pulled his arm over her shoulder, and they walked faster.

She helped him to climb into his seat over the gearbox. He tried to conceal it, but his leg was hurting more, his whole body ached and his breathing had become snatched and shallow. He glanced at Liv, wondering if she'd noticed. The last thing he wanted was for her to freak out and take him to a hospital before they found the containers. She didn't look at him but he had a strong feeling that she knew. And now he thought about it, she looked exhausted herself.

The pickup rattled as they drove on the uneven ground, as though its component parts had begun to disarticulate. Carl felt like his bones were jiggling and that he, like the pickup, would fall apart if they didn't get onto a better surface soon. It was twelve thirty but he decided to take his painkillers now.

"Like driving a tin of nails," he said.

As they sat in traffic before the turn to the main road, Carl noticed a young monk standing barefoot at the side of the road, next to his bike, staring from afar at the busy entrance to the temple complex. Carl vaguely remembered seeing him when they arrived, right where he was now, holding his bike with both hands, his arms tense, agitatedly glancing around – not daring, perhaps, to enter the temple grounds. He hadn't seen that expression in monks before – fear mixed with confusion. It made the man look human. There had been far fewer monks around the temple this time, as though there was nothing else they could do for the souls of the victims but to let the men in hazmat suits butcher the remains. There was no smoke anymore from the crematorium at the far end of the temple grounds. The bell tower stood in silent witness to the invasion of mortals.

Carl thought of the serene temple with chipped walls in the coconut grove outside Kuraburi, where the grass was up to his knees and the paths were unmarked. After Carl had collected Kristoffer and Eva's death certificates from the police station, Jack had taken him to the temple for the cremation of his friend Georgio and some of the others who'd died at Golden Buddha.

They had travelled from Kuraburi in the back of a pickup,

following two open trucks carrying the coffins. Julia had asked him to hold a basket with small floats made from banana leaves carrying incense, candles and flowers which later they would float out to sea. She said they were called *krathongs* and there were fourteen of them, for everyone who perished at Golden Buddha.

He recognised Jonas as the famous Swedish chef whose show he had watched once with Kristoffer and Eva in their flat in Stockholm. Heavy snow had kept them inside and they had spent the day in pyjamas, drinking wine and cooking. Carl didn't tell him that, and expressed his condolences about his partner Jose.

When they got to the highway, they had stopped to pick up a red-haired Scot whom Carl remembered from Vachira Hospital. He said his wife Linda had begun to recover and they would be able to fly home in a week. He said he owed Kristoffer a drink because he had lost every pool game they played.

A Spanish woman sat next to Jack, her eyes vacant and her face the colour of dried earth. Jack introduced her as the fiancée of his friend Georgio. She hadn't spoken since identifying her fiancée's body. Her lacerated hands rested on her knees, and Carl noticed there was no engagement ring, just a telltale white line on her finger.

Carl asked Julia if she remembered whether Eva and Kristoffer had been wearing their wedding bands. She didn't. Peter too shrugged his shoulders. Carl couldn't settle in his mind why the bodies had no rings. Jonas said that Jose's ring had been stolen, and that his two diamond earrings were gone too. But Jose's body had been found in savannah – it was far from the resort but not difficult to access. Who would go to the mangrove thicket, even for the sake of gold?

315

The pickup stalled at traffic lights. Liv turned the key a few times before it started again. Carl leaned his head against the window frame and closed his eyes.

"Are you okay?" he heard her say. He nodded.

Monks had stood behind the coffins, which were draped in white cloths, making a continuous murmuring sound. They looked composed and graceful with their orange robes over one shoulder. There were eight of them, two of whom were very young – no older than fifteen, their heads neatly shaved, a contour line around their lips. Tongues of flame from torches threw a flickering light on their peaceful faces. It was the peace of children's faces, signifying youth and purity. The monk with the bike near the temple might have been one of them, had not his eyes been stripped of virginity.

"What are they chanting?" Carl had said to Jack.

"*Aum*. It's a Sanskrit word, a syllable."

"What does it mean?"

"For Buddhists, *aum* is the mother of all sounds. It symbolises the universe, where all things find manifestation."

Jack had sat with his feet crossed, his hands folded in the praying position. He wore large white linen trousers wrapped around his hips in the Asian manner, and a thin white shirt with the top three buttons open. White, he explained to Carl, was the Asian colour of mourning.

"The concept is fascinating," Jack said, his eyes narrowed as he watched the flicking flame of a ceremonial candle. "It's the cycle of birth, of coming into being and of dissolution. The silence surrounding the syllable is the unknown: it's called simply 'the fourth'. The syllable itself is God as creator-preserver-destroyer, but the silence is God Eternal, uninvolved but underlining everything. Our life is *aum* but the silence that underlines it is immortal."

At various points they were asked to lean forward and touch the back of the person in front of them, creating a chain of compassion, spreading it to those most in need of it. When Jack touched Carl's shoulder, Carl reached in turn to touch Julia's back.

Why Kristoffer? he remembered thinking. The low stone bench felt cold against his hot palms. The fever was already consuming his body.

A monk poured water from a clay jug into a platter, wet his hands and touched Jack's forehead. Jack folded his hands and bowed his head. The monk simply knelt in front of Carl.

"The ceremony of burial," Jack explained afterwards, "of going into a tomb, is symbolic and is more for we who are alive, to give comfort and hope. Death is the beginning of a new life. The basic principle for all believers is that there is a beginning in the end. To enter the tomb is to return to the womb, to be born again."

After more prayers, the chief monk invited all to move to the funeral pyre in the yard behind the temple. As they walked through the tall grass, Carl felt the dew from the stems, the sensation of cold on his burning calf. Led by the monks, holding a sacred thread connected to each coffin, they walked one after another in a circle around a log pyre. When they had repeated this three times, villagers helped them to lift the heavy coffins to the top of the pyre, placing the heads so they faced west. On each of the coffins was a photo – of Georgiou, Jose, the Thai employees – decorated with candles and garlands of orchids and bougainvilleas. The still night air was thick with incense.

The flames blazed and hissed. The flowers shrivelled and melted away, and the white cloths burned in an instant. The sputtering sparking of burning wood from the pyre filled the air. Sparks soared into the sky. A Thai turned on a gas blower, adding to the fire. The flames went wild.

The heat blasted into Carl's face and he stepped back, covering himself with his arms.

Twenty-six

"Not allowed."

A policeman, a face mask over his mouth, lifted his hand in front of Carl. He stepped aside to let out two women in disposable gowns, with shoe caps over their sandals, escorted by a man in a white coverall, then returned to his position in front of the barrier.

"We are looking for Swedish refrigerated containers," Carl said. Wat Yan Yao site looked more organised than Wat Bang Muang, with its chaos of rotting bodies covering the ground. Behind the barrier, he could see only containers and temporary constructions; there were only a few people not wearing hazmat suits and rubber boots.

The policemen waved them to his left.

"Go to tent one."

At the end of a row of portable toilets along the temple wall, there were three long tents where most people were being sent.

Carl suspected he didn't understand his question. "Can you—"

Liv interrupted him and spoke Thai to the guard who very soon changed his frown to a smile. Carl wondered how he would have got around without her. He repositioned his feet so that she wasn't taking so much of his weight.

"No Swedish freezer containers. Only Thai and Australian DVI are working at the site," Liv said as she led him away. "The guard says the area is restricted to DVI personnel. This morning, police in Phuket issued a directive advising all friends and relatives of the missing or dead to refrain from visiting tsunami-affected locations, temples and all operational sites. They are getting more organised."

Carl hopped, trying to keep up with her, but lost his balance and hung on her with most of his weight.

"Where do we go now?"

"To the pickup."

"And then? Where do we go with the coffins?"

"Hospital first and then back to Kuraburi?" She readjusted his arm and they trudged on.

"No, please … wait."

Carl didn't know what to suggest, but he didn't want to leave the coffins anywhere and he was getting paranoid that the ice would melt before the end of the day.

"If we are lucky," Liv said, "when I drop you at the hospital, they may agree to store the coffins in their morgue."

"The morgues are full. They will send them here or, worse, Wat Bang Muang and we will lose track of them."

"We can't keep trailing the coffins around in this heat. And I can't carry you on my shoulders either. You happen to be a bit heavier than I thought. I haven't been a human crutch before and had no idea it was such hard work."

Carl sighed. He couldn't blame her and wondered if they should leave the coffins at Kuraburi temple. Jack had said that all the coffins from Golden Buddha were still there, in the shade of the temple wall, and that no embassy representatives had come to pick them up – Swedes were not the only ones.

"Let's check what's happening in tent number one,"

Carl said, glancing at the long queue that started inside and stretched far out of the tent. There was nothing to be done there, but he wanted to delay going back to the pickup. Several people in the queue looked Swedish and he hoped that maybe they'd heard something about the containers or had some other useful information.

Inside the tent, plastic fans attached to steel poles produced a steady current of air and at least temporary relief from the heat outside. Liv leaned Carl against a wall of plywood coffins covered with condensation. He felt the refreshing coolness on his back. If they had ice inside it meant there were corpses. He glanced at Liv, who leaned back and pressed the back of her head against the cold wood. He decided there was no need to tell her about his suspicion.

"What if we go to the Swedish temporary embassy," Liv said, "and leave the coffins in the hotel's lobby, which is air conditioned? They're hardly going to put them outside, are they? You need to go there anyway, for your passport."

That was one way to lose the coffins, Carl thought, but instead he said, "Do you remember that lanky guy working for the embassy you were hanging out with him when I met you in Phuket the first time?"

"Fredrik? I didn't hang out with him. I was speaking to him about a Swedish family who needed passports to leave Thailand asap."

Carl sniffed; he knew how a man looks at a woman when he wants to get her into bed.

"Do you think you could call Fredrik and ask about the containers? I don't think the woman I spoke to will call me back, certainly not with anything new. You heard her – she kept repeating that the containers were at Wat Bang Muang."

Liv scrolled through her phone, pressed Call and held it to her ear.

"He's not picking up. But he will call me back, he knows my number."

Fredrik knew her number? That meant they knew each other well enough. But why be so defensive?

"I'll get us some water." Liv walked outside the tent, to a cart selling beverages.

Carl spotted a crutch lying on the ground next to a table and worked his way over, using the coffins for support. This single table was at the endpoint for the long queue and was manned by a Thai woman, whose little boy hid underneath. '*DNA collection*' was written on a sheet of A4 taped to the table. A tall, skeletally thin Thai man dressed in a doctor's coat over his jeans was standing beside the table, taking samples with a cotton swab from inside the mouth of an Indian woman. Just above her *bindi* she had a scar across her entire forehead, roughly sewn up with the ends of the sutures sticking out like tiny antennas. He put the swab into a plastic bag, meticulously sealed it and passed it to the Thai woman, who began asking the Indian woman questions and filling out a form. The Thai woman then asked for a sample of hair, explaining that for a good DNA match of a sibling a saliva swab was not enough. The Indian woman spoke in sobs, at times wailing and raising her fist in the air, but she pulled some hairs out by the root and handed them over.

Carl leaned down and picked up the crutch. The underarm pad was ripped, the foam crumbling out, and the tip was split in two, but it was better than nothing.

"Excuse me, do you know if this crutch belongs to anyone?"

The woman at the table shrugged and spoke to her male colleague in Thai. He shook his head, and several people in the queue did likewise. Carl transferred his weight to the crutch and glanced outside to the cart, where he assumed Liv had joined the queue, but he couldn't see her.

"I know you."

An Asian-looking man with a large camera on his chest was waving. He stepped closer, lifted his camera and took two snaps of Carl against the wall of coffins. Carl was about to protest when he remembered the man. It was the Korean Australian journalist he had met at the taxi rank at the hospital in Phuket.

The man put a cap on his camera lens and leant against the stack next to Carl. His eyes were red. He yawned.

"Did you find your friends?"

"I did."

"Alive?"

"No."

"Sorry."

The journalist turned his back to Carl and began taking pictures of a tall blonde woman in a floral blouse who was sitting at the DNA collection table. She had a perfect manicure and her wedding band was incrusted with diamonds, which glittered as she moved her hand to fill out the form.

Carl hoped the conversation was over.

"You are lucky," the journalist said and let his camera hang on his chest.

"Oh?"

"There are tons of Swedish running around looking for their relatives." He took out a pack of blue Camel from his chest pocket.

"There are all sorts of people looking for their relatives."

"But only Swedes are running around with coffins looking for containers."

Carl stared at the journalist, who was flicking his thumb on the lighter wheel. Only sparks came out. He shook the lighter and tried again.

"What containers?"

The flame broke and the tip of the cigarette began glowing.

"Refrigerated containers." The journalist inhaled deeply, sucking his cheeks in, all the time looking straight as Carl. "Some mad Swede has been going around with his wife in a coffin for the last two days—"

"Eric?" Carl gaped. "Baldish, tall?"

"Yes, bald Eric." The journalist smiled.

"Did he find the containers?"

"No, he didn't. I don't know why he was looking for them here, there are no Swedish officials." He rubbed the side of his nose with his thumb. "I felt sorry for the man and took his coffin to the Australian containers for storage."

"How did you manage that?"

"I'm Australian. Our guys built the most advanced mortuary site here in a day." He blew smoke high in the air.

"How many missing Australians are there?"

"Seventy, eighty, something like that."

"Missing or dead?"

"Missing. Thirteen confirmed dead."

"Is that all?"

"That is a lot," the journalist said.

Carl knew he hadn't expressed himself correctly. But he had read that morning that more than three thousand Swedes were missing – a disproportionately large number.

The journalist pointed to his leg. "What did you do to yourself?"

"Accident."

"Accident?"

"Stepped on broken glass."

The journalist crinkled his eyes against the smoke and looked at him sideways.

"*Har ar ditt vatten*," Liv said, and tapped him on the shoulder with the cold bottle.

Carl was glad to be rescued. "*Nu gar vi*," he said. He raised his crutch for her to admire, then leaned on it and took a step.

"Wait, not so fast." She opened her own bottle and took several large gulps.

She wiped her mouth with her arm and glanced at the journalist, who had been studying her. She smiled her usual big grin, the one that created dimples in her cheeks, and said, "Hello."

Carl wished she hadn't.

"Dylan." The journalist smiled, tapped his open hand into his chest and gave a little bow. The smile lit up his face and Carl had to admit that he didn't look malevolent anymore.

"Liv," she said. "Any good stories?" She pointed to his camera.

"There are a lot of stories. But they're all sad. What's your story?"

"I'm just helping my friend." She gave a closed-lip smile.

Dylan pulled his card from his pocket and handed it to Liv.

"Just in case," he said. He bowed for the second time and walked away.

"That guy is so intrusive," Carl said, watching as Dylan took pictures of a teenage boy who was being swabbed. The boy was on his own.

"Is he?" Liv got two bags of fresh pineapple from a plastic bag and offered one to Carl. "He's just doing his job. I'm sure his readers are delighted with all the gory details from the tsunami-struck coast."

"He said other Swedes are looking for the refrigerated containers too."

She nodded, chewing on a piece of pineapple and holding her hand in front of her mouth. "The containers are stuck in Bangkok."

"What?"

"I spoke to Fredrik. The containers were supposed to be here two days ago; that is why they told everyone to take the bodies to Wat Bang Muang. But for some inexplicable reason, they are still in Bangkok."

"That is so poor. So poor."

"I agree. But they are under such pressure; part of me feels sorry for them."

"I feel sorry for all the people they misinformed."

"I suppose. But it's not really their fault. There is still very little real help from Stockholm. There are no resources, they are understaffed and nothing is coordinated. They are like headless chickens."

"I thought you said Laila Freivalds flew to Thailand?"

"That is what I read in the Swedish papers," Liv said. "She has come in for a lot of stick in Sweden. People want her to step down, so I guess she's trying to compensate for the inadequacy of her initial response to the tsunami."

"It's a tick for her that she visited the region. An interview here and there. She's doing her best to restore her reputation."

"Fredrik said he can put us in contact with Jonas Hastrom."

"Who is …"

"The ambassador to Thailand."

"How is he going to help us? Get more ice for the coffins?" Liv looked away.

"I'm sorry." He touched her shoulder. She didn't respond. "I know you are trying to be helpful, and you are. I just don't think we can hope for help from the temporary embassy people. They just take our time and mislead us."

He thought about Nok and the forensic pathologist he met at Wat Bang Muang the first time he went there. He thought about the nurse in Takuapa Hospital, and Anna, and many other people he had met in the last week who were out there helping, saving lives, making changes without orders from above but in response to a call from within. Even journalists were making a difference, Carl thought. He scanned the queue searching for Dylan but couldn't see him.

"Fredrik said to take the coffins to the temporary embassy," Liv said finally, "and he will call Rescue Services Agency to arrange the embalming. And he said once the containers arrive, they will store the coffins."

Carl raised an eyebrow.

"He thinks they should arrive tonight."

"Did he say they'd left Bangkok?" Carl yanked up his oversized shorts.

"No, he didn't."

He glanced at her but didn't say anything.

"Fredrik said the military plane will land tomorrow." Liv paused. "But he also said they won't take off the next day. They want to fill it with coffins to make it worth flying."

"But they don't have any bodies …"

"They have twenty-six confirmed dead."

"But where are they? They don't know. They don't know where their containers are."

"He said it's a huge plane. They have to fill it to take off. It kind of makes sense."

"It will be a Hercules. They *are* huge – I flew in one in the army. With their efficiency they won't fill it in a month."

Carl glanced around the tent again, looking for Dylan. "Where's the card the journalist gave you?"

Liv picked it, wet and sticky, from the plastic bag containing the remains of the pineapple.

"Please, can you ring him? I think he can help us."

"My battery is dead."

"Let's find him."

He leaned on his crutch and slowly began to walk. The

crutch rubbed uncomfortably under his armpit, but it was solid enough and increased his speed. He was glad to be able to move on his own.

"Why the urgency? I thought you wanted to get rid of him."

"He knows someone working for the Australians. They're storing a Swedish coffin in their refrigerated containers."

Carl went to check inside tent number two and Liv checked the third tent. They met at the entrance to the site. Carl could see their pickup parked on the other side of the road, and the pool of water that was gathering underneath it. The asphalt didn't absorb the melted water like the clay surface near Wat Bang Muang. He glanced at Liv; she was staring at the pickup too.

"Why you didn't you ask this guy to help straight away?"

"I wasn't sure. I thought he was a bit of a pain. I didn't want to share anything about Kristoffer and Eva. He would have made a story of it."

"And now?"

"Now, I'm thinking about directing his investigative efforts to the Swedish temporary embassy rescue effort."

Liv raised her eyebrows and stared at him. Carl wasn't sure if she would approve of his idea – he hadn't given any thought to it himself.

A truck pulled off the road and was reversing in front of the barrier. Through the mix of dust and fumes, Carl caught the smell of rotten flesh. His eyes went to the flatbed. It was filled with rough plastic cocoons, large chunks of ice scattered between them.

"You know that Australia reported only seventy-something missing and thirteen confirmed dead?" As he spoke, he wondered if he was trying to justify his intentions to himself. "There are one hundred and fifty-nine British missing and forty dead accounted for. And there are three thousand Swedish missing and only twenty-six confirmed dead. The question is, what is the real number of Swedish fatalities? That is the question I want him to ask. I think many Swedes would like to ask that question."

"What is the real number do you think?"

"Three, four hundred?"

"That is too many."

"That is the best case scenario," Carl said. "With the numbers that countries have reported so far, the ratio between missing and dead is about five to one. Or less. So, between five and six hundred dead is a more realistic number."

Liv shook her head, frowning. She pushed a stone around with her foot, and her lips moved slightly as if she was talking to herself.

"I know the editor in chief at *Aftonbladet*," she finally said. "I can put them in touch."

Carl pointed over the barrier. "I think that's him. Dylan!"

The Australian looked over and waved.

Twenty-seven

The temporary mortuary was within the main temple building, built of plywood on a pine stud frame. There were other structures at the back of the temple, and work in progress around the *sala* and the open pavilion. In a deep trench along the side wall of the temple, Thai workers were installing pipes coming from below the temple, and connecting them to a row of large tanks.

"The Australians constructed the mortuary in thirty-six hours," Dylan said proudly, as if he had been involved himself. "But they still need efficient drainage for the waste from the sinks and the mortuary floor. You can't just build a big soakaway because of potential contamination of the ground water, so they have come up with an ingenious cascade system of septic tanks."

"They do seem well prepared," Carl mumbled.

Water trickled from the coffin containing Kristoffer's body, over the shoulder of the shorter of the two faceless men in hazmat suits when they squatted to lower the coffin to the ground. They put it next to three white body bags, beside the door to the mortuary. A tragic and silent queue.

"I think they got a bit of training in the Bali bombing." Dylan stepped into the narrow shade of the building. Carl stood next to him and leaned with all his weight on his crutch. Two chairs on the other side of the door were taken by mortuary staff, and a third squatted next to them. All were smoking in silence.

"Were you there?"

"My hostel was two blocks away from the night club in Kuta. I was one of the first with a camera at the night club, which was completely shattered."

"Did you fly to Thailand when you learned about the tsunami?"

"No, I was on my Christmas holiday. I was about to go and have breakfast and took pictures of the wave from my balcony as it crashed into the café."

"I guess you could call yourself lucky?"

"I am." Dylan kissed a little wooden talisman that hung from a string around his neck.

He said the Australians had rapid response kits consisting of pre-packed, containerised and air portable equipment designed to allow full field forensic or DVI operations for seven days before resupply. The kits even included portable dental X-ray machines and all the necessary dental mortuary equipment and PPE. However, they were never designed to deal with anything on the scale of the tsunami and there were all sorts of minor problems, like the provision of enough 110v equipment.

A man in a disposable gown walked out of the mortuary, accompanied by a woman who was sobbing uncontrollably. He took off both their gloves and masks and threw them in a gigantic bin near the door, already full with disposable rubbish. He said something to her and she covered her face with her hands. He stepped back awkwardly, tapped a row of pockets on the thigh of his green cargos, found a pack of cigarettes and offered her one. She stopped crying, looked at him blinking, then shook her head.

Snatches of the man's words reached Carl's ears. The woman had lost her son and husband, and he was talking to her about transportation of the remains and what documents he needed from her. Carl followed them as far as the gates, all the while keeping an eye on his coffins at the door to the mortuary.

When the woman had left, Carl approached the man.

"Excuse me, I overheard your conversation. You said you were organising air transport for her relatives to Sidney?"

"Yes." Carl sensed he was in a hurry.

"I need to transport my two deceased friends back to Sweden. Is it a private air service?"

"The company is Kenyon International Emergency Service. We're contracted to the Australian Department of Foreign Affairs and Trade to support the international disaster response operation in Thailand. I'm Ben Steel, by the way." He put out his hand.

Ben had probably been in special forces in the past, Carl thought, judging by his posture and the air of authority. He had wide shoulders and muscly arms.

"Can I consign the bodies to you? They have all ID papers. I'd pay, of course."

"We do repatriate bodies to countries of origin. Our priority is Australian citizens, but we do. Why don't you ask at your embassy? It might be easier."

"Swedish representatives have been unhelpful. They still haven't arranged refrigeration facilities, for example. That's why I'm storing my friends' bodies in the temporary morgue."

"Why so?"

"I don't know. The Swedish Rescue Service Agency, which is the central supervisory government agency for rescue services, have very limited resources on the ground here. I don't know whether it's to do with financial support from the government, or internal disorganisation, or whether the disaster is beyond the scope of their expertise. The temporary embassy in Thailand is pointing fingers in all sorts of directions. And in the end, nobody does anything." Carl spoke fast, running out of air. "Swedish tour operators chartered flights within two days for the tourists without accommodation. The first government-chartered evacuation plane and air ambulance arrived only on the night of the 30th, four days after the tsunami."

"I did read about your foreign minister's trip to the theatre the night it happened."

"Yes – unbelievable. Incoming calls to the Swedish Ministry for Foreign Affairs were not used as a source of information. They were seen as a disturbance that caused the switchboard to collapse. The Prime Minister didn't return from his holiday until the next day. The Health Minister went on holiday shortly after instead of supporting medical relief efforts. As for the Finance and Defence Ministers, they said it wasn't their job."

Ben shook his head. "I did notice a lot of Swedes around and it seems nobody is helping them." He removed his sunglasses, holding the thin frame with two fingers, and wiped them with the corner of his shirt.

"So, can you help me?"

"To be honest." Ben clicked his tongue. "It'll be much easier for you to use your embassy, even if you have to wait. Because we've more work than we can manage – or afford – to do. It won't exactly be asap with us either."

"Can you even look into it, please?"

"We do repatriation according to internationally recognised protocols for the transfer of human remains across borders. We'll need all appropriate documents like death certificates, burial transit permits, permission to take bodies from the country, funeral agencies who will receive the bodies in Sweden. And something else – you will need to request most of the papers from your embassy. So, you will need their assistance anyway."

"How much would transportation cost?"

"I can't tell you now. I need to enquire. It will certainly be a pretty decent amount if you get the sponsorship of the Australian government. Call me tonight."

"I will. Thank you." Carl took the card Ben handed to him. His number in Thailand was written in blue ink on the back.

"Do you prepare the bodies for travel? Embalm them?"

"The bodies do have to be embalmed before the flight, and we might be able to help with it. At the moment I know there is a shortage of embalming fluid, but I guess there will be more in the next few days."

"Where's your office here?"

"We are located between this site and Thachatchai, near Phuket International Airport. We already have more than a hundred people in the region. We supplied Wat Yan Yao and maintain two mobile mortuary facilities, with equipment and personnel. We provide specialist advice on chemical use, protective equipment, DNA collection, data management process, everything really. We provide comprehensive IT support to the Victim Identification Information Management Centre – that's where they coordinate all forty-plus countries involved."

Carl stood with Ben's business card in his hand, watching him march away to the temple gates, his leather boots raising bits of sand. He thought about the newspaper photo of Göran Persson shaking the hand of a man with a head bandage. '*The Prime Minister meeting first survivors arriving home.*' Carl smiled wryly and shook his head. He had only one pocket in his shorts; the other one had a hole. He made sure to put the card in the right pocket, next to his mobile phone with no credit and no battery.

"I'm Dr Deer, forensic pathologist, Australian Federal Police."

The man lowered his mask. His handsome face was tanned, with a pale line on his temples from wearing sunglasses. He looked athletic – like a surfer in a hazmat suit. He removed a plastic apron with drying brown blotches and threw it into the bin.

"I was told you would like to store two bodies temporarily in the Australian refrigerated containers."

"Yes, the Swedish containers still haven't arrived."

"You marked them well." Dr Deer pointed to the two coffins on the ground. On each side, Carl had written name, nationality and his own phone number with black paint.

"I was afraid of losing track of them," Carl said. "You know, so many bodies everywhere …"

"I'm afraid that to meet Interpol protocols for victim identification we have to get them out from the coffins and make a record of each body. We will then place them in secure tagged bags in the facility."

Carl dug his hands under his armpits. "I have all ID papers. I just need storage."

"We follow the same procedure with every corpse. Do you know if they have a record in the international DVI centre register?"

"They are registered with the Swedish temporary embassy in Phuket."

"Your embassy list may not be synchronised with the DVI register yet."

Carl could quite believe it. He blew out his cheeks.

"They were registered at Kuraburi police station two days ago and they issued identification papers and death certificates."

"The international DVI Coordination Centre, led by the Royal Thai Police, was established only yesterday." Dr Deer sat down on one of the two plastic chairs outside the door. He took off his heavy rubber boots and put his feet on the other chair. "When we pick up a body from a pile, we don't know which country it belongs to. With a large number of international teams, it is a great challenge to adopt a common strategy. It's crucially important to follow the same procedure."

"What is your procedure, exactly?"

"We record everything – clothes, features, fingerprints if still available. We take pictures, make dental records and perform autopsies if necessary. We may even take sample tissues for DNA."

"What is the point of an autopsy? To confirm the cause of death?"

"No, the autopsy is limited to the abdomen. It's for identification purpose only. We aim to find typical results of surgery, such as a missing appendix or gall bladder."

"Can I be present during the procedure?"

"Yes, if it's not too disturbing for you. Normally, we won't allow civilians in the mortuary but taking into account your situation I'm happy to make an exception."

At first, Carl was disorientated by the blazing fluorescent lights on the low ceiling and walls, as though he had walked onto a stage. The room was packed with forensic personnel, gathered in groups around steel trolleys, investigating corpses. The air con was blowing cold air but the room still had the stomach-churning smell of disinfectant and rotting flesh.

He followed Dr Deer to a trolley on which a flaccid corpse seemed to deliquesce all over the metallic tray. Large blisters on the ballooned stomach had ruptured, oozing a brownish liquid. Two mortuary technicians were cleaning the body, one with a wet sponge gently tapping the skin on the ribcage, another with tweezers picking out bits of leaves and needles from the hair and between the layers of skin on the neck.

Carl felt the blood drain from his face. "It's not Kristoffer, is it?"

"It's a male body from one of your two coffins."

Carl pressed a hand over his face mask. He shook his head and stepped back.

"Is it possible that one of your staff confused bodies when they got them from my coffins?"

"No," Dr Deer said sharply. He put on his safety glasses and leaned over the corpse. "Was the identification confirmed only visually?"

"Yes." Carl felt his chest tightening as if in an iron claw.

For the first time, he began to doubt. When he had found him, he knew in his own mind it was Kristoffer. The length of the corpse. His straight, jet-black hair, almost long enough to get in a hairband at the back. His face, though grey and distorted, seeming to hold something of the man he knew. And then there was the woman's body, with blonde, shoulder-length hair. He had not doubted for a moment that it was Kristoffer and Eva.

"Yes," he repeated, more loudly. "I'm his best friend. They had been staying in a resort and I found them near the ruins."

"When?"

"On the 30th of December."

"Four days after the tsunami. We believe that at that stage of decomposition, with so much heat and humidity, facial identification alone is not reliable. I working on the Bali bombing, and a third of the facial IDs were proven wrong."

"There's no doubt about their identity." Carl squeezed his hands into fists, his nails piercing his palms through the gloves. "Fourteen people missing from the only resort hotel on a secluded island, and everyone else found apart from a four-year-old child – how could there be any doubt?"

"I'm just stating the facts," the doctor said evenly. "It's undeniably in your interests to get the right body."

"Eva …" Carl cleared his throat. "The woman's body. She was pregnant. I guess the autopsy would be helpful in her identification."

"Yes, good to know. Because there are no clothes or jewellery. There's no mention of a pregnancy in the documents you gave us?"

Carl nodded. He decided not to mention the missing wedding rings.

"Were they in the water when you found them?"

"In a mangrove creek."

"I can see fish bites all over his skin. Unfortunately, warm stagnant bodies of water will break a body down quicker because they tend to breed bacteria and the body will attract various kinds of carnivorous sea life. It would be different in a cold ocean." Dr Deer gently rotated Kristoffer's head from side to side. He pulled over the long arm of an adjustable lamp to get more light. "He probably had a fatal head injury."

Carl leaned forward and squinted at the area behind the ear, to which the doctor was pointing. There was a distinct swelling, and the flesh was darker.

Carl pulled back, trying to control his breathing. Trying not to retch.

"How on earth can you see that?"

"It's my job. Besides, most people didn't drown as such, they were lethally injured by sharp, heavy objects hitting them with great force. It reduced their chances of fighting the actual water."

The doctor bent down to the corpse to continue the examination. Carl watched him moving methodically along, his assistant making notes and another technician taking photos – a bizarre and silent mortuary dance. He remembered not being able to move the body from the spot where he found it. It was as heavy as a stone and the skin was so thin, spongy. If he found Kristoffer now, though, he would scarcely recognise him as a human being.

"Look, here is another significant wound – low down on the chest."

Carl didn't look. He didn't want to know the details of Kristoffer's death. He didn't want to hear the torment he had gone through before he died.

"You don't need to be here, you know," Dr Deer said. "When I'm done, our odontologist will take dental records. You can wait for the paperwork outside."

Carl nodded.

The assistant used a cable tie to attach a plastic tag marked with indelible ink to Kristoffer's left wrist.

"We will seal the body in a bag with another tag attached to the zip. That will have the body number and will indicate the position of the head. You will be given the container number on the post mortem form. We won't lose him, don't worry."

"To get the bodies back," his assistant added, "you will have to get the signature of Federal Agent Hamish Ross – he's in charge at the Yan Yao site."

Carl nodded again.

"I'd recommend you request his and his wife's dental records, just in case," the doctor said. "It's one of the most reliable identification methods for Westerners; most have pretty good records."

"Better than DNA?" Carl remembered the long queue at the DNA data collection table.

"DNA is time- and cost-consuming. Usually, DNA samples are taken from a piece of muscle from the arm but autolysis is already highly advanced so we're tending not to take flesh samples anymore, but to go for a piece of bone, perhaps from the femur. And it works only if comparative data is available. We have records of whole families missing or sometimes a victim has no close relatives, so then DNA fails."

"Kristoffer has no blood relatives," Carl said.

The doctor fixed his eyes on him. "You were very lucky to find his body. If he had ended up in Kao Lak his body would have been separated as Thai and at best buried in a mass grave. Everyone's telling us now that there must be many foreigners to whom that happened, like Japanese, Singaporean, and even Australians of Asian origin. But of course, we have to deal first with all the bodies we have available here on the ground and only then will we go through exhumation and final inventory. Which means much hope will rest on DNA."

Twenty-eight

From outside the window of the Western Union, Carl watched as Liv was handed four stacks of banknotes. She set one aside and began counting the other. She was flipping the notes quite fast but halfway through the pile she stopped and held a note in the air, hesitated, and returned it to the pile, starting from the beginning. Carl couldn't believe they had given her four thousand US dollars in what looked like notes of ten. And why was Liv counting it in there? She should have just taken the money and left. Who cared if it was a couple of notes short?

There were two Western men behind her in the line. One was a head taller than her and had a ragged scar above his ear, from which hung four hoops. He stood watching her, his hands in his shorts pockets. The second man was shifting on his feet, rising up and down on his toes, scratching his chest, then his back, then rubbing his nose.

Carl had come out to relieve himself in the bushes, and had noticed the pair going in. He immediately thought they looked suspicious and regretted that he'd left Liv alone. They had already spent almost a half-hour waiting for the Western Union agent to locate the transfer, made in Liv's name by Carl's friend, and he had finally confirmed that the transfer had come through and the cash was available. Now, Carl wondered if the agent herself had called the two thugs. She would have seen that Carl couldn't manage without Liv's support.

Carl held his crutch tightly. What if the men followed Liv outside? He was not fit to defend her, even from the smaller of the two. It was getting dark, and the bank branch was a small cabin next to a post office that was already closed. There were just two street lamps, one at the entrance to the bank and another down the road near a 7-Eleven – the only place there might be a few people. He glanced at Liv's Yamaha in the parking space to the left of the door, and at the men's more powerful Suzuki. They couldn't even drive away from them.

The agent offered a rubber band to Liv and she wound it around the two stacks at once. The shorter man stepped closer to Liv and said something. She said something back, looking over her shoulder. The man laughed and nudged the bulky guy, who smirked and rubbed his beard.

Carl hobbled over to the door but stopped with his hand on the door handle. They wouldn't do anything while they were inside; there was a camera in the far corner, facing the window. Likely they would follow Liv outside. They knew it was dark and empty on the street.

He might be handicapped, but he would certainly be a surprise. Carl hopped to the corner of the building and back, looking for a good spot to approach the men from behind. When they opened the door, he would let them out, then hit the bulky guy over the head with his crutch and smack the short guy with something heavy. He peered around, looking for a stone or an empty bottle. A lorry thundered along the road, and Carl glanced in its direction as it disappeared, wondering if he had time to attract the attention of one of a few cars that passed by. His common sense was wrestling with his urge to rush inside. His breaths became fast and short.

He watched Liv open her backpack and drop in the stacks. The men watched her too. She zipped her bag. The short one said something and both men laughed, stepping closer to her. What if the Western Union agent was in on the deal and had switched off the camera? The short man brought his hand to Liv's face but she slapped it away before he touched her. The big guy moved right in front of Liv and Carl couldn't see her anymore. Carl jerked the door open. He would give them the money straight away. He couldn't risk Liv being hurt. They could be dangerous. They could have knives. He would ask Rob to send him another transfer.

He swung the door with a loud bang. The big guy stepped aside, and all three stared at him.

"Hi baby," Liv said loudly, her face tense. She marched towards him.

The men didn't move.

"Sorry I'm late. George and Rob are parking the car." He scooped her in his arm and drew her to his chest. Suddenly her body was so tight against his, her face so close, that he felt her warm breath on his neck. She looked into his eyes, half-frowning with confusion. He was confused too.

And he kissed her. His lips mashed against hers, burning; his tongue thrust into her mouth.

The walls shook. Everything shook, the floor, his body, the air.

He felt dizzy. He was losing his balance. He had left his crutch outside so as not to give the impression that he was weak. She must have felt it because she gently pushed against the small of his back with her hand. He stared into her wide-open eyes, catching his breath. Her lips were still half-open, the edges red and plump, wet. There were marks around her mouth from his stubble. His ears were drumming, blood rushing in his veins.

"You are one lucky dick!"

The grating voice behind Carl brought him back to reality. Suddenly the room was again filled with light, and he was aware of the muffled music coming from a small radio tucked into the corner. The two thugs were staring at them.

"I know." He mustered a lopsided grin. He began pushing Liv in front of him to the door. "Nice to meet you." He waved with his free hand.

Once they were outside and the door behind them shut, Liv clasped her hands in front of her face and, stuttering through her giggles, said, "That was a hell of a strategy."

"Get on the bike, I want to get out of here," Carl said, avoiding her eyes. His heart was still racing.

"They are just bullies. They won't do anything."

"Can we leave, please?"

"Where do we go?"

"Just away from here."

The rush of the wind in his face calmed him. It blew the heat from his face, the burning from his lips. But his mouth was still full of her taste – sweet, juicy, intoxicating. The kiss had turned everything upside down. Suddenly he felt as if he had been beaten by the big guy, and he couldn't think straight. He stared at the lights ahead of them, his mind taking flight, crashing to the ground, then taking flight again. His damp T-shirt flapped against his body.

The deserted road climbed uphill and after a long curve, Liv slowed down and turned into a petrol station. As she stopped, a car drove away from one of the two pumps and there was nobody left – just a stray dog sleeping at the steps of the convenience store. The lights inside were dimmed and the store seemed unattended.

"Are you looking for trouble?" Carl burst out, even before Liv got off the bike. "What are we doing at a dark, abandoned petrol station?"

She put up the kickstand. "Most of the petrol stations near the beach are destroyed or closed. I don't have enough fuel to go very far." She sounded calm. Perhaps she didn't share his anxiety.

"It won't take long." She shoved the nozzle into the tank.

Carl walked around the bike, peering into the darkness of the trees and bushes around the station. He spotted two people on the darker side of the store, away from the only street light. They leaned against the wall, not moving. Could it be the guys from the bank? How hadn't he seen their bike behind them? He pulled himself up straight and stepped back to the bike, shielding Liv with his body. He glanced at the wall again. There were two garbage bins side by side, with a pile of folded cardboard boxes between them. The breeze was lifting the corner of one of the sheets of cardboard. He wiped his palms on his T-shirt.

"How ridiculous to give us four thousand dollars in tens. Now what? I'm going to need a bag." He stood next to Liv, with his back against the pump, watching the turn from the road to the station.

"A bag is useful," she said. "You can use it for your phone, charger, your bottle of water, your medications. You'll soon see how it fills up. And mine gets lighter. But why did you ask for so much money, in the first place?"

"Well, I don't know how long I'll be here for." Carl stared at his oversized Nikes. His feet were sweaty and sore. Socks and new shoes would be his first buy. "And I enquired about arranging private air transportation for the bodies."

"That will be more than four thousand."

"I know, but there are ways to reduce the cost. The guy from Kenyon called me. Said I should be able to get partial sponsorship from the Australian government to repatriate the bodies. He is looking into availability for a flight to Sweden, but it's unlikely in the next few days. Probably by the end of the week. He gave me the number of a company in Singapore and said they might be able to do it faster."

Earlier he had made a number of calls to Sweden to arrange the paperwork for the bodies to leave Thailand. He had considered calling Kristoffer's law firm and suggesting they get involved. They were the biggest in Sweden and the owner, Jonas Karlsson, whom Carl had met once at a charity dinner, was friendly with Queen Silvia. He wished he had his London phone with all the numbers and emails. He knew he had Jonas's private email and it bugged him that he would have to call the main office first, explain who he was and why it couldn't wait until Jonas returned from his Christmas holidays.

"Wait for the Swedish military plane. It's more straightforward."

"I want to get going. I want to get out of this damn place as soon as possible."

Liv didn't say anything. He looked at her, waiting for her response. She always had something to say. Now, she stood silently watching the pump nozzle. Her hair slid over her face and he couldn't see her expression. When the hiss of petrol stopped, she pulled the nozzle out and hooked it onto the pump.

"Let's go for a drink and something to eat," Liv flipped the petrol cap closed. "Then maybe buy a bag and after that, hospital."

"Sounds like a plan to me." Carl slapped a mosquito on his forearm and it left a bloody trace.

"You happy with something local?"

"Very. But I'd like a few more lights than there are here, more people and no stray dogs."

She fastened her helmet. "You are so high maintenance."

"Yes, I want proper forks and knives. I haven't had those since I arrived in Thailand."

With one arm, Carl dragged a heavy wooden chair from under the table while trying to maintain his balance. A waiter trotted around but instead of helping him with the chair, he took the crutch once Carl had flopped into the seat, cautiously leaning it against the table. He grabbed a napkin from the table, flapped it in the air and placed it on Carl's lap. Before rushing away, the waiter shoved a tri-fold laminated menu into his hands.

"Please, a large bottle of still—"

But the waiter had gone.

Carl searched for Liv. The Thai man with the Santa hat at the entrance, who had hugged her and spoken in hushed tones, was now catching a crab in a fish tank at the entrance stall. Carl saw Liv squatting with her arms on her knees, talking to an older blonde woman who sat at a table with a teenage girl. The girl was wearing a headset, mouthing words and nodding to some unheard music. Liv had said the restaurant was favoured by many of her expat friends and was off the tourist track. Carl liked this kind of place since the food would be better if they relied on returning customers. Everybody knew Liv, he thought, growing impatient. Every table, apart from two at the back, was occupied, mostly by foreigners. On second thoughts, he hoped that not *everybody* knew Liv.

Carl swiped a dead insect from the sticky surface of the table. The tartan tablecloth was tattered at the corners and smelt of a strange mix of beer, curry and disinfectant.

Why did he kiss Liv? He was stupid. It was unnecessary.

It complicated things. He couldn't understand how it had happened. He didn't want her to misunderstand him, to think that he was interested in her. He wanted to explain himself but he didn't know what to say.

"Your Jack Daniel's." The waiter plonked a full glass with large cubes bobbing above the rim in front of Carl.

"You read my mind," Carl said.

"Liv told me," the waiter said shortly. He placed a glass of white wine on the other side of the tale and left.

Carl frowned. Was it personal? That was the second time the waiter had turned his back on him. He didn't care what was in his head but he wanted to order food. He scanned the restaurant for another waiter. There was only one older Thai woman, slowly trudging towards the back with a tray of dirty dishes. It would be a while before she returned. Carl took a fork from a wooden jar in the middle of the table and hooked most of the ice from the glass, throwing it on the ground behind him. He took a large sip, feeling a burn in his throat that spread to his stomach. He placed his elbows on the sides of his chair and glanced above his head, where threads of tiny lights stretched on trees branches wrapped everything in a soothing yellow light. He sipped again.

He had kissed Liv because he hadn't had sex since August. It was as simple as that. She was very sexy and he had simply lost it. Overreacted. Carl took a large gulp and crunched a piece of ice with his molars. He shook his head. The wrong time and place even to think about sex. He felt a pang of guilt. How could he spare a thought for anything besides his grief? He glanced along the tables. Liv was walking towards him, and she smiled when their eyes met. It suddenly became hard to breathe. Carl dropped his eyes to his glass and slurped his whisky.

"Sorry, I had to speak to a friend." Liv sat down. "Well, more of an acquaintance."

She picked up Carl's glass and brought it to her mouth. She touched the glass rim with the tip of her tongue before taking a sip. It aroused him, that brief moment, the more so because she hadn't seemed conscious of it.

"Are you enjoying your drink?" She put the glass on the table next to his hand. "I guessed a guy like you would order a whisky when he says he needs a drink first."

Carl turned his almost empty glass in his hands. "A guy like me prefers his whisky without ice, for next time. But thank you for ordering it for me. I felt totally ignored by your waiter."

"By Anurak? Impossible."

"In that case, can we order food, please? I haven't been able to get his attention."

"I did order. I don't know why it's not here." She waived to the waiter, who immediately spotted her as if he had been waiting for her to call him.

Carl raised his eyebrows. "You ordered food for us?"

It felt strange that she had decided for him again. It wasn't a big decision but he wasn't used to someone taking care of him. He often felt sorry for his male friends when their girlfriends would take care of them and order something they believed was healthy or good. And the poor guy would have to eat bland fish with broccoli on the side, when the only thing he wanted was a rib-eye with French fries.

"It was on the list, wasn't it?"

For a moment, Carl wasn't sure what Liv meant. And then he tried to remember what else was on the list. "You are not the kind of person who follows a list," he said.

"But you are, aren't you?" She winked.

"Your green chicken curry." The waiter placed a large ceramic pot in the middle of the table and lifted the lid. Steam, and the rich curry aroma, exploded into the air.

"It's very good here. I hope you like it," Liv said, taking a bowl of rice from the waiter's hands.

"I love green curry." Carl dipped his spoon in the thick liquid and poured it over his rice. It had the perfect consistency. He took a couple of spoonfuls.

"I cook a mean green curry," Liv said with her mouth full.

"That's cool, mine always comes up just okay." With his napkin, he wiped around his nose and forehead. He scooped large dollops of chilli onto his plate.

"I only cook it well in Thailand, I think it's all about the ingredients."

"That is what I always said, so I bought everything from a Thai shop. But it just never worked. Kristoffer, naturally, cooked it only once and it was perfect first time. Thick, like this one." Kristoffer used to joke that maybe he was half Thai. He preferred Thai food to Korean. Nobody, it occurred to Carl, knew his real roots.

"I wish I'd met Kristoffer and Eva," Liv said in a low voice.

Carl felt a tightness in his chest. He wished the same but didn't say it out loud. It was already awkward, having a cosy dinner under that stars, Mariah Carey drifting over from speakers hidden among trees, talking about cooking and things they liked as if they were on a date. He put a full spoon of curry in his mouth and chewed it slowly.

"Your cold Singha." The waiter placed a tall glass covered in droplets on the table.

"*Skål.*" Liv raised her glass of white wine. "For …?" She tilted her glass from side to side.

"*Skål.*" Carl lifted his glass and fleetingly looked into her eyes before taking a mouthful of beer. He didn't want her ask what they were toasting. He was afraid to know what was in her head.

A short silence grew into an uncomfortably long one.

"What wine do you like?" Carl said.

350

"This one, as a matter of fact. The grapes are grown here in Phuket."

"There are no good wines in Thailand."

"Have you tried this one?" She tilted her head to one side.

"No, I just know. Wines made in this hot climate are too low in acidity, too ripe in the fruit, and with a high alcohol content, which means they likely lack structure."

She rolled her eyes. "You sound like my father."

Carl cringed inside. He didn't know the guy but he didn't want to be compared to her father for good or bad. And from her tone, it was rather bad. It sounded like a summing up of everything that was wrong was with him.

"He is a man of theory rather than experience," she quickly added and glanced somewhere over her shoulder.

"Are your parents still together?"

"My mother died."

"I'm sorry," Carl said. "Were you … were you a child when she passed away?"

"No, it was five years ago." She traced the squares of the tablecloth with her finger. "And my father remarried after eight months. I can't blame him. She was in many ways the reason I left home. But I thought he could have waited a little." Liv rolled her eyes and shook her head. "He married his assistant. The same assistant who came to our house and helped me with my maths in my last years in school. He was never home. I always thought he was married to his work. Well, I suppose he was. And all the while, my mother kept the perfect façade of the happy family."

"I'm sorry you were in the middle of it."

Liv shrugged. "How about your family. Tell me about the skeletons in your closet."

"There aren't any. Mum and Dad are still together. They have been working together since they met, they were teachers at my local school. Dad still makes her breakfast in bed every weekend day. They play golf together. Meet with their friends. I think they are happy together."

Liv held her glass between her slender fingers, moving it around the table, lost in her thoughts. Then she glanced at him and said, "So why can't you enjoy the ordinary?"

The question, at first, confused him; he didn't understand what she meant. And then he felt a light tremble in his chest. Did she just put her finger on something that had always nagged him, especially at night when he couldn't sleep, but couldn't find the words for?

A bat passed above her head and disappeared into branches braided with threads of light.

"Is it because you couldn't fit in?" Liv said.

He stared at her. She slowly ran her fingers down her long neck, tucking her hair over her shoulder. In the dim light her skin glowed a warm gold. He pushed his chair back and it dragged against the stone tiles. He was glad that it was dark, otherwise she would see his cheeks flush. He wondered if she knew that he regretted kissing her. He wondered if she knew that his whole body was burning with desire.

She opened her bag and got out a plastic bottle of pills. "Take your medication."

He pulled himself together, but his heart was still pounding as he if he had just taken the stairs two at a time.

"You would be a good wife."

The words had rolled off his tongue before he realised that it might give her the wrong idea. He was not looking for a wife and he definitely hadn't considered her for the role.

"I would be reprimanded by your doctor for allowing you to swallow these with whisky."

"My doctor told me that alcohol has no impact on the

352

efficiency of antibiotics." Carl put a capsule in his mouth and drank half glass of water.

Liv raised an eyebrow. "It's good to have an alcohol friendly doctor."

"But he did say that was not the case for painkillers, and that alcohol increases the burden on your body, which has enough to do fighting disease." Carl laced his hands behind his back, pushed out his chest and said, "I feel better."

"I think it's the anaesthetic part of the alcohol."

"Possibly. And food too. But I do feel better. I don't want to go to the hospital. What is the point? I'll find a hotel, take a shower and sleep in a comfortable bed instead of a glorified trolley."

"What if you suddenly feel worse? The fever goes up? You lose consciousness?"

"I won't. Probably."

"Isn't that how you ended up in the hospital in the first place?"

"Yeah." He rubbed behind his head. He was lucky that Jack had been in the room when he collapsed unconscious. He should have gone to the hospital before the cremation ceremony – he had fever already then but hoped it would go down with paracetamol.

"By the way. It's not that easy to find a hotel," Liv said.

"Most tourists have left by now, haven't they?"

"But there are a lot of officials, volunteers, people like you who have arrived. And of course fewer hotels."

"You know your way around. Can you call a few hotels and find me a decent room?"

"I feel like I'm your unpaid secretary." She said it with a girlish laugh that did not quite ring true to him.

"Sorry I made you feel that way. You have saved the day for me, more than once." Carl moved his empty plate to the side and leaned over the table, looking straight into her eyes.

"Your help has been priceless. Without you, it would have been impossible."

"Why don't you just sleep at my place?"

Carl tensed. "Maybe that's not the best idea. I'll be fine in a hotel."

"You might be. But it would save me a lot of time. And tomorrow morning we'll go together to Kao Lak."

"I have money. I can get a taxi. You don't need to drive me around."

"Carl, I'm tired. My place is a ten-minute drive from here. You can take a shower and be in bed within an hour. And if you suddenly feel worse, I can call the hospital." She spoke like many of his male friends when they tried to convince girls after few drinks that their place was better for the night, that they had tea they brought from a monastery in Japan or a book they wanted to share – even though Carl knew they had never been to Japan and there wasn't a bookshelf in the flat. Often, he envied them because he wasn't good at all at saying things that weren't true.

"I'll give you my bed and I can sleep on the fold-out—"

"Liv, please. Listen to me." He fixed his eyes on her. "I know you like me. But there can be nothing between us. I do find you extremely attractive. But I don't want to give you the wrong idea. We are different. You have a very different life from mine. I'll leave in a few days. I don't want to feel guilty that I slept with you because I wanted to and not because I was really interested in you, that I wanted something more than just one night. I don't want to take advantage of the situation."

Liv rolled up her napkin and slowly twisted it in her hands. A heavy silence hung between them. A tea light placed in a glass jar in the middle of the table died, and a thin strand of smoke like white twine curled around something invisible in the night. When she looked up, Carl noticed first that her eyes were swollen and raw. And then he saw in them a wounded rage, and his heart sank. Maybe, just maybe, he had fucked up the best thing that could possibly happen to him.

"Why would you tell me all that?"

"Because I like you. And I'm very grateful for all your help. That is why I want to be honest with you." He felt lightheaded. He couldn't bring himself to look her in the eyes again.

"I offered you help. Not sex." Her words were stilted and cold.

"Don't you think that is how it would end up if I stayed at yours?"

"You know yourself better than I do. It was you who jumped on me at Western Union."

"I … was protecting you from those thugs."

"I wish they'd protected me from you."

Carl wanted to say that he was sorry for kissing her, but the waiter came to their table and began collecting their dishes.

"Anurak, do you have a plastic bag?"

The waiter looked confused.

"I would like to do a takeaway. These rice crackers." She picked a basket with the crackers from his tray.

"I pack it and bring it for you." He tried to pull the basket from her hand.

"No, no. Leave it and bring us a plastic bag," she said. "Two plastic bags, please."

There were bits of rice where Carl's plate had been, and a pool of green curry. The waiter wiped the table but not Carl's side. Carl took his napkin from his lap and wiped the rest of the food away. He probably deserved it.

"I'll call around the hotels myself. And you can go and rest. I'll get a taxi. I … I'm sorry I kissed you." His lower lip quivered. He knew his voice was trembling. He bit his lip hard before continuing. "I didn't mean to hurt you."

"And you didn't," Liv said woodenly.

The waiter brought a white foam food container.

Carl saw the corners of her mouth curl up and she gave a little snort of laughter. He felt his own lips spreading into a smile. One of the things he loved about her was that a tiny thing would bring a smile to her face and she would throw it at him, like a mirror that catches a sunbeam.

The waiter looked from one to the other, perplexed. "You wanted a takeaway, Miss Liv."

"It's fine. Thank you," she said. She took the box from him and said to Carl, "It might work better. So you don't need to buy a bag."

She pushed her chair back and swung one leg over the other. "Anurak, please bring us two double whiskies. One with ice and one without. And one Diet Coke."

Carl sighed. He wished she hadn't ordered more drinks. He wished he could go right now. But he owed it to her to stay.

"It's not good for my medication," he said.

"Your doctor said it's fine." She slipped the box under the table, and Carl heard the zip of her backpack and a rustle of paper. When the box reappeared, it was bulging, and Liv held it closed as she pushed it across the table towards him.

"The cash, your antibiotics, and the receipt for your passport."

"Thank you," he said. On top of the box was a large paperclip. He picked it up and looked at Liv.

"And this?"

"For luck."

"How did you learn to use it?"

The waiter brought their drinks. Liv added the Coke to her whisky and mixed it with her finger. She sucked the tip of her finger and took a mouthful of her drink.

Carl lifted his glass and tilted it from side to side. The rich amber reflected the lights. He really wasn't sure if he should drink more tonight. He put the glass on the table untouched.

"It was my first year in Thailand," she said slowly. "I had no money left and no place to stay. I'd seen how they do it in the movies and always wondered whether it was that easy." She sipped her drink again, thought for a moment and poured more Coke, almost up to the rim. "I slept on a beach for a few days, on a stack of sunbeds under a big wooden umbrella. It was the end of the rainy season and one night it poured continuously and I was completely soaked, despite the umbrella. Behind me, there was this stunning villa with a tidy garden and an infinity pool. I thought, there's nobody there, no guards or dogs – why not go inside, sleep in a comfy bed and have a nice shower? I played with a lock on the patio doors and managed to get them open. I stayed in that villa for nearly two months. Until one day I came back in the evening and there were lights on. I always kept my bag with the important stuff under a shrub in the garden, so I didn't lose anything apart from a toothbrush and maybe a box of tea that I left in the kitchen."

Liv rested her head on her hand, leaning over the table.

"For the next two years, I lived in luxurious villas all along the coast here. I would move away if the owners returned or the location wasn't convenient for me, or water didn't run in the shower, or a toilet began to smell bad. Until finally one day a guard caught me. I'd just moved into a villa, very modern, took a bedroom with a sea view. Not the master bedroom, I always thought it was dangerous to stay in the master bedroom. I don't know how I didn't see the guard living at the property, because of course many properties do have guards. He didn't notice me straight away either. It was only the following day that he knocked on my door."

She slapped a mosquito on her elbow but missed it. When she removed her hand there was already a small pink bump. Carl wondered if she had to sleep with the guard to get away. He took a long gulp of his whisky.

"I gave him fifty dollars. You know, they have a tiny wage, these guys. Then we talked a bit. Me speaking Thai helped of course, and for fifty more he allowed me to stay for another six weeks. The owner came for a holiday with his family and when they left the guard called me and said I could stay any time for thirty dollars a month. That is when I learnt that if you have spare money it's easier to make some arrangement with a guard, an official, whatever."

"Why did you tell me all that?"

"You asked me how I learned to use a paperclip." She sipped and moved her glass from one hand to the other. "Anything else you'd like to ask?"

"Did you sell your body?"

"God no! Why would you ask that?"

"You are very beautiful," he said lamely.

"That is not a reason to sell your body." Liv rubbed the middle of her forehead with her fingers. "You know, you can be quite offensive sometimes."

"I didn't mean … I'm sorry."

Carl wanted to say more but stopped himself. He tensed his toes in his sneakers, feeling the small, sharp stones that were lodged there. He stared at the space between his feet, unable to look her in the eye, his cheeks burning. He was still trying to figure out who she was. She was so different from anyone he had ever known. He had met her with Luka, whose reference he wouldn't trust, but she had saved his life twice. She was smart but was wasting her life backpacking. She was brave but was hiding in Thailand from something. She was reckless but thoughtful. He glanced at the scar on her wrist. He didn't believe the story she'd told him about the bike accident.

"Did you ever take drugs?" he said.

"Oh, that's a softie compare to the previous question." She chuckled. "Yes, I did. Pretty much all of them. But I took a vow never to touch anything again. Come on, next question. You're good at this."

"Did you steal?"

"Yes."

"What did you steal?

"I stole food because I was hungry." She looked at him reflectively, playing with her turtle pendant, moving it along the string from right to left. Carl knew instinctively that he wouldn't like what she said next. "And I stole hearts, men's hearts. Because I am beautiful and I can."

He winced. "Truly?"

"What do you think?"

"Yes."

"Bingo."

"What do you do with them?"

"With the hearts? I eat them," she said flatly. "I also fake documents."

"Why are you telling me?"

"Because I did it for you, remember? At the embassy. Does it make me a forger?" She curled a strand of her hair around her finger.

Carl swallowed. At the temporary Swedish Embassy they had met up with Fredrik, who was very apologetic about the confusion with the refrigerated containers. He said it would take longer to verify Carl's identity and issue him a temporary passport to leave Thailand, since he hadn't been in the country during the tsunami and the procedure was slightly different. Fredrik had taken Liv aside and Carl overheard him whispering something about how he looked like many of the Turkish he had met in his years working in the embassy in Istanbul, trying everything possible to get a visa to enter Sweden. Fredrik said Carl had probably known that Carl Lundmark was missing and was using his name; he had probably even met him and picked up some information about him. Liv told him she had known Carl since childhood because their parents had been friends.

When they got outside, Carl told her they could check his identity through the Ministry for Foreign Affairs – they had his photograph from his last passport application. He didn't say how much of the conversation he had overheard, embarrassed that she too might have doubted him.

"They prioritise tsunami victims," Liv said. "He wanted me to vouch for you in writing, so I did."

"Well, thank you for lying on my behalf," Carl said.

"You know, it's not what you call something, it's why do you do it."

"So why did you help me?"

"Because you needed help. I think it's a good reason to help someone, no?" She shook the remains of the ice in her glass and raised it to her lips. "Or did you think that I helped you because I liked you? Because I wanted to sleep with you? Don't you think that's a bit too much trouble to go to for sex?"

Carl couldn't collect his thoughts for a coherent answer. He opened his mouth but words didn't come out. Anyway, it was safer to not say anything. He already felt like an asshole. He was getting himself in trouble every time he said something. He peered at the base of his fingernail, from which he had picked a piece of skin. It was bleeding and he pressed his finger against it.

"You are not so good at answering blunt questions, are you?" Liv said.

Most of the tables were now empty and the light above the crab tank was off. Anurak was wiping down tables and glanced in their direction several times. It would be obvious to him, Carl thought, that they weren't having a cheery conversation. He wondered if the waiter was happier now.

Liv leaned over the table. "I helped you," she said, "because my friend, Achara, is still missing. She is Luka's brother's fiancée. His family, who has all the money in the world, did nothing. Nothing. They didn't even fly out to check on him. They paid others to do it. They organised a private plane and he is now in Singapore, recovering at the best hospital. But they didn't do anything for Achara."

Carl realised he hadn't asked Liv if there had been any news of her friend – he had forgotten she was even looking for someone. She hadn't said much and he only vaguely remembered the connection with Luka.

Liv tilted her chair back onto its back legs. "You know, they have been together for six years. His family came here two weeks ago to choose a venue for the wedding. It was to be in April. They all said how much they adored Achara, how lucky they were to have her in the family. They said they wanted a wedding the island would remember for years. The fireworks alone were going to cost fifty thousand."

That all sounded like Luka's family. Carl guessed Achara was Thai.

"And here, I meet you going to the forgotten island, looking for your friends against all the odds, risking your own life. I liked that. I helped you because I thought you were different."

"Thought? Not *think*?"

"You are so full of yourself."

Carl flinched.

"Worse, you are weird. Luka was right about you. You are weird."

His face flushed and he stared at her, hurt and angry.

"You don't know me," he said.

"Well, you don't know me."

"But I want to know you."

"I have a feeling you want to prove something to yourself and until you do, you don't want to know me," Liv said, and got up. "Don't worry about a bill. And don't read anything into that. The owner of the restaurant owed me."

She stumbled over a root as she walked towards the exit.

"Maybe you shouldn't drive?" he said weakly.

She didn't look back. "I'll be fine."

He wanted to run after her and order a taxi. But he didn't dare. He knew she wouldn't let him. He also knew that she would be fine.

He wondered if *he* would be.

Twenty-nine

Carl raised his coffee cup to his lips and found it cold and nearly empty. He put it down, and the black flecks swirled, found a pattern, and settled in the remaining quarter-inch of liquid. He briefly calculated how much money was left on his phone after all his morning calls.

The Singaporean company had offered him a plane for the bodies' transportation on the evening of 5th January, but the price was steep and the deposit was to be paid by the end of the day if he wanted to secure space on the flight. He spoke with Ben from Kenyon but he still couldn't confirm their next availability. Eva's mother emailed dental records for both Eva and Kristoffer, and he forwarded it to Wat Yan Yao mortuary for comparison.

After that, he called Luka to get an idea of the situation with Ralf, and whether he still had a job so he could cover the cost of transportation. They had signed the contract with the investor just before New Year, and Luka and Ralf were in Vegas celebrating. Luka said that Ralf didn't seem angry with Carl anymore since they'd got what they wanted anyway; but Luka was now in charge of the fund which meant that at best Carl would be given a lesser role when he got back. Strangely, it didn't bother Carl. What unsettled him was that he realised he would prefer to have heard he was fired, rather than have to choose whether to continue working for Ralf. As he listened to Luka telling him about the size of the investment they had secured, he decided he would pay for the transportation costs from his savings. He wrote 'Call bank' at the end of his long to-do list. By the time it opened it would be late afternoon in Thailand, and he hoped there would be more clarity with Kenyon.

Carl asked Luka how his brother was and Luka said he had been transferred to a clinic in Switzerland and was getting better, but that he hadn't seen him yet. They all assumed that his fiancée had died since there was no news about her, and he said how sad they all were. When Carl asked him why they hadn't tried to find her body, Luka said he wasn't sure what they could have done or whether it would change anything. Then he said he had to go.

When Carl looked into the half-collapsed tunnel of his past, things became blurred. Usually, the past was certain. Now, it confused him. Carl had a chilling feeling that it was the past of someone else, someone who had been lost forever in the mangrove creek on the island.

Carl was sitting at a round table in the back courtyard of his hotel. Lush palm trees covered the ugly concrete wall of the building. The table was rusted, and rocked every time he touched it. He had sat at a similar table, with an identical problem, in the Rodin Museum Garden with Kristoffer and Eva, eating croissants with latte; they had folded a street map and put it under one of the table legs.

Jack had come by the hotel, and the ashtray in the middle of the table still had his Marlboro stubs. When the waiter attempted to clear it away, Carl asked him to leave it. That morning at the Rodin, Kristoffer had bought a pack of Marlboro and declared that he would smoke while they were in Paris. Carl had thought it silly at that time, but Kristoffer had said it was decadent and Hemingway-esque.

Jack had said he found the clubhouse safe buried in the sand where the yoga *sala* used to be. He had taken a leather pouch from his pocket and tipped two silver rings into his open palm and offered them to Carl. Carl recognised them instantly. He had offered them in his open palm to Kristoffer at the church. Carl stared at the rings for a long moment, then wiped his eyes with the back of his hand.

"I guess this also belongs to Kristoffer."

Jack placed a book with damp-stained cover on the table. It was the first edition of *The Old Man and the Sea* that Eva had given to Kristoffer as a wedding present. Carl flipped through the creased and stiffened pages.

Now is no time to think of what you do not have. Think of what you can do with what there is.

That was what Kristoffer always quoted. That was how he lived. But Kristoffer would never become old.

He closed the book and moved it to a shaded spot on the table. He wished life had dealt Kristoffer – and him – a different hand. He was still unable to grasp his new reality. In his mind, he still was making deals and hopeless offers to destiny. And he was still asking, Why?

According to the newspapers, the earthquake had been magnitude 9.3 on the Richter scale – the second-largest earthquake in recorded history. It had lasted for close to ten minutes, an eternity in seismological terms. The tectonic plates had readjusted themselves. The India plate, part of the great Indo-Australian plate, had slipped further into the earth and the Burma plate, a portion of the great Eurasian plate, had snapped upwards. The megathrust was unusually large in geographical and geological extent. An estimated 1,300 kilometres of fault surface had ruptured and moved, shifting

365

between five and fifteen metres at different spots along the subduction zone – the longest tear in an ocean seabed that scientists had ever seen.

For Carl, there was some comfort in the numbers, in the science behind an event which at first seemed meaningless, random. But in the same way that scientists, with all their knowledge, were unable to predict whether the next earthquake would create a tsunami, nothing that Carl read could answer his question: Why Kristoffer and Eva?

He read that the waves reached the African coast eight hours after the quake but caused no damage. That in Indonesia alone the death toll was already above 100,000, and in Sri Lanka – where he'd visited the previous Christmas with his parents – 18,000, mainly locals. And that children accounted for one-third of those missing. He thought about Marcus's daughter, who perished in Koh Phra Thong; and about Eric's son. Their tiny bodies might never be found.

Later in the morning he met Eric at Phuket International Hospital when he went to change his bandages. Eric was alert and decisive; he didn't ask questions anymore. His daughter was in intensive care. Carl remembered her sitting in the taxi between them, clasping the edges of her skirt. Eric said that yesterday she had suddenly stopped talking and her left arm and leg had become paralysed. A chest radiograph revealed air and pus outside the lining of the lungs and a brain scan showed four abscesses. It was a type of aspiration pneumonia that occurred from inhaling saltwater contaminated with mud and bacteria. It had entered her bloodstream and spread to the brain, producing abscesses and neurological problems. Dr Green said they already had more than twenty people with different aspirational problems due to near drowning, which they were calling tsunami lung – something that could develop even a month later.

In a strange way, his daughter brought Eric back into the world. She was the only fragment left of his broken family and he was fighting with her for her to stay alive. She gave him a reason to live.

Carl glanced at the open book.

"Think of what you can do with what there is …" he said aloud.

A sparrow was collecting breadcrumbs from under the table. A second sparrow flew down and they began to fight. Then two more landed and without any fuss started collecting the crumbs until Carl's foot moved into their territory. All four were gone in an instant.

Carl opened the *Phuket News* with its cover of a photo of a woman with spiky, dye-streaked hair, punk style, and rows of bracelets around her wrists, dressed in a khaki T-shirt, tight jeans and rubber boots. She was standing with a group of men in hazmats, and Carl immediately recognised the coffin wall in Wat Yan Yao behind them. 'The voice of death', the paper was calling her – Dr Porntip, Thailand's top forensic scientist. He peered at the woman's face, at the line of piercings in her ear. If he saw her again, he would certainly remember her.

He skimmed through the pages. There was a story about a French family of five, reunited seven days after the disaster. A list of the beaches in Phuket that were left untouched by the wave. An article about the King's grandson, who had died in the tsunami.

Carl stopped at the headline on page seven: THE INSTINCT CANNOT BE TAMED. He stared at the black and white photo of a crocodile in front of a huge aloe plant with thorns almost the size of the crocodile's teeth. The plant leaned over the edge of a pond, like a gigantic octopus creeping back into the water. When he looked at the crocodile again, he noticed barefoot legs sticking out from its half-open jaws. At first, Carl thought it was a trick – tamers sticking their heads into the open jaws of crocodiles was a common form of entertainment in Thailand. But looking closer he saw a black pool on the ground below. '*This crocodile killed the keeper who fed it every day of its life,*' was the first sentence of a short article. He didn't read the rest of the article and closed the newspaper. He noticed the story was flagged on the front page, above the masthead. Under a tiny picture of the crocodile, with the trainer kneeling in front of it, smiling, was the caption, '*Instinct is the monster hiding under the face of humanity.*'

"Do you know what is the most powerful human instinct?"

Carl hadn't realised Dylan was standing behind him. The Australian put his cigarettes and phone on the table. He'd shaved, Carl noticed immediately, and his hair was combed.

"Survival?" he said, and moved a chair for Dylan to sit.

"No, the urge to procreate. Where is your girl?"

"Taking a day off."

"Did you fight?"

Carl stared at him. How the hell did he always know what was going on? The sign of a good journalist, he decided. He wondered if he should stop avoiding Dylan's questions, just to save time.

"No, why?"

"You look like a truck ran over you."

"Well, yes, there was a tsunami and I lost my best friend, my hotel room was full of mosquitos and the air con didn't work, from six the sun was beating in my window – which has no curtains – and the air became so hot and humid that I felt as if I was breathing through a dishrag. My leg still hurts, and the coffee is rubbish here. Is that enough reasons to look like shit?"

"On the positive, you are finally wearing clothes your size."

"That is the best thing that's happened to me today." Carl rubbed his hands on his knee-length jeans shorts, bought at the market near the hospital. To wear proper underwear felt good too.

"Why you didn't stay at her place?"

The question surprised Carl.

"Because she is not my girlfriend."

Dylan raised his eyebrows. "I kinda wasn't sure." He fidgeted on his chair. "Because she is a very cool chick, you know. I kinda like her."

A waiter brought Dylan his coffee and collected Carl's empty plates.

Carl didn't like Dylan calling Liv a chick, but he only said, "Welcome to the kinda club." He picked up a butter wrapper, crumpled it with his fingers and put it into his empty coffee cup. "Any success with *Aftonbladet*?"

"My article is in print, will be in today's newspaper. Thanks for putting me in contact with them. I'm writing another two pieces for them."

"I'm glad. It's Liv's contact, you should thank her not me."

"I did, I went this morning to her flat and gave her a copy of the article." Dylan sipped his coffee, looking straight at him. Carl realised he'd held his breath for too long. He exhaled. "Her coffee is much better than this."

Carl leaned back on his chair, his cheeks flushed as if he had been slapped. He wondered if Mister Investigative Journalist noticed it. He felt a mixture of relief and confusion, and something else that bubbled inside him. He had called Liv twice during the course of the morning, left a voicemail and texted his apologies for being rude. She hadn't replied, which he thought was understandable. But as time went by, he became anxious that something may have happened to her on her way home. He had called the restaurant but nobody picked up. He decided not to call Fredrik meantime, hoping that he would hear something from Liv. He hadn't thought about Dylan.

"You know that she is a teacher at a private school," Dylan said, "and then spends her weekends at a school for stateless children?"

Carl didn't know that.

"What kind of a job is that anyway?" Dylan picked up his Camels from the table and, without taking his eyes off Carl, pulled one with his teeth from the pack. "It's a charity. Fine. But, you know, she could do so much more with her life. She is smart and beautiful." He lit up his cigarette and took a drag, shaking his head. "She said her life turned upside down after her injury in Nagano in 1998."

"Yes," Carl said, not moving his lips. He felt as if Dylan had stolen something that belonged to him, even though he didn't want it.

"How well do you know her?"

"From childhood. Our parents were friends," Carl said, making sure that he didn't blink.

"Oh, I see, that is why the two of you look so close." He crinkled his eyes against the smoke.

"Yes."

Dylan's phone pinged and he put his cigarette into the ashtray and began texting, his foot bouncing on the ground.

"What is your next article about?" Carl said, staring at the cigarette as it slowly turned to ash. He wondered if Dylan was texting Liv.

"The plane. Hold on … It just landed."

"Which plane?"

"Swedish military plane. I thought you knew. Liv said that Fredrik would call you."

"No, I didn't know. Nobody called." Carl checked his

phone. There were no missed calls. He had been on to the temporary embassy earlier, enquiring about embalming the bodies, but no one had mentioned it. He wrapped the Hemingway in a clean cotton napkin and put it into the side pocket of his backpack. He gathered up the newspapers and notepad, and grabbed his crutch – a new one acquired from the hospital that morning. "Are you coming with me?"

"Of course, it's my next assignment for *Aftonbladet*."

"I want to speak to someone senior," Carl said to a man in loose jeans with a skull ring on his middle finger. The lanyard badge around his neck stated that he worked for the Swedish consulate. The place was even more crowded than the last time, and from the bits of conversation he overheard, Carl realised many people had just arrived in Thailand, eager to find missing relatives.

"Perhaps I can help?"

Carl sniffed. "When does the plane take off with bodies being repatriated?"

"Oh, I don't know." The man pulled up his jeans. "I think you need to go to the queue at that table in the corner. Ulrika will help you."

"I don't want to speak to Ulrika or anyone else at a table, I have been through all that already. I want to speak to Jonas Hastrom. I know he's here."

"I don't think I know who that is."

Dylan stepped in. "He's the ambassador to Thailand. I'm Dylan Williams, from *Aftonbladet*. We agreed he would do an interview."

The man rubbed his pierced ear. "Right, let me see if I can find someone."

He wandered off and returned in a few minutes with a woman in her fifties, dressed in grey trousers and a white shirt.

"I'm Emma Ostberg, I work for the Swedish Ministry for Foreign Affairs." She reached out her hand. "I heard about you and your deceased friends. Fredrik warned me. My condolences."

Warned me? It sounded like a less than enthusiastic introduction, Carl thought.

"The plane will take off when we fill it with coffins. There is nothing you can do to speed it up." She looked at him over her glasses. "And please tell your journalist friend to stop sniffing around here. You are doing your country no favours in these difficult times."

Carl's first reaction was to disagree. He thought he was helping his country, even if not the government of his country. But the conversation wasn't about that and he bit his tongue.

"How many bodies do you have right now, ready to load onto the plane?"

She hesitated before saying, "Three. It will be five with your friends."

"That is how many bodies you were able to bring together, a week after the tsunami?" Carl stared at her. "Do you realise it will take you a month to fill it up?"

"Do you understand that it doesn't make any sense to fly a huge military plane back with five coffins? It's expensive and a waste of resources." She crossed her arms.

"Do you know where to look for bodies?"

"Yes, they are stored at various locations like temples and hospitals. We already have fifty-two people confirmed dead."

"Do you know what is required with each body to get them to the airport in a coffin ready to fly?"

"No, it's not my responsibility here on the ground. Other people deal with that. I believe they are competent enough to do it without my interference."

"I don't think they are, since this is the third of January

and you have only three bodies ready out of fifty-two. Fifty-two known, that is."

Her pale face flushed with anger. "It's easy to criticise when the only thing you do is go around telling people what to do."

Carl bit his tongue for the second time.

"First, you will need to get a death certificate," he said evenly. "I got one for my friends on the 31st. However, since then the rules have changed, visual identification is no longer allowed. Now, you need a DNA test or dental records, and this slows down the process a lot. Then you have to transfer each body from their location, whether it's a local temple or a hospital, to a central area with refrigerated containers. This is also time-consuming and Sweden doesn't have the logistical capability on the ground—"

"We deployed the Swedish Rescue Services Agency for transportation and other logistics," Emma Ostberg said.

"I don't think they're doing their job very well so far. I waited for their refrigerated van from the thirty-first, when I called them, to the second. In the end I had to sort it out myself."

"I'm sorry to hear that you didn't have enough help."

"Then, you need to embalm the bodies to preserve them during air transportation. I'm still waiting for the embalming specialist to contact me."

Carl looked at her expectantly, and she seemed to be weighing her response.

"Your feedback is valuable to us," she said, and adjusted her glasses.

"It will take you a while to round up fifty-two bodies. Most countries have already begun to repatriate their deceased citizens and it's not a secret here or in Sweden that the Swedish government's response was weak and disappointing." Carl paused. "You have to fly the plane back immediately to show that you are at least doing something."

"Thank you for sharing your opinion. The decision as to when the plane takes off is made in Stockholm. We don't make such decisions here."

"If you don't fly the plane immediately, I will use private transportation that I have already organised. It will be very embarrassing for the government when my friends arrive home as the only dead Swedish citizens to be brought back. There will be a lot of questions from the media about why the Swedish government seems unable to bring home its own dead."

There were four people in front of Carl for a blood test and progress was slow. The back of his chair was broken and he tried not to lean on it. He rested his elbows on his knees and glanced at his clean nails. He wondered if Liv would find him more attractive when he was shaved and wore clean clothes.

Before going to the hospital, he had popped into a barbershop on a side street. It was an industrial-style place with exposed concrete floors and rough walls covered in mismatched posts and rusted metal cabinets, run by a tattoo-clad Chinese barber with a fake American accent. He asked Carl if he wanted a manicure while he was having a shave. His nails were long but, worse, he still couldn't get the creek mud from underneath them and from the sides of his nails. And so, at first reluctantly, he agreed and sank into a soft leather vintage-style chair.

Afterwards, he walked to a nearby street market, where he bought himself a bag of fried bananas – the same as Tanawat had cooked for Liv.

There was little chance that he would bump into Liv again, as had happened so many times before. Carl ran the back of his hand along his jaw. The skin was smooth and soft – the barber did a good job. He remembered the red marks he had left around Liv's lips when he kissed her. It would not happen again.

A woman in the seat beside him, waiting her turn, glared at him and he became aware of the sound of his own feet tapping against the floor.

He wondered what sport Liv did. She was too tall for skating but maybe skiing? Or fencing, even though it wasn't big in Sweden. Why hadn't she told him? Carl felt his ears burning. Why would she? He had made it clear he didn't want to know.

Eric brought him iced tea. Droplets were clustered on the paper cup like tiny see-through pebbles.

"Are you one of the Sami people?" He sat next to him and shoved a straw into his cup.

The question came out of the blue, and at first Carl didn't understand what Eric meant. The Sami were an indigenous people living in the north of Sweden, synonymous for many with reindeer herding. From Carl's modest encounters, he knew them to be heterogeneous in terms of their physical characteristics, many having darker Mongoloid features, others light-coloured skin and hair, with blue or brown eyes, slanted or not and with high, low or medium cheekbones. Sami spoke the Finno-Ugric language, which closely linked them to Finns, who were also extreme genetic outliers from the general European population. For most of the twentieth century, Sami were considered an inferior race and were dehumanised and even subjected to cultural genocide. It was a topic that Swedes didn't talk about, other than in human rights activist circles. Kristoffer had once said that Swedes knew more about Native Americans than about their own indigenous population.

"No," he said. "Why do you ask?"

"Because you don't look very Swedish."

The first and really the only time Carl remembered someone asking him if he was Sami was on a train to Lund with Kristoffer. A man with thin blond hair, in his sixties, was sitting across from them but instead of looking out his window he kept staring at Carl, his eyes gleaming through lenses of pink alcoholic wetness. Kristoffer suggested moving seats and they went to the other end of the carriage. The man duly followed them and, holding onto a rail to balance himself against the movement of the train, he asked if Carl was Sami. Carl said no.

"I know you are," the man hissed through his teeth, and left.

The incident left Carl confused. He wasn't sure if he preferred to be of Sami, Balkan or Turkish stock, or something else entirely. With Kristoffer's encouragement, he hired a woman to trace his genealogy, and she returned with a list of very Swedish names from the last two hundred years on both sides of Carl's family. He didn't want to investigate further or speculate as to whether the records were accurate. If someone had changed their name in the past to save his family from oppression, it was worth it. He felt it would change nothing for him. He said he didn't care.

He knew that Kristoffer had understood, even though they never spoke about it – not even when Eva began work on an appeal to the United Nations to return ancestral lands to the Sami people. In this respect, he and Kristoffer were similar. Kristoffer never tried to find his real parents, to go back to his people, to discover his country, unlike some of his Korean friends from Sweden. The difference was that Carl knew his real parents but didn't want to rub an old wound; whereas Kristoffer didn't have a wound.

"My great-grandmother on my maternal side was Sami," Eric said. "Did you know that Sami people have three hundred words to describe snow?"

Carl didn't like the snow. Maybe he didn't have Sami blood after all.

His phone was ringing. It was Dylan.

"The plane will take off at 8 p.m. tonight," he said.

Carl felt a chill in his bones. "How reliable is this information?"

"As you well know, nothing is reliable with these guys. I'm still at the temporary embassy. The announcement just came out, and the woman you spoke to found me to tell me personally. I think she was concerned about the newspapers from the conversation you had with her."

Carl felt a trembling in his chest. Was he really coming to the end of his journey – his mission, as Jack would mockingly say?

"Are you there, Carl?"

"Yes, I'm here. Thanks for letting me know."

Carl's phone rang again. It was someone from the Rescue Services Agency. An embalming technician was available to take care of the bodies, and they were sending a refrigerated van to collect them.

"There are three bodies to embalm and transport from Wat Yan Yao," Carl said, and Eric whispered, "Thank you."

"So, you did persuade them to take the plane back," Eric said when Carl hung up.

"I'll believe it when I see it."

Thirty

Like the shadow of a winged giant, the Hercules blended into the night. Six coffins draped in the colours of the Swedish flag were lined up in front of the ramp. Carl could barely see through the tears. He didn't know in which coffins Kristoffer and Eva's bodies lay – he had said his last goodbyes in the van on the way from Wat Yan Yao, placing his hands on the cold plywood. The raw pain in his chest was so strong that he crumpled to the ground and sobbed like a child, inconsolable in his grief.

From the other side of the ramp came the melody of a violin from the small orchestra that someone from the embassy had thought to organise at the very last moment.

A woman, whose oldest son was in one of the coffins, knelt next to Carl and asked if he was alright. Her breath smelled of alcohol. Without lifting his head, Carl nodded. She stood up and walked back to her husband, who was speaking in hushed tones to a priest.

Emma Ostberg stood apart from the cluster of grieving relatives, with a small group of officials. She had thanked Carl for his help before the ceremony, shaking his hand and giving him a smile which ended at the end of her lips.

Fredrik motioned forward some Swedish journalists who had come to record the bodies being loaded into the plane.

They hadn't allowed Dylan onto the airfield, but every time Carl glanced towards the perimeter fence he could distinguish the glowing end of his cigarette in the darkness. He thought it ironic that journalists, musicians and a priest should outnumber the coffins.

Only when the plane had disappeared over the distant lights at the end of the runaway did Carl begin walking away. Almost at the gates, where he had arranged to meet Dylan, he heard the pounding of someone approaching at the run from behind.

Fredrik pushed an envelope into Carl's hand.

"These are your temporary passport and flight tickets. You fly home tonight."

Carl immediately thought of Liv. "Oh," he said. "That was … fast. I didn't expect—"

"If I'm honest, I'll be glad to see the back of you." Fredrik put his hands on his hips and his Adam's apple went up and down with special vigour. "Let's say I used all my powers to speed up your passport."

Carl watched Fredrik running to his car and only when he had driven away did Carl look at his tickets. Tomorrow. Tomorrow he would be in London. He shifted from foot to foot. The tears threatened to return and he struggled to keep his composure. When he thought about the future, all he could imagine was a world from which everything he counted important had been banished or had willingly fled.

"To your friends."

Dylan lifted a large hip flask into the air and wiped his lips. He offered the flask to Carl.

"What is it?"

"Jack Daniel's, a friend I always take with me." Dylan lit his cigarette.

Carl rubbed the end of his shirt over the flask mouth and took a small sip, then a bigger one. He offered the flask to Dylan.

He didn't take it.

"Have more." He blew silver rings into the thick night air.

Carl leaned on Dylan's bike and took a large slug.

"To everyone who died," he said, rubbing his burning tongue against his gums. "May they live forever."

"When is your flight?" Dylan said.

"At midnight."

"At which point, all your knight's armour is going to turn to dust?"

"As long as my plane doesn't turn into a washtub, I'll be fine," Carl said, as planes queued on the runaway, the tiny dots of their wing lights blinking. "When are you going back to Australia?"

"I'm planning to stay in the region for as long as people want to hear what is happening here." Dylan threw the stub of his cigarette on the ground and crushed it with his foot. "Or until destiny takes me somewhere else?"

"How does it feel to trust …" Carl cleared his throat. "To trust your destiny?"

Dylan stretched his arms high in the air and locked his hands together behind his head.

"Like when you float on the surface with your arms and legs spread apart," he said, looking up, his head tilted back. "In the sea. Because it holds you better. You know how it feels?" He glanced at Carl.

"No." His legs would inevitably begin to sink and water would always get into his nose and he'd choke and begin floundering and trashing his arms and legs to stay afloat. Kristoffer always said that he was making too many movements, that he had to relax.

"Can you take me to Liv's flat?" Carl tightened the flask's top. "I promised I'd pass by to say goodbye on my way to the airport."

He didn't look at Dylan.

Carl fastened his helmet under his chin. There was a good chance Liv wouldn't be home, but since she still hadn't contacted him it was his only hope of seeing her. He didn't believe Dylan would help him to find her if he knew the truth – he obviously wanted to be in her good books. Marco might be willing to help him. When Carl was in a taxi on his way to the hospital for his blood test, he recognised the Shell petrol station, and then the two-storey motorcycle shop where Liv turned onto the side street to Marco's garage. Now, he could easily find the turn, though he was less sure he would find the gate to the garage in the dark.

And what would he tell Marco anyway? That he had said things to Liv that no man should say to a woman? That he'd like to apologise? If Marco was sensitive – or perhaps selfless – enough to understand, he would ring Liv and pass the phone to Carl.

At all costs, the apology had to be in person. He would thank her again for all her help and he would say that he was truly sorry for offending her with his stupid questions. What else was there to say?

They passed an ambulance, and at that moment Carl remembered that he'd left his crutch leaning against another bike at the airport.

"Wait." He tapped Dylan's shoulder.

Dylan changed lanes and slowed down on the side of the road.

"If we return you won't have much time to go to Liv's before your flight," he said. "We are five minutes from her house."

Maybe he didn't need to see her in person. Carl rubbed his cheeks. They felt numb. He could send her another text and avoid the embarrassment of showing up at her door without an invitation. What if she was not even at her flat? In the end, it had been her choice not to respond. He already texted her a long apology. He had tried. He could text when he got home and ask her to call him when she was next in London.

Carl stared at the two rivers of red and yellow lights. "Let's go back to the airport."

She wouldn't call him when she was in London – he knew it. He knew her. He knew he would not call her the next time he was in Thailand, should he ever return. If he left now, he was unlikely to see her again, unless they bumped into each other by chance. But what were the odds that destiny would offer them that chance?

He remembered what Kristoffer had said. Destiny has a way of taking you to the right place at the wrong time, maybe to test whether you deserve the blessing.

"Wait." Carl put his hand on Dylan's arm just as he was turning the key. "Please, take me to Liv's flat."

"Are you sure?"

Carl wasn't at all sure.

Reaching the top of a long hill, Dylan reduced speed, driving steadily along a residential street with apartment blocks on one side and the roofs of villas poking up through lush greenery behind high fences on the other.

"It all looks the same in the dark."

Dylan squinted and slowed near a wrought iron gate to an apartment building, but then he hit the throttle again and they drove further, to an identical gate, the walls on either side overgrown with creepers.

It was a five-storey building with large terraces like nests set into a cliff. Parallel rows of elegant palm trees ran from the ends of the façade to the street. There were bright lights at all the windows on the top floor, and two softly lit windows on the third.

Carl hobbled to the door at the side of the iron gates, on which were twelve residents' buzzers and one for the concierge.

"I forget which flat." Carl turned to Dylan.

"I don't remember either," Dylan said evenly. "Call her. I have to go," he said, and sped off the way they had come.

Carl peered through the gate's wrought iron bars at a cobbled driveway with neatly trimmed bushes on both sides. He glanced back at the deserted road behind him. Everything was quiet, save for the chorus of crickets. How was he going to find a taxi here? He hadn't expected her place to be this far from the main road. Without his crutch, it would take him forever to get to the nearest intersection, and any chance of a passing taxi.

He pushed concierge's buzzer. When nobody responded, he pressed it again several times. He had to be at the airport at ten thirty to have enough time to limp to his gates. If he left now and had to waste time looking for a taxi, he might not get there before eleven.

He pressed the first apartment's buzzer. When nobody responded, he pressed the next buzzer up. And then the next. He wondered if the buzzer system was even working. Where were all the residents? Was it the right building? Only when he got to flat number 12 did a man responded, in Thai.

"Sorry, my mistake," Carl said into the intercom.

He heard the hum of a car engine getting closer, and stepped away from the buzzers. Lights flashed into his face and momentarily blinded him. A 4x4 turned off the road and stopped in front of the gates. The driver's window slid down, and a Thai woman stretched her hand out with a garage opener and activated the gates.

"Are you here for Liv?"

"How did you guess?" Carl peered into the woman's face to see if he knew her.

"There aren't many Western visitors."

"I think her buzzer doesn't work."

"Did you try to call her?"

"My phone battery died."

"Go on in," the woman said. "There are lights in her flat, so she might be home."

"Third floor, right?"

"Yes," the woman said, driving through the gates.

What if Liv was not alone, and that was why she hadn't responded? Keeping one hand on the wall for support, Carl limped from the lift. His calf had begun throbbing as soon as he had put weight on it on the driveway. There was no way he would get to the intersection without help.

He stood still in the middle of the hall between two brown doors, 8 and 9, listening, but all he could hear was his own panting. The paint around the doors was chipped and there was a long crack on the wall between them, in the shape of a flash of lightning. The carpet was thin and had lost its colour. It smelled of last year's rain.

After a while, the light in the corridor switched off automatically and Carl stood in complete darkness. Slowly he began to distinguish a soft light coming from under door 9. He stood still for another minute or two. It was a different silence to the street below, it was lifeless, it thickened around him and seemed to press in upon his burning eyes. He flashed his phone on. It was ten fifteen. The light in the corridor went on, and he shuffled up to the door and knocked.

He crooked his arm against the door frame and waited. At first he heard nothing; then he made out the soft slapping of bare feet on a wooden floor. He breathed out very slowly, composing himself.

"Who is it?" Liv said from the other side of the door.

"It's me. Carl."

There was a long silence before he heard a scraping of the metallic latch.

Liv slowly opened the door as far as the safety chain allowed, and Carl stepped closer and peered in.

A breeze rushed through the door gap and rippled the silk of her coral nightdress, revealing and concealing her figure. Strands of hair floated around her face. She said nothing.

"I wanted to say sorry."

His tongue felt too heavy to let words he had planned to say roll out. He stared at the oval links of the steel chain between them. He wished she would remove it but didn't dare ask.

She yawned. "I read your texts. All good." The wind blew again, skimming her breasts. "I thought you were already on your way to the airport."

"I am," he croaked. "Can you order me a taxi, please?"

"What?" She slapped her hand against the wall and laughed. But not in the way that would make the world around her dance. She laughed as if someone had punched her in her stomach and she was trying to get her breath.

"I can't believe you came here to ask me to order you a taxi …"

Carl wished the floor would open beneath him. He wished he was already at the airport, in the plane, on his way London, as far as possible from her. He stepped back, balancing on his good leg, and glanced at the lift door.

"Come in." She removed the chain. "I'll order you a taxi."

She turned her back to him and walked into a room on the other side of the hall.

He paused for a moment at the door, then limped inside.

The living room was dimly lit, spacious, with a gigantic mirror in a lacquered frame leaning against the wall on one side and a long, black-lacquered sideboard opposite, with a crimson vase and a row of tea lights in glass jars of different shapes. On the wall above there was a row of framed black and white portraits.

There were stacks of books all over the floor, like pebbles in a mountain stream.

He felt an insane desire to turn on the light, to roam through the whole flat, to see the titles of the books and the faces on the photos, to know who she was, what she liked apart from green curry and fast driving.

Liv stood in the golden pool of the floor lamp, facing the open doors to the terrace, holding her cordless phone next to her ear. He could hear a recorded voice offering her a menu of choices. Warm, humid air infused with salt and the fragrances of the streets below moved through the room, playing with the linen curtains as if they were sails. She pulled her silk strap onto her shoulder, but it slid down again.

Carl stepped closer and pressed the Off button on the base.

She stared at him with a closed, unreadable expression, her brows creased in a slight frown. He took the receiver from her hand and placed it on the base. She opened her mouth but before she was able to say anything, he softly put his hand against her lips.

"I'm sorry for what I said." He breathed out. "But I'm not sorry for kissing you."

And just like that, he finally said what he felt and not what he wanted to say. His heart didn't run for its life anymore. It tapped rhythmically in his chest. He felt adrift.

"You will be late for your flight."

"It doesn't matter."

A wry smile touched her lips.

"You can afford to get another ticket then?"

"No, I want to stay with you."

She lifted her dark blue eyes and stared at him.

"And then what?"

He saw a storm in her eyes. He saw fear like that day on the pier in Kuraburi.

"I don't know. We will figure it out, right? Together. But if I leave now, we will never know. I will never know."

"Where are you going to live?"

"Here," he said, and made a small step towards her, close enough to touch her lips with his. Too many questions. He didn't want to think any more. He wanted to feel. He wanted to feel alive.

Thirty-one

Today at 3 a.m., the first plane carrying the bodies of six Swedes killed in the tsunami landed at Arlanda Airport. Met by mourning relatives, King Carl XVI Gustaf, Queen Silvia, Mr Persson and other officials …

His head lay on her arm. He could feel her every pulse, every heartbeat.

Indignation and criticism over the government response to the tsunami continues to grow …

She reached out and switched off the television.

A shaft of late afternoon sun fell across the side table below the window, and he watched as the dust particles danced.

The breeze coaxed the white linen curtains into ceaseless movement.

Afterword

Every few weeks afterwards, as the tsunami faded from the international news, the official death toll climbed. Not until the following spring were the final numbers estimated by the United Nations at 230,000 lives lost – a milestone that might have been marked by a great memorial service but went essentially unnoticed.

Thailand experienced the largest runup height – defined as the maximum inundation point above sea level – of any location outside Sumatra. It measured 19.6 metres at Ban Thung Dap, on the southwest tip of Koh Phra Thong Island, and 15.8 metres at Ban Nam Khem, a fishing village in Kao Lak, where two and a half thousand lives were lost in a heartbeat.

More than 8,000 people are estimated to have died in Thailand. Of those, a third are still unaccounted for – the result of a combination of mass graves, bodies not identified, and children and others never found.

Sweden was the hardest-hit country outside Asia. Five hundred and forty-three Swedish tourists, mainly in Thailand, died, and the tragedy had a severe and lasting humanitarian and political impact in the country.

Acknowledgments

Thank you to my editors, Helen Baggott and Sheena Billett for your eagle eye and attention to detail, and thank you, Michael Faulkner, your touch made my book shine.

This book turned out to be a long journey and one that took me to where I didn't want to go. Like the main character, I thought it was the story of my friend; instead, I was searching for myself. As in a bent mirror, I was able to see a different me, the person I didn't realise I was. I am grateful for that.

To Alexander, my wonder, who changed my life forever.

To Nicolai, my little sunshine, who joined me on this journey.

To Jocasta, my amigo, my first anchor in London, who has always believed in me. I wish you were living closer.

To Glyn, my Scottish friend, who has become my family. Thank you for your advice and guidance and for all the time we spend together, all the adventures and laughs we share.

And my deepest gratitude is to Henrik, my Mr Right, who holds me tight when I'm falling asleep, who guards my dreams. Thank you for sharing your story and letting me write it my way.